MASK MORTEM

ARUN RAJAGOPAL

To Cioci,

Enjoy the book!
I have enjoyed having
you in our lives!

♡

Arun Raj

PROLOGUE

One Thousand Years Ago

The priests had made their choice for the sacrifice in the Rebirth ceremony after a thorough vetting process. Fifteen finalists assembled in the main plaza, fifteen men in their early twenties, each waiting with a sense of anticipation for the announcement. After going through the formalities, the head priest lifted his hands, ready to announce the young man selected for this honor. He paused for a moment. Fifteen anxious pairs of eyes studied his lips, waiting.

"Atoc," he announced.

One man gasped as the other fourteen finalists clustered around him, patting him on the back and offering their congratulations, some tinged with envy. Atoc beamed with pride, pleased at being chosen for such an honor. After the announcement, one priest draped a ceremonial robe around Atoc's shoulders and escorted him to a designated room in the great pyramid. For the next twelve days, until the day of the Rebirth ceremony, they lavished him with silk garments and treated him to sumptuous meals including roast wild pigs, fresh passion fruit, herb-crusted fish, and llama milk.

On the morning of the Rebirth, Atoc lay on a pallet in his room halfway up the great pyramid. Matching the shape of the pyramid, the outer wall angled into the room. Drops of condensation had collected in a damp patch on the floor. He stirred in his sleep, shivered, and pulled the cover over him. A shaft of bright sunlight entered the room through the narrow window, crawled across the floor and crept onto the pallet, bathing his face. He awoke with a start. He rolled off the pallet and stood, stretching away the stiffness in his muscles. Goosebumps erupted on his arms, and he pulled the cover off his bed and wrapped it around his shoulders as he moved into the sunlight. He stood at the window facing east, absorbing the sun's warmth. He gazed at the central plaza and lush tropical forest that lay beyond the city's boundary. A tongue of mist lapped at the edge of the clearing as it retreated from the sun. In anticipation of the Rebirth ceremony, a few of the citizenry had already assembled in the main plaza and gazed in awe at his young figure in the window.

The single door in his room opened to a central hallway. A thick curtain, woven from the same coarse material as his cover and with the same vivid herringbone pattern, hung in the opening. The curtain bunched to one side as one of the priests pushed it aside and entered the room.

Atoc bowed in deference to the older man.

"Did you sleep well?" the priest inquired.

"Yes." Atoc nodded.

"Today is the Rebirth."

"I am ready."

The priest had a tall and stooped frame, his wrinkled skin and a semicircular halo of white hair showing his age. He wore a bright multicolored robe with a feathered headdress adorning his head. He held a goblet in his right hand and now proffered it to the young man.

"Drink this."

Atoc accepted the goblet. The liquid inside, a brownish extract of several herbs, had been steeped for hours. A wisp of steam rose from the goblet as Atoc held it up to his nose and breathed in its flavors. He wrapped his fingers around the goblet, savored its warmth for a moment, swirled the contents, and downed it in one gulp. It felt bland and soothing on his tongue but after a moment, he felt the bite of a tart and acidic aftertaste. A few seconds later, he felt the inside of his mouth tingle. The priest took the goblet and smiled.

"We are ready for the Rebirth," the priest said. "Today we go to the Valley of the Sun."

Atoc nodded.

"I am ready," he repeated.

The priest left. Atoc sank back on the pallet; his head swam from the effects of the drink.

A few minutes later, the curtain parted again as two women arrived. They appeared to be the same age as Atoc. The first woman through the curtain carried a folded item of clothing. The material looked crisp and new, the pattern a similar style as the cover and the curtain. The second woman carried small bowls containing pigments in various colors. They spent the next thirty minutes helping Atoc get dressed in the ceremonial clothes. They outlined his face with the pigments and painted in his face, creating colorful solid patterns.

A few minutes after they finished, an entourage of twelve older men arrived outside his room. They were the high priests of the kingdom. The oldest among them entered the young man's room. The two women bowed and stepped back.

"It is time," the priest intoned. He had the most elaborate headdress and robe and thus had the most stature among the priests, indicating his position as the head priest.

The sun had burned off the morning chill as the twelve priests and Atoc set off. One priest carried a cube-shaped box sixteen inches on each side. He had placed the box in a leather satchel that hung across his shoulder. Another priest carried a flat box some twenty inches long by six inches wide and two finger breadths deep. The procession marched down the stone steps of the pyramid where the people of the city had gathered. A celebratory roar rolled through the crowd as the priests turned toward the jungle that abutted the edge of the clearing from which the pyramid rose.

They started on the long hike, pausing for refreshments every thirty minutes and to give Atoc a drink of the same concoction he had drunk earlier. Despite the drink's effects on him, Atoc was able to maintain a reasonable pace.

They marched in single file through the dense jungle with the trail sloping upward in a shallow incline. They marched in silence, their pigmented faces glistening from the exertion and from the sun's increasing intensity. The rhythmic crunching of their footsteps against the foliage maintained a cadence against the constant background chirps of insects and the intermittent screeches of the howler monkeys and birds. The green canopy provided a respite from the sun. A few hours later, the sounds faded as they emerged from the jungle. They stepped out from under the canopy and stood for a minute, chests heaving, surveying the plateau. Their robes fluttered around their ankles as they stood on the rocky surface. They had another round of refreshments and a drink of the potion for Atoc. A short fifteen-minute walk across the plateau brought them to the base of a set of towering cliffs.

A crack in the rock face, about the width of two men, disappeared into the mountain. The crack led to a passage through the mountain through which the procession walked, still in single file. They emerged on a ledge some sixty feet wide flanked on either side by cliffs. There was a sheer drop of fifty feet off the ledge after which the valley floor sloped several hundred feet down to the bottom of a verdant valley. The valley's orientation lay in an approximate east-west direction so for most of the year, the sun traversed the sky along the length of the valley, thus giving it its name, the Valley of the Sun.

Atoc stared, transfixed by his first look at the spectacular panorama. From their vantage point on the ledge, the floor of the valley looked like a ruffled dark green carpet. Far below, birds resembled gnats jumping in and out of the carpet.

The group stopped on the ledge. In the middle of the ledge, a natural outcrop in the bedrock had been carved into an altar. It was waist high with several planes and angles and a flat irregular rectangular top. At one end, a section of rock had been carved into the shape of a squared dorsal fin. It pointed skyward and cast a wedge-shaped shadow on the altar. Markings chiseled around its base indicated its purpose as a sundial.

"We have arrived," the head priest said. "The Valley of the Sun."

The effects of the drink had worn off, and Atoc looked at the altar, his brow furrowed. After another drink and some soothing conversation from one of the other priests, his expression relaxed.

The priest unslung the leather satchel carrying the box and placed it on a stone ledge. He lifted the box out, placed it next to the satchel and untied a leather clasp. A thick, woven fabric lined the box. A dome-shaped object lay nestled inside. The priest reached in and lifted it out, revealing a mask. It was a dark grey-green color with a rough texture and an irregular mottled surface. The top of the mask formed a dome-shaped extension that fit over the head. The face plate was the same color and texture as the dome. A ridge separated the dome from the face plate, which extended far enough to cover the upper half of the face. There were two black, almond-shaped eyeholes.

"Behold," the priest said. "Mask mortem, the healer of life."

The priest held the mask over Atoc's head and chanted a brief prayer as he lowered the mask and helmet onto his head. The drink had relaxed him, but he still recoiled when he saw through the mask that the priest leaned toward him. The group saw only the mask's black eyes.

The priest opened the flat box. A knife, gleaming and sharp, lay nestled in cloth. The ornate, jeweled handle glinted in rainbow colors, and its long, straight blade ended in a point. He took the knife out of its case and stood straight, chanting another prayer.

As directed, Atoc climbed onto the altar and lay supine, elbows by his side, fingers crisscrossed on his abdomen. Sunlight bathed the mask. The priest motioned to the head priest, who took his place next to the altar at Atoc's side. The head priest murmured a few soothing words to Atoc. The shadow cast by the sundial had shrunk to a mere sliver as they prepared for the Rebirth.

The priest holding the knife stood by the altar next to the head priest. He continued chanting a prayer as he lifted the knife over his head, gripping the handle with both hands with the sharp point aimed forward. Atoc's breathing had

quickened in anticipation. The top of the robe had
separated, exposing his heaving chest. His fingers tightened
across his stomach.

The priest looked at the sundial; its shadow had
disappeared.

Time for the Rebirth. *The head priest glanced at the priest
holding the knife and nodded.*

The priest pivoted to the left and swung the blade into
the head priest's chest, driving it in with such force that only
the jeweled handle protruded from his chest. The head
priest gasped and let out a shriek of pain.

The priest jerked the knife out of the head priest's chest
with some effort, the blade rasping against a rib. Now
glistening with streaks of blood, the blade came out, drops
of blood dripping off its sharp point. The head priest
collapsed, blood spurting out of the wound in his chest. The
feathered headdress toppled off his head and he fell on top
of it. Atoc sat upright and lifted the helmet off his head. The
mask seemed to glow from within, although in the bright
sunlight it could have been reflected light from the sun.

Atoc stared at the dying priest, his face devoid of
surprise. The head priest lay on the ground writhing, his face
contorted in pain, a look of uncomprehending horror on his
face. He rolled on the ground, moaning as his strength
ebbed, clutching his chest in vain. The dark, damp circle on
the ground beneath him expanded as the other priests stood
watching him. No one said a word. No one offered to help.
After a minute, his last breath came in a wet wheeze. He
stopped moving.

Two priests walked to the body and bent over. The
feathered headdress, mangled and bloody from his death
throes, protruded like he had smashed a bird as he fell. They
lifted the arms and legs and dragged the body close to the
edge. Another priest chanted a prayer. As the prayer
concluded, they pushed the body of the head priest off the
ledge. A series of receding crashing sounds through the
foliage marked the body's path to its final resting place at the
bottom of the Valley of the Sun. Another priest swept the
remains of the headdress off the ledge with his feet. They

wiped the knife's blade clean and put the mask and knife back in their boxes. They marched out of the valley in single file, this time led by Atoc.

ONE

Present Day

Art Marlow sat at his desk at home one Monday morning in
early April, sipping his coffee and staring at the computer
screen. Kidneys preoccupied his mind this morning.
Scattered gray clouds dotted the sky outside. The
intermittent bursts of sunshine mirrored his mood; gloomy
but punctuated with bursts of optimism. Later today, his lab
would unveil the latest results of his research. He expected a
big day for his staff and himself.

He reviewed his data again, for the umpteenth time,
considering all variables in his research into creating organs,
specifically kidneys, from a single pluripotent stem cell. He
had tried five times over his career to produce a kidney and
each time, the kidney had not worked as it should. Funding
constraints imposed by the investors meant this could be his
last attempt. If this attempt failed, it would be difficult to
continue this line of research. He would have to switch
gears, step back, and consider other options for creating
organs that maintained genetic compatibility with the host.
The time required to create a new program would be
lengthy; the effort involved tedious; and the chances of new
funding after these failures would be difficult at best. It
would also create a serious impediment in his chances of
achieving tenure. A sense of urgency and mild desperation
pervaded his thoughts.

His wife entered the study.

"Ready for a refill?"

He handed his coffee mug to her.

"How's your schedule today?"

funding his lab and as such, the office of translational research at the university had already created an affiliated limited-liability corporation. He had three graduate students and several lab assistants. At least for now.

The big day had arrived. After years of research, they had arrived at the stage in which they had studied every step of the life cycle from stem cell to organ.

A few weeks earlier, they had harvested a single stem cell from an umbilical cord blood sample donated by a healthy volunteer. They had placed the stem cell in a controlled environment that changed every few days per their protocol. As the stem cell divided, the change in environment guided its division. And now, after several weeks, in the apparatus lay a small human kidney. It looked like any small human kidney, normally formed. But would it function like a normal kidney?

Previous attempts had failed. They knew how cellular division proceeded along genetically predetermined pathways and the complex interplay between various hormones steered organogenesis, the process that resulted in organ formation. Dr. Marlow had attempted to replicate this process in a dish. Earlier attempts did not even resemble specific organs. Through years of trial and error, he felt he had conquered all the variables and could now steer the development of specific organs.

"The microtome is ready, so I'll get to work," Burt said.

The cryostat microtome, a device that looked like a chest freezer with a glass door, sat next to the microscope. It could flash freeze a tissue sample in seconds, and Burt could cut razor thin serial slices only a few micrometers thick to view through the microscope. These sections would then be analyzed under a microscope by his staff over the next few hours to determine if the cellular structure replicated a human kidney. A lengthy, tedious, and critical process.

"OK, I'll be in my office. Let me know how it goes."

Dr. Marlow walked out of the lab and toward his office, his brow furrowed. Previous attempts had failed as the task he had set for himself years ago had proven to be more difficult that he had imagined. After millions of years of evolution, the natural process seemed effortless, but why specific cells went a certain way during differentiation remained a mystery Dr. Marlow hoped to solve.

A considerable amount of money rode on the success of this attempt. The office of translational research had already created the limited-liability corporation, CellGenEX, LLC, a portmanteau of "Cellular" and "Genesis"; the "EX" added on for marketing purposes. Based on his burgeoning reputation and the potential of his research, angel investors and others had funded his research to the tune of millions of dollars.

*   *   *

Back in the lab, the kidney lay in a flat glass dish. Burt picked up the dish. The kidney, glistening and rubbery, slithered from side to side, bouncing against the walls of the dish. He balanced the dish on his palm as he carried it to the microtome. A couple of the other technicians followed at a distance, to observe this crucial step. On a table adjacent to his work area sat a microscope with a video screen.

He opened the lid of the cryostat microtome and using a pair of tweezers, lowered the kidney onto a metal disc. A gel-like medium formed a circular ridge around the edges of the disc. He slowly lowered the entire apparatus into liquid nitrogen. As the warm apparatus contacted the liquid nitrogen, a hissing sound accompanied puffs of bluish white vapor rising out of the cryostat. The kidney froze solid in a few seconds. Burt donned insulating gloves that resembled oven mitts. He lifted the kidney out and placed it on the slicer. He dialed the thickness of the slicer to a few micrometers and started working on the sample. After obtaining a few slices, he left the rest of the kidney in the cryostat and placed the thin sections on glass slides. He added a few drops of a special stain and covered the sample with a glass slip. He placed the slide in the microscope and peered into the eyepiece, focusing on a few areas of the kidney sample.

most recent electronic trappings completed the opulent look.

He undressed and pressed a button on the wall. A wood panel silently rose, and he tossed his workout clothes into the laundry chute. He stepped into the shower. He touched a button and warm water sprayed over his body from many directions. He barely enjoyed the shower as the upcoming events occupied his thoughts. Soft clouds of water vapor rolled out of the shower stall. He took the handheld sprayer down and held it over his right buttock to soothe the sciatica. After ten minutes of daydreaming, he touched a button and the water stopped. He wiped off his arms and legs and wrapped the towel around his waist.

He stepped out of the shower and looked in the mirror. Condensed water vapor obscured the upper half of the mirror. He did not like what he saw in the lower half. He wiped the mirror and stepped back.

From a distance, some signs of aging were less obvious. His chest hair had more than a "touch of grey," as did his temples. *At least I still have most of my hair*, he thought, eyeing the thinning spots around his temples. He felt around the crown of his head and fingered his scalp there. He held a handheld mirror over the back of his head and grimaced at the expanding circle of shiny skin.

He leaned closer to the mirror. The exhaust fan had cleared most of the condensation. Up close, the wrinkles seemed more numerous and creased deeper than ever. And those annoying longer hairs in his eyebrows and ears rankled him. He sucked in his gut and pushed out his chest, looking at his profile in the mirror. He had never liked his weak chin. He let out his gut, and his chest sagged. His paunch extended out farther than his penis, a *dick do*, he thought. That old joke popped into his mind. *What's a dick do? It's when your belly sticks out farther than your dick do.*

I need to take better care of myself. Maybe work out more. He made a mental note to lift weights along with the cardio routine. *But I sure as hell could use a cigarette today!*

After shaving, he stepped into his closet to get dressed. He dressed as usual in a starched and pressed pair of slacks and a white shirt. The splash of color from his tie and matching cufflinks offered the only daily difference in his appearance. He never dressed casual at work, not even on Fridays. At work, he was all business. Except for today. He had other plans.

He exited his house through the back door to the garage and grabbed the handle of his ostentatious Mercedes sedan. The key fob triggered the built-in proximity sensor, and the car chirped once, unlocking the doors.

He snapped his fingers in annoyance before climbing in. He went back into the house and into his bedroom, grabbed a pill bottle off the dresser, stuffed it into his pocket, and went back to his car. He climbed into his car, aware of his moist palms; they had left an imprint on the door handle. He wiped them on his pants legs. He opened the garage door, reversed out of the garage, and drove down the shady, tree-lined driveway of his house, pausing at the automatic gate while it slid open. He turned right and accelerated, driving past the "Welcome to Highland Park" sign on his way to the office.

As he exited Highland Park, he passed by one of his neighbors, Dr. Jick Arnsson, waiting on his driveway as Peter passed by. Peter waved to him and Dr. Arnsson lifted his travel mug in acknowledgment. He knew Dr. Arnsson was an anesthesiologist, divorced, lived alone, and was about fifteen years older. He idly wondered if Dr. Arnsson had similar issues of anxiety over growing old and wondered how he coped with it. He wondered if Dr. Arnsson had ever contemplated doing what he planned to do later in the day.

chain around her neck. Sensibility all around. She was a spinster; Peter had no idea what she did in her spare time. She owned a cat, which was not a surprise.

At nine o'clock, Lidia announced Art Marlow's arrival. Peter rose to his feet. Marlow reached across the desk and shook Peter's hand.

After taking a seat and exchanging a few pleasantries, Marlow brought up the subject of his visit.

"I won't take up too much of your time, Mr. Northrup. As you already know, your firm owns a twenty-one percent stake in CellGenEx, LLC. Our research is proceeding along very well, and we have made great strides in organ regeneration. However, we need some additional funds. Before discussing this in a meeting with the university and other investors, I wanted to offer your firm the opportunity to acquire an additional thirty percent stake in the company, which would give you a majority interest. Fifty-one percent."

"How much additional funding do you need?" The bullshit meter in Peter's head chimed a warning as the needle jittered toward red. Peter was shrewd at evaluating people and he was surprised Marlow was willing to give up a majority interest in his company. He detected a hint of desperation.

"I'm working on a prospectus for the additional research we need to do. As a ballpark estimate, I would say around one million to one and a quarter."

Peter's eyebrows rose.

"According to your last quarterly update, you were quite close to the holy grail. Why do you need this much additional funding?"

"We ran into a minor glitch and need to repeat some bench research. But the need for funding is somewhat urgent. Hence the immediate offer of a majority interest in the company."

The bullshit meter needle in Peter's head swung further toward red.

"Minor glitches do not result in such dramatic funding needs, Professor."

"I know, but…"

Peter interrupted, blunt and to the point.

"Has something gone wrong with your research? It sounds like it has. You are offering a majority interest in your company, and you need a lot of money. The bullshit alarm in my head is going off. Therefore, I must decline the offer. You have a meeting soon; my firm will also be represented. There will be experts in the field, and we can discuss it as a group. Once we have their input, I will make a decision."

Marlow did not answer the question about his research.

"But if you wait until then, the majority interest offer will be off the table. I put together, for your review, this presentation of my research and where the additional funding will go."

He pushed a folder across the table. A thumb drive in a plastic bag was taped to the corner.

"I would appreciate it if you would look it over and let me know as soon as possible. What I am offering you is a golden opportunity to acquire most of the company for far less than what it will be worth someday. You shouldn't pass it up."

Peter's irritation level increased with Marlow's hard sell. He sensed Marlow wanted to lock down funding before experts in the field had a chance to review his data. He pushed the folder and thumb drive back.

"As I said, I must decline the offer. We will talk about this at the appropriate time. Bring your presentation to the meeting. And now if you will excuse me..." He tilted his head toward the door.

Marlow clenched his fists on his lap. He did not stand.

"Mr. Northrup," he tried again. "This is a once-in-a-lifetime opportunity. Your firm could afford the additional funding with ease, and you would be the sole majority owner. Think about it."

"Professor, this meeting is over."

Marlow's face took on a more intense hue. He stood. "You're making a mistake."

He walked to the door, opened it, and let himself out. The folder and thumb drive lay on the table.

He walked over to the drawn curtains and noted the little button pad to open and shut the drapes. He pressed the open button and with a soft whir, the curtains parted, revealing a majestic view of the Dallas skyline. He could see cars, silent and orderly, crawl along the streets below like ants in a procession. He tried to focus on random thoughts to stay distracted. He wiped his hands again, just in case. *Time for a third drink. I shouldn't, not yet. I'll just pour it.* He filled his glass with the third bottle and glanced at his phone. Almost time.

Shortly after one o'clock, he heard a knock at the door. He walked over to the door, looked through the peephole, and saw a woman standing outside. He opened the door, once again pausing for a second to wipe his moist palms on his pants leg. The woman standing outside was attractive, a bleach blonde with dark roots, pale complexion, and hazel-green eyes. Many tattoos.

"Hi, my name is Candy," the woman said.

You certainly are. A simultaneous thought flashed through his mind. *My God, she's only a few years older than Pauline.*

"Hello, come on in." He cleared his throat.

She sashayed into the room and walked over to the bed, dropping her handbag on the floor. She wore a sleeveless black dress with a partial-sleeve tattoo over her right shoulder and elbow. The front of her dress plunged halfway down her chest, displaying another tattoo. As she walked, her chest sparkled with body glitter. A whiff of a warm floral scent and an undertone of tobacco trailed in her wake.

Should have got a Smoking room.

He shut the door and walked over to her. He stuck out his right hand, first wiping it on his pants leg.

"I'm Peter."

"I know. The agency told me. Hi Peter. Pleased to meet you." She shook his hand and smiled.

He did not quite know what to say next, not having done this before. Candy knew the expected routine and guided their interaction.

"Are you having a drink?" she asked, eyeing his wine glass.

"Yes."

"I wouldn't mind one, too."

"What would you like? We have beer, wine, and mini bottles of gin, vodka, and rum. Do you want me to make you a mixed drink?"

"No, thanks. White wine would be good. Whatever you have."

He took out a chilled bottle of chardonnay from the minibar, unscrewed the top, and poured her a glass. They clinked glasses together.

The hell with it. I need one.

"Do you have a cigarette?"

"Isn't this a Non-Smoking room?"

"Yeah, but I don't care."

She reached into her bag and pulled out a pack of cigarettes. She jiggled the carton and offered Peter one, then held the carton to her lips and pulled out one for herself. The tip of the cigarette flared with Peter's long first drag. He held it in for a few seconds and slowly exhaled, twin streams of smoke swirling out of his nostrils.

My first in four years. Damn, that is so good.

"So, how's your day so far?" she asked.

"It's good."

"Good. Weather's been good so far today."

What if she's a police officer? He dismissed the thought as he had gone through an agency. *But I could be wrong about that,* he second-guessed. He had read that police officers sometimes conducted sting operations, especially targeting high profile individuals, and Peter was well-known around the metroplex. He discussed various unrelated topics, and idle chatter soon followed. He decided she was not a police officer.

After a few minutes, hoping to segue into the next step, he asked her about her religious background.

"Those tattoos are way cool," he said, trying to adopt the vernacular of the younger crowd. "That one on your arm kinda looks like a religious symbol."

"It's not a religious symbol. It's a pattern I saw that I thought looked good. I'm not religious."

"You're not?"

"No."

"You might do well to discover a little religion. Hey, why don't you start now? I see a book there. It's probably a Gideon's Bible; they're always in hotel rooms. You should read it for a little while." He winked.

"OK."

She took the hint and picked up the book. Almost immediately, she noted the "gift" between the pages. She took out the notes, riffled through them and put them back in the Bible. She shut the book and handed it to Peter.

"Do you want to have a shower?" she asked. It was rhetorical.

"OK."

He had read that some escorts prefer their clients have a shower first. She had counted the money and handed the Bible back to Peter. He knew he had to take the money into the bathroom during his shower so a dishonest escort would not abscond with the gift while the client showered. He would give it back to her afterwards. He took another long drag on his cigarette, tapped the ash into a glass, and snuffed it out.

He went into the bathroom and shut but did not lock the door. He undressed, feeling a little self-conscious. *Should have finished that third drink*, he thought. He had a quick rinse-off shower from the neck down. He toweled off, cinched the towel around his waist, and came back into the room.

He placed the Bible on the table and walked over to the bed, sitting with the towel wrapped around his waist. She took the money out of the Bible, placed it in her bag and walked over to the bed. She placed her hands on his shoulders and applied gentle pressure, pushing him back so he sank into the mattress. He caught a whiff of her perfume mixed with stronger cigarette smoke as he fell back onto the bed.

As she stood by him, he once again felt the vague thrill in his chest and once again thought he heard a voice saying "Petey." It seemed to come from his right.

He jerked upright in bed, startled, and looked to the right. The bathroom door had been left ajar.

"Did you hear that?" He looked at Candy, who showed no sign of having heard anything.

She shook her head.

"I didn't hear nothing. Now lay down again."

He lay down, Candy applying gentle pressure on his chest as he sank back. She ran her fingers on his chest, scratching over his abdomen and around his nipples with a light touch. A tent-shaped bulge rose in the towel still wrapped around his waist. *Thank goodness for the blue pill*, he thought. She stood up, reached behind her back, and unzipped the dress. She let it fall to the floor around her ankles, revealing a sheer black bra and black thong panties. *Tattoos or not, she is hot*, he thought. Peter had never been a "tattoo person" but hers had artistic merit. Two moles on her chest had been incorporated into the eyes of a fairy with wings extending over each breast, the nipple incorporated into the wing design. The fairy came alive, trying to escape the confines of her bra. He became aroused. She glanced at the towel loosened by his erection, smiled, and climbed into bed and lay next to him, her head propped on her elbow.

The thrilling sensation in his chest flared again, this time more intense, accompanied by a dull ache, and the same Petey voice.

"Stop playing with your food, Petey," the voice said.

"Mom?" he said out loud, looking around.

"What?" Candy asked. "Did you call me Mom?"

When he did not answer, she flipped back the towel, exposing him, holding his erection as it deflated. Candy looked at him, puzzled, then winked as if understanding it was apparent that this was his first time with an escort.

She removed her bra and panties and allowed him to survey her body. As her breasts moved, the fairy's wings came alive. She had generous breasts, *definitely Ds*, he thought, and she had shaved her pubic hair, *de rigueur* for today's generation. She placed his hand on her pubic area. The visual and tactile input had its desired effect and his flaccid penis pulsed back to attention. She rolled over on top of him and, reaching down into her bag, extracted a condom in its foil wrapper. She tore open the package and started unrolling the condom on his penis.

He felt a much more intense ache and pressure-like sensation in his chest, and this time the ache persisted. He clutched at his chest as the same intonation of his mother's voice returned in his head: "Don't stay out too late, Petey."

"Mom, what the fuck, I'm going crazy."

"What is the matter with you?" Candy asked. "Are you OK?"

Candy's voice sounded different to him. She seemed to be speaking in slow motion and the timbre of her voice dropped.

"No. My chest is hurting, shit. What the hell is going on?"

Candy rolled off him and stood next to the bed, a concerned look on her face. Peter's hair was matted to his forehead, and he breathed like a fish out of water in short, labored gasps. The erection had subsided. The thrill in his chest had progressed to a pounding, each beat of his heart transmitting a pressure wave to his ears. The drumbeat continued in his ears as he felt a wave of dizziness. It seemed the world around him slowed to a crawl.

A heart attack? As soon as the thought crossed his mind, he realized with a shock what had been going on all morning. *Is my life flashing before my eyes?*

"Life flashing…" he managed to get out.

Candy's look of concern had turned to one of alarm. He could hear her, but her speech had slowed so much that he had difficulty focusing on what she said.

"I---a-m---g-o-i-n-g---t-o---c-a-l-l---9---1---1…" she said, her voice now sounding to his ears like she stood behind a whirring propeller and spoke through its spinning vanes.

As Peter's world faded to black, he heard a cacophony of voices in his head, random words and phrases from not only his mother but others in his life, being replayed from his childhood through adulthood. Against that backdrop, he saw Candy walk toward the phone. Through the babble of

voices in his head, he heard Candy's voice whirring in the background, "Y-o-u---h-a-v-e---t-o---h-u-r-r-y!"
I don't want to die.

*   *   *

Meg sat at the registration desk at the Regence hotel. About an hour ago, she had registered Peter Northrup and had assigned him Room 2904. He had made no particularly memorable impression on her. She had noted with some amusement that he had looked flustered when she asked him about his baggage. She had seen the type and knew what he had planned. No professional businessman-type arrives right after lunch and checks in without bags unless their wives are out of town. She continued working on paperwork from the morning's registrations.

On a typical day, things slowed after lunch. Between noon and three, the checkout rush had finished, the maid service crews cleaned the rooms, and the check-in rush had not yet begun. The registration desk saw very little activity during this period. The only exceptions were the occasional Peter Northrups of the world who had requested an early check-in and the hotel accommodated these requests at noon. Although hotels frowned on overt prostitution, they tolerated this behavior with a "see no evil" attitude.

The hotel manager, Tim Murtaugh, stopped by her desk. Meg knew Tim was married and knew his marriage had hit a trough. Meg thought Tim was the most socially inept person she had known, let alone worked for. He would often make comments on the edge of being inappropriate and most of the female staff had rejected his advances. He seemed oblivious that, as manager, he could not engage in any relationship with a subordinate.

"Hi, lassie," he said as he sauntered to her desk. "What's up? Or should I say, 'good day?'"

He said "good day" in an imitation Australian accent. Meg groaned inside.

"Nothing much. Finishing paperwork from the morning."

"Anything exciting?"

"No, the usual. One early check-in today, but otherwise it's a routine day. We're about ninety percent full. Not bad for a weekday."

"That's good," Tim said. "Got any plans for the evening?"

"Yes." She always said she had plans, regardless of the status of her social calendar.

"You always have plans," he complained.

If there was anything positive about his behavior, it was that he was not the type to use any rejection as a basis for reprisals later.

"Well, I'll go check on housekeeping," he said and sauntered off.

The phone rang at her desk. It was Room 2904. She glanced at her screen and saw "Northrup, Peter". She wondered what he wanted. It had only been about an hour since he had checked in. Usually, this type of customer arrives, takes care of his business, and leaves even though the room charges are prepaid through the next morning. Also, they are disinclined to draw any attention to themselves and seldom call to complain about things like the air conditioning or the contents of the minibar.

She reached over and picked up the phone.

"Regence front desk, how may I help you?"

"You have to hurry!" said a frantic woman's voice. "I think this guy is having a heart attack. Can you call 911?"

"What?" Meg exclaimed.

"I'm here with this guy," the voice was more insistent. "He started complaining of chest pain and started talking crazy shit. Now he's blacked out. Please call 911 right now."

The woman's voice conveyed the gravity of the situation. Meg agreed and hung up. She immediately called 9-1-1 and advised the operator of what had transpired at the hotel.

"Please hurry!"

After what seemed like an eternity but could not have been more than a few minutes, red lights strobed the foyer of the hotel as she heard the wail of sirens announcing the arrival of an ambulance and a police cruiser.

SIX

Four paramedics jumped out of the back of the ambulance and behind them, a gurney followed, its collapsible legs straightening and locking into place. A police officer emerged from the cruiser and together, the five of them rushed to the glass doors, pausing for a second as the automatic doors swished open. Meg had commandeered an elevator with an override key, and she waited with the door held open.

As the elevator door closed, Meg turned the key and pressed 29. This bypassed all the intervening floors, and the elevator raced straight to the 29th floor. As the elevator door opened, Meg noticed Tim and hotel security had arrived in another elevator. She had notified Tim as she waited for the ambulance. They rushed to Room 2904 with the paramedics. Using a master key card, Meg opened the door and she and Tim stepped aside, allowing the EMS crew and the officer entry into the suite. Meg, Tim, and the hotel security officer stepped in behind them and closed the door.

Candy sat by the window, looking a little frantic and almost hyperventilating. Peter Northrup lay supine on the bed, splayed out flat, naked, and unconscious. The covers of the bed were not pulled down. He lay on a towel on top of the duvet. Meg thought he looked a little gray already. With a sense of controlled urgency, the paramedics went through the airway, breathing, and circulation protocol, doing their best to resuscitate him.

The paramedics grasped Peter and lifted him off the soft bed, placing him on the firm gurney. One of them felt Peter's neck for a pulse; she looked at the others and shook her head. Another paramedic, a burly man with a ruddy complexion, started chest compressions, pushing down his chest at a rate of about once every second, grunting with the exertion. Someone applied sticky pads to Peter's chest and then requested a pause in the compressions to assess the rhythm. Someone said, "v fib."

"Keep doing the compressions," another voice said.

A third paramedic, a woman who looked young enough she could have been a recent graduate, grasped Peter's left arm and started an intravenous line.

"IV's in," she announced as she taped it into place.

They stopped the compressions as one of the paramedics took out a face mask and clamped it to Peter's face. Two elastic straps secured it to his face. A short length of accordion tubing led to an Ambu bag. Another paramedic took a turn doing compressions. The young female paramedic took over squeezing the Ambu bag.

The police officer, Meg, Tim, the hotel security officer and Candy watched the proceedings with interest, Candy looking somewhat distressed.

They attached wires to the pads on Peter's chest, and the one paramedic, presumably the team leader, called "Clear." They stepped back, and someone pressed a button. Peter's body convulsed on the gurney as a high-pitched whine signaled the defibrillator recharging. No response from the patient. The compressions continued.

"Milligram epi," the team leader called out. Someone injected a medication through the IV. After a minute, they paused compressions and checked Peter's pulse. Nothing.

The team leader announced "Clear" followed by another shock. Peter's body convulsed again on the gurney. This time, the rhythm strip changed, and one of the paramedics called out, "We have a pulse. Stop compressions!"

Within seconds, they loaded him onto the gurney. One of them spoke on a phone, communicating with a physician at the nearest hospital. Another covered him with a blanket to preserve his modesty. In a few minutes, they rushed him out of the room, leaving Meg, Tim, Candy, hotel security and the police officer behind.

*   *   *

A sudden silence filled the room. No one said anything. The nearer bed was the one Peter had lain on. A crinkled condom wrapper lay on the floor next to an unrolled condom. Next to the bed, a woman's bag lay partly open. Candy wore a hotel robe and still sat by the window.

The police officer sat at the circular table by the window. Candy got up, walked over to her bag and reached into it. She extracted a cigarette and a lighter; her hands shook as she lit the cigarette.

She walked back to the window and sat down, looking a little defiant. She realized the awkwardness of her position, being an escort in a hotel room with a wealthy and well-known client. Tim frowned at her as the room was "No Smoking". Given the circumstances, he decided not to say anything. The officer broke the silence.

"I'm Officer Sylvia Bentley. Want to tell me what happened, who you are, why you're here, and all of that?"

Candy recounted what had happened, describing his comments about hearing his mother's voice and then complaining of chest pain.

"It was like, weird. I guess he set up this, uh, meeting, and the agency sent me here to meet him at one o'clock.

"Within a few minutes of me being here, he sits up in bed and looks around the room, like he heard something. A few minutes later, he looks around the room and was like 'Mom'? I thought he had called me 'mom.'" She left out any parts that may have implicated her in any sexual activity.

"Then, he complains about his chest hurting and he's like 'I'm going crazy' and 'what the hell,' shit like that. Then he blacked out.

"The last thing I says to him was that I would call 9-1-1 and I did. Just before he blacked out, he tried to say something," said Candy. "I think it was 'life flashing' or something like that. I couldn't make out what it was. That's pretty much it.

"Nothing else happened between me and him," she insisted.

"Calm down, hon," Officer Bentley reassured her, "I'm not arresting you."

After Candy finished her narrative, the officer jotted down her contact information.

"You can go," Officer Bentley said to Candy. "Now would be a good time to consider another line of work."

Candy did not say anything. She gathered her clothes strewn about the floor by the side of the bed. She scooped the condom and wrapper and went into the bathroom.

Officer Bentley conducted a brief interview with Meg and Tim. Meg did not have much to add other than recount Peter's arrival and details of the phone call from the room. Neither Tim nor the security guard had anything to add. Candy came out of the bathroom and left without looking at any of the others and without saying another word.

*   *   *

As the ambulance sped to the hospital with sirens blaring, Peter's rhythm strip continued to show an irregular rhythm, but he had a palpable pulse. The end-tidal carbon dioxide monitor on his breathing tube showed a wavy line.

As they turned onto the hospital's driveway, an alarm went off and the rhythm strip again deteriorated. The CO_2 tracing also flattened.

"Oh shit," said a paramedic. "We're losing him again."

The ambulance had pulled up in the porte cochere of the emergency room by now. The back door of the ambulance opened, disgorging two paramedics. They took one end of the gurney and pulled it out. Two other paramedics soon followed and as the gurney came out, two sets of wheels straightened and locked into place. The other paramedics grabbed the far end of the gurney and they raced into the emergency room.

The patient on the gurney was comatose. The portable monitor registered random sawtooth lines. There was no ordered rhythm. Which meant no cardiac output. Which meant no blood pressure. The paramedics raced through the entrance and the emergency room staff waited to meet them.

"We had him for a while but as we pulled in, we lost him again."

"Bay 4," someone barked. They rushed the patient to bay 4 through the controlled chaos.

Like a well-oiled machine, the emergency room staff took over the code. Everyone knew their assigned task.

"On three," someone said. "One, two, three" and on three, everyone standing around the gurney lifted Peter to a bed with a CPR board. Someone connected the EKG leads to the monitor and someone else did a quick IV line survey. The paramedics gave report to the emergency room staff as the physician took over running the code.

The emergency room physician, Dr. Paul Simms, went to the head of the bed. The patient's chest did not move much, although it was difficult to assess. *Not ventilating very well,* Dr. Simms thought.

"Call anesthesia," Dr. Simms said. While examining the airway, he barked orders for various resuscitative drugs and shocks.

Another round of drugs later, one of the ER staff held the defibrillator paddles against his chest and Dr. Simms announced "Clear." Everyone took a step back. Peter jerked on the bed in response to the shock. Everyone looked at the monitor as the defibrillator recharged with a whine. The monitor continued to show an irregular combination of sawtooth lines.

SEVEN

Jick entered the operating room lounge to exchange news and gossip with his colleagues.

"Jick," he heard a chorus as he walked in. "You're back."

"Yes, I'm back. And glad to be back."

"Glad to be back? At work?" It was Tom Lowery, one of his colleagues. "How was the cruise?"

"Great," Jick said, in a voice that showed it was anything but. "By about day four, I wanted to lower a lifeboat and row back to shore."

"What happened?"

"I found it boring. The activities were not my deal, and the people were not fun to talk to. I should have gone on one of those organized tours for singles to one location and spent a week on the beach. Like to one of the Caribbean islands, for example."

"Well, welcome back. The Rangers are on a four-game winning streak," Tom stated. He loved talking about the Rangers. Jick had outgrown watching baseball years ago.

"Great," Jick said in the same voice.

After a little more chatter with others, he walked off to check his cases for the day. For the rest of the morning, he immersed himself in the routine of getting cases started, relieving staff for breaks, and making sure there were no anesthesia disasters. Pretty much a typical day. For most of the day, the nurse anesthetist and he worked with a surgeon who did lower extremity orthopedic cases. He did the first three with a spinal anesthetic and the fourth with a laryngeal mask airway.

After lunch, Jick's cases were underway, and he stood by the Big Board at the nurse's station. Dr. Bob Foster, "ran the board", making changes that coordinated the various surgical procedures, scheduling surgeons, relieving staff for lunch breaks, and making sure things progressed through the day. Jick wandered into the lounge and dropped into a chair.

The phone at the front desk rang. The charge nurse answered it.

"Dr. Foster, it's the emergency room. They need anesthesia down there for an airway. It's not STAT but they would appreciate an assist ASAP."

Dr. Foster leaned behind the nurse's desk and peered into the lounge. Jick was the only one there.

"Jick, the ER called. They need us for an airway. Wanna go?"

"No problem."

Jick picked up the bag of various airway management tools kept handy so they could, at a moment's notice, respond to urgent calls. He walked to the elevator and went down to the emergency room.

As the elevator doors opened, he saw some ER staff standing by Bay 4. Scattered commands for various drugs could be heard from inside the room. Every now and then, the command "Clear" punctuated the air, followed by a popping sound and a whine. He walked quickly to the room.

"Hi, Jick," the ER doctor said.

"Hi, Paul, what's up?" he asked.

"This guy arrived in full arrest. We've done pretty much everything, and he keeps going in and out of v. fib. Cath lab is ready if we can bring him back. His airway is not great. Want to have a look?"

One of the ER staff stopped squeezing the Ambu bag, and Jick stepped over to take a look. The patient had an airway whose position was "anterior," as well as a weak chin which rendered it more difficult to intubate him. Jick used one of his advanced airway management tools and in a few seconds, secured the airway with a proper endotracheal tube.

"Thanks," Dr. Simms said. "We'll keep going for a few more rounds."

As he left the room, Jick glanced back at the patient. He lay pale and motionless, except for movement from the compressions and the occasional jerk during shocks. As he walked to the nursing station, he heard a shout from someone in Bay 4.

"We have a pulse!" It sounded like Dr. Simms. "Call the cath lab. We're taking him straight there."

He walked over to the nursing station and picked up the patient's chart to jot down a quick progress note about the intubation. He noted with a start of recognition that the patient was Peter Northrup, whom he had seen that morning as he drove by. Jick had not recognized him in the emergency room. He had attended Peter's fiftieth birthday a few months ago. He knew Peter had two college-age children, a boy and a girl, who attended college somewhere in the Pacific Northwest. Jick sighed and shut the chart.

One of the emergency room nurses sat on the chair next to him.

"That's Peter Northrup," she said.

He glanced over.

"Hi Mallory," Jick said.

Jick thought Mallory's best attributes were her cheeks. She had the most perfectly shaped bubble butt known to man. If there was a beauty contest for ass cheeks, she would not have been an ER nurse. She was also aware of this, wearing scrub bottoms one size too small.

"Yes, I know, I realized that just now. He's one of my neighbors. I know him."

"He's your neighbor? Did you know the triage call for his arrival came from the Regence Hotel downtown?"

"Oh," Jick was surprised. Why would he be at a downtown hotel in the middle of the day? Maybe he had a meeting to attend.

"He may have had a meeting to attend," Jick ventured.

"The call came from a hotel room," Mallory said, poker-faced. "That's where they found him."

"Oh."

"He was already in cardiac arrest. He did not make the call." She maintained the same expression.

"Oh," he said for the third time.

"Who did? Oh, never mind, there's no use speculating. It will get the rumor mill wound up. I'm sure we'll know more details in due time."

He watched Mallory walk away and then went back upstairs to the operating room.

His stomach growled to remind him he had skipped lunch. He headed back to the lounge where Mireille Lavoisseur sat alone, having finished her day. Mireille was one of the recent hires; she had joined the department about three months ago. She was a nurse anesthetist, about thirty-five he guessed, single, and very good-looking. She hailed from Canada, from somewhere in the French-speaking part, and had moved to Dallas to start work. Jick had spoken to her a few times but knew very little about her. What he did know was she was not seeing anyone.

She had a striking appearance. She stood about five-eight, one-twenty-five, with a well-proportioned physique. Jick had always been partial to a pretty face and with her black hair, tan complexion, and brown eyes, he thought she was one of the most attractive women he had seen in a long time.

I would have loved to have Mireille along on the cruise, he thought. *But then again, if Mireille had been with me, I wouldn't have needed to go on the damn cruise.*

"Hi, Mireille," he said.

"Dr. Arnsson," she said, acknowledging him. "How are you?" Her voice had a slight Canadian lilt.

"Fine. A little hungry. I'm going to the cafeteria for a late lunch."

Then, without thinking, "Would you like to join me?" and inside *What the hell, Jick?*

Her answer surprised him.

"Sure," she replied. "I planned to work out but that can wait for a bit. I didn't have lunch either, so I'll get a snack before working out." Her "out" came out like "oat." *Charming.*

They walked downstairs to the hospital cafeteria. For a hospital cafeteria, the food was not bad. Many hospitals nowadays compete for better patient satisfaction scores, so improving cafeteria services is a good way to make a favorable first impression. He chose a cheeseburger and fries, and she chose a bowl of seafood gumbo with cornbread. On an impulse, he offered to pay, and she accepted. *Hmmmm*, he thought. In the dining area, she picked up a bottle of Tabasco and splashed a generous amount of Louisiana's finest hot sauce over her gumbo.

They chose a table near one of the large windows with a panoramic view of downtown Dallas. As they ate, she started the conversation.

"So, who was the code?"

"Believe it or not, it was Peter Northrup. You know the guy; he's always giving to this or that charity. Nice guy. He's only fifty."

"Never heard of him. But I moved to Dallas only a few months ago. I heard something about this on the news. I didn't realize they had brought him here. I didn't know he was well-known in the area. I heard the police and paramedics responded to a 9-1-1 call at the Regence Hotel."

"I knew that. The triage nurse in the ER told me."

"Word is already spreading on the grapevine that the call came from a certain woman in the room with him."

"Certain woman?" Jick asked. "Not his wife?"

"Well, let's say she was like a parking meter. Paid by the hour."

He smiled at the joke even though it was not very good.

"Oh," he said. "So, he was there with someone, and he coded while they ...?" He lifted an eyebrow.

"Seems that way."

He took a bite of his burger and thought about that while chewing. Peter was a nice guy. As he was well-known in the Dallas area and had been a neighbor, Jick knew about his wife and two children. Things would be difficult when they found out.

"I know he has a wife and two grown kids. It's possible they had problems. Or a midlife crisis thing. I can relate. I'm having a latelife crisis."

"A latelife crisis?"

"Well, a midlife crisis happens in your fifties. I went through a divorce and had to focus on my work then. So, I didn't get a tattoo, buy a sports car, get into risky relationships, or do any crazy shit like that. But now I'm in my mid-sixties and I still don't have a tattoo or own a sports car. But I wouldn't mind getting into a crazy relationship. So now when I sometimes I feel like I'm either having, or about to have, a crisis, 'latelife' seems to fit."

"So, Dr. Arnsson, what crazy things are you contemplating?" Mireille asked with a smile.

"It'll take too long to explain." He took a breath. "How about we get together one evening after work and go to happy hour at Julio's? I can tell you all about the crazy things I'm contemplating." *Time to throw caution to the wind*, he thought, followed by *Shit, Jick, you have to work with her. What the hell are you doing?*

She surprised him again.

"OK."

"Oh. Good. And you can call me Jick," he said. *In for a penny, in for a pound.*

"What kind of a name is Jick? Is it a nickname?"

"I don't know. My first name is Jayant. It's Indian. My mother was English, of Indian descent, and my father was from Texas of Swedish descent. I am not sure where Jick came from, but my kid brother, who's ten years younger than me, called me Jick, I think. I'm not sure if he came up with it or just heard something. And it stuck."

He steered the conversation back to Peter Northrup.

"Wonder what went through Northrup's mind when he realized he was in trouble? I wonder if he had some thoughts about his wife finding out."

"Well, they say your life flashes before your eyes. Hope he had some pleasant thoughts toward the end," Mireille said.

"He did not look good, but he may still pull through. It would be interesting to talk to him and see if he had any near-death experiences.

"I'm not a neuroscientist but this life-flashes-before-your-eyes thing is interesting. Our brains maintain memories by the continuous infusion of energy in the form of glycogen. I guess it's like shining light on a phosphorescent object. When the light turns off, the brain cells depolarize, or discharge all their memories right away, in a process that takes a few minutes at most. I imagine memories from your past could get replayed before the end."

"Would that make it fluorescent or phosphorescent?" Mireille asked.

"Well, with fluorescence, as soon as the light source turns off, the glow stops immediately. With phosphorescence, there's a period of time as the glow fades away."

"I see."

This was not a particularly scintillating conversation, but he was glad Mireille seemed enthusiastic.

The conversation paused again.

As Jick ate his burger and glanced at Mireille, she unfolded a napkin and dabbed at her mouth.

"Hot gumbo," she commented.

A single bead of perspiration emerged from her hairline near her left ear and inched its way down the side of her neck. As Jick watched, it came to life. The drop seemed to have a mind of its own, pausing and changing direction as it encountered the moist skin of her neck. It clung to the side of her neck, indecisive about its direction. Then it gained enough inertia to dart down her neck and upper left chest before disappearing into her scrubs over her left breast. A small darker green wet spot appeared on her scrubs where the drop had landed above her left breast. A second drop appeared, navigating a different route down her glistening neck.

Lucky drops, he thought. *I feel like such a horny dog watching her eat.*

That, and that he was sixty-four. And single. And deprived.

Mireille finished her gumbo. Jick took another bite of his burger.

"Perfect time for me to go work out, eh? I'm already sweating like a pig."

Oh God. She could be sweating like a pig but at this moment, I sure as hell feel like un vieux cochon.

"OK. I'll finish and head back to the OR." He couldn't stand at this moment. Maybe in a few minutes...

EIGHT

Jick bounded out of bed the next morning, the pain from his right knee banished by his euphoric mood. No more smacking the snooze button, his reluctance to get out of bed having evaporated with Mireille saying yes to going out after work. He wondered if this evening would be too soon to see if she wanted to go to Julio's after work for a drink.

Jick went through his morning rituals of pills, coffee, shower, and breakfast. Today's microwave offering consisted of *idlis* and *chutney*. This time, to increase his protein intake, he also fried two eggs. He looked forward to today.

As he drove down the driveway, he paused at the end. Yesterday, at about this time, he had seen Peter Northrup drive to work. He wondered what had been going through his mind. He wondered if Peter had been having a midlife crisis thing or if there had been problems developing in their marriage. His life may have come to an abrupt and sordid end, leaving his wife with many unanswered questions and likely some regrets. Jick's thoughts wandered around about the transitory nature of life and as soon as he went down that rabbit hole, the Black Cloud threatened to return. He shook his head, raised the volume on the radio for distraction, and turned right toward the hospital, fingers tapping on the steering wheel to the rhythm of the song.

He pulled into the hospital at about six-thirty and made his usual brief morning pilgrimage to his office. He had not looked at today's assignments. In the excitement of being involved with Peter Northrup's possible failed resuscitation, it had completely slipped his mind. He decided he would check on Peter. He logged in and noted with mild surprise that Peter was now in the coronary ICU, still intubated, having survived his ordeal. The survival odds for someone this far along the resuscitation algorithm were not good.

He's lucky. Somehow managed to get as close as possible to death without crossing the threshold.

He noted with a grimace that his assignment today was the pediatric ear, nose, and throat room. It was not one of his favorite assignments. He went to the lounge. Mireille was there.

"How was your workout?"

"Great," she said. "Important to stay in shape. You should get into the habit of working out at least three or four times a week."

Is she inviting me to work out with her? No way could I do that.

His mind conjured images of her running on a treadmill, her tight workout clothes wet with perspiration, her hair stuck to the nape of her neck, the exposed skin of her upper back and shoulders glistening. *No way...*

He snapped out of his reverie. Mireille had said something.

"I'm sorry, what was that?"

"Are you going to Dr. Madison's retirement party?" She pointed at the bulletin board where the department secretary had posted a flyer about the upcoming party.

Walter Madison, M.D. was one of the senior members of the anesthesiology department. His retirement was imminent and at age sixty-five, he and his wife had bought a motorhome to drive around the country. He was one of Jick's colleagues who had rhapsodized about cruising and his enthusiasm was one reason Jick had considered it. *He'll go on a seniors-only cruise with the missus, and they'll play Bingo*, he thought, still a little sour over the cruising experience.

"I don't want to, but I guess I should. He's sixty-five and I'm a year behind. Next year they'll be throwing something similar for me. Christ, Mireille, I'm sixty-four. I've been doing this for thirty years, and what do I have to show for it? The last thing I want to do is go to someone's retirement party and everyone is wearing black and acting obnoxious, making grim reaper jokes. It's as bad as a turning fifty or turning sixty birthday party. I'm sure for his retirement presents he'll get a rocking chair, reading glasses, maybe even some spoof presents like male vitality pills or incontinence underwear. No, I do not want to go."

"Wow, glad I asked," she joked.

Jick had not planned to vent and cringed that he had. There was nothing dumber than asking a younger woman out and then telling her what a cranky and old man he really was. Maybe discovering he had been assigned the pediatric ENT room had left him irritable. Maybe he just *was* a cranky old man. He glanced at Mireille and found her nodding in support and understanding. But he would wait to ask her out. He did not want a sympathy date.

Work was hectic this morning, doing a string of quick cases with a rapid turnaround. His schedule listed nine cases, six involving placement of ear tubes and three involving tonsillectomies and adenoidectomies. For the ear tube cases, if the children had not yet developed stranger anxiety, it was straightforward. They would carry the kids, make some cooing sounds as they whisked the kids to the operating room, and then place a mask that allowed them to breathe a combination of nitrous oxide and an inhaled anesthetic. They would drift off to sleep in a few seconds. The anesthesia team would hold the child's head turned one way and then the other and the surgeon would use a microscope to place the ear tubes. These surgeries took only a few minutes.

For the older children, the ones who would scream at the sight of a stranger, a mild oral sedative in the holding area smoothed things out. The usual cocktail was a dose of midazolam dissolved in acetaminophen syrup. Even sedated, the children were scared, sleep deprived, hungry, and irritable. To make things worse, these rapid turnaround cases meant little to no downtime in the OR lounge.

The longer tonsillectomy cases presented a different challenge. The little bastards had massive tonsils and obstructed breathing, making the induction of anesthesia more difficult. These kids also needed an IV line placed after the midazolam and inhaled anesthetic knocked them out. Not only that, after surgery, they were at risk for developing a bleeder from the tonsillectomy site, so the anesthesia team tried their best to minimize gagging and retching on the breathing tube while they came out of anesthesia. All things being equal, Jick felt he could do without dealing with this type of anesthesia.

After the last case finished, he went to the OR lounge and sprawled on a chair. Bob Foster wandered in behind him.

Bob Foster was a little BMI-challenged, which was the politically correct way of saying he was fat. The lounge chairs were black vinyl with a U-shaped seat padded on all sides by the same vinyl in a wraparound design. Someone had once joked that Bob would need a running start to fit in the chairs. Someone else had shown no mercy in writing "Running Start" in fluorescent red paint on one of the chairs. Bob took it in stride. He walked over to "Running Start" and sank heavily into it, a huff of escaping air from the cushions signaling his descent.

"How was your day?" he asked.

"Shitty. Thanks for asking," Jick said. "That pedi ENT room has to be the worst. I would rather do half dozen stat sections."

"Doing anything later?"

"No, nothing planned. Why?"

Walter Madison entered the lounge as they spoke, so Bob did not answer Jick immediately. Jick helped himself to a glass of Dr. Pepper from the soda fountain and sat back in the chair. Walter had stopped to check the next day's schedule, pinned to the bulletin board.

"Looks like I'm covering OB tomorrow," he said.

"Shouldn't be too bad," Bob said. "The census has been on the low side up there. But you never know. Some grand multip will show up in breech with fetal decels and the shit will hit the fan."

"I'm getting too old for this," Walter said.

"Don't worry. Your retirement is almost here. We have to give you a grand sendoff by having you cover the shittiest assignments. So, I guess OB it is."

"Oh, I don't mind," Walter said. "It's funny when all the midwives and nurses appreciate us being there but also treat us like crap because we represent MAN, the evil being that caused the women to be in pain. But then we get that epidural in and the women, the patients I mean, are so thankful."

"Well, I'm heading out for today. 'Bye guys." Walter left the lounge and headed upstairs to the labor and delivery area.

Bob turned back to Jick.

"The department wants to get together and buy Walter a retirement present. We thought a rocking chair with an engraved plate with an inscription thanking him for the years of service would be appreciated. And maybe a little something else."

"Got something in mind?"

"No, no specific item. I know he's into clocks, golf, and going on cruises. I figured one of us could get something meaningful to go with the rocking chair. Do you want to do it?"

Jick did not want to but explaining why would only prove he was that cranky old man.

"Sure," Jick said. "I'll drive around, stop at one of those stores with gag gifts and maybe get him an obnoxious T-shirt. You've seen those shirts with 'Old Guys Rule'. I'll find him one with a cartoon and caption 'Old Guys Drool.'"

"Well, if you're thinking gag gift, how about a penis pump?" Bob suggested with a grin.

Jick responded with a laugh to avoid showing his own discomfort at the whole aging thing. He left the hospital late that afternoon in a foul mood because it had been a long and tiring day. Or maybe his mood was foul because of the way he had vented at Mireille in airing out his anxieties about growing old. He had not even thought of asking Mireille if she wanted to have a drink at Julio's after work. Now he had to get Walter a present on the way home. He took a detour on his way home and drove a few miles to Deep Ellum, the historic and one of the oldest areas of Dallas.

They have unusual shops there. Maybe I'll find something interesting.

NINE

As Jick approached Deep Ellum, he noticed a few scattered
groups of homeless people loitering about. The individual
homeless stood by intersections as if they were declaring
their turf, holding signs requesting money, food, or anything
else to help. Those who were not actively panhandling
clustered in small groups near bridges and overpasses. He
did not hand out money because given the desperate straits
they faced, too often they would use the money to buy a few
minutes of escape from their predicament, in the form of
cigarettes or alcohol and sometimes, harder drugs. Jick's
mother had taught her boys to be generous. But she had
always advised Jick to be generous with materials rather than
money.

One homeless man, standing outside a McDonald's,
held a sign that said, "Visions of a cheeseburger." Under the
caption was a picture of a giant Venus flytrap that resembled
the carnivorous plant from "Little Shop of Horrors." Under
the picture of the plant, he had written "Feed Me Now!"

The man stood straight and would do an occasional
pirouette, jiggling the sign and waving at passersby. His arms
and legs jerked like an invisible hand was pulling at strings
attached to his limbs. He made eye contact with as many
drivers as he could, making it more difficult for drivers to
ignore him. Jick smiled at the sign. He pulled into the
McDonald's and as he turned in, rolled down his window
and shouted out to the man, "Wait here."

He navigated his way to the drive-through window and
eyed the menu. He chose a double cheeseburger combo, size
large.

"One double cheeseburger combo, large fries, and a coke," Jick said to the McDonald's high school age employee.

Jick drove around to where the homeless man stood and rolled down the window. The man stopped his marionette routine and walked over.

"Here's your vision realized: double cheeseburger, fries, and coke." He handed the bag and drink to the man.

The man's eyes lit up.

"Thanks, man, I sure appreciate this." He took the proffered meal. He folded the cardboard sign, tucked it under his arm and made his way back to his roost below the overpass, bag in one hand and drink in the other. Jick watched him sit, open the bag, take out a fry and study it with appreciation before eating it. He took a long draft of his Coke and leaned back, eyes closed. Jick could almost hear the sigh of contentment. He felt good.

As he drove around the block, an antique shop caught his eye. This would be a perfect place to get Walter something like an antique pocket watch or mantelpiece clock, or some other retirement trinket. He knew Walter had a collection of old clocks, a hobby of his, and an antique pocket watch would be the perfect complement. The antique shop was large, its facade taking up much of one small city block. It looked to be about a third the size of a football field. Jick parked by the curb and alighted from his car.

The early evening sounds and smells of Deep Ellum were in the air. He heard a jazz band playing in the distance and from the opposite side, he was downwind from some restaurant's kitchen. He closed his eyes and breathed in the unmistakable aroma of smoked seasonings on meat. *Definitely slow-smoked barbecue*, he thought. He dropped a few coins into the meter and went inside.

The lighting in the antique shop was subdued. The clatter of an air conditioner fan struggling to keep up provided an aural backdrop. Fluorescent lights hung in parallel rows from the high ceiling. Many were unlit and a few flickered, signaling their imminent demise. The shop was cavernous, organized into loose sections with each area emphasizing a certain type of antique or a certain era. The sections he could see comprised a furniture section, an Old Americana section, a jewelry and coins section, and a section of books and magazines. To the right, a set of full-length saloon doors led to an annex containing miscellaneous goods. Jick explored that area first, finding most of the items in the annex looked like junk. They included random items like old appliances, old swords, children's wagons, tricycles, etc. More like a junkyard than an antique store. He went back into the main store, inspecting a few items and dismissing them as suitable presents. It was not busy this evening. Given the size of the shop, he had the impression he could have been the only shopper in there.

As he walked around, a wizened man wearing a navy blue apron approached him. He introduced himself as the proprietor.

"Is there something in particular you're looking for or that I can help you with?" he inquired.

"I'm browsing. One of my colleagues is retiring, he's sixty-five, and I'm looking for a retirement present. He's into antique clocks and I understand he has quite the collection. I thought about something like a mantelpiece clock or pocket watch."

"Our pocket watches are toward the front of the store on the left side. We have a very nice collection of railroad pocket watches and some mantelpiece clocks. You should be able to find something to your satisfaction."

"Let me browse around back here for a bit and I'll head to the front in a few minutes."

"Please take your time. Let me know if you have questions." He walked off to attend to other customers.

Toward the back of the store, a magazine rack with many older magazines leaned against the wall. It was flanked on either side by boxes containing more old magazines. An edition of the Journal of the American Medical Association from the 1890s, displayed on the rack, caught Jick's eye. He thumbed through it, marveling at the utter lack of medical knowledge and how far medicine had progressed in just over a hundred years. Anesthesiology as a distinct medical specialty had not even existed in those days. The administration of anesthesia was crude, consisting of chloroform or ether dripped on a piece of gauze embedded in a mask. Anesthesiology had been organized into a specialty only in the early 1900s. The edition he picked up had an article about rendering people insensate for surgery. The article described a precursor to his specialty, so he decided he would buy it.

Jick thumbed through a few more magazines. One of them, a Popular Mechanics from the late 1950s, caught his eye. He looked at the articles about radio tubes, amplifiers, and car designs with large tailfins. Advertisements done in those days embodied a paternalistic style that, by today's standards, would be sexist if not downright misogynistic. One advertisement showed a woman draped across her husband's lap as she is about to get a spanking for buying the wrong coffee. Realizing he was born when these advertisements were acceptable, the Black Cloud reared its head. He took a deep breath, exhaled, and went back to browsing around.

As he wandered around the shop, on one shelf toward the back, he spotted something that caught his eye. On a shelf, placed at eye level, a dome-shaped mask stood propped against a collection of other artifacts. Jick picked it up to examine it. Its substantial weight surprised him. He turned it around, studying its inner surface. It appeared to be a simple mask, a uniform dark grey-green, large enough to cover his face, with two black, almond-shaped eyeholes. A layer of dust formed a skullcap over the dome. He blew the dust off. There was no hole for the nose or mouth. The top of the mask was dome-shaped so the entire mask would fit over the head with the faceplate suspended over the face. He tried it on. It fit well. He looked out of the eye holes and surveyed the store.

The proprietor had wandered back to where Jick stood inspecting the mask. Noting Jick's interest, he said, "That mask is called the Healer of Life."

"Healer of Life?" Jick's professional interest was piqued by the reference to a healer. He lifted the mask off his head.

"Yes, that is its name, the Healer of Life."

"I'm surprised it's called a 'healer'. Aren't these antique masks usually funerary objects, like death masks?"

"*Mask mortem*," the proprietor murmured. "The mask of death.

"You are correct. In ancient Egypt, death masks were meant to strengthen the spirit in the afterlife. In more contemporary times, the death mask was used to make a sculpture of the deceased, for mementoes, museum pieces, etc.

"I don't know its source," the proprietor continued. "We think it may be Central or South American. Brunca is a possibility, although the color scheme seems too drab. Brunca masks always sported vibrant colors. It could be Incan as well. No one is sure where it came from. It was part of the Ingersoll estate sale in the 1930s. If you're not an archeology buff, you wouldn't know the name. Bartholomew Ingersoll was an archeologist who made his name and reputation exploring parts of Central and South America in the eighteenth century. He hailed from the Northeast. He retired back home to somewhere in New England."

The proprietor droned on.

"After he passed away, his sons inherited parts of his estate. One of them moved to Texas in the early nineteenth century and when he passed away, the trustees auctioned off the estate. Most of the valuable pieces went to various museums. Some lesser known and less valuable pieces sold off to individual collectors or antique stores. This mask was part of the estate, so, like I said, I assume it's Central or South American. I do not know why it is called the Healer of Life. I am not sure how one 'heals life' as such. Life is life. You live it once and it is done, right? There is no healing, no do overs."

He must have realized he had been rambling.

"Sorry, is this too much information?"

"No, no, it's fine. Some background trivia always makes it more interesting."

"It has been here for years and if you like it, I can make you a good deal," he added, a touch of eagerness tinging his voice as he hoped for a sale.

"How did you get it?"

"Now and then, when someone wealthy dies, their estate approaches us to take some less valuable artifacts. We are one of the oldest antiques stores in Dallas, with a solid reputation. A trustee of the Ingersoll estate approached us years ago."

"I see."

"This might look good in my office," Jick added. He walked over to a shaft of sunlight streaming in through one of the front windows of the shop. The sun streamed in at an angle, casting odd shadows around the store. He held the mask in the light, examining its texture. The sunlight accentuated the irregularities in the mask's inner surface. Its shadow formed a solid outline, distorted as it fell across other artifacts in the store and across the counter. It looked well-made but he could not make out the material. It looked and felt like some very dense wood. He placed a fingernail along the inner surface and pressed firmly, trying to make a mark on the surface. His fingernail grated along the material but did not leave a mark. He turned the mask in his hands. Motes of dust swirled and sparkled in the twin beams of sunlight from its eye holes.

Jick strolled over to the jewelry and coins section and set the mask down as he perused the case. A collection of old pocket watches lay on a dark red felt-lined tray. None of them worked, but he assumed they had not been wound regularly. He asked the proprietor about the watches.

"Since you are buying it as a present, let me show you some of our nicer specimens," he said. "These are specimens that still work well. If this isn't quite your price point, we have others." He unlocked the cabinet, reached in and took out two of his best specimens.

"These are railroad pocket watches," he said. "Back in the day, keeping trains running on schedule was of utmost

TEN

On the way home from the antique store, Jick stopped at the
Indian store to replenish his stock of frozen TV dinners and
other necessities. It always amused the shopkeeper that Jick
spoke some Hindi to him. Being Anglo-Indian, with his
father's tall stature and light brown eyes, he may not have
been able to discern from Jick's appearance that he would
know any Indian language. He was not particularly good at
it, but at least knew a smattering of words and phrases, even
if it might smack of a bit of an accent.

"Aap kaise hain?" Jick asked the shopkeeper how he
was.

"Mai teek hoon," he replied with a smile that he was
well.

A bit later the headlights automatically turned on as Jick
drove home, the evening already settling in. He parked the
car and went through the back door, carrying the bags of
groceries and the bag with the mask and present for Walter.
He put the bag on a side table and stacked the frozen meals
in the freezer. His friend Cabernet was finished but friend
Shiraz was present. He made a mental note to go to the wine
store tomorrow. He pulled the cork on a bottle of fine
South African Shiraz and poured a glass.

Jick settled on the couch with dinner and flipped on the
television to watch the evening news. He was in a
contemplative mood. It had been an unsettling couple of
days. Peter Northrup, age fifty, had almost died in the
emergency room earlier. Walter was about to retire at sixty-
five and his colleagues found the aging situation gag worthy.
To Jick it was just gagging.

At sixty-four, what did he have to show for his
accomplishments? In college, one of his favorite poems was

Shelley's *Ozymandias*, about a powerful king who wanted his empire to last forever. And it did not. Only a ruined statue lay among the sands, its sneering visage pushing back against time in defiance and futility. No one can overcome the remorselessness of time.

On the opposite end of the spectrum was Jick's father, whose favorite poem was "The Bull" by Ralph Hodgson, a poem about the cycle of life as a bull, ostracized from his herd, as he awaits his demise. Jick's father was an atheist who did not believe in an afterlife, realized nothing was permanent and almost seemed to look forward to his demise, choosing to exercise his right to self-determination at age seventy-five. Jick reached for his friend Shiraz for a top up.

A veil of moroseness covered Jick tonight. The Black Cloud had parked right over his head, waiting to unleash its pent-up storm. His thoughts turned to his childhood, his parents, and his decisions in life that had led to his choice of medicine as a career. And here he sat, sixty-four, divorced, few friends, a bottle (or several), and fantasizing about much younger coworkers. The cruise had been a dud, only reinforcing the reasons he had taken it in the first place.

Jick was born and raised in Dallas. His father was in the military and worked as an attaché in charge of embassy security, at one point stationed in England. There he had met his wife, part of the extensive Indian diaspora in the United Kingdom, during a diplomatic social gathering. They married and moved to the United States. After his military service, he had worked for a private security firm as a consultant, traveling often. He was an expert in krav maga, the Israeli army's street fighting based martial art. He taught both Jick's brother and him self-defense tactics.

As kids, Jick had spent some Christmas vacations in India with his grandparents in what was then called Bombay, now Mumbai. They did not visit in the summers because of the dreary weather and relentless Indian monsoons. But at Christmas, they enjoyed the trips thanks to the drier weather and cool winters. His mother had several relatives around the area, so the visits turned into mini reunions.

Jick spoke a little Hindi, of the Bombay Hindi kind. A good analogy is speaking English, of the hillbilly English kind. You could get your point across and most people understood it. But purists tended to look down on Bombay Hindi speakers. However, with the proliferation of Bollywood movies, this type of Hindi gained a gradual acceptance.

They also went to Sweden once, to see the part of Sweden from where his father's ancestors hailed. After three generations, he did not know any relatives there, but it was still fun to explore the country. In July, Sweden was a mesmerizing place with ten o'clock dinners under sunlight.

His mother gave his brother and Jick their first names, Jayant and Vikram, both meaning victorious. For reasons he did not know, everyone knew the boys as "Jick" and "Vic." Jick's brother was born ten years after him, so they did not have the typical close relationship with horseplay, sibling rivalries, or fights. However, as adults, a bond developed, and Jick enjoyed having a kid brother in a different line of work that he could "shoot the shit" with.

Jick did not know what he wanted to do with his life until college. He did not have an epiphany that resulted in his choosing medicine, although he had the grades to get into medical school. Until the last minute, he remained undecided. A girl he knew in college also wanted to get into medical school, but her grades and qualifying exam scores did not measure up to gain admission. She exhorted Jick to go with the grades he had, so he did. For his personality—not that much of a people person—anesthesiology turned out to be the perfect fit.

Then he met Dorothy, a nurse. They had married but could not have any children. After twenty years of marriage, they had drifted apart and got divorced about ten years ago. Dorothy remarried, lived in Florida, and Jick and she rarely spoke.

His thoughts turned from the gloomy to the physical. A better word would be carnal and involving Mireille. As the wine had its desired effect, he could not stop thinking about Mireille. *But shit, Jick, you're almost thirty years older than she is,* he thought, as his friend Shiraz placated any concerns about the age difference.

And so, he whiled away the evening with his friend Shiraz, thinking about Mireille, relieving himself into a relaxing torpor, and falling asleep on the couch.

ELEVEN

Two weeks after his heart attack, Peter Northrup was back at work. Paula and the children had rushed back from the Pacific Northwest and the first few days after he left the hospital were pleasant. But for someone as well-known as Peter, the circumstances around his heart attack could not be kept under wraps. From media narratives and police reports, Paula soon found out what had happened. Peter and she had a few explosive rows followed by a strained silence. Paula had stopped talking to Peter, so he stayed late at the office to avoid returning home.

As Peter drove home from work, a familiar vehicle ahead of him turned left into a driveway. Peter still reeled from Paula's phone call earlier in the day, and he felt he needed to talk.

Oh, what the hell, he thought. On an impulse, Peter steered his car onto the driveway.

*   *   *

Jick alighted from his car and paused as a car pulled into his driveway. The headlights washed over him, and he turned to see who it was. He recognized the car.

"Hi, Peter," Jick said as Peter got out of his car.

"Hi, Jick. How's it going?"

"Fine. I just finished a long day at work, and I was about to kick back and have a drink."

"Care for a little company? I won't stay long."

"Sure, come on in. Give me a minute to kick off my shoes and change and I'll meet you on the patio."

Wonder why he doesn't want to go home. I can guess...

Jick came out of the house a few minutes later, carrying two wine glasses, a bottle, and a pewter serving bowl filled with cocktail peanuts. He flipped a switch and simulated candle lights turned on, casting a soft, flickering yellow glow over the patio. He pulled the cork out of the wine bottle with a deft twist and poured two glasses.

"Cheers," Peter said.

"To your health," said Jick.

They touched glasses and Peter leaned back, swirled his drink. He took a sip of wine and glanced at the glass.

"This is very good. What is it?"

"A South African shiraz. Saxenburg is the winery. I'm partial to fine shirazes from South Africa."

"It is excellent." He swirled the glass again and took a more generous sip.

For the next minute, they did not say anything. Peter studied the label on the bottle. The bug zapper let out a resounding crack as a flying insect met its demise. Then Peter placed the bottle on the table, took a deep breath, puffed out his cheeks, and began.

"Paula wants out."

"Wants out?"

"Divorce. She called me at work today and said she's done."

"Oh-kay." Jick did not say anything else, waited for Peter to continue.

"We've been having problems. I won't go into details. She had gone to visit the kids and you know what they say, 'When the cat's away, the mice will play'. I went to an escort service."

He stopped, waiting for Jick to say something. Jick filled the pause with a slow, deliberate sip. He scooped a few peanuts and popped them into his mouth.

"I'm sure you had your reasons."

"Did you ever do anything like that?"

"Go to an escort service? No. Just not my thing."

"I never did before either. Guess I wanted to do something wild and exciting."

He swirled his glass and contemplated the wine, its legs sparkling against the glass in the faux candle lights.

"She was gorgeous. Young, tattoos, body glitter, her smell. And fuckin-A, Jick, her name was Candy. *Candy*. Probably not her real name but still. I'm sure she did all the things I have fantasized about. I planned out every contingency except for the goddamn heart attack. And now it's all out there and Paula wants out."

He tipped his head back to drain the glass and reached for the bottle to top up his glass.

"So, what are you going to do?"

"I don't know, Jick. I mean, I guess I'll get a lawyer. She is really mad at me; guess I can't blame her. But it is still a kick in the balls."

"Do you remember any of it?"

"The heart attack?"

"Yes."

"I'm not sure. The whole day was weird. I was stressed about it all day and kept hearing things."

"Like what?"

"Just shit replaying in my head from my childhood. My mother telling me stuff. Probably my voice of conscience."

"They say your life flashes before your eyes when you're about to die. Maybe that's what it was. Your brain being weird and replaying your life."

"Yeah, maybe. Last thing I remember was she was holding my dick and then I blacked out."

"You almost died, Peter. Hell, you were dead there for a while. They took you to the cath lab and put in a stent; I'm sure you already knew that. The part you probably don't know is where the stent was placed in your heart."

"Where was that?"

"Let me put it this way. The lesion you had is called the Widowmaker."

"I see."

"We don't often see people that far into a code pulling out of it. You are in that magical 'less than five percent survival' category."

"I did not realize that. The first thing I remember was being in the hospital and the nurse telling me it was three days later."

"You don't remember anything else? No pearly gates, white lights, or even red creatures with pitchforks and pointy ears?"

Peter looked at Jick.

"Nope, nothing like that. Just my whole life replaying in my head, then the gorgeous girl, then game over. And now it really is game over. Certainly for my marriage."

Jick changed the subject.

"Why are you already back at work?"

"Why not? I feel good. Just a little tired every now and then."

"Your heart took a pretty good whack, Peter. I haven't looked through your chart, but I would have thought you would need longer to recover. Does your cardiologist know you're back at work?"

"Uh, no." Peter looked sheepish.

"But there is work to do, Jick, and I enjoy it. Every time I do a winning deal, it's an adrenaline rush."

"Just what your heart doesn't need right now. An adrenaline rush."

"I'll try to take it easy."

He paused for another sip of wine.

"How do you do it, Jick? You've got a few years on me."

"Do what?"

"Cope with getting old. You seem more laid back about it."

"I'm not. For what it's worth, I was also about fifty when I got divorced."

"You were married?"

"Yes, no kids. After the divorce, I focused too much on work. Now I'm sixty-four and there's not much to show for the last fifteen years."

He nodded toward the bottle of wine.

"This is my friend."

"It's not fair," Peter mused, staring at his glass. "I'm fifty, what have I got, maybe another fifteen or twenty good years? Then what?"

This conversation had awakened the Black Cloud. Jick went into the house and came back with another bottle.

"No, it's not fair," he said. "No matter what path we're on through life, everyone converges on the same point."

"It's fucked up, Jick," Peter said, downing the rest of his wine and waiting for Jick to top up his glass.

Despite being almost fifteen years older than Peter, Jick felt a wave of sympathy for the younger man. Peter was too ego driven to ever slow down and enjoy life.

"I would ask you to stay for dinner if you want but I'm having a TV dinner. We can order something."

"No, that's OK. I won't stay. I should get home. I'll probably have a TV dinner too.

"Thanks for letting me intrude on your evening."

"Not a problem. I enjoyed it. But you should try to take it easy with work."

They finished their drinks and Peter stood up.

"But I feel good, Jick. I really do."

            *   *   *

Art Marlow sat at his desk on a Tuesday morning some three weeks after he had realized the most recent attempt at synthesizing organs from a single stem cell had failed. A dense cloud front had rolled in, both on the horizon and in his mood. Later today, he had agreed to meet with the university's office of translational research and representatives of various institutional and individual investors. Another university administrator, the liaison between the university and the semi-independent CellGenEX, the limited-liability corporation created to market the process, would also be present.

Art sipped his coffee, but the upcoming meeting preoccupied his thoughts too much to savor its flavor. Ever since he realized his research had probably reached a dead end with organ synthesis, an overshadowing dread about today's meeting had pervaded his thinking.

"Are you feeling OK?" his wife asked.

"Yes, I'm fine," he said. "I have a meeting today and my primary goal is to develop a strategy to convince the investors to give me more time. I'm working on a Plan B that should be successful but to see it through to fruition will take about six more months, at least, more likely a year. We are working like crazy in the lab."

"Well, good luck at the meeting," she said.

The meeting would begin at nine o'clock in the administration building. Art left home at eight o'clock and went straight to his office first. Members of his staff were present in the lab.

"Good morning, sir," one of them said. They all knew what was stake today, or at least suspected it, and all eyes turned to him.

"Anything we can, um, help you with for today's meeting?" one ventured.

"No," he said. "I'm working on a model that differs from what we have been doing, and I just need time to think it through. These types of meetings are an enormous distraction. But we need the money and cannot afford to jeopardize it by pissing off the investors."

One of the research assistants voiced concern. "I am worried about our lab, sir. It would suck to have to look for another job, but I could find something. I'm more worried for you. You've been good to us."

"Well, let's not panic," Art said. "We need another year so I need to convince these guys we can get something done in the next year."

"But what? Trying to get organs to grow all the way from a single cell has been way more difficult than you thought."

"Yes, it has. But don't worry, I have a Plan B."

He left for the meeting at eight forty-five and walked from the lab building to the administration building. He made his way to conference room C on the third floor. He

entered at exactly nine o'clock and noted that all the other
attendees had arrived already.

A circular conference table in dark mahogany sat in the
middle of the square conference room. The other attendees
had clustered in a semicircle on the far side. On the near
side, bottled water, a pen, and a small notepad had already
been placed, marking his spot. Thus, he would sit facing all
of them. *Feels like an inquisition*, he thought. *Only things missing
are the naked light bulb and the restraints.*

Richard Hardman, the administrator for the office of
translational research, sat across from Art. Art thought Dick
Hardman was a great name for a porn star although this
Dick Hardman did not look the part. But he could be a dick
sometimes. He adjusted his glasses, flipped open a folder,
and opened the meeting.

"Good morning, everyone," he began. "We are here
today to discuss Professor Art Marlow's research and to get
an update on where things stand. As I recall from our last
meeting three months ago, we are on the exciting cusp of
being able to create organs from single stem cells. So,
without further ado, I'll turn things over to Professor
Marlow."

Art cleared his throat. From the neutral and hopeful
looks on the faces of the investors, it was clear there had
been no leak of his failure. He had to tread with care now.
He believed the direct approach was best.

"Good morning, everyone," he said. "Thanks for taking
the time to attend today's meeting. The news I have to
report is exciting but unfortunately, not as good as I would
have liked. I'll get straight to the point.

"We had five attempts at organogenesis from single
stem cells and with each attempt, we got closer to the holy
grail. On our sixth attempt, we had hoped we addressed and
solved all the variables. But this was not the case. This most
recent attempt improved on the previous attempt and a
kidney did form as planned. Everything about it, from size
to shape to weight, looked perfect. But, under microscopic
analysis, we identified several abnormal cells. To put it
bluntly, we cannot move forward with these results. But," he

paused with an encouraging smile as he gazed across the semi-circle of now concerned faces, "I have a different plan of attack to solve the problem, and I am excited to discuss that today because I would need the support of the investors."

A slight murmur of astonishment rose from the group. The representative for the investors spoke. He first introduced himself as Timothy Bryan. He had a doctorate in molecular and cell biology. He worked for industry as a scientific liaison.

"Let me see if I understand what you said. Are you saying your research has reached a dead end?"

"Well, I would not put it in such drastic terms," Art Marlow said. "But we are at something of an impasse and the only way to move forward is to modify the plan."

"And how do you intend to, as you say, 'modify the plan?'" Bryan asked. A hint of skepticism crept across his expression.

Art Marlow paused for a moment and cleared his throat. He sipped some water before clearing his throat again and began.

"The major difficulty we have been having is unwanted cells forming in the structural matrix, the scaffolding, if you will, in the organs. There is something about the structural proteins that hold organs together that we could not solve with our current approach."

"This whole process of growing organs from single stem cells was bound to be difficult anyway," Bryan agreed. "This is a process that has taken millions of years of evolution and you planned to do it in days to weeks in what is little more than a glorified Petri dish, right?"

"Well, not a flattering description of our research but the gist of what you said is correct," Marlow admitted.

"So what's the modified plan?" asked someone from the group.

Marlow continued. "All organs go through a process of cellular regeneration during the organ's lifetime. Toward the end, cells undergo apoptosis which, for the layperson," he nodded toward the administrators, "is a term for programmed cell death. With the knowledge we have already gained from years of this research, we would like to take an existing organ and hasten the process of cell death while creating new cells at the same time. The stem cell would, of course, generate the new cells. Therefore, the structural matrix would remain as is and new cells would take the place of the old."

He paused. Tim Bryan's facial expression had changed from skepticism to incredulity. Everyone else blinked or looked at one another with a neutral expression, displaying a lack of understanding.

"Let me get this straight," Bryan said. "You're telling me you will take an existing organ that I presume is a donation from someone. You're going to introduce a way to hasten the organ's 'demise,' if you will, at a cellular level by increasing the rate at which cells undergo apoptosis. As the native cells die off, the stem cell, using your proprietary method of guiding cellular differentiation, will generate 'normal' cells that will take the place of the dead cells, bypassing the issues you've had with the structural matrix. In the presence of like cells and your proprietary method, the hope is that these cells will differentiate into the proper cells and not result in creating these extraneous and incorrect structural cells. These newer cells will have the DNA of the stem cell and thus, you would have an intact organ that is genetically compatible and in a structurally sound matrix."

"Correct," said Marlow.

"My first impression, if you will excuse my saying so, is that this is absurd." Bryan leaned back in his chair.

A flash of anger gleamed in Art Marlow's eyes.

"Absurd? I would respectfully disagree.

"We have a body of knowledge that spans years and has allowed us to create organs, almost to the last step, starting with a single stem cell. That, in itself, is remarkable and would have been called absurd only a few short years ago. True, this last step has proved challenging and therefore, with a slight modification in approach, we need to use an existing organ to provide the required matrix as new cells are generated in it to replicate the recipient's DNA."

"But, Art," Bryan leaned forward, "what you're suggesting is hardly a 'slight modification'. This is, whole cloth, a different field of research. Even if you could demonstrate viability, and I have my doubts, I represent investors whom you have promised for years your research would yield genetically compatible organs from a single stem cell. Now you're saying you want to start with an existing organ. You would need to keep this organ alive at the cellular level while your concoctions or potions do their work. Who knows how long that will take? You do not know the kinetics of cellular replacement or even if it is viable. We are talking about growing another organ in an existing one as the existing one dies off at the cellular level. This process could take weeks to months. During that time, do you expect the intended recipient of the donated organ to sit around twiddling their thumbs while this donated organ's DNA changes to match theirs? And if that's the case, why bother at all? Why not continue with the status quo of using existing organs and using immunosuppressant drugs?

"And finally, where do you plan to get these 'existing organs?'" Bryan added.

"Well, we would approach the organ bank to keep any organs unsuitable for transplant and give them to us. Or we could try an animal model."

"Animal model?" said Bryan, looking dubious. "Oh please. Everyone knows that animal research does not always translate into viability in humans. Now we are talking years more before any of this becomes viable, if it ever does. Sounds like you are clutching at straws."

"I find your lack of imagination regrettable," Art tried to control his anger, knowing that Tim Bryan, as the scientific liaison for the investors, influenced the investors and controlled the purse strings.

He continued. "What we are requesting is a one-year extension to show the viability of our premise. Our lab is working around the clock and then some and we plan to have concrete data within six months."

Bryan looked around at the other faces, all of which looked concerned at one level or another. "I will go back to the investors after this meeting and present today's discussion. However, be prepared that they could decide to pull the plug.

"Plus, you will need a lot of luck. You cannot just order the organs you need. You had better hope the organ bank has an extra kidney or heart lying around that you can have."

Bryan shook his head and continued, "Art, we are both scientists here. And talented scientists need to know when to push ahead when it's feasible and when to cut bait when things become futile. But I'll do my best to get you the one-year extension."

"OK, thanks," Art said.

The meeting adjourned. Art rose from the table and left, leaving the others mumbling behind him.

$*$ $*$ $*$

After he left, the remaining members sat around the table for a few minutes before wrapping things up.

"What do you think?" one of the administrators asked Tim Bryan. "Think he's got something here?"

"No," said Bryan. "This is nuts. There is no way what he is proposing is feasible. I'll lay it out and see what the investors say. They are in it for many millions and for the next six months to a year, there might be some willingness to take a gamble. I'll call Peter Northrup when I get back to my office. He's the main guy with Chariot and if he decides to stay in, I'm sure enough of the others will go along. I bet they will slash some funding, regardless. But this is his last shot. I don't know what he is planning to do next. He needs to acknowledge that this is not a viable line of research. I know he is trying to get tenure but maybe he needs to realize this type of bench research is not for him. Not every field of research ends with a Nobel."

$*$ $*$ $*$

Two days after the meeting, Art sat in his office brooding. He had skipped his customary visit to the lab and went straight to his office. His staff had been stressed after the meeting when he updated them. Now they were waiting to see if their employment would continue beyond the next few months.

He sat in his office, chin in hand at his desk, staring at the computer screen as various news items flashed by. His right hand was on the mouse, idly rolling the wheel.

The phone rang. It was Richard Hardman.

"Good morning… Dick," said Art. The pause was deliberate.

"Good morning, Art. I thought I would give you a couple of days to recover after the meeting. I must say it surprised everyone. And not a pleasant surprise."

"I know, but we are confident this Plan B will generate meaningful data in about six months."

"That is what I called about. I just got off the phone with Tim Bryan. He said he spoke to Peter Northrup late yesterday and Peter has decided to pull the plug. He is advising other investors of his decision and it is expected that funding for your research will be terminated."

Art felt his throat tighten as he exhaled. He stopped rolling the scroll wheel on the mouse as a headline caught his eye. He noticed the word Northrup in the headline, *High society divorce? Does Peter Northrup's wife…*

He clicked on it.

As he spoke with Dick Hardman, he glanced through the article.

"He can't do that. He *shouldn't* do that."

"What do you mean he shouldn't? He assessed your research based on Tim Bryan's recommendations and decided he was not willing to fund it further."

The article mentioned the Northrup scandal. *Scuttlebutt on the street is that wealthy hedge fund manager and Dallas philanthropist's wife Paula Northrup wants a divorce. She has apparently had it, and the scandal involving Mr. Northrup and the escort was the last straw…*

"What I do has the potential to save lives. What he does is shuffle papers in the world of finance and make money." He scanned further in the article. "And screws escorts."

"What? What's that about escorts?"

"Oh, nothing. There's an article about Peter in the news."

"So what's your point, Art? He did not become wealthy squandering money. He evaluated your research and decided he was done.

"You have enough funds remaining to continue for another four, maybe five, months at most. If you are that excited by this Plan B, I would suggest you get to work. Maybe if you can generate meaningful data, you may attract funding."

The rest of the article mentioned rumors of Peter Northrup's wealth and how much Paula would get in a divorce. As Art continued reading the article, he felt a rage build within. He had swallowed his pride to ask Peter for additional funding. He mentally compared the amount he had asked for with Peter Northrop's reputed net worth. *Shirt buttons*, he thought. *I asked for shirt buttons.* He had swallowed his pride and asked for only a million and had agreed to give Peter a majority interest in his company. A company that represented much of his research and was near and dear to him. And now Peter was cutting him off and advising others to consider doing the same.

Hardman had continued talking as Art was distracted by the article. His attention snapped back to what Hardman was saying.

"In the meantime, we will have to mothball CellGenEX. We'll put the limited-liability corporation on hold, stop filing statements, stop having meetings, etc., as there is nothing to report."

"Well, do what you have to do."

He hung up and sat in his office, staring at the phone. He knew what came next. The office of translational research would have to file a quarterly report with the university and afterwards, the demise of his lab seemed certain. His lab would be on the chopping block for closure if nothing meaningful developed in the next few months. He also knew his chances of making tenure were now in serious jeopardy. In academia, careers were built on two things, publishing and attracting funding. He was about to lose his funding and without funding, the publishing would also wither.

I need to move quickly, he thought.

He turned toward his computer. The hypnotic screen saver had replaced the Northrup article, random symmetrical patterns resembling a fluid Rorschach. He jiggled the mouse to awaken the computer; the Northrup article appeared on the screen again. A picture of Peter Northrup from some years ago smiled at him. Marlow clenched his fists and clicked the window shut. He logged into his e-mail account. He sat there for about thirty seconds, staring off into space at the blinking cursor. Finally, he decided on a course of action. He took out his cell phone and flicked through his contacts. He scrolled down until he saw the name he wanted. The name had an e-mail address, no phone number, no street address.

He clicked on "New" and typed in the e-mail address. In the subject line, he typed "Greetings from Art". He typed out a brief introductory message and hit "Send".

Nothing in life is more irreversible than the Send button.

He leaned back in his chair and cracked his knuckles.

I just crossed the Rubicon.

TWELVE

Tiffany Jensen stared at the screen, bored. Jonas, her
husband, had already gone to work. She sat at the computer,
leaning back in her chair. Her eyes jittered from side to side
on the screen as her right index finger clicked the mouse
button. She perused web pages, checked her Facebook and
Instagram accounts, and scanned the other usual assortment
of sites designed to while away time. As she clicked through
various sites, provocative banner ads appeared, each trying
to tempt her to buy something related to a recent search.

One such banner ad, known as "click bait" in today's
vernacular, caught her attention. Its tagline blinked, "Want
to meet that special someone?" Smaller print under the
tagline touted the site's dedication to privacy, the discreet
nature of any encounters, and their "no strings attached"
policy. She held the mouse pointer over the ad, the index
finger cursor poised over it. A string of text appeared for a
few seconds next to the cursor: "Come on in, give it a try."
She swirled her mouse pointer around for a good fifteen
seconds, index finger hovering over the mouse button. Then
she was overwhelmed with curiosity and clicked on it. The
site went through several pop-ups requesting a birthday,
gender preference, preferences for various anatomic
characteristics such as weight, color, and size, and then
asked for an email address. Here, Tiffany paused. *Why an e-
mail address*, she wondered. She clicked the "X" in the corner,
sighed, and stood up.

"I'm bored," she said out loud.

She was born and raised in Provo, Utah, in a family of
practicing Latter-Day Saints, and her life had been scripted
from a young age. The veneer of outward piety that suffused

members of her faith had glossed over and covered any stressors in life.

Then she met Jonas Jensen.

She met him at a church-sponsored social gathering for LDS singles. He struck up a conversation, and from there, things progressed over the next several months. He had grown up in the Salt Lake City area and, after an LDS mission in Colombia as a young man, had returned to go to college for computer science. He fit the stereotypical description of being tall, dark, and handsome. His father was a native Utahn, and his mother, fifteen or twenty years younger, was Brazilian, thus explaining his beautiful olive complexion.

Over the next few months, they dated regularly. One day, he pleasantly surprised her when he "popped the question." She felt a sense of relief when he suggested getting married in a secular location rather than going through the sealing ritual in the Mormon temple and a couple of months later, they married. She had turned twenty-one and he was twenty-eight.

The wedding was a well-attended affair. Tiffany discovered that Jonas' father had been married before, when he lived in Texas, and his ex-wife continued to live there. Even though his first wife did not attend the wedding, several of Jonas' father-in-law's relatives from his first marriage attended. Tiffany discovered that Jonas had at least one, and possibly more, half-siblings. The entire wedding and reception had been a whirlwind affair and afterwards, Tiffany settled into wedded bliss.

Within a few months after their wedding, things changed. She had been aware that he liked to have the final say in most things, which she had not minded. But after the wedding, he became more controlling, especially with their finances. He also started drinking and when he drank, incidents of verbal abuse that skirted the edge of becoming physical abuse became frequent. When drunk, he had also alluded to disturbing events in his past, events he had participated in. She wrote these off as alcohol-induced ravings; when sober, things were fine. At one point,

Tiffany's concern grew enough to ask her mother-in-law if there had been any trouble with Jonas during his childhood years. His Brazilian mother had stated there had been some incidents, but she did not elaborate. She dismissed such concerns as "well, boys will be boys."

Reading between the lines, Tiffany realized Jonas had some dark chapters in his past that his family did not want to talk about.

Within two years of their marriage, Jonas accepted a job with an IT consulting firm in Dallas, Texas. He would cover several healthcare-related facilities, including the University and a group of clinics that served the underprivileged. There would be a slight salary increase, but the primary draw was a chance to try something different and live someplace else for a while. Tiffany had agreed with reluctance, as much of their family lived in Utah, although Jonas presented it to her as a *fait accompli.*

They had now lived in Dallas for four years. Without her friends and family nearby, she found it more difficult to cope with her chronic boredom. Jonas earned enough money and discouraged her working outside the house. He became more controlling. They tried to have children but had been unsuccessful. At one point, they had a dog, a Great Dane named TJ, their initials, but he died after an unexpected illness. So, for the past six months, Tiffany did little except go to the gym, surf online, shop, and try to stay busy.

Then she stumbled across the "click bait" article. She was not particularly computer savvy but knew enough about computers to create a new e-mail address. She went back to the site, answered all the screening questions, this time entered her new e-mail address, verified it with her phone number, and logged in. The site asked her to build a profile of herself and a profile of the type of person she sought.

Within a few days, she had met several men who wanted to strike up conversations with her. "John," "Harold," "Vincent," and "Simon" had matched the profile she constructed. It began as an all-purpose chat room with members signing in and out, engaging in group chats or sometimes messaging one another in private. For the next few days, she engaged in group conversations with several men. Most of the topics discussed were innocuous, about her likes and dislikes, types of cuisines she enjoyed, whether she watched sports, went to movies, etc. The site whiled away her boredom.

Of the men she chatted with online, "Simon" seemed to be the most receptive and engaging.

Simon, like Tiffany, had plenty of spare time and little to do, so she commiserated. It began innocently enough with questions plied at each other about their lives. Tiffany had used "Madeline" as her screen name. Tiffany used Simon as an escape valve to talk about her ennui. He listened. He communicated back. He empathized.

"So, Madeline, what do you do?" he wrote.

"I stay at home," she wrote back.

"Stay at home mom?"

"No, just stay at home."

"How come?"

"My husband doesn't like it when I work. Or do anything outside on my own. Sometimes I feel like I'm one of his possessions instead of a person."

"I'm sorry."

"How about you?"

"What about me?"

"How's your wife?"

"She works a lot and stays at work longer than her shift. Good overtime, I guess."

"Any kids?"

"Two daughters, both teens now. They don't want to be bothered by dad. And one of them drives now. So, I'm useless. Not much to do around the house."

This morning, of the four men who had been communicating with her, only Simon was online. So, she requested a private chat with him, and he agreed.

"Hi, Madeline," came from Simon, almost as soon as she requested the private chat.

"Hi," she wrote back.

"Whatcha up to?"

"Not much. You know who has gone to work and I'm here at home, alone and bored as usual."

"Same here. Kids are at school, and wife is off working. Same as yesterday. Same as the day before that."

"What do you do?"

"I was a welder. I got disabled. My left arm. Other parts still work." His reply was appended with a wink emoji.

Tiffany smiled. "Someday I'd like to check those parts," she wrote, attaching a different wink emoji. She felt herself blush the second she hit the "send" button. But what was the harm?

"Hmm," from Simon with a thumbs-up emoji.

"How's things with your wife?" from Tiffany.

"Meh."

"?"

"We growed apart." He did not go into further details. "Also growed apart as man and wife, for months, if you know what I mean."

"Yes, me too, kinda." She did not go into details.

After about thirty minutes of chatting, Tiffany wrote, "Gotta go. Need to go make dinner."

"OK. Not sure when I'll be on tomorrow but I'm looking forward to it, Madeline."

She logged off with a sigh. Simon seemed like such a likeable guy, she thought.

She went through the motions of making dinner and later that evening, Jonas returned from work.

"How was your day?" she asked. The question was innocent enough, but she had an uncomfortable tingle as if he could read something into her normal greeting. Today was the first day in which her online conversations had moved beyond idle chitchat and the first day in which she had started the private conversation. Not only that, the conversation had already taken a turn toward the risqué. She felt guilty for having feelings for this unknown "Simon."

Jonas did not say much except for a brief greeting. "It was fine. What's for dinner? I'm hungry."

He poured himself a drink and settled on the couch to watch TV. He pulled a keychain out of his pocket and started twirling it on his left index finger. It was a mannerism he had; having something to fidget with helped him focus. He watched TV for a few minutes and would pause to watch the twirling keychain, his eyes darting as he watched the keychain spin.

Tiffany had made sloppy Joe sandwiches and a salad and she served him his dinner. Jonas was ravenous as he worked his way through dinner. During and after dinner, he also worked his way through several drinks. After watching some reality TV show until about nine, he called Tiffany over.

"Come on over here, honey," he said.

Tiffany felt herself tightening inside. She knew what he wanted and in recent months, had found it less enjoyable. Jonas wanted to make love on the couch.

"Jonas, I don't want to tonight," she said. "It's close to that time of the month and I feel bloated and I have a headache."

Jonas scowled at her. He stuffed the keychain back into his pocket. He was on his sixth drink and he looked belligerent, if not downright angry.

"Come on, honey," he said, trying to cajole her into agreeing. The corners of his mouth rose into a forced smile. Tiffany recognized the look. He would make one attempt to be nice and then, especially after a half-dozen drinks, he would become unreasonable.

To placate him, she endured the experience.

Later, as she lay in bed, she thought back to her chat session with Simon.

He's such a nice guy.

THIRTEEN

The next morning, Jonas wandered into the kitchen at his usual time. Tiffany had already set the coffee maker. It burbled louder as it neared the end of its brew cycle and with a final cough of steam, signaled its completion. Both he and Tiffany had lapsed from their Mormon upbringing in Utah and drank coffee. As they sipped their coffee, Jonas said he would be very busy for the next few days.

"What's up?" Tiffany asked. "How come you'll be so busy?"

"We have a contract with the University to install servers in a lab. It will be many hours of server installation, configuration, testing, and verifying that it's ready to go."

"Oh, ok."

After a shower and breakfast, Jonas left. As soon as Tiffany saw the car disappear down the road, she went to the computer and logged in. John and Vincent were logged in. She spent the next thirty minutes chatting with them and then signed off. She hoped Simon would log back in later in the day.

She went to the recreation center near their neighborhood and swam and worked out for about two hours. After doing some grocery shopping and having lunch, she returned home. As she put away the groceries, she noticed the bottles of wine. On an impulse, she opened a bottle and poured a glass even though it was midday, something she only rarely did.

She logged in to the chat room, and this time, Simon was also logged in. She spent the next couple of hours chatting with him and sipping her wine, finding both more enjoyable as the time passed. By the end of that first week, their messages had progressed from bland topics about each other's lives to more intimate topics. Simon first broke the ice by asking Madeline about her measurements.

"Your thumbnail pic looks good," Simon wrote.

"Thanks." She typed her reply.

"But it's only your face."

"Yeah?"

"What about the rest?"

"What about it?"

"Are you an A student?"

"?"

As soon as she typed the question mark and sent it, she realized he had made an allusion to her chest size. She giggled and rocked back and forth in her chair.

"No, I'm a poor student."

"Huh?"

"I'm a D student."

"Wow," Simon typed, followed by a "wow" emoji, wide-eyed and tongue sticking out.

She cheekily replied by asking him about his measurements.

"What sandwiches do you like?"

"Huh?"

"Six inch or foot longs?" This was followed by a "wink" emoji.

He joked that he would send her a picture. After a few minutes, Simon sent her a picture of a jumbo hot dog, accompanied by a "face with tears" laugh emoji. A few moments later, he sent her a picture of a banana peeled halfway with the caption "I Like My Fruit Naked". A different laugh emoji accompanied it. He had browsed the internet and cropped the picture from some site.

Tiffany opened a second window in her browser and did a quick search. She found what she wanted. She sent him a picture of a woman suggestively eating a hot dog. She attached a wink emoji to it and a caption, "Wonder what that hot dog tastes like..."

She leaned back in her chair with a sigh. She reached for her wine glass and took another sip. *He's funny*, she thought, appreciating his ability to banter back and forth online with double entendres.

He changed the subject.

"How often do you do it?" he asked, with a wink emoji.

"Do what?"

"You know. Take matters into your own hands."
Another wink emoji accompanied the text.

"Oh, I get it. Three or four times a week." she wrote. "Self-help is the best help, right?"

"You should let me watch."

"You wicked boy," she wrote with a wink emoji.

She reached for her wine glass and had a sip. Then another one.

"How about you?" she asked.

"Often enough," he wrote with a smiley face emoji.

Their chat session became more serious. She told Simon she and Jonas had been drifting apart, and when their lovemaking happened, she had not found it enjoyable anymore. He commiserated and said likewise. His relationship with his wife had deteriorated over the past few years.

"Things were great there for a while," he wrote.

"But then I went on disability, and she had to work more to pay the bills."

"She'd be home all tired, and I was rarin' to go. After a while, I guess she kinda got fed up. For me, it's been months."

Tiffany wanted to ask him what had happened to him to cause his disability but skipped that until she knew him better.

"My husband comes home from work, drinks too much, decides he wants some. Most of the time, I'm bored with being home all day. And I guess resentful that he doesn't like it if I work."

"How come he doesn't like it when you work?"

"I don't know. Could be a cultural thing. We're not practicing, but we used to go to the Mormon church growing up."

"Oh, I get it."

"Or it's because he is a controlling jerk."

"I'm sorry, Madeline." A pouty-faced, sad emoji accompanied this last message.

"Ever thought of leaving him? Y'all don't have any kids."

"Thought about it," she wrote. "But he's got a bad temper, especially when drunk. I'd worry he would do something."

"Is he the violent type? Has he ever done anything to you?"

"Sort of. But I talked to his mother once. He did some nasty stuff when he was a kid. Didn't know it when I married him."

After a few more exchanges, Tiffany signed off. Her online intimacy with Simon had gone well, and she looked forward to her future exchanges.

By the time she hung up, she had filled her glass two or three times and she felt the effects of the wine. A wave of disenchantment about her life, marriage, and future washed over her and she burst into tears, hard sobbing tears. She continued to cry for several minutes and when she finished, she went to the bathroom, washed her face, and went to the kitchen to get dinner ready.

FOURTEEN

The operating room schedule was lighter than normal. At lunchtime, Jick removed his surgical cap and shoe covers and donned his white coat. He went to the auditorium to attend the Grand Rounds presentation out of a sense of necessity rather than interest in the subject. The lunches served at Grand Rounds were good; the subdued lighting, cozy atmosphere, and the droning speaker had a relaxing effect. *Splendid place for a nap, er, downtime*, he thought. The OR schedule had not been taxing and he had spent much of the morning staffing the pre-operative evaluation clinic. Getting an hour of meaningless continuing medical education credit was a bonus.

Jick walked to the foyer of the auditorium and surveyed the repast. Today's lunch consisted of orzo pasta topped with garlic chicken. A pan of orzo pasta sat next to a steaming serving pan of chicken, both kept warm by a small burner. Next to the pasta a tureen sat on a hot plate; it contained a creamy sauce dotted with button mushrooms. *I'm glad it's orzo and not spaghetti*, he thought. Trying to twist spaghetti on a plastic fork while sitting in a conference room would have been messy. *Someone thought this through*, he thought. *However, they could have thought of something other than garlic for the chicken, for the sake of the docs who still had to see patients in their afternoon clinics.* For the vegetarians, slices of eggplant parmigiana formed rows, neatly arranged in a serving pan, cushioned on either side by a red marinara sauce. Sauteed asparagus spears, a chilled salad, soft rolls with chilled florets of butter, and a rich-looking chocolate torte rounded out the offering. The drink selections consisted of iced water, chilled punch, or iced tea. Jick's stomach growled in anticipation.

After helping himself, Jick walked into the auditorium and chose a seat toward the back and against the aisle. Effortless way to make an escape if he wanted to. He took out his phone and went to the application for signing in for medical education credit. Thanks to recent changes in requirements for maintaining his board certification, collecting meaningless continuing medical education credits, even in unrelated disciplines, had become an essential component.

The tables formed rows angled to facilitate viewing the screen. Jick placed his meal and iced tea on the table, unfolded a napkin on his lap, and tucked in.

Four lines of text appeared on a large screen behind the stage. "Genetic Genesis, Fact or Fiction?" appeared at the top, followed by "Organs for All?" in a smaller font. "Art Marlow, MD, PhD" and "Assistant Professor of Surgery and Professor of Genetics and Cell Biology" appeared next. In the lower right-hand corner the logo of the institution was depicted in a reddish-brown. In the lower left-hand corner, a stylized logo of a cell with an exaggerated gene in the shape of an X appeared in aqua blue. The letters "CellGenEX" appeared below the X-shaped gene.

This dry topic had no connection to Jick's practice. *Hope they dim the room lights or maybe I'll duck out after eating.*

The department head introduced Dr. Marlow. He went through some of Dr. Marlow's professional achievements, including the creation of a separate company called CellGenEX through the university's office of translational research. Angel investors and venture capitalists had already contributed significant amounts of money to further fund this exciting new frontier in genetics. After the introduction, Art Marlow stood up and walked to the podium; a polite round of applause accompanied his walk. Jick saw a man of medium height, heavy-set, appearing to be in his mid-forties. A suit that appeared to be one size too snug, square dark-framed glasses, and unruly hair rounded out the stereotypical appearance of a young, eager professor. He adjusted his tie and tapped on the microphone; the sound thumped across the auditorium.

The first few slides provided background information about his research. Despite his unfamiliarity and earlier skepticism, Jick found the topic interesting. Dr. Marlow had taken stem cells and controlled the cellular environment to steer differentiation in a specific direction until his lab had created an organ.

He began his presentation with a question. "What is a pluripotent stem cell?"

He went on, "A pluripotent stem cell is a stem cell that has the ability to differentiate into any specialized cell down the line. This is how we are all born. We start as fertilized eggs and then zygotes. As the cells keep dividing, stem cells differentiate into specialized tissues resulting in organs such as the heart, brain, skin, kidneys, or liver. The process is fascinating and complex.

"After millions of years of evolution, the process seems simple. But it's not. As cells divide, several factors affect their local microenvironment. It is most likely hormones that steer differentiation. Somehow, in this organic soup of hormones, specific cells express specific receptors. Simple genetics drives this process. Based on which receptors the cells express on their surface, even though the organic soup seems to be homogenous, their effects on certain cells depend strictly on which receptors the cells express on the surface. Here's where our research comes in."

Marlow went on to explain that the current state of affairs in the research of stem cells had identified certain cellular factors that certain cells expressed. This allowed stem cells to differentiate into specific tissue types. Dr. Marlow had identified and controlled the cellular environment to steer stem cells to differentiate into specific tissue types, similar to what occurs in nature.

The model his lab had developed so far was the kidney. Marlow was candid about the difficulties that lay ahead. For example, the organs would have to grow to a certain size to be viable. It was one thing differentiating the cells into specific organs. It was quite another to grow them to an adequate size. They could not grow through normal developmental cycles and initially such organs would only be suitable for a newborn. At some point, science would need to grow the organs in an accelerated process to achieve adult size.

He continued for about thirty-five minutes and then asked audience members for questions. Several hands shot up.

Someone asked him if he had grown an organ yet and he replied in the affirmative, eliciting a slight ripple of interest from the audience.

"You've created an organ. Which one?" someone asked.

"Well, let me hedge a bit," he said. "We have created a kidney, but we are still trying to fine tune its function. It is very close."

"What do you mean by 'very close'," someone else asked.

"We have made significant strides in modifying the cellular environment to allow the specific cells to differentiate. We can change the environment for stem cells to differentiate into cardiac cells or into renal cells.

"We have an organ that is almost a normal functioning kidney. But that last step has proved to be more challenging than we had expected. We are trying to work out the kinks. We expect to address these last few hurdles soon."

The Grand Rounds presentation concluded after a few more questions, and Jick went back to the operating room.

The operating room schedule had wound down. There were only three or four rooms running and the staff had already set up the trauma rooms. The preoperative evaluations clinic had finished screening the upcoming day's schedule.

Jick was in the operating room lounge, about to head out, when Mireille came in. It was about two-thirty so if she had finished her work, Jick assumed she would go work out. He took the plunge.

"Doing anything after your workout?" he asked.

"No, nothing in particular," she said. "I still have to get something for Walter. Weren't you planning to get him something earlier in the week?"

"Actually, you won't need to get him anything. We will do it as a department-wide present and the staff need not contribute. I already got him something: An old railroad pocket watch. Early 20th century, I think. It's quite a nice present and should go well with his collection of old clocks. The department is also getting him a rocking chair with an engraved plate thanking him for his years of service.

"And, since you won't need to do any shopping after working out, how about going down to Julio's for happy hour?" *This is it, unto the breach,* he thought.

"Sounds good," she said. "I'll finish working out by about four."

"Perfect. How about we meet by, say, four-thirty? Their happy hour runs until five-thirty."

"OK, see you then."

She headed to the women's locker room, next to the OR suites. Jick stood dazed. That had gone about as well as he could have hoped.

"Wow," he breathed out.

He had also finished his cases for the day. He headed home on a cloud and alighted at his house. He had a quick shower, change of clothes, spritz of cologne, and floated to Julio's. He wore a pair of jeans, button-up shirt, and sneakers.

Jick arrived at four twenty-five. Mireille had not arrived yet. He sauntered over to the outdoor bar with the faux Mexican beach look, complete with thatched grass roof, gaudy neon cerveza signs, and signs in Spanish nailed to the wall. The lively music lent a festive ambiance to the outdoor dining area. Several people had already congregated at the bar. Jick ordered a Corona with a slice of lime, one of his favorite drinks except for his friends Cabernet and Shiraz, and perched on a barstool.

At four thirty-five, Mireille arrived, dressed in a pair of shorts and a T-shirt with half-length sleeves rolled up. Casual leather sandals completed the ensemble. *Was that a tattoo on her right arm?* Jick thought. He had only seen her in scrubs at work and now, in shorts, he could appreciate her legs. Her left ankle sported a small tattoo of a maple leaf.

"I've never seen you in street clothes before. Is that a maple leaf tattoo?"

"It is. A moment of youthful indiscretion in my early twenties, like this one on my arm." She pushed up her right sleeve further to reveal a stylized *fleur-de-lis*. "I'm Canadian but second-generation French."

"I see. What would you like to drink?"

"The same as you."

Jick beckoned to the bartender and ordered another round of Coronas. They continued talking.

"So, how do you like it here in Dallas so far?"

"It's great. Work has been enjoyable. I miss Quebec since most of my family is there."

"What made you leave Canada and move so far away?"

"Things had become stale in Canada, and I wanted to try something new. I had been in the Quebec area for most of my life and felt ready to start exploring the world. I'm not sure how long I'll be here, but for now, I'm enjoying it. How about you?"

Jick told her about his background, his family, and outside interests. It surprised him to find out she had also trained in krav maga. It had become more mainstream among the martial arts.

"Why krav maga?" he asked.

She paused as a motorcycle roared up the street.

"I wanted to learn a martial art some years ago. I chose krav maga because of its efficiency. As a woman, often traveling alone, I felt that any martial art that emphasized physical aggression and disarming an attacker or turning their weapons on them, would be better. Not that other martial arts, especially the ones from Asia, are bad. It's that those martial arts also emphasize principles of respect, obedience, moral behavior, etc., as a way of life. All I wanted was to learn to kick someone's ass."

"I see." He envisioned Mireille taking down a bad guy with a ferocious and well-placed kick to his ball sack.

"How about you?"

"My dad was an expert at krav maga and wanted us to learn a martial art. I haven't kept up with it as much as I should but at one point, I had an E1 rank."

"That's good. I'm not that far along yet." She pushed the slice of lime into her drink. "I should find a good krav maga training place here and move higher in training."

Jick finished his beer and beckoned to the bartender for another round. As he finished his beer, he let his thoughts wander to Mireille engaged in krav maga training, once again visualizing her in tight training clothes, working up a glow as she pummeled bad guys. She interrupted his thoughts by asking a question.

"I'm sorry, what did you say?" he said as he picked up his beer for a swig. He pushed the slice of lime into the cold bottle and watched the bubbles cluster around the slice. He tapped the bottle with his fingernail and a cluster of bubbles detached from the slice and raced to the top. More bubbles formed almost immediately. He took a long swig and savored the tartness of the lime against the cold beer.

"I said, do you know a suitable place to go for krav maga training?"

"No, but I can look it up for you."

"Thanks. That would be great. If you want to go with me sometime, that would be great too. It would be nice to have a friend to spar with."

Oh shit, he thought. *I would love to spar with her.*

"Uh, yeah, that would great."

She had a swig of her beer.

"So, how did you decide you wanted to be an anesthesiologist?"

"Well, it came about in a roundabout way. It's not a specialty we do any rotations in as part of the core curriculum in medical school, like surgery, internal medicine, or obstetrics, for example. I stumbled across it because the department had offered jobs for medical students to work in the operating room setting up anesthesia equipment between cases at night when fewer anesthesia technicians worked. It was a fantastic job; on some days it could best be described as sleeping for dollars on slow nights.

"It's a unique specialty. We're the only specialty that doesn't diagnose a problem and fix it afterwards. For example, if you're a surgeon, a patient comes to you with a problem and you fix it. Or if you're an internist, a patient sees you for problems like hypertension or diabetes and you either fix or manage it. In anesthesia, we try to prevent problems *before* they occur.

"My dad used to always din into my brother and my heads that anticipating trouble and preventing it is the key to survival. I try to plan several steps ahead in much of my decision-making in life. That mindset is perfectly suited for anesthesiology. Most of the time, we try to anticipate and head off trouble.

"So, for lengthy periods of time, it's watching monitors and assessing patients in real time while a surgeon is inflicting severe trauma. The closest analogy would be an airline pilot. Takeoffs and landings would be analogous to induction and emergence from anesthesia. In the middle, it's on autopilot with careful monitoring. If the shit hits the fan, you want the best-trained person watching the monitors.

"Also, no continuity of care with patients. We arrive at work, do the job, and go home, not having to worry about being called for ongoing care. From a lifestyle perspective, it's a great job."

He paused, then added, "There are drawbacks, though. Many people, including other physicians, don't see us as 'real' doctors. Maybe it's professional envy as we're not encumbered by the same patient care requirements as they are."

"I see," she said. "I hate to say, but for me, it was money and some adventure. I had been an ICU nurse in Canada for about a year and wanted to try something new. So, after nurse anesthetist school, I applied in the United States."

They chatted about various other topics for about an hour and a half. She had wanted to get in some other shopping, and earlier in the day Jick's brother had asked him to dinner at his house, so they called it an evening.

"I'll get this," he said.

"You also paid for lunch that day," she said. "It's my turn."

Jick agreed with some reluctance. They had had some beers and the happy hour prices at Julio's were very reasonable.

"OK," he said. "Next time is on me then."

"Right on."

Jick walked out to the parking lot with her and accompanied her to her car. They ended the evening with a wave and a "see you tomorrow."

Not bad for a first outing. He walked back to his car, climbed in and drove off, a smile on his face, the Black Cloud banished for the evening.

FIFTEEN

Jonas drove toward downtown. The morning rush hour had thinned by mid-morning. As he approached downtown, he spotted an auto parts store. He made a quick stop to get a five-gallon gasoline container and engine oil, followed by a stop at a gas station to top up his car and fill the gasoline container.

He drove through an industrial area, past several warehouses, their corrugated sides bleak and gray in the morning sun. In the distance, he could see the greenbelt surrounding the Trinity River. He kept driving for a few hundred yards. The double yellow line disappeared; the surface became uneven and several patched cracks appeared in the asphalt. Wispy tufts of grass struggled to thrive in the cracks. His car bounced along as he made his way to an isolated lot close to the river, the last lot on the road. As he turned right onto the lot, he could see ahead that the pavement ended, and the road meandered into a trail that disappeared into the greenbelt. He stopped at a locked gate and got out of his car. He unlocked the gate, swung it open and drove in. He shut the gate behind him. There were four dilapidated sheds on the lot and Jonas drove around to the back of the shed on the far left, closest to the greenbelt. He got out of the car and stretched. It was mid-morning and the air already felt stifling. But there was work to be done.

He took out his phone, scrolled through his contact list, and tapped the screen.

"I'm here," he said. "Yes, I'll get to work right away. This will take most of the morning. You can bring the rest of the stuff later."

He listened.

"OK, I'll let you know when I'm done."

He hung up and surveyed the lot. From his vantage point, standing behind the shed at ground level, he could not see any of the warehouses he had driven past. To the north and a little west, the greenbelt stretched along the river. To the south and also a little west, more greenbelt. He had come from the east. The only witnesses would be from the west, where some jogging trails could be seen along the river. But more than a hundred yards of greenbelt separated the joggers from the lot; he had also planned to reinforce the fence to reduce visibility. As he stood there, he felt the first beads of sweat form around his neck and on his face. A mosquito whined as it flew past his ear.

He unlocked the door and with a slight creak, slid the door open. The shed's dilapidated appearance was deceptive. He had been at the site before, dropping off boxes and installing locks on the doors.

Several cardboard shipping boxes and some wooden crates had been stacked on one side. He took off his shirt and hung it on a nail. He picked up a crowbar and set to work. He placed the crowbar against the edge of one of the wooden crates and grunted with the exertion, prying open the wooden top. It yielded with some difficulty, the metal nails screeching in the wood as the top came off. Inside was a gas-powered generator, wrapped in thick shipping plastic. He found a box-cutter and slashed the plastic wrap off. He removed the packaging and using the edge of a hand truck, pried the heavy generator off its base. By maneuvering one side of the generator and then the other with the edge of the hand truck, he got it off its wooden shipping pedestal. He filled it with gas and engine oil. After getting it set up, he squeezed the rubber bulb to prime the engine. He turned the key; it started on the first try. He let it run for a few minutes and turned it off. Its ticking sound as the engine cooled was the only sound in the shed other than Jonas' exertional breathing. The air felt muggier as the morning sun rose in the sky. The lack of breeze made the inside of the shed stifling despite the door being open. He wished he had brought a fan. He had brought several bottles of cold water and he took a few swigs out of one.

By now, it was almost eleven, and the temperature was unbearable in the shed. Rivulets poured off his face as he opened the other boxes. One set of large boxes contained parts for an aluminum table, about six feet long and two feet wide. He assembled the table in half an hour. Other boxes contained various tools unfamiliar to Jonas. He dragged his forearm across his face and continued working.

"Damn!" he roared as a mosquito's whine past his ear ended with a stinging sensation on the back of his neck.

Three shipping boxes contained an unusual item. Each box contained a plastic tub with hoses and tubing, electrical cords, and what looked like a small motor. There was an instruction manual that wilted as he pawed through it with his damp hands. He opened a box containing what looked like three battery packs. Each pack needed a full charge before first use, so he restarted the generator and plugged in each battery pack to the standard outlets on the generator's frame. He glanced at the sign stuck to the generator's frame showing its specifications. More than enough to charge the battery packs.

Finally, at about twelve-thirty, he stopped for a break. He stepped outside the shed. A welcome breeze had started which took the edge off the heat and mugginess.

He sprawled under a shady nearby tree to eat his lunch. He had brought lunch, and he took a long draft out of another ice-cold water bottle. As he sat under the tree, he squinted and surveyed the jogging trails in the distance. He could see a few joggers and people walking their dogs in the distance, their outlines shimmering in the midday heat. A biker went by, his or her silhouette merging with and then separating from the joggers' and dog walkers' silhouettes. He could not make out any details, which meant they could not see him either. There would be no reason for any of them to leave the trail and head towards the shed, across the greenbelt. But just to make sure, he decided to fortify the fence after lunch.

He finished his third bottle of water and stood. He walked back to the shed and looked at the batteries. Their

charge status light glowed yellow. He walked over to the
fence.

On second thought, I'll leave the fence as is, he thought. If he
added more planks to the fencing and made it hard to look
in, it would create two problems. He would not be able to
see if anyone approached and new boards could attract
attention.

He spent the next two hours breaking down the boxes
and crates, arranging things as he had been told to do. When
he finished, he took out his phone and tapped the screen.

"It's done," he said.

He listened.

"I tested the generator, and the battery packs are still
charging for, what are they called, oxygenators?"

He listened again.

"Oh, ok. If we won't need it for another few weeks, I'll
shut down everything for now. I can come back in a few
days and check on things."

He listened again.

"It went good. Wished I had brought some mosquito
spray."

And after a moment.

"No, I won't get into any trouble. Yes, I'll be careful."

He went back into the shed, turned off the generator
and unplugged the battery packs. The display read eighty
percent charged. He locked the shed doors and pocketed the
key. He got back into his car and headed home.

He parked and went inside his house. Tiffany wrinkled
her nose as she greeted him.

"Honey, what have you been doing?" she asked. "You
smell like you've been sweating it out all day."

"Nothing much," he said. "I installed several servers.
They had been stored in the loading dock and I had to haul
them upstairs by myself. The loading dock on a day like this
is how come I got all sweaty. I'm going to have a quick
shower."

He jumped into the shower, rinsed off, and put on a
clean set of clothes. It had been a tiring day and the warm
shower had a soporific effect.

*   *   *

Tiffany served him dinner. As usual, Jonas began the evening with a drink. And as usual, with each drink, Tiffany felt her emotions tighten more and more. But his day's apparent hard work had exhausted Jonas. After dinner and several drinks, he passed out on the couch. His fidget trinket slipped off his finger and fell on the floor.

Tiffany felt a sense of relief. She left him on the couch and retired to the bedroom.

As she lay in bed, she thought over the day's events. The long online conversation with Simon, interspersed with wine and double entendres, had left her with a warm and satisfied feeling. But after she had ended the chat session, a wave of disenchantment had washed over and she had had a crying session. For the first time, she thought seriously about leaving Jonas.

Wouldn't it be great, she thought, *if I could leave Jonas and be with Simon?*

She had a fitful night's sleep as she drifted off thinking about Simon, Jonas, her lot in life, and what she could do about it.

SIXTEEN

Jick left Julio's and headed to Vic's. In some ways, the first
outing with Mireille had been better than he had hoped. She
seemed to enjoy his company, and it was easy to talk to her.
He daydreamed about her, and the phrase *Horses sweat, men
perspire, and women glow* popped into his mind. First the
working out, now the krav maga. He would enjoy being with
her, but his interests in her seemed prurient. *Nothing wrong
with that*, he thought.

He stopped at the wine store on his way to Vic's house
to restock for home and pick something for dinner tonight.
He perused the collection of South African wines; he was
partial to South African Shiraz. They had a nice collection,
and he picked a few. He wandered over to the California
section and chose a few cabernets and even an Oregon pinot
noir, to round out the case.

Jick arrived at Vic's house at six-thirty. Vic had texted
him earlier in the day and asked him if he wanted to come
over. He had mentioned Sam had planned a leg of lamb for
dinner. Jick agreed to visit before the happy hour with
Mireille; he was grateful neither can caused a scheduling
conflict.

Of course, he would have loved continuing his evening
with Mireille, but the happy hour had been a pleasant first
outing. Jick went with it casually as there were two big issues
he knew would be a problem. The first, and more obvious,
was their age difference. Although Jick didn't look sixty-
four, Mireille was in her mid-thirties, and he was close to his
mid-sixties. The second issue was her employment. In the
pecking order of the operating room and in their
department, nurse anesthetists were subordinate to

anesthesiologists. Their fraternizing could cross into a professional and ethical gray area.

Jick did not have any direct ability to affect her employment. He was a member of a private practice group that had an agreement with a staffing company to provide nurse anesthetists. Therefore, she was an independent contractor hired by a staffing company. And, there were no specific rules that forbade relationships between the anesthesiologists and nurse anesthetists. But this could still be a problem. *Sometimes you have to say, what the fuck?* he thought, glossing over this inconvenient fact.

He scanned the case and picked one of the South African Shiraz wines. It would go well with lamb. He rang the doorbell at Vic's front door and Samantha, Vic's wife, answered.

"Come on in, Jick. Vic's in the shower."

Samantha, Sam to her friends and relatives, had an easy Southern belle approach to people, with only a hint of accent, that everyone found charming. She worked for a company called MicroEye, supposedly managing databases. Although nominally a private company, many if not all of their contracts originated through the U.S. government, so for all intents and purposes, the company served as a front for the government. She specialized in investigations involving any computer-related malfeasance. MicroEye had a nationwide presence, and she often had field assignments that required some travel.

Jick had asked her once about her job.

"So, Sam," he had said, "you do a lot of online snooping. Do you work for the NSA?"

She had shrugged her shoulders.

"Ask me no questions and I'll tell you no lies."

Vic and Sam had married three years ago after meeting at some cybersecurity conference. Between her cyberspace investigative work and his investigative reporter work, both could be considered professional snoops. Jick had never asked her age; he assumed she was in her early to mid-forties. Vic hadn't been the settling down type, but at fifty-two, something had clicked when they met.

Their wedding had been a no-nonsense affair at the courthouse. On Vic's side of the family, Jick was the only attendee. On Sam's side, her parents and younger sister Jan attended. Several of their friends also attended. A small but lavish reception followed at one of Dallas' most recognizable landmarks, Reunion Tower. During their childhood, Jick and his brother had a German shepherd. Sam also had dogs as a child.

Sam had wanted to have children, but they had been unsuccessful so far. Jick knew this had been a source of some stress and did not bring it up when he was with them. He did discuss it at times when he was alone with Vic; he knew they were in the early stages of investigating *in vitro* options.

Sam stood about five-six, one-twenty, with sandy brown hair and blue eyes. In her early forties, she was attractive, and a few early wrinkles had added character to her beauty.

"Drink?"

"Thanks. I'll help myself. I brought a very nice South African Shiraz that should pair well with dinner. Vic said you made a leg of lamb?"

"I did. Shiraz sounds great."

Jick betrayed his allegiance to his friends, Cabernet and Shiraz, and opened one of Vic's bottles of a full-bodied California zinfandel. He poured out three glasses and handed Sam one.

Vic came down the stairs, dressed in a casual pair of shorts and a Dallas Mavericks T-shirt. Like Jick, Vic had the light olive complexion of their half-Indian ethnicity. He stood about an inch shorter than Jick. His glasses had slipped down his nose, and he reached up with the back of his index finger and pushed them up. The Mavericks logo bulged slightly around the gut.

Jick handed him the other glass of wine and raised his for a round of cheers. They clinked glasses and headed out to the patio where three lounge chairs sat on one side, next to a rectangular glass-topped patio table surrounded by six nylon mesh outdoor chairs. The backyard was small but well-maintained. A raised hot tub was mounted on a deck off the patio and the obligatory barbecue sat next to the patio. The backyard faced west, so at six-thirty, the sun flickered orange-red through the trees.

Jick settled into a chair and leaned back against the warm backrest. Vic leaned over to his left, pushed up his glasses, and opened a small storage chest. It contained various odds and ends, including cans of bug spray and mosquito coils. Vic extracted a green mosquito coil and lit it, placing it on its stand. Tendrils of smoke rose in a straight line and then jittered into random patterns in the setting sun. He leaned back in his chair.

"Red sky at night, sailor's delight," Jick murmured.

"What does that even mean?" Vic said.

"If the sky is red at night, it reflects a higher concentration of dust particles, which apparently indicates a higher-pressure system, thus better weather."

"You know, Jick, you are a nerd. Ever thought about going on Jeopardy?"

"As a matter of fact, yes. I tried out once but didn't make it past the first stage."

The conversation paused as they gazed at the sunset and had a few sips of the wine.

Sam soon after excused herself and went back into the house, disappearing into the kitchen. A tantalizing aroma swirled from that end of the house. There had to be something in the oven. *Sam the foodie has outdone herself again,* Jick thought.

Vic sipped his wine and smacked his lips with appreciation "This is good stuff."

He moved his chair as a shaft of sunlight had settled on his face.

"So, Jick, what's new? We haven't seen you since you got back from the cruise. How was it? Exciting? Meet anyone? Did you behave well? If you didn't, don't name it after me."

"No, the cruise didn't excite me. In fact, I made a mental note not to go on a cruise again."

"Why, what happened?"

"Well, nothing specific. And that was the problem. My fellow passengers were a bunch of people who weren't particularly interesting to talk to. I hung out with a couple of women doctors for a while, but mostly, it was a dud. I have Walter Madison, and a few others in the department, to thank for going on the cruise.

"And speaking of Walter, he's retiring soon, so I bought him a pocket watch for his retirement party. The department will present him with it, and a rocking chair, after a retirement dinner. Other than that, nada, nothing else new, just back to the routine of work."

They paused for another sip of the magnificent zinfandel. The sun had sunk below the horizon and orange-red ribbons lit up the western sky.

"Oh, I went to a Grand Rounds earlier today. It ended up being more interesting that I would have thought."

"What was the topic?"

"One of the faculty members at the university, Art Marlow, has been working on growing organs from scratch."

"No shit. How does he propose to do that?"

"This will sound technical but bear with me. When we're at the embryonic stage of development, there are these stem cells called pluripotent stem cells. That means they have the potential to differentiate into anything. As we grow from the zygote stage, which is a clump of cells that all look alike, to an embryo where things differentiate, or look and act differently, it is these stem cells that change over time, forming specialized cells that form specific organs."

"How do stem cells know how to differentiate?"

"From what little I know, our genes control the local environment around a cell, or groups of cells. Genes are sort of like program code. They code for certain hormones, and receptors on cells only bind to specific hormones that act like triggers to allow specific organs to form. This is not my area of expertise, by any means, so if you want to know more, you'll have to look it up."

"And this guy has controlled the environment all the way to making an organ?" Vic whistled. "That's impressive.

I'm a layman, but to me, that would seem almost impossible. It's one thing to take out the DNA, make a cloned cell, and allow nature to run its course and make an entire organism. It would be quite another to take out a cell and steer it toward a specific end organ."

"Yeah, I did find that impressive," Jick agreed.

Should I mention Mireille, he wondered. He decided he would.

"Changing the subject, I went to a happy hour earlier today at Julio's with one of our nurse anesthetists, Mireille Lavoisseur. She's quite the hottie."

"That's great, Jick. Thought you said there was nothing new going on." He winked.

"That's quite an exotic name. Italian?" he bantered. "Well, you haven't been fooling around much since you and Dorothy broke up. And you said the cruise was a dud. Then you come back home and voilá, Mireille. *Trés bien*."

He took a sip of his wine.

"So, how old is she?"

Jick mumbled something unintelligible under his breath.

"What?"

"Thirty-five... I think."

"Thirty-five? Christ, Jick, what are you, seventy?"

Jick leaned over and delivered a playful punch.

"I'm not sure why she even agreed to go out with me, even if it was just happy hour at Julio's. Besides the age difference, we work in the same department and based on the departmental hierarchy, I'm her superior but not her supervisor. So, I can't ever let any relationship interfere with her work."

"I'm not sure why she agreed to go out with you either." Vic continued needling him. "What does she call you when you're not at work? Daddy-O? Sugar? Or, wait for it, Sugar Daddy-O?"

Jick flashed Vic a withering look and changed the subject.

"So, how's your work going? Still reporting on crime?"

"Yeah. It goes through ups and downs. For the past couple of weeks, things have been slow. A spate of petty crimes that are not even worth reporting. Even a routine murder, like a lover's quarrel or a drunken bar fight gone bad, doesn't register in the news cycle anymore. Fazio usually keeps me in the loop, but it's been slim pickings."

"Oh, well, hang in there. It'll pick up."

Sam came out of the kitchen.

"You guys want to help set the table?" she said. "Let's eat outside. The weather's great."

They went inside to get the items to set the table. Jick assembled three sets of dinner plates, cutlery, and napkins. Vic started taking the dishes out to the patio dining table. Tonight, Sam had made a spiced boneless leg of lamb that she had marinated the night before. From the aroma, it had a mild curry flavor. Yogurt combined with powdered almonds, seasoned with honey and a touch of saffron, formed a crust over the meat. Whole roasted redskin potatoes and blanched asparagus spears rounded out the dinner. Jick opened the bottle of Shiraz while Vic did the honors carving the lamb. A large jar candle with outdoorsy scented wax sat in the middle of the table and Vic lit it for ambiance. As always, with Sam the foodie, she outdid herself. The pairing of South African Shiraz with the lamb was a match made in culinary heaven.

After dinner, they sipped a delicious South African port wine. Vic turned on the television. The often hapless Texas Rangers had a game this evening and having nothing else more interesting to watch, they chatted and watched the game. The Rangers won. Since it was a weeknight and he had to work the next day, Jick called it a night at ten o'clock and went home.

Today had been a magnificent day. Memories of the happy hour rolled around in Jick's head as he drove home. As he went to bed, he wondered what tomorrow would be like with Mireille.

SEVENTEEN

Most mornings, Jick began the day with the gloomy sentiment of routine. Another day in the trenches, knocking people out for their surgeries and making sure they awakened without complications, Jick thought, as he went through his morning ablutions. Another day of placating surgeons, hospital administrators, and other staff. Unlike his usual routine, today he felt invigorated.

As he headed for the back door on the way to work, he noticed the bag with the mask, still lying on the side table. Going to that antique store for the present for Walter's retirement had been an unsettling experience. Everything in that store seemed to remind him of how little time he had left. Perhaps it was because he was next for a party.

Jick picked up the mask. *The Healer of Life would look good in my office*, he thought. He put it on and looked out of the eyeholes. He stood by his wine cabinet, and he could see his reflection in the smoked glass door, his silhouette framing the wine bottles visible through the glass.

This thing is weird, he thought, and took it off. After he took it off, he felt unsettled again. The mask looked fine, but... something was not right. He shook his head. He wondered if it was an age thing with him or something else. He put it back in its bag and decided he would take it to work.

He arrived at work by six-fifteen a.m., perfect timing for a seven a.m. start. He went to his office and sat at the desk for a few minutes, scanning through his work e-mails. None needed his attention right away.

He had some picture hangers in his desk drawer, but the helmet-like shape of the mask precluded hanging it on the wall. He tried using two picture hangers with a wire strung between them, but the aesthetics did not satisfy him. The dome shape of the top of the mask was at a ninety-degree angle to the face plate, so he abandoned trying to hang it on the wall and placed it on a bookshelf, hanging it over the edge. One wall of his office was floor to ceiling bookshelves. The weight distribution of the mask allowed it to hang unsupported off the edge of the bookshelf. Behind that wall were the operating rooms. He stood back and stared at its neutral expression and black oval eyes. *I think it's staring at me*, he thought as he left to go to the operating rooms.

He left his office, turned to the right down the hallway, walked about fifty feet, and pushed the square metal button to open the doors to the operating rooms. Two large operating room doors swished open, and he turned right and walked through. The first hallway to the right led to operating rooms one through four; his office was behind Rooms Three and Four. Room Three was today's designated trauma room.

He went through his morning routine, scanning the schedule of cases in his rooms, thumbing through preoperative evaluations and making sure no issues needed his immediate attention. Today he would supervise two rooms and they designated him to cover trauma. Except for complicated cases, like when using a cardiac bypass machine, once the induction was done and surgery began, an anesthesiologist could hand off the care for that patient to a nurse anesthetist and either start another procedure or take a quick break before the surgery end process. None of the procedures today would require his constant attention and he would work with a nurse anesthetist in each room. Each of them would have already pulled the drugs needed for the day. *Would Mireille be one of them?* he wondered.

Focus, he thought. *You're at least thirty years older.*

Today's schedule seemed reasonable and straightforward. He covered two rooms assigned to general surgeons. The first room had five scheduled cases and the second room had four. In the first room, the first two cases were laparoscopic cholecystectomies to remove a gallbladder, followed by an exploratory laparotomy for a suspected malignancy. The last two were by a plastic surgeon, both elective breast augmentations. It was Mireille in the first room.

Yes!

The second room was two umbilical hernias, another laparoscopic cholecystectomy, and a wide excision of a lipoma. If the latter was an obvious cancerous lump, it could lengthen the procedure. The second room had two add-ons by another plastic surgeon doing a tummy tuck and a liposuction. The liposuction was the only case that needed extra attention as fluid overload situations can sometimes arise. Ten cases, all routine. He settled in for the day.

The day started without a hitch. The orderlies wheeled the first patient into the room. She was an otherwise healthy woman scheduled for a cholecystectomy.

After induction of anesthesia, the surgeon made four small puncture wounds for a light source, camera, surgical tools, and an insufflation port. Pressurized air injected through the insufflation port inflated her abdomen, which looked like a doughy loaf of bread rising. This facilitated viewing her gallbladder. On the camera, it looked like a view into a dome-shaped 'room' with a pile of entrails lying on the 'floor'. It took about twenty-five minutes for the surgeon to pick through the entrails, isolate the gallbladder, and tie off its blood vessels. When the offending organ was finally untethered, it looked like a limp dark red balloon hanging off a metal straw.

After the induction in the first room, Jick went to his second room. The induction in this room, for the first umbilical hernia surgery, also went well. After the surgeries were underway, he strolled to the lounge. He planned to return to the rooms in about fifteen minutes to check on things. *Sure beats the pedi ENT room*, he thought.

He went into the lounge and sprawled on a chair. Bob Foster, who was not running the board today, had shoehorned himself into "Running Start," having a cup of coffee and perusing the Wall Street Journal, reading glasses perched at the end of his nose. Jick sat down next to him.

"What's new?"

"Nothing much," he said. "A typical Thursday. Walter's party is this Saturday. Are you going?"

"Yes," Jick said. "How can I not go? I need to see how obnoxious everybody will be to an imminent retiree. I'm the next oldest guy in the department so I need to know what to expect next year."

"Don't worry, Jick," he reassured Jick. "Whatever you see this weekend for Walter is nothing like what we're going to do for you next year. You see, you are our department's resident aging bachelor. Since you're not married, we can make it a special event." He grinned at Jick in a way that made him suspicious.

"Well, if you're planning something for an aging bachelor, how about we do it at Alley Cats," Jick said. Alley Cats was a stripper club.

"Really?" Bob said. "All the other guys in the department, except for you and a couple of the younger guys, are married."

"So? You guys should be able to read all the menus you want as long as you eat at home," Jick quipped.

Bob looked a little wistful. He shook his Wall Street Journal and folded it back.

Jick was about to go check on his rooms when the overhead intercom system blared.

"Trauma hot!"

Shit.

"What the hell? It's not even seven-thirty. Maybe a motor vehicle accident. I'll head over to three and get things ready. Can you do a quick peek into my rooms and make sure they are OK?"

"You bet." Bob hefted himself out of Running Start and ambled out of the room.

Jick made his way to Room Three, the designated trauma room. Ray Martinez, a nurse anesthetist, bustled around, getting everything ready. Bob arrived a few minutes later and said Jick's other rooms were fine. He stayed to lend a hand. Trauma cases were always frantic and chaotic at the beginning and an extra set of hands was always welcome.

They waited in the room for a few minutes and the elevator dinged as the door opened. The commotion in the elevator spilled out and the emergency room trauma crew rushed out, pushing a patient on a gurney. One person squeezed an Ambubag, another looked at the monitor and called out instructions, and three others handled steering the gurney. Three IV bags jostled against each other; each hung off an IV pole clamped to the 'head' end of the gurney. Each bag's tubing snaked through an infusion pump. The ER crew swarmed into Room Three and within a few seconds, the trauma resuscitation was under way.

Jick shook his head; not a motor vehicle accident. A gunshot victim. Young guy, mid-twenties, shot in the chest and throat. He had bled profusely and looked ashen.

Jick did not need to tell Ray what to do next. The orderlies and Jick moved him to the table. They applied monitors and using a rapid sequence induction protocol, intubated him. As Jick intubated him, an operating room nurse splashed his chest with betadine and unfurled a blue drape. He handed its sterile edge to Ray. As soon as she gave the go signal, the surgeon asked for the bone saw and they began. Ray clipped the edge of the blue drape to two IV poles at the head of the bed and watched as the surgeon started. The operation was quick and in operating room vernacular, a "peek and shriek." There was not much they could do for someone who had been shot above the heart through all the major vessels.

When he had arrived in the operating room, his first set of vitals showed a rapid ventricular rhythm that still generated some cardiac output. By the time the surgeon had opened his chest, the rhythm had deteriorated into a ventricular tachycardia and then ventricular fibrillation. He was dead at this point. Despite their best efforts, which entailed the surgeon trying to stanch the bleeding, it was futile. They pronounced him and ended the surgery in a matter of minutes.

Jick chatted with the surgeons for a minute, then left Ray to finish and reset the room for the next trauma. He took a brief detour to his office to unwind before checking on his other rooms.

As he walked up to his office, a wave of uneasiness swept over him. *There's someone in my office*, he thought. He could feel it. The door was closed. He pushed the door open and stood in the hallway, leaning in for a look. There was no one there. But the feeling of a presence in the room was now even stronger. His gaze swept across the room and stopped on the mask. Despite the bright room lights, the usually drab colors of the mask seemed more vibrant, more pronounced, a little brighter. Its black eyes stared at him. He went in and shut the door behind him. He looked at the bookcase. Behind it was Room Three and in there, someone had died a few minutes ago. He glanced around his office. There was no place for anyone to hide. He sat down at his desk, took a deep breath, held it for ten seconds, and exhaled.

I need to go check my other rooms.

He sat for another minute and then left, going back to the operating rooms.

As he left, that same nagging feeling he had experienced in the antique store returned. He could not place it. It was something about the mask.

The cases in his other rooms neared completion. He helped extubate the laparoscopic cholecystectomy, finished a case in the other room, and strolled back to his office. He had fifteen minutes of downtime before he had to start the next case.

This time, as he approached his office, nothing. No feeling of uneasiness that someone was in there. As he was about to open the door, the operating room doors opened and the morgue staff pushed out a coffin-shaped gurney, covered in a thick dark green plastic cover. It was the recently deceased occupant of Room Three. Jick pushed open his office door and looked around. Nothing. Everything was as it had been about thirty minutes earlier. He looked at the Healer of Life. It seemed drab, lifeless, and less vibrant than earlier.

Must have been my imagination.

EIGHTEEN

The next day was a routine day at work. Jick started the day with his usual preoperative assessments. The operating room was a little short staffed and two of the nurse anesthetists had called in sick. He would do a room by himself, prepping the patients and staying throughout the procedures. His assignment was to work with an orthopedic surgeon who had a light schedule. Today would be three knee arthroscopies followed by a knee replacement. The surgeon would finish by lunchtime.

The first patient was a healthy young athlete from one of the local high schools. He had the physique of a Grecian sculpture, marred by the bane of all teenagers, a face speckled with acne. He had torn an anterior cruciate ligament in a freak soccer-related injury. His medical history had no red flags.

"Good morning, I'm Dr. Arnsson," Jick said to the young man. "Are you Myron Stenhouse?"

Who names their kid Myron nowadays, Jick thought.

"Hi," Myron said, his expression stoic. He glanced at Jick and then averted his gaze. "Yes, that's me."

Jick glanced at his hospital bracelet. Today's generation seemed to have difficulty with eye contact. Probably too much time socializing through their phones and not enough time learning actual social skills, he thought.

"So, what happened to your knee?"

"I tore my ACL playing soccer."

"Hmm, nasty break, son," Jick said. "Let me describe how we'll do the anesthetic. Don't be too nervous."

"I'm good."

"We'll start an IV here and take you back to the room. On the operating room table, you will roll over and pull your legs up and tuck your chin. Curl up like a boiled shrimp. I'll scrub your lower back with three cold swipes of betadine and then you'll feel a slight pinch. That's it. You'll feel a tingly sensation from about the chest down and they you'll go numb. Everything above the chest should be normal. If that weird feeling makes you nervous, we'll give you something through your IV and you'll be in la la land. Sound good?"

"OK," he said.

Myron did not seem nervous in the holding area when Jick described the procedure for a spinal anesthetic. Since he was eighteen, Jick did not need to talk to his parents although they had accompanied him. In the operating room, he rolled over on his side and obligingly curled into a fetal position when asked. Jick cleaned the area and placed a sterile drape over it. It took less than a minute to numb his skin and place the thin spinal needle in the right place. Jick removed the stylet, the small inner wire in the needle, and noted the crystal clear spinal fluid. After injecting the local anesthetic, he took out the needle, wiped off the iodine cleanser, and placed a Band Aid. Within a few minutes, Myron lost all feeling in his legs.

"This feels weird," he said. "I'm OK but this feels super weird." Jick added a very light IV anesthetic regimen to keep him calm.

The second case was a little more challenging as the patient was in his mid-sixties and had several medical comorbidities. His nose looked like someone had squashed a cauliflower floret on his face and painted it dusky red. His fingertips bulged at the tips, a sign of clubbing, and had a dusky pallor, all signs of a chronic smoker. As Jick walked up to him, he stared at him with an unfriendly expression. His demeanor was surly because he couldn't eat breakfast or have a cigarette. *We should have scheduled this guy first,* Jick thought.

"Hello, I'm Dr. Arnsson," Jick said. "You must be Marion Thibodeaux. I'll be your anesthesiologist for your surgery."

Myron and now Marion.

Marion did not say hello. He started with a complaint.

"Hey, how come I can't have a cigarette or a little something to eat?"

"If you have food in your stomach, your stomach produces acid," Jick explained. "When you fall asleep with the drugs, sometimes that acid can back up in your esophagus and go into your lungs. That's called aspiration. It can lead to pneumonia. You do not want that.

"So, what happened to your knee?" he asked.

"I did something stupid. I was out in the garden carrying a bag of fertilizer and stepped into a hole. My knee twisted as I went down."

"I see. Well, let's talk about your health. This is from your new patient questionnaire. You're a little overweight, you've had a heart attack, you're a diabetic, and you smoke. Sound about right?"

"Yeah, so?" He sounded defensive.

"Anesthesia is safe, and it looks like you haven't had any recent issues with your heart. So, don't be too nervous about this surgery."

"I'm not," he said. "Can we do it using a spinal? I don't want to be knocked out for this. I hate the way my throat feels afterwards."

Jick thought about having this surly patient awake in the operating room. He would have to keep him somewhat groggy regardless of how they anesthetized him.

The patient had had previous back surgery and access to his lower lumbar spine for a spinal would have been challenging. Jick convinced him to have it done under a general anesthetic but promised he would use a specialized airway to minimize throat discomfort afterwards.

"You've had back surgery in the past," Jick said. "I'm concerned that placing a spinal can be a little challenging. An easier option would be to knock you out and use something we call a laryngeal mask airway. It's not a breathing tube like you found uncomfortable before. For this kind of surgery, you're knocked out and we can keep you breathing on your own."

"Hmm, well, you're the doc," he said.

"Also, the surgeon will use a long-acting local anesthetic, so you'll be comfortable for at least the next day or so."

His case was uneventful. Placing the laryngeal mask airway was easy, and the surgery was under way in a few minutes.

By lunchtime, they had finished all the knee arthroscopies, and the knee replacement was about halfway done. One of the nurse anesthetists relieved Jick for a lunch break. Since the case was more than halfway done, the surgeon would finish by the time he finished lunch. Jick went to the trough for lunch.

The trough was an annex to the main hospital cafeteria. It was in a parallel hallway and was a reserved dining area for physicians, accessible by their key card IDs. The hospital provided meals gratis for the physicians as a perquisite.

Jick went to the trough and held his keycard against the reader. The red LED turned green, and he pushed the door open. Two small Italian flags were mounted on table stands to highlight today's Italian-themed offering. It was a self-serve pasta bar consisting of three fresh pastas, four different sauces, parmesan chicken and Italian meatballs, and all the trimmings such as freshly grated cheese, garlic bread, and crushed red pepper. A salad bar rounded out the lunch. Jick assembled his lunch and went to the dining area. The trough was nearly full, and he noticed one table that had only one occupant. It was Art Marlow, whose Grand Rounds Jick had attended yesterday.

Jick walked over to Marlow's table.

"Hi, I'm Jick Arnsson."

"Art Marlow."

"May I join you?"

"Sure, please do." Art waved his fork at the chair across from him.

"I was at your Grand Rounds last week. The subject was completely out of my bailiwick, but I still found it very interesting. A fascinating field of research."

Art looked at Jick with frank appreciation. He glanced at Jick's name stitched over the left front pocket of his lab coat. The department's name was underneath his name.

"You're one of our anesthesiologists," he said.

"Yes, I'm more of a clinical guy. Research was never one of my strong suits."

"It's not for everyone," he said. "I began as a researcher, first getting my PhD before medical school. In medical school, I thought about clinical work and finished my residency in surgery before I decided surgery was not for me. I enjoyed the research lab more. I guess I'm not a people person. So I gave up clinical medicine and went straight back to the lab. Having an MD opens doors, but I am not a clinician type. But, since I'm on faculty as a cell biologist, the university gave me a dual appointment in surgery."

Jick nodded. "Not everyone is cut out for clinical medicine. Did you know that Michael Crichton, the well-known author, was an MD and never practiced medicine? He wrote The Andromeda Strain while he was in medical school."

"I knew that," Art said. "He was quite a brilliant writer. I write a lot but it's all journal articles or book chapters, things that don't resonate beyond the halls of academe."

"How come you're here today?" Jick asked. "Aren't you usually based out of the university?"

"Yes," he said. "I only come here once in a blue moon, like when I did the Grand Rounds presentation. Believe it or not, I am here today to see my doctor. It was time for my annual checkup. I figured I'd stop off afterwards at the trough for a quick bite."

They continued chatting for a while. Jick asked him some questions about his research and he was happy to delve into details about his research, how he had started in this field, and how he hoped to revolutionize the field of organ transplantation.

"I must admit that, although I find the science exciting and challenging, it has also been a struggle."

"How so?"

"Well, for one thing, there's always a struggle for funds. My lab is well-capitalized but as I said, I'm not a 'people person' and often, I find myself trying to sell my research to wealthy assholes so they'll continue to fund us." His voice took on a hard edge.

"Wealthy assholes?"

"Yes, you know the type. Venture capitalists, hedge fund managers, speculators, etc. Guys who contribute nothing of any value to society but make tons of money pushing paper. They have the funds, so I have to try to appease them."

"What about government sources? Aren't there funding sources within the government for your type of research?"

"Yes, there are, but those funds are more competitive. For my area of research, because it's considered speculative, the private sector is more risk tolerant and more willing to give more."

Jick did not say anything. He thought Marlow was a little unreasonable, wanting the juicier funding from private sources without working at convincing the sources.

Marlow finished before Jick and after exchanging some parting pleasantries, he excused himself and left to go back to the university. Jick finished eating a few minutes later and headed back to the operating room.

By the time he returned to the operating room, the surgeon had finished the knee replacement. That patient was already in the recovery room.

Jick wandered back to the operating room lounge. It was his turn to be an early out and he had finished his cases for the day. It was almost two o'clock. He debated whether he should see if Mireille had any plans for the evening. It had been five days since their happy hour outing, and he was eager for an encore. Or more.

"Busy tonight?" he texted.

A few minutes later, "No, going to work out. Work done early."

"Want to do something?"

"How about we see Spring Fever?"

Jick thought about this for a moment. Spring Fever was a silly romantic comedy about a May-December romance. The two protagonists, both of whom were well-known actors, had an approximate twenty-five-year age difference.

Is there a message here?

"Uh, ok." he texted.

"Great. I'll meet you at the theater." She texted the theater location and said there was a six p.m. showing. Jick said yes with some hesitation.

This was a lot of food for thought. Meeting at a theater was more like meeting a friend, rather than something more involved if he had, for example, picked her up at her house.

A famous movie quote flashed through his mind. He thought back to "When Harry Met Sally," when Billy Crystal famously said: "No man can be friends with a woman that he finds attractive. He always wants to have sex with her."

Shit, he thought. Perhaps she viewed their relationship as just a friendship. *Oh well, maybe I'll enjoy the movie.*

NINETEEN

"So, what happened, Peter?"

Jick had come to work and found out Peter Northrup was back in the emergency room. He had arrived just after midnight. Since he had some time before starting his cases, he went to the ER to visit Peter.

"Maybe you were right, Jick."

Peter lay in an ER bay. Random beeps punctuated the air from the monitors that were hooked up to him. He wore the usual attire of the hospital: underwear, socks with dots of rubber underneath for traction, and an immodest hospital gown. His face was pale and drawn.

Jick waited.

"Maybe I shouldn't have gone back to work so soon. Should've taken it easy for a while. There were too many things to juggle, and I had already dropped a couple of them. I guess I didn't realize how busy I had been all these years until I tried to slow down."

"So, what happened?"

"I woke up last night with this heavy feeling in my chest and called 911. That's it."

"Do you have chest pain now?"

"No, they gave me something and I feel pretty good. I have a trip to the cath lab scheduled pretty quick. I guess they want a quick look or something. They didn't like something on my EKG when I came in."

Jick glanced at the monitor. Normal sinus rhythm.

"Looks good now. I have to head back upstairs so I'll stop by later to see how you're doing. Next time listen to your doctor."

"I promise." Peter looked like he meant it.

As Peter had been lying in the emergency room for much of the night, he longed to sneak outside and have a cigarette.

As he lay in bed, a boyish man with a white coat and the bearing of a physician entered the room.

"Hello, Mr. Northrup. I'm Dr. Howard Charnov. I'm the on-call cardiologist. I understand you've been having some chest pain and shortness of breath?"

"Yes," Peter said.

He eyed Dr. Charnov.

Everybody looks younger and younger every day.

"Yes, I had some chest pain and mild shortness of breath. I was in the hospital about six weeks ago and they put in a stent."

"I know," Dr. Charnov said. "I looked over your chart. You've had no problems since then?"

"No, I've been fine since. Until last night."

"So, what happened this time?"

"I don't know. I was fine until yesterday. Then I woke up last night, thought I had a nightmare. Then I realized my chest was aching and felt pressure in my chest. I was also a little short of breath. Dr. Arnsson is my neighbor. He thinks I went back to work too soon."

"Did you?"

"Yes."

"How do you feel now?"

"Good. I gave up smoking four years ago but fell off the wagon a few weeks ago. Right now, I'm wishing for a cigarette before we go."

Dr. Charnov frowned at him.

"You may want to rethink that. After we get done, leave the cigarettes out."

"I will. I have fallen off this wagon a few times. This time I am going to quit for good."

At exactly eight-thirty, two hospital staff arrived from the cath lab to get Peter. They collected his chart, said some reassuring words to him, and wheeled him toward the elevator. His portable monitor continued to report his vitals and beeped every few minutes. They exited the elevator on the second floor.

Unlike six weeks ago, he was awake this time. As they wheeled him down the hallway, Peter saw the sign for the operating rooms and further down the hallway on the opposite side, "Cardiac Catheterization" was affixed to a set of double doors. The orderly smacked a metal square on the wall and the double doors flipped open. The cath lab was a cold, sterile and forbidding environment. He took a deep breath and exhaled, puffing out his cheeks. *This time I will give up smoking*, he thought. *I sure do not want to come back here.*

The cath lab staff members wheeled Peter to a room and pulled alongside the procedure table. Three orderlies grabbed the sheet he lay on and transferred him supine to the procedure table. His skin erupted in goosebumps from contact with the table. Additional monitors were placed, and the nurse checked his vitals. A warm blanket was placed across his legs. He saw Dr. Charnov, who was in the adjoining room, conversing with the nurse. Peter could not make out what they said but shortly afterwards, the nurse injected something into his IV and he felt woozy and disconnected from reality.

The last thing he remembered was seeing two staff members bending over him as he drifted off. Their faces formed a silhouette against the overhead lights. His brain registered that a woman was on the left and a man was on the right. The man standing to his right leaned over him and pulled a strap over his abdomen. He shook his head, turning to the left and right. To his right, he saw a wall cabinet with glass doors. The labels were legible but unintelligible. To his left was a large C-shaped machine. His eyes fluttered and closed.

*   *   *

The cath lab staff prepared his groin area for vascular access. After they cleaned and draped the area with large blue towels, Dr. Charnov appeared, wearing a cap, mask, a surgical gown with a lead apron underneath, and sterile gloves.

"Local," he said.

An assistant handed him a syringe. Dr. Charnov injected local anesthetic around the site. Peter winced in his sleep and tried to draw his leg back. Dr. Charnov ordered more sedation and more local. Once the area was numb, he made a small skin nick with a scalpel. He blotted the bead of blood that welled up from the nick. Leaving a wad of gauze at the site, he took a larger bore needle on a syringe and using anatomic landmarks around the head of the femur, lifted the gauze and inserted the needle into the skin nick. He placed the needle into the femoral artery. A sterile wire followed soon afterwards, and the procedure was under way.

An x-ray machine, shaped like a large letter C poised to embrace Peter, loomed over his chest, its positioning optimizing the view of his cardiac vessels. An operating room table next to the procedure table was covered with various sterile catheters. Under intermittent periods of continuous fluoroscopy, Dr. Charnov first obtained an arteriogram to map out Peter's cardiac anatomy. He then mapped out which vessels had narrowed, and which needed a stent. The previously placed stent was visible, bobbing with each beat of his heart.

About thirty minutes into the procedure, as Dr. Charnov placed another catheter, an alarm sounded an insistent beep, continuous, high-pitched, and penetrating. Peter's blood pressure had dropped below a critical level. Coincident with the alarm going off, the rhythm strip changed, from sinus tachycardia to short runs of ventricular tachycardia.

"What the hell?" said Dr. Charnov. He ordered the immediate administration of pressor agents to bolster Peter's blood pressure. Peter's blood pressure spiked in response but within thirty seconds, peaked and headed down again.

"Call the OR," he barked at an assistant. "I'm not sure what's going on, but he may have a dissection or perforation in the left main or LAD." He had been working around the patient's left main artery and the left anterior descending artery, the two most important blood vessels that feed the left ventricle.

Peter's rhythm changed to ventricular tachycardia and on the arterial line tracing, his blood pressure plummeted further. Dr. Charnov glanced at Peter's neck veins. They were visible and swollen.

"We need to get to the OR right away," Dr. Charnov said. "I think he's developing a tamponade." Too much fluid, like blood, around the heart, would result in a dangerous compression of the heart and impede its regular motion.

The staff had already made the call to the OR, and they transferred Peter off the table and onto a gurney. The crew wheeled him out of the room, racing down the hall. The operating room was next door; one of the cath lab staff ran ahead and banged on the square metal plate to open the door. They wheeled him through and one of the OR staff called out, "Room Four!"

The entire process of transfer had taken less than three minutes. Peter was still in ventricular tachycardia and was now hemodynamically unstable. The cardiologist ran the code as the ER staff prepared for surgery. While the ER staff prepared, Dr. Charnov grabbed a syringe with a large needle. He placed the needle below the sternum and aimed it in the general direction of the heart. He guided it by feel and after a reasonable distance, blood filled the syringe rapidly. Almost immediately, there was a slight positive response in Peter's blood pressure.

"He has a tamponade," Dr. Charnov confirmed.

As the pump technician primed the bypass pump, the cardiothoracic surgeon arrived on the scene.

"Hi, Howard," she said to the cardiologist. "Give me a minute to get scrubbed and you can talk while I get started."

"Hi Joan, sounds good," said Dr. Charnov. "I'm still not able to get a stable rhythm. I'm worried he may be tamponading from a dissection or perforation."

The surgeon, Joan Latham, scrubbed and came back into the operating room. The anesthesiology crew was also ready. The cardiac anesthesiologist was not yet available so one of the available anesthesiologists would start the case.

         *   *   *

Jick came into the room.

"I'll get things started," he said.

Oh, shit, he thought when he realized it was Peter.

He intubated Peter and connected him to a ventilator. After a quick prepping and draping, Dr. Latham asked for a bone saw to do a sternotomy incision. The surgery was under way.

Dr. Latham and another surgeon, whom Jick did not know, opened Peter's chest in what seemed to be record time. Within a few minutes, Peter was on bypass. The pericardium was tense and distended. Dr. Latham incised the pericardium and blood rushed out. She quickly applied suction to empty the sac while she looked for the bleeder.

Dr. Charnov had been right. Peter had bad atherosclerotic blood vessels and one of them, unfortunately the main one, had developed a rupture from the cardiac catheter. Blood had filled the pericardium.

Dr. Ross Mortimer, the cardiac anesthesiologist, appeared in a few minutes, and Jick signed off the case to him. He went back to the OR lounge and settled in a chair. He had told Peter to take it easy, but it may not have made a difference anyway. Stent thromboses, the development of a clot in a recently placed stent, was a known complication and despite being on blood thinners, it seemed a likely diagnosis. He sighed.

About thirty minutes later, there was a commotion near Room Four. Peter was not doing well. There were already two anesthesiologists, two surgeons, and many support staff in the room, so Jick stayed away. He decided there were enough skilled personnel involved in this resuscitation and sometimes it was too many cooks.

Jick found out later that even though Dr. Latham had drained the tamponade and had sewn the ruptured vessel shut, Peter had bad vessels, and it appeared he had thrown a plaque in another vessel. This triggered another round of arrhythmias that Peter could not survive.

They coded Peter, but he died on the table about fifteen minutes later. Jick headed back to his office to catch up on tasks until it was time to go home. He strolled around the corner, pressed the metal square to open the operating room doors, and walked toward his office.

The same feeling he had experienced a week earlier was back. *What the hell? There is someone in my office.*

He opened the door of his office and looked in. As it had been last week, there was no one there. Again, the mask caught his eye. It seemed more vibrant. On an impulse, he took down the mask from the bookshelf and studied it. It almost seemed to invite him to put it on.

He lowered the mask on his head and immediately felt a rush of disorientation.

I'm supine, looking up at fuzzy outlines of two people, a woman standing on my left and a man on my right. Each wears a surgical mask and bends over me, their faces silhouetted against two bright lights. The man leans over me, pulling a strap across my abdomen. I shake my head, turning to the right and left. After a brief glimpse, the image is now black and ... wait a minute ... I can see my office.

Jick jerked the mask off his head. He felt a mild vertiginous sensation and a sheen broke out on his face. He walked to his desk, carrying the mask, and dropped into his chair.

What the hell was that? Jick thought. That image looked like had been lying on his back on a procedure table, looking at operating room lights. From the labels on the cabinet and the C-arm x-ray machine, he had recognized the inside of the cath lab.

The mask was now drab again. That vibrancy he had noted in its appearance from a few moments ago had faded away. He hesitated, then put the mask back on. Nothing. He could see his office through it. Yet for a moment, he had felt like he had seen something else altogether. It had lasted for a second or two and then vanished. The sensation of vertigo had also faded.

Jick did not know what to make of it, so he hung the mask back on the edge of the bookshelf. The feeling of someone being in his office had also disappeared. He looked back at the mask. Its black eyes stared at him.

He went to check on his rooms. As he left his office, the same feeling of disconcertedness he had experienced before was back.

What is it about that mask?

He went back to the operating room lounge. Dr. Mortimer was there.

"So, what happened in there?" Jick asked.

"Not sure but if I was a betting man, I'd say he threw a plaque, and this one was the bad one. It wasn't a stent thrombus. His left main was perfed, but he was doing great on bypass. Joan had finished sewing the perforation, and we had got him off bypass when he coded again. We tried to crash back on bypass, but it was not gonna happen for him today. We couldn't get any rhythm back."

"And he came straight from the cath lab."

"Yes, he did." Dr. Mortimer looked at Jick. "Something bothering you?"

"Oh, no, nothing," Jick said. "I was thinking about something else. He was my neighbor. I knew him, got to know him better in the last few weeks."

Did I see the last thing Peter saw?

"Sorry to hear that."

Jick looked at the schedule for the next day, which was Friday. He was on call. That meant he would return to work at three o'clock and stay until seven on Saturday morning. He resolved to take the mask home and do some research into it.

He went back to his office and threw himself into his chair. Peter had said he had maybe fifteen good years left. And he was dead. The Black Cloud swirled around his head.

I need to go home to my friends.

TWENTY

Jonas had left for work as usual. Tiffany Jensen's routine for the past month was to wait until Jonas left and then log on to her online chat room. The conversations between Simon and her had become more explicit and they had begun exchanging pictures. Tiffany felt a thrill as she logged in. She felt today was the day something was going to happen between them. She wasn't sure what, but a part of her hoped Simon would concoct a way for them to meet in person.

It was 10 a.m. and Tiffany poured a glass of wine. She sat at the computer, sighed, and turned it on, immediately going to her online chat room. She took a sizable gulp of wine and logged in. She felt a warm flush from the wine and almost immediately on logging in, noticed that Simon had sent her a picture of his computer setup with a glass of wine next to the screen. Tiffany looked at it and giggled. She wore shorts and a T-shirt without a bra. On an impulse, she pulled the neckline of her T-shirt away from her body, held her phone at her neck looking down, and took a picture. It showed the valley between her breasts in the middle of the picture and each breast arced toward the side of the picture. The picture was hazy from the light that filtered through her T-shirt. At each edge of the picture was a hint of exposed nipple.

She giggled again and sent it to Simon.

"Better than wine?" she typed a caption.

After a few minutes, he sent a picture back. It was a close-up and she could not immediately make out what it was. It was cork-colored, cylindrical, with wavy linear ridges.

"Not a wine cork... what could it be?" was the caption with a giggle emoji. When she read the caption, she realized with a pleasant shock that it was a close-up of the shaft of his penis.

Tiffany pulled her shorts down a little and aimed her phone at her pubic area. She had kept it cropped but not shaved completely. Jonas liked it that way. She took a zoomed in picture and looked at it. Close up, it looked like a brush with a cleft at one end. She sent it to Simon.

"Not a brush, what could it be?" was the caption with another giggle emoji.

"Next time I'll let you watch the whole thing," she wrote as she started rubbing herself. She lifted her T-shirt and took a picture of her breasts and sent it to him with another giggle emoji. She stood and dropped her shorts. She sat, took a picture of her exposed pubic area, and sent it to him. A second picture, this time with her finger on her private area, followed the first.

"Oh, Simon, I wish we could be together," she wrote.

"I'm ready," was Simon's reply. "Let's do it."

She ended her chat session with Simon with a deep sigh. She logged off the chat room and leaned back in the chair. She poured a glass of wine and downed it in a few generous sips.

In his last exchange with her, Simon had shown he wanted to relieve himself with the image of her pubic area and breasts. Tiffany felt the same and had asked him for another picture of the "cork". He had sent her a picture of his chest and belly, looking toward his penis. His lower half was exposed and, in the picture, she could see his shorts gathered around his feet.

She continued rubbing herself. Afterwards, she felt relaxed and settled down to read a book and take a nap. She had closed her browser windows, logged off her computer and powered it down.

*   *   *

Jonas arrived at work deep in thought. He pulled into one of the parking spaces behind Second Chance and went into his cubicle in the healthcare clinic where his computers served the facility. He had noticed a change in Tiffany's behavior over the past few weeks and wanted to find out the reason. It bothered his controlling nature that he did not know exactly what she did during the day. So, without her knowledge, he had installed a keylogger that tracked all her keystrokes and had installed software that would allow him to turn on her computer camera from his office and without her knowledge. He sat at his cubicle and turned on his computer. He pulled his keychain out of his pocket and started twirling it as he stared at the screen.

Within a few minutes, he had accessed her camera and keylogger. There was nothing on the screen. He spent the next two hours catching up on work as he had backups and server maintenance scheduled. Second Chance had three satellite clinics, and a remote location housed the servers. His office was at one of the satellites, but he could remotely assist any of their facilities.

Tiffany's camera feed was in a small window that he had not quite minimized on the desktop but was visible if there was any activity. Shortly after 10 a.m., he noticed a movement. He stretched the window open to get a better view. He also opened a window to look at the keylogger's streamed data.

As he watched, Tiffany lifted a glass of wine to her mouth and took what seemed to be a large gulp. Jonas frowned. He drank alcohol but did not like it when Tiffany drank, especially alone. Not to mention in the morning.

He could not see what was on her screen. She leaned forward and pulled the neck of her T-shirt open, holding her camera over the opening and taking a picture. Jonas' eyes widened. The keylogger tracked keystrokes in both directions but not image files from the phone. Those files were sent from the phone straight to the recipient's computer, most likely as an email attachment. As soon as she had sent the picture somewhere, the keylogger reported 'Better than wine?'

He wondered what email account she used.

A few minutes later, a picture appeared on her phone. She looked at it and rocked back on her chair, giggling. The person on the other end of whatever chat room she was in sent back a message "Not a wine cork.... what could it be?" to which Tiffany pulled open the front of her shorts and took a picture, sending to this other person a picture of her pubic area. She sent a message "Not a brush, what could it be?"

Jonas felt a slow fury building inside. He felt his breath and pulse quickening and clenched his fists. He forced himself to unclench his fists and continue watching.

As he continued to watch, she lifted her shirt and exposed her breasts. She took a picture and sent it to her online contact. She stood, took off her shorts, and stood naked from the waist down. She held her phone facing toward her to get a "selfie" and her fingers typed a message as she sent it.

She leaned back in her chair and poured another glass of wine. She gulped it. He could only see her from the waist up but judging from her splayed position on the chair and her expression, Jonas could see she was masturbating.

"Next time I'll let you watch the whole thing," the keylogger reported. She took another picture, this time with her finger suggestively against her most sensitive area and sent it.

Her last comment was like a dagger to him.

"Oh, Simon, I wish we could be together."

The recipient's reply twisted the dagger.

"I'm ready, let's do it."

She leaned forward and logged off the chat room. She drank another glass of wine.

Jonas sat motionless and expressionless, watching her. After a few minutes, she finished her wine, and she reached down with both hands to button up her shorts. She stood, picked up the empty glass of wine, and reached for the mouse. The window went black as she logged off.

Jonas remained motionless, staring at the black window, for a full two minutes. He exhaled as he realized he had been holding his breath. His keychain was clenched in his left hand. He stuffed it into his pocket and walked over to the clinic's manager's office.

"I'm not feeling well. Think I'm coming down with something. The backups will finish on their own, so I'm taking off early. I'll be on my phone."

He left the clinic and walked over to his car. He climbed in, shut the door, and started the engine. At the realization that she planned to leave him, his pent-up anger released as he let out a howl of rage and slammed both fists on the steering wheel. He grabbed the steering wheel with both hands and squeezed it as hard as he could, his forearms shaking with the effort. He breathed hard, and his face was red, beads of perspiration forming on his forehead. He felt a throbbing vein down the middle of his forehead.

She was going to leave him.

"Fucking bitch!" he yelled out loud.

He put the car in reverse, backed out of his parking spot, and drove away. For the first few miles, he drove aimlessly, deep in thought. After about thirty minutes, he turned toward the University, with a new purpose. After a brief stop at the University, he was back in his car. He drove to the Spanish-speaking part of downtown Dallas and surveyed the shops. A sign on one shop caught his attention. He parked and went in.

Signs in Spanish advertised many items, including cheap cell phones and calling cards. A young Hispanic man stood behind the counter.

He pointed to a cheap Android smartphone and asked, "¿Cuánto por este teléfono celular?" He had maintained a working knowledge of Spanish after his Mormon mission in Colombia.

"I speak English," the shop clerk said. "Fifty dollars."

"I'll take one and a fifty-dollar calling card."

The clerk produced a phone and gave it to Jonas to inspect. Jonas scanned the back of the box. It was a cheap Chinese made Android phone. There was a sticker on it showing its compatibility with U.S.-based cell phone networks. The clerk rang up the sale for the phone and calling card. Jonas paid in cash and left. He drove back to the clinic and went in.

"False alarm," he said to the manager. "I'm not feeling that bad so I'm back."

"OK," she said. "It isn't too busy today, anyway. If you feel worse, you can take the rest of the day off."

Jonas sat at the computer and logged into his and Tiffany's cell phone account. He clicked on her number and reviewed the recent text history. The screen showed several text messages sent this morning to a 713 area code. None of the content was visible, but he knew the number that had been sending her messages. Nowadays, area codes are not always specific to geographic areas, but Jonas knew the 713 area code was somewhere in the Houston area.

He opened another window and set up his burner phone, adding the fifty-dollar card to the account. He opened the Google Play store app and perused the apps for a cell phone number spoofing application. For someone with his computer-related expertise, this was child's play. In a few minutes, he had set up his phone to display the 713 area code number. He test-dialed his office and noted with satisfaction that it had worked. The caller ID showed the same number as the person who had been texting, or sexting, Tiffany.

He opened the keylogger window again. It had archived every keystroke on Tiffany's computer and kept a running archive for up to five days. He hit the page down button several times, pausing on each page, scanning the lines of messages until he found it. Her login information.

He went to the online chat room Tiffany had been on and logged in. He looked at her chat history from days earlier, his mood darkening further as he read the explicit messages. It seemed she had been chatting with someone named "Simon," not likely his actual name. A small thumbnail picture of Simon accompanied his replies. The picture was a hot link, so when he clicked on one thumbnail, it went to Simon's account page. Most of the information was general but some of it was specific, including the fact that he was a stay-at-home dad and that his wife worked in airline reservations. There was no other personal information.

Jonas took a shot in the dark. He clicked on the button to open a chat with Simon. Simon's thumbnail showed he was still online. He may have forgotten to log off. Or he was still there.

"I enjoyed this morning," Jonas typed.

There was no response for a minute and then a series of dots blinked in sequence, showing someone typing.

"So did I," from Simon.

"Don't have much time. You-know-who will be home any minute. He's out of town next week for work and, you know, wondering, you know, if I could, you know, see more than, you know, the cork?" Jonas typed, pretending to beat around the bush.

"Wow," from Simon. "My wife is taking the girls to New Orleans to visit her mother. I sure as hell ain't going to see that bitch. Would love to see you. But we only got one car."

"I'll come to you. After this morning, I'm desperate," Jonas typed.

"Me too," from Simon. "I'm in North Houston. Aren't you in Dallas?"

"Yes," Jonas typed.

"All right," from Simon. "Here's my address. She'll be gone all next week."

His address followed.

"I can be there on the 21st," Jonas typed. "Oh God, I'm so looking forward to seeing you. Gotta go. Bye."

Jonas logged off and stared at the screen, hardly believing his luck. *What a dumb fuck*, he thought. He leaned back in his chair. For a few minutes, he sat in his chair motionless. His mind went through several options. Different expressions flitted across his face before ending with a cold smile. After deciding what to do, he walked out of the clinic. He got back in his car and drove back to the Spanish part of town. He chose a different shop and went in.

He repeated a similar transaction and left with a second cell phone and cash card. He returned to the clinic to set up his other burner phone, setting it up to show Tiffany's cell phone number on the caller ID. He turned off the phone, cleared his computer's browsing history, logged off, and went home.

*   *   *

Jonas came home from work as usual. He seemed quiet and contemplative. Tiffany assumed he had a tough day at work.

"How was your day?" she asked with a hint of cheeriness in her voice.

"OK, I guess." His answer was brief.

"I made dinner," she said. "Are you hungry?"

"Sure."

She served his dinner. Conversation was sparse. He did not have a second helping.

Jonas had his usual four or five drinks with dinner, and Tiffany felt herself tightening inside, as usual. But thankfully, Jonas did not seem to be in the mood for any intimate activities.

"I'm tired," he said after dinner. "I'm going to bed.

"By the way, I'm going out of town for a few days. The company is trying to get a contract with a hospital group in Houston. I'm leaving tomorrow and I might be back in a day. But it could be two days."

"Oh," Tiffany said. "Ok." She looked forward to tomorrow's chat session with Simon. Maybe she would get to see more than his "cork". She giggled inside.

TWENTY-ONE

Tiffany looked forward to the evening with some
anticipation, excitement, anxiety, and some guilt. The scales
tipped in favor of anticipation and excitement over anxiety
and guilt. Her relationship with Simon had progressed
beyond suggestive texts to actual sexting. At her last session,
she had expressed a desire to get together and he had said he
was ready. But she was still surprised at how soon he had
agreed to meet in person. She had received a text from him,
apologizing for the short notice, asking her if she wanted to
meet. She could hardly believe her luck as it was the same
day Jonas was going to be in Houston.

She did not know where Simon was, although the online
meeting websites usually suggested contacts close to each
other. She assumed he was in the Dallas area even though
his messages had come from a Houston area code.

They had pushed their online relationship as far as they
could, and Tiffany, as bored and unhappy as she was, agreed
to a meeting in person. And Jonas had said he would be out
of town. Even better.

Simon had suggested meeting near a bar in Deep Ellum.
He had also told her not to contact him by phone until the
meeting as he didn't want his wife finding out. Tiffany was
not too familiar with that part of Dallas but knew it was a
well-populated and vibrant area and she was not too
concerned. Simon had also proposed Tiffany park her car at
a pay-to-park lot near the bar and he would jump in and
they could go to the bar together, leaving his car there to
avoid his car being spotted at the bar. Reading his text
outlining this proposal created a slight flutter of anxiety, but
she brushed it off. She thought of asking him where his wife
and kids were if he planned a meeting at night, but also

brushed that off. She assumed his wife and kids were out of town. *In that case, why would he even need to meet in a pay-to-park lot nearby?* she thought.

That morning, Jonas had assembled an overnight bag for his trip to Houston. He loaded his bag into the back of his car and took his laptop. After breakfast, he gave her a perfunctory kiss, and drove off. Tiffany waved goodbye and immediately went to her computer and tried to log in. Simon had told her not to text but had not told her not to chat. She could not log in and her computer produced an error message showing there was no internet connection. She frowned at this but decided she would keep busy running errands until the evening. She decided she would shop for a new dress.

By early evening, her excitement increased as she was about to meet Simon for the first time in person. She spent the next hour getting ready, inspecting every minute aspect of her makeup and clothing. Her new dress was black and sheer, snug in all the right places. She poured a glass of wine and downed it in a few gulps, dabbed her lips on a tissue, did one last makeup check, and left.

*   *   *

Jonas had spent the day driving around and brooding. He went over in his mind everything he had arranged. Every time he thought back to what he had seen the previous day on his computer, his rage swelled and his grip on the steering wheel tightened.

At seven o'clock, he pulled into the parking garage at the University. He had the burner phone he had programmed with Simon's number in his pocket.

He walked through the campus and went to a lab. He pushed open the door and went in. A few staff members worked late, bent over their desks. They looked at him and waved in recognition. He was an IT guy who visited the lab occasionally and did some work.

"Doing some late work?" one of them asked.

"Yeah," Jonas said. "There are some problems with a server, and I'll check it out and see what's wrong."

"Sounds good," the staff member said. "We're going home in a few minutes. You have a key card, right?"

"I do. I'll let myself out. Thanks."

"There's some leftover pizza in the fridge from lunch. You're welcome to have some."

"Thanks."

He walked through to an inner office. There was a desk and some chairs. He took out his phone and left it in a desk drawer. Then he turned and walked out but did not leave the building the same way he had come in. He went down the stairwell to the basement and looked for a service door. There was an emergency exit with a "Do Not Open, Alarm Will Sound" message. He reached up to the door frame and slid a piece of tape on the contact button. He pushed it open and stepped out into the now darkening evening. He let the door close behind him, wedging it in the open position. He made his way back to his car.

He drove downtown from the University and parked his car on a side street, about fifty yards from a parking lot. It was a few minutes shy of eight o'clock. He opened the trunk and took out the overnight bag he had packed earlier in the day. He walked to a bus stop and waited. The next bus was punctual, arriving five minutes later. He changed buses once and at closer to nine o'clock, alighted near his neighborhood.

His phone dinged a text message. He had left his regular phone at the University but had forwarded text messages to the burner phone. Depending on the texting app he used, the other person would either see Jonas' number or Simon's number.

"Hi, Jonas," from Tiffany. He had planned to call her when he arrived in the neighborhood.

"Hi," he texted back.

"How's it going?"

"Good. Hang on a second."

He dialed Tiffany's number. She answered immediately.

"Great timing, I was about to call you. I'm in a hotel near Bush intercontinental airport in Houston."

"Did you have a pleasant drive?"

"Yes, it was not bad. Meeting some hospital groups tomorrow. Should be home late. May need to stay another day. I'll let you know."

"OK, good night," she said. "Love you."

"Good night. Love you."

He arrived at his house. The light outside the garage was on, casting a yellow cone over the driveway. The garage door was closed. He avoided the cone of light and walked around to the back, skulking along the bushes. A sliver of light shone between the master bedroom curtains. He leaned close to the window and through a small opening in the curtains, he could see Tiffany in a black sheer bra and panties. She wriggled into the dress and looked back over her shoulder at the mirror. She wriggled her butt and giggled. She did not have makeup on yet. Jonas felt a wave of rage building and he clenched his fists.

He sank into the bushes and walked in a semi-crouch to the side door of the garage. He inserted his key into the lock, opened it without a sound, and went in. Tiffany's SUV was there. The motion sensor in the garage door opener sensed his presence and the light flashed on. He froze, startled. But Tiffany was busy in the master bedroom. He opened the back, climbed in, and pulled the back shut with a soft thud. He reached into the overnight bag and pulled out his gun. He had two guns, a revolver and a Glock. He had brought the revolver, chambered in 357 Magnum rounds. Thirty seconds later, the garage went dark again. He leaned back, his gun next to him, along with a thin gauzy cloth he had brought along. As he waited, he fished a keychain out of his left pocket and started twirling it. He waited.

*   *   *

Tiffany backed her SUV out of the garage and waited until the garage door closed. She paused, wondering if she should do this. It seemed to be too late to back out now. *I'm a little nervous*, she thought, as she turned the air conditioner knob down a few notches. She guided her Honda SUV through the streets of Dallas. She had asked her phone to navigate her to the address. It was a pay-to-park lot that stretched along a cross street connecting Main and Elm Streets. As she pulled in, her phone dinged and the message, from Simon's phone, said "I'm almost there." She flipped open the visor mirror, and the light illuminated her features. Her nose shone and there was a nervous sheen to her features. She hastily fished a powder compact out of her purse and dabbed her face. She turned her head to one side and then the other, inspecting her makeup again, making sure everything was perfect.

She put the car in Park, turned off the engine, and opened the driver's door.

Her phone dinged again and this time, there was no message, just an attached picture. She looked at it, puzzled. It was a black screen with a gauzy, out-of-focus neon green and red/yellow splash on one side. She stared at it and her phone dinged again. "Running late. Be there in two minutes."

She felt something twist in her guts and felt a twinge of fear. *What's with the picture?* she thought. The scales had swung in favor of fear over anticipation and excitement.

Before she could reply to the text, her phone dinged again and this time, once again there was no message. Just another attached picture. She looked at it, both puzzled and now alarmed. The picture was the same, but the neon green and red/yellow splash was in better focus. She could barely make out some letters in the red area of the picture. *Maybe a D and an E?* she thought.

Her phone dinged again, and the message was: "I'm here, Madeline."

She looked around the car, using the steering wheel as leverage as she craned her neck from one side to the other. There was no one there. Small patches under the streetlights were lit but most of the parking lot and the street were in darkness. She leaned out for a better look. Faint music throbbed from a side street but there was no one in the parking lot. The feeling of fear crept out of her guts and seeped through her limbs.

She pulled the door shut and pressed the lock button on the fob. All the doors locked with a reassuring click and a red light began blinking on the dashboard. She loosened her grip on the steering wheel.

About fifty yards in the distance through her front windshield, off to the left, was a glowing neon green and red/yellow "DEEP ELLUM TEXAS" sign. Something in her brain clicked. With a sudden shock, realization hit her, and she gasped. The fuzzy pictures she had received were of the Deep Ellum sign.

Whoever took the pictures and sent them to her was in the car, behind her.

She spun around in her seat in fright. A figure hiding in the third-row seat of the SUV sat upright, still in darkness but silhouetted against the dim streetlight entering through the back window. The unmistakable twirling in his left hand left no doubt in her mind. The figure's right hand held a gun.

"Jonas?" she said, puzzled. "Is that you?"

The figure in the back shook its head.

"No, Madeline, I'm Simon."

Tiffany gasped as a sudden explosion, unexpected and deafening, reverberated in the confines of the Honda. She had no time to react.

In an instant, the large-caliber bullet tore through the backrest of the driver's seat and hit Tiffany over the left eighth rib. It deflected by a few degrees, its shock wave and mass tearing through the compliant left lung, nicking the pulmonary artery, through her right lung, and ricocheting against her fourth rib as it exited. The bullet then hit the horn and it chirped for an instant, like someone had clicked the lock button twice.

Tiffany coughed and tried to speak. No words came out as blood leaked out of her pulmonary artery and into her bronchial tree. The only sound she made was a wheezy gurgle. She slumped sideways and fell across the passenger seat.

*   *   *

Jonas scooped up his phone, stuffed his keychain back into his pocket, and jumped forward between the seats.

He unlatched the back door on the left side and pushed it open with his foot. Since Tiffany had locked the doors, opening the back door triggered the alarm and a loud staccato of honking started.

Jonas reached between the front seats and picked up Tiffany's phone. Tiffany lay slumped sideways, her breaths coming in short, wet gasps. He jumped out of the SUV and ran to the back. He opened the back door and reached in for his overnight bag. He slammed the hatch shut and fired a single round through the back window. He tossed the phones and gun into the overnight bag and took off running.

He trotted up the block for about fifty yards to where he had parked his car, his heart pounding. He could still hear the car alarm and by now, it drew attention. He jumped into his car and looked through the windshield at Tiffany's SUV. As he watched the scene unfolding in front of him, he powered off Tiffany's phone.

*   *   *

Two passersby ran up to the SUV. The first one arrived a few steps ahead of the second. He peered into the car and jumped back, waving his arms.

"Holy shit, Bill, there's a gal in there. I think she's been shot."

One of the passersby glanced into the SUV as he pulled out his phone. As he tried to dial 911, his hands shook, and he dropped the phone. He bent over to pick it up.

"I'm going to call 911," said Bill.

The operator answered immediately.

"911, please state your emergency."

"Hey, come quick, there's a gal here who's shot!"

"Please state your location," the operator said. "We'll get someone there right away."

More animated talk ensued between the men, with lots of hands signals and the second man relating more information through his cell phone.

"What do we do now, man," said Bill. "We can't leave her in there."

They opened the door. Tiffany moved weakly in the seat, still slumped over to the side, still breathing in shallow gasps. Blood spatter covered the seats and center console, coming from an obvious chest wound. Some blood trickled out of her mouth. A pool had collected on the floor. Her eyelids fluttered but remained closed.

Bill reached in and grabbed Tiffany's arm, trying to pull her out. She made another wheezy gurgling sound. Her eyes opened wide for an instant, unfocused, staring. She coughed once, a deep wet cough. Bill let go of Tiffany and recoiled as a spray of blood hit his arm.

The wailing of sirens interrupted any further attempt on their part to help Tiffany. They stepped back, relieved, as the paramedics jumped out of the ambulance.

*   *   *

Jonas watched the scene unfold from his car. He started his car, executed a U-turn, and drove off.

He drove back to the University and parked. He got out of the car and jogged around to the lab building he had left a few hours earlier. As he went past a dumpster, he tossed in Tiffany's phone. He powered off the burner phone and tossed it into the dumpster. He went to the emergency exit that he had pushed open some hours earlier. It was closed and there were no handles on the outside. He wedged his fingers against the door. By pulling hard, he could open the door. He peeled off the tape over the alarm button and shut the door. He made his way back to the office and sat on the couch. He sat still for a few minutes and when he had calmed enough, took out his phone. He edited selected messages and the call history on his phone using an app he

had found. Then he settled back on the couch and closed his
eyes.

TWENTY-TWO

Jick arrived at work on Friday shortly before three. He changed out of his clothes, splashed cold water on his face, and put on a pair of clean scrubs. He was on call, which meant it was his turn in the barrel. Warm Friday nights usually meant at least one, and sometimes more, knife and gun club events or drunk driving events. The regular operating room schedule for Friday had finished and most of the staff had left. As the on-call attending physician, his shift started at three o'clock and ended the following morning at seven. One attending physician, two nurse anesthetists, and two residents from the nearby medical school comprised the on-call team. There was also an on-call physician upstairs in labor and delivery, in case the shit hit the fan. Mostly, the staff they had downstairs was enough for trauma. The hospital also had a policy of going on divert, which meant sending patients to a different hospital, if things spiraled out of control with trauma cases.

Jick lounged in his office on a futon. He had just finished an unsatisfying dinner from the hospital cafeteria. Visiting hours were finished by the evening and hospital cafeterias operated a skeleton crew, if they were open at all. Most of the offerings were leftover specials from earlier in the day. There was no evening meal service in the trough.

He took the mask down from the bookshelf to study it. It was eleven o'clock.

"Trauma hot!" signaled Hot Potato, pealing an alarm as he settled in his futon. Hot Potato was part of the trauma alert system, a signaling device passed around from one on-call physician to the next like a hot potato. The intercom in the operating room also signaled an incoming trauma.

"ETA 3 minutes," said the mechano-voice inside Hot Potato.

Three minutes? Jick thought. *That's close. Where the hell was he shot? In the hospital parking lot?*

He climbed out of his futon, put the mask back on the bookshelf, and left his office. He walked the few feet around the corner to the operating suites where the designated trauma room was already set up: Room Three.

Stepping into Room Three was like stepping into a sauna. In preparation for the arrival of a trauma patient, the thermostat had been set to ninety. Bodies cooled rapidly when blood poured out or if the surgeon needed to crack open a chest and all the innards were exposed to ambient temperature. A cooling body created all kinds of problems for resuscitative efforts so the best way to keep a body warm was to not let it cool in the first place. So, Trauma Hot meant hot trauma, miserable for the staff but better for the patient.

Probably another damn Friday night knife and gun club gang banger, he thought.

Mireille was also on call. She was already in the room with the resident, scanning all the anesthesia equipment and drugs. She looked hot, in more ways than one, and there was an erotic quality in watching her work with perspiration running down her nape and staining her scrubs in erogenous areas.

Jick let his thoughts wander and then put them resolutely out of his head as the elevator doors opened with a ding and an orderly called out, "Coming in hot."

The "knife and gun club gang banger" was anything but. It was a young woman, Jick guessed mid-thirties, dressed for a night on the town. The front of her dress was drenched and from her pallor and half-lidded expression, Jick knew she was almost gone. EMS personnel had already intubated her, and he did a quick assessment of her intravenous line situation. There appeared to be two medium-bore IVs in her arms. *Not enough*, he thought.

Since she was intubated, the resident attached her endotracheal tube to the ventilator and turned it on. Jick glanced at the monitors to make sure there was an end-tidal CO_2 signal, to determine the tube was in the correct place. There was … for now. Working with a practiced efficiency, Mireille positioned the patient's outstretched arms on the boards and placed an arterial line in her right wrist.

Jick angled the table so the patient's head was tilted down, in the so-called Trendelenburg position. By using bony landmarks such as the sternal notch and mastoid process, by feel and with years of experience under his belt, he placed a large-bore central line on the right side of her neck.

Mireille clipped the pressure transducer to the arterial line; the first blood pressure on the waveform was fifty over thirty. The blood bank had already sent blood, and the resident worked on hanging the first bag with a pressure infuser as Jick hung pressor agents to increase her blood pressure.

"Too soon for gas?" asked Mireille.

"Yes," Jick said. "She's not stable enough yet. Let's give her a small dose of midazolam and wait. We may introduce the gas in a little."

"OK."

While they got her ready from an anesthetic standpoint, the operating room staff had prepared her chest with a generous splash of betadine. They placed a blue surgical drape over the clean area and passed one end to Jick. As he clipped the end of the drapes at the head of the bed, he glanced over at the patient's chest. There was a ragged hole in the left side at about mid-chest, along the left hemithorax and about ten centimeters to the left of her breast. On the right side of her chest, there was an exit wound higher up. He already knew by the trajectory of the bullet that this was probably an exercise in futility. He nodded to the surgeon to proceed.

"Bone saw," the surgeon said. The surgeon, Dr. Kessner, was a trauma surgeon. Since her injuries also involved the thoracic area, Dr. Latham, the cardiothoracic surgeon, was also present.

As the bone saw whirred to life, Jick noted the patient's pressure had crept up to about sixty over forty. Not good. With the amount of pressors and blood they had pushed in, this was not good.

The surgeons opened her chest cavity. The inside was a mess. The bullet had torn through the lungs and nicked the pulmonary artery, leaving a trail of ragged destruction. Jick was surprised to see the extent of the damage on a still living patient as these types of injuries are usually fatal on the street and seldom make it this far.

"What's the story?" Jick asked.

"As far as we know, she was in her SUV near Deep Ellum when someone walked up and shot her. The bullet hit the horn and because of the noise, some passersby discovered her within a minute. We're just down the road so they got her here as fast as they could. The only reason she even made it this far is because of how they discovered her. And because it took her a while to bleed out."

Opening the chest had the effect of turning a bloody mess into a gusher. The blood pressure dropped as the heart struggled to maintain its output. Then it quit beating: the patient was gone. There was nothing the surgeons could do.

"Jesus," said Dr. Kessner. "We're done here, guys."

"Agreed," said Dr. Latham.

One of the operating room staff announced the official time of death. Mireille said she would finish and get the room set up for the next trauma. Jick walked to his office and let Mireille finish the paperwork and general cleanup. As he left the operating room, he heard the hiss of the residual gases as Mireille turned off the anesthesia machine. She silenced the EKG's flatline alarm sound.

He arrived at his office fifteen seconds later. As he reached for the doorknob, the feeling of that presence was back, again from inside his office. *There's definitely someone in there*, he thought. He opened the door and walked in. The feeling was much stronger and this time he noticed an unmistakable glow from the mask.

Jick walked over to the mask and without hesitating, lifted it off the bookcase and put it on. A rush and a feeling of disorientation hit him as soon as the mask settled on his head.

Looking around through the mask, I realize I am not in my office. I am in a vehicle, sitting in the driver's seat. All the surroundings are a grayish haze, like I am in a swirling storm cloud, and as I watch, the cloud begins to coalesce or evaporate, and the surrounding images come into sharper focus. There is no sound. From the logo on the steering wheel, I can see it is a Honda SUV. I canot hear anything but see myself looking down at a phone. The text is in focus, "I'm almost there."

I pull down the visor and flip open the mirror. I look at myself in the mirror, then dab at my face with a powder compact, inspecting my face on one side and then the other.

I can't hear anything but look down at the phone again. This time, an image appears, a small black square with a neon green and red/yellow splash in the corner. I look down again, this time the message is "Running late. Be there in two minutes."

I continue looking down. Another picture appears, the same black area with the neon green and red/yellow splash in the corner, now in sharper focus. Another text, "I'm here, Madeline." I pull the door shut and press a button on the key fob. I glance through the windshield and notice a neon green and red/yellow sign. The words "DEEP ELLUM TEXAS" are clearly visible. With a sudden move, I twist around to face the back of the car.

I look at the back seat, at a figure rising in the darkness, silhouetted against the dim light coming in through the back window, twirling something in its left hand. The object alternates between light and dark from the dim incoming light through the rear window, giving it a soft strobe-like appearance. It resembles a keychain with something on the end. The figure holds an object with an unmistakable silhouette in its right hand. The figure shakes its head, as if saying no.

There is a flash of light from the back of the SUV, and I feel myself jolt and fall back and to the side. The imagery clouds over in a grayish haze that turns to black as I fall onto the passenger seat. For a brief second, the clouds part to reveal a man bending over me in the driver's seat. Then the imagery ends for good as the inside of my office swirls into focus.

Jick pulled off the mask, gasping, and steadied himself against the desk. He was nauseated and drenched. His eyes had visualized the movement, but his head had not moved, and his brain triggered waves of nausea in protest. But everything was back to normal now.

He stared at the mask in shock. He had recognized the face when he looked in the visor mirror. He realized it was the woman in Room Three, the woman who had died in there a few minutes ago. There was a *joie de vivre* to the features that had all but vanished when he first saw the face with its death pallor and half-lidded eyes, now lifeless in the room behind the adjacent wall of his office.

He put the mask back on. His office was visible through the mask. Whatever he had seen through the mask had faded away.

He lifted the mask off his head. *Jesus H Christ*, he thought, looking at the mask. It no longer glowed. It was just a mask, an inanimate object, molded out of some material years ago. This thing had somehow channeled the last minutes of the victim's life as her memories faded to oblivion.

I was inside her body and saw her murderer.

Its black eyes stared at him. It was then that Jick realized what had unsettled him in the antique store and earlier when he was in his office after taking care of the gunshot victim.

The mask's eyes. They should not be black.

In the antique store, he had held it up to the light, and the sunlight had struck the inside of the mask. The mask's outline was a solid black with no light passing through from the eyes. When he had turned it around, he had subconsciously noted the beams of sunlight through the eye holes. The slight discrepancy had triggered his internal alarm.

If the mask was on him, he could see through it. Light, it seemed, only passed from the front of the mask to the back and not in the reverse direction. He also recalled the day he brought the mask to work. He had tried it on at home and looked in the mirror. He could see himself in the mirror, but when looking at the mask's eyes from the front, they had been black.

When it hung off his bookshelf, there was a row of books behind it. So, its eyes should not have been black. He should have been able to see the books behind it. But he could not.

Jick stared at it again. He turned it around, and he could see through it. He put it on. Nothing. He put the mask back on the bookshelf. His scrubs clung to his body. He changed into another set of scrubs in his office and walked back around the corner to the operating room.

There was no one in the operating room, at least, no one alive. A soft background hum and a whisper from the air vents were the only sounds in the room. Someone had turned down the thermostat. The victim lay on the operating room table, her face now covered in a sign of respect. Blotches of red had soaked through the white sheet in several places. In a few minutes, the crew from the morgue would arrive.

Jick pulled the corner of the sheet off her face and looked at her. Her face was serene, eyes taped closed. Her eyes had been lubed and taped closed to prevent inadvertent injury during anesthesia. Jick peeled off the tape and thumbed open her left eye. It was blue. Without the vitality of life, it looked like a doll's eye, glassy, fixed, and staring. Her face was ashen from the catastrophic blood loss. Streaks of dried blood still lined her chin and neck. The end of the endotracheal tube, held in place by a soft wraparound holder, protruded from the right side of her mouth. It pulled her mouth askew to the right in a partial rictus.

"I saw him," Jick murmured to the victim. "I saw the guy who did this to you."

There was a sound at the door as the morgue crew arrived. Jick pulled the sheet back over her face and walked out of the operating room.

TWENTY-THREE

The victim died before midnight on a Friday. By the following morning, the investigation was in full swing. The police had impounded the car for forensic analysis; they had run the license plates through the database, and the police had tried to locate next of kin. The victim's name was Tiffany Jensen. She lived in Oak Cliff with her husband, Jonas. Just them, no children.

On Saturday morning, an unmarked car stopped outside Tiffany Jensen's house and two men emerged. One was middle-aged, tall, and thin, the other younger, shorter, and stouter. They parked outside the house and noted the car parked in the short driveway.

"Wonder if the husband's home," said Tall One.

"Let's find out," said Stout One.

They walked up the driveway, eyes surveying the landscape and the windows. In the early stages of a murder investigation, there was no way of knowing if it was an isolated murder or part of something bigger. They kept their hands close to their firearms.

Tall One rang the doorbell and took a step back. A tall, dark-haired man with disheveled hair answered the doorbell. He looked like he had not slept all night. *Looks like he got back from killing someone*, thought Stout One.

"Jonas Jensen?" queried Tall One.

"Yes."

"May we come in? I'm Detective Fishburn, this is my partner Detective Cook. We're with the police." He held out his ID for Jonas to inspect.

"Oh, thank goodness, I was about to call you."

"Why?"

"I got home about thirty minutes ago, and my wife is not here and she's not answering her phone. I was about to call the police."

"Actually, that's why we're here, to talk to you about your wife."

"Why? What's wrong?" Jonas asked, looking alarmed.

"May we come in and sit for a minute?"

"Yeah, sure, come on in."

They walked into the living room. Fishburn and Cook sat on opposite sides of the room and Jonas was between them.

"Can I get you something to drink?" Jonas asked.

"No, thanks," said Fishburn.

"Mr. Jensen," began Cook. "I'm afraid we have some terrible news. It appears your wife Tiffany is dead."

Jonas stared at him, eyes widening, the color ebbing from his face.

"What?" he almost shouted. "What happened?"

"She was in her car last night in Deep Ellum," Fishburn said. "Someone shot her."

"Oh. My. God." said Jonas, holding his head in his hands. "Oh, no."

He rocked in his chair.

"Are you sure it's her?"

"We'll need you to please come with us to identify the body and also to answer some questions," Cook said.

"What?" he said, looking startled at the suggestion. "Oh, of course, of course. Like I said, I got back home about half an hour ago. One of our clients had a server crash in his lab and I was there all night. I slept in the lab and when I got home... Sorry, I'm not quite with it yet. Sleeping on a couch isn't easy."

"You weren't home all night?" Fishburn said.

"That's right. I was working. Oh, I'm an IT support guy. One of our clients at the University had the server problem."

"Do you have any idea why your wife was in Deep Ellum at around ten o'clock last night?" Cook asked.

"I have no idea. When I left to go to work yesterday morning, she didn't mention anything. I called her to let her know I would have to work late. Maybe she went to a bar with one of her girlfriends?" Jonas suggested. "Oh my God, Tiffany." He buried his face in his hands. His shoulders jerked.

The detectives said nothing for a moment to let the spasm of grief pass. "If you could come with us, we would be very much appreciate it."

"Give me a minute to freshen up. I'll be right out."

*   *   *

Jonas went to the bathroom, splashed some cold water on his face and dragged a comb through his hair. He looked in the mirror. A day's worth of stubble shaded the lower half of his face and his eyes looked bloodshot with dark circles underneath. His face was expressionless. He went back into the living room.

"OK, I'm ready, let's go."

Jonas locked the front door behind them and got into the back seat of the unmarked police car. They made their way through the streets of Dallas and stopped at a nondescript large gray concrete building near downtown. Office of the Medical Examiner was in brass letters at eye height on a plaque outside the building, near the main entrance. They went in, footsteps clattering on the concrete floor. There was no carpeting in this type of building. Easier to clean and easier to keep smells out.

Fishburn stopped at a computer at the desk and typed in some information. The computer told him which area of the building housed their victim. They walked down the hallway and stopped at a service window. Fishburn showed his badge to the attendant.

"We're here to do a positive ID on last night. Name is Tiffany Jensen."

"Case number please?"

Fishburn flipped an iPad open and swiped through some screens. He showed the iPad to the attendant who copied the case number on a yellow sticky.

"Give me a few minutes to get the viewing ready. Please have a seat. I'll call you." The three of them sat on the hard plastic industrial chairs.

In a few minutes, the attendant buzzed open a door from the inside and motioned them in.

"We're going to viewing room two." The detectives and Jonas clattered down the floor, their footsteps in unison.

The attendant opened the door to viewing room two and motioned them in. Inside, the decor was stark, with whitewashed walls and a shiny antiseptic floor. Bright white, fluorescent lights completed the stark look. The attendant had wheeled a metal table into the middle of the room and on it, a body lay covered in a white sheet. Four hard plastic chairs flanked two small, molded plastic and aluminum end tables. A box of tissues was on each table.

"This won't be easy," Cook said kindly. "We'll be brief."

Jonas walked to the head of the table and stood there, looking down. Fishburn held one corner of the sheet and peeled it back until the face was visible. Tiffany lay there, pale, with a waxy countenance, eyes closed. All signs of trauma had been cleaned and she looked like she might have been asleep. Except for the unnatural pallor. Jonas stifled a gasp and swayed. Fishburn steadied him by placing a hand on his shoulder.

"Tiffany?" Fishburn asked.

Jonas nodded, mute. He reached out, touched her cheek with the back of a finger, then turned away from them and reached for a box of tissues. He pulled out three in rapid succession and held them to his face.

"OK, thanks," Cook said to the attendant, and they left, clattering back down the hallway.

Outside, they all stood by the car. Jonas dabbed at his eyes and sniffed.

"We'll need you to come with us to the police station and make a statement," Cook said. Jonas nodded.

They drove from the morgue to the police station. Cook parked the car in one of the reserved stalls and they walked in. Fishburn waved his badge, and they bypassed the reception area, heading straight back to the interrogation rooms. Cook closed the door behind them and Fishburn directed Jonas to sit in a chair that faced the camera. Fishburn and Cook, along with a stenographer, sat on the other side.

"Please state your full name and date of birth," Fishburn said.

Jonas complied.

"Tell us a bit about where you work, your normal schedule."

Jonas complied, explaining about his tech work for Second Chance and the University, and his varied schedule due to putting out brush fires when problems arose.

"Please narrate the events of last Friday, starting with the morning and through Saturday morning."

"Well, let's see," Jonas began. "I left the house as usual in the morning and there was nothing out of the ordinary that day. In the evening, I want to say around six, one of our clients at the University called me to report one server had malfunctioned. I got there around seven and went to work. It had been a bad crash, so I did data recovery. That took about three hours. Then I had to rebuild the operating system and reinstall everything. I finished around midnight and was too tired to drive home, so I slept on the couch in the lab. That's about it."

When he got to the part about the server crash, Fishburn interrupted.

"So you left Second Chance at about six-thirty, drove to the University, went straight to the lab, and stayed there until midnight?"

"No, I stayed there all night. I finished repairing the server by midnight and stayed there."

"You didn't leave to get dinner or anything like that?"

"No. I stayed there with our client the whole time. Actually, our client went to get dinner for both of us."

"Did you leave for any other reason?"

"No."

"So, when your client went to get dinner, he left you alone for a while. What time was that?"

"Why? Are you implying something?"

"No, Mr. Jensen, gathering data. What time was dinner?"

"I'm not sure. I think he left at about seven-thirty and returned about fifteen, maybe twenty minutes later. There was some leftover pizza from earlier in the day, but we were not in the mood for it. He went to a place around the corner from where we worked to grab a couple of burgers and fries. After that, we worked until midnight. He went home after midnight and I fell asleep on the couch."

"Why didn't you go home?" asked Cook.

"It was late, and I was wiped out, so I lay down on the couch for a few minutes. Next thing I knew it was morning."

"When was the last time you spoke to Tiffany?"

"It was after the client called. I knew I would be late, so I called to let her know."

"Did you speak to her?"

"Yes, we had a brief conversation."

"Did you tell her you planned to work late?"

"Yes."

"Did you tell her you planned to stay there all night?"

"No, I didn't plan to stay all night."

"She didn't tell you she planned to go out later in the evening?"

"No."

"That's odd, Mr. Jensen. It's after six and she's planning to go out at nine and she doesn't say a word to you? Don't you find that odd, Mr. Jensen? I find it odd."

"Yes, that is odd. I can only guess that after I spoke with her, one of her friends called and wanted to meet."

"And she didn't text you about this? Or call you?"

"No."

"Any idea who that friend might be?"

"No."

"Do you have your phone with you?"

"Yes."

"May we have it? We'll get our guys to back up the phone and give it back to you asap. Your information will be secure."

"I'm not sure about this," Jonas said. "I have several confidential emails from various clients."

Fishburn frowned.

"Mr. Jensen, we're trying to locate your wife's murderer. The quicker we can gather data, the more likely we are to solve this crime."

"Yes, of course. I just… can I at least first contact my employer? I need to ask them what the protocol is for handing over a company-owned phone."

"Fine, you do that. But we expect you to hand over the phone by later today."

"OK, no problem."

The questioning session continued for another fifteen minutes. Afterwards, Fishburn stayed at the police station and Cook drove Jonas home. As they drove home, Cook chatted with Jonas about personal things, such as where he was from and why he moved to Texas. He also asked him about his job and how he enjoyed working as an IT support guy. Jonas answered in short words or phrases, keeping his answers neutral.

"I'm sorry for your loss," Cook said as Jonas got out of the car at his house.

"Thanks. I appreciate it."

"This investigation is starting. Please make sure you're available. We may have more questions as we investigate this further. And we need the phone by the end of the day."

"OK."

He walked up the driveway and went into his house. He went into the bathroom and stripped off his clothes and had a long, hot shower. After showering, he popped open a cold one and sat at his desk. He thought about what to say as he drank his beer.

He took out his phone and called a number.

"Hello," said a female voice.

"Hi, Norma, it's Jonas."

"Hi, Jonas, how are you guys doing? We miss you here in Utah. I wish you hadn't moved so far away."

"Norma, I have some terrible news," Jonas did his best to sound subdued. He heard a sharp intake of breath at the other end.

"What's going on? How's Tiffany?"

"Norma, I'm afraid Tiffany is dead."

"What?" Tiffany's mother said, disbelieving.

Then realization hit and he heard her wail.

"Oh my God, oh my God, oh my God, what happened?"

"She had gone to Deep Ellum. It's an artsy neighborhood near downtown Dallas, last night, I think to meet a friend. Someone shot her while she sat in the car. The police think it may have been a random killing."

"Wait, I'm getting Ron." He heard the phone clatter as she tried to put it down and dropped it. The connection was still on.

"Ron, Ron." He heard her shrieking for Tiffany's father. In the distance, he heard a reply.

"Yeah, what is it?"

"Come here, quick! It's Tiffany. She's dead. Shot. Jonas is on the phone."

Jonas heard running footsteps. Then a sound as Ron picked the phone off the floor.

"Jonas, what's going on?"

Jonas repeated what he had said to Norma.

"Oh, God," A pause. "The police think it was a random killing? What the hell was she doing out there alone? Where were you, Jonas?"

"I had to work late. I didn't know she went out. I got home this morning after falling asleep in the lab where I had worked, and she wasn't here. The police arrived just as I was about to call them."

"Are you sure it's her?" Ron asked, clutching at straws.

"Yes. The police wanted me to go to the morgue and identify her. I can't believe this is happening."

"Oh, God," said Ron again. He paused, his voice breaking. They spent the next couple of minutes in disconnected sentences about how wonderful she had been, how this could not happen, what a shock it was, etc. When the conversation petered out, Ron let out a shuddering sigh and asked, "Any idea what we should do for funeral arrangements? I can't believe I'm doing this."

"We want her to come back home," Norma said from the background, between sobs.

"Jonas, can you make the arrangements to have her sent back?" Ron asked.

"I'll talk to the funeral home."

"Thanks, Jonas, we'll talk again. I guess there's no point in us coming there, is there? Jonas, you'll be coming here for the funeral, right?"

"Of course," Jonas said, sounding a little choked up. "I'll stay with her all the way."

They ended the call.

*   *   *

Cook drove back to the police station. He went to Fishburn's office and knocked on the door.

"Come in."

He went in. Ed Fishburn sat at his desk. Cook dropped into one of the chairs.

"Well, Ed, what do you think?" he asked. "I think something's fishy."

"I think so too.

Fishburn continued, "Let's walk through this. We'll start from Tiffany's point of view. When the husband goes to work in the morning, she expects him to be back at the usual time. He calls her, or texts her, and says he's running late, but she doesn't know exactly how late because neither Jonas nor she knows how long it will take to rebuild a server, assuming that is what he did. She also expects he will be home at some point and if he ran late, he would text her or call her to let her know so she won't worry. So, what does she do? Gets dressed like she's about to meet a guy and goes out. Makes no sense. If she planned to meet a girlfriend and hang out for a while, that's the kind of thing you tell the husband, most likely in a text, so he won't worry when he gets home. And you go dressed casual."

"Right," Cook said. "And she goes out at nine o'clock, when she knows Jonas could get home any minute."

"It would make more sense if she thought Jonas would be gone all night," Fishburn said. "She sure as hell acted like that. Like she thought Jonas was out of town and she was fixing to meet some guy there."

Cook nodded. "And instead of coming home when he is done with his task, what does Jonas do? He doesn't go home at midnight to discover his wife is missing. He sleeps on the couch and is gone all night. It is almost as if he planned it so that he wouldn't need to report she's missing until the morning at the earliest."

"But somehow the car alarm goes off and she's discovered right away.

"We need to go through all her phone records, online contacts, and social media stuff. Find out where she worked and who she could have met, either online or in person. We also need to go through the University's security cameras and see if Jonas was there in the evening. And check that client of his who was supposedly with him at the lab most of the night.

"All right, let's get to work."

TWENTY-FOUR

Jick could not focus on work after the shock he had experienced with the mask, and the rest of the night was an endurance test of trauma cases. Between cases, he tried to put together in his mind what exactly had transpired in his office. That mask had a glow to it, a presence that seemed to replay the last few minutes of Tiffany Jensen's life. He was there to catch the tail end of it.

Did it replay her entire life? How far back does it go? he wondered.

"His life flashed before his eyes;" an expression commonly used in near-death experiences. Is this what happens? Our brains preserve memories like a computer's random access memory, or RAM. When the power shuts off, that memory disappears. But unlike computers, when our brain power shuts off, the memories might take time to disintegrate before there is nothing left.

How long does that take? he wondered. *And does this mask have the ability to replay those memories and if it does, then what?* This process is not immediate. The memories don't disappear in a flash, at least he didn't think so. They likely persist and fade over some time, like a phosphorescent object that continues to glow and fade when the light source turns off. Probably takes a few minutes.

The only way to answer these questions would be to keep the mask with him. He had planned to keep it in his office as a decoration but after the odd episodes, he decided to take it home and do some research on its background. He had forgotten to take it home on Thursday after work.

He could not get close to bodies that had recently died except sometimes at work when they lost someone during a Trauma Hot or when there was a disaster in the cath lab.

He thought about recent occurrences; there had been that incident the first day he took the mask to work, when they had that gunshot wound victim in Room 3. He had felt a presence in his office and the mask seemed to look a little more vibrant. *Was that the victim's presence in my office? What if I had put the mask on? What would I have seen?*

Jick thought back to the incident of Peter Northrup, who had died on the table after the cath lab disaster. He had been in the operating room and when he had coded and died, Jick was not part of the resuscitation effort. He had stayed to help clean and so had gone to his office a few minutes later. As had happened earlier with the gunshot victim, he thought he felt someone in his office. He had put on the mask, but by then, maybe it had already replayed most of the Peter's life. He caught the tail end, when staff bent over him in the cath lab, like apparitions bending over him, before everything faded to black. Now, with this young lady, Tiffany Jensen, he had put on the mask to catch the last five or ten minutes of her life—and had seen the person murder her!

This line of speculation opened up more questions. *What if I had been wearing the mask at the moment someone was killed and I was nearby? Would it replay their entire life? In slow motion, regular speed, or sped up?* There was no way to replay someone's life in its entirety in regular time. He wondered if it replayed the earlier years of someone's life in a sped-up manner and slowed toward the end, like an exponential decay curve. That would explain how, within a few minutes, the mask returns to being a drab and lifeless object. He wondered what the mask would show if someone was shot in the head and the bullet obliterated the memories in an instant. Disjointed memories that lacked any semblance of coherence?

He had been on call Friday night, so they relieved him of duties on Saturday morning. He passed off Hot Potato and went home. He took the mask home. He sat at his desk to consult today's oracle, Google.

He ordered a pizza for breakfast. *Why not?* One pizza place nearby opened early and had a full menu all day.

Something quick and convenient so he wouldn't have to do anything in the kitchen.

He was too agog with excitement in anticipation of doing some research on this mask. What had the antique shop owner said? That the mask may be Brunca? Or Inca? He poured a glass of Cabernet and settled at his computer. He did not drink in the mornings unless he was post-call. Or was he rationalizing a dangerous habit? He put it out of his mind and focused on researching the mask.

He jiggled the mouse, and his computer awakened from sleep mode. He logged in, opened a browser window, and went straight to Google. He typed in "Brunca" and read an article that matched in the search results.

The Brunca, or Boruca, are an indigenous people living in Costa Rica. They are known for distinctive masks made from balsa. Every year they have a three-day celebration called *Danza de los Diablitos* or Dance of the Little Devils. According to Brunca folklore, the mask empowered the wearer to fight and vanquish the Spanish invaders, represented by a little bull.

Jick found several other fascinating articles about the Brunca, but nothing in their folklore or traditions suggested anything about masks channeling the dead. Jick learned about Brunca culture, but it was not helpful in his attempt to learn about this mask.

As he leaned back in his chair to try something else, the doorbell rang.

"Pizza delivery," a voice announced from the porch.

Jick opened the front door, took the pizza and paid the driver a generous tip. Back in the kitchen, he surveyed the pizza. *Just what the doctor ordered,* he thought with satisfaction. He had been in the mood for a Chicago style deep-dish pizza even though it was barely ten. He ordered it with his preferred toppings; black olives, mushrooms, bell peppers, onions, and last but not least, anchovies. *Onions and anchovies. Oh, what the hell. I'm not going anywhere for the rest of the day.*

As if on cue, his phone dinged a reminder for Walter's party at six o'clock.

Crap, he thought. *Forgot about that. Oh well, no worries, I'll brush and use mouthwash.*

He put two slices on a plate, drizzled on crushed red pepper and parmesan, topped up his wine glass, and resumed the search.

He searched for Healer of Life. There was nothing besides a few random sites about spiritual healing or religiously affiliated sites about healing. He tried Lifehealer with no better luck.

He then searched Inca masks. This showed some promise. Incan masks did superficially resemble his mask. But beyond that resemblance, there was little else. The Incans engaged in child sacrifice and the thought crossed his mind that maybe a mask like his could have seen uses in some sacrificial rituals. *But for what?*

It was not a fruitful search. He finished his wine, put the rest of the pizza in the fridge, and lay down on the couch. He debated whether to take the mask back to work on Monday and decided against it. Another Tiffany Jensen was not likely.

He made a mental note to call his brother and see if he could include him in any of his work-related outings in an interested onlooker role. Vic rarely got to murder crime scenes immediately after a murder, but it was better than nothing. In an ideal world, Jick would have liked to have gone with EMS personnel on their emergency calls. But that was not likely, and it would look odd for him to tag along with EMS personnel and as soon as they arrived at a cardiac arrest or gunshot situation, put on a mask. He would look like some kind of witchdoctor! So Vic was the best bet.

As he continued his fruitless research into the origins of the mask, a question popped into his mind. As his awareness of the mask's abilities had increased, he had been too agog with the excitement to realize he did not know the answer to this simple question.

Why?

Why did the mask exist? Why would anyone construct a device such as this? What purpose did it serve other than replaying a dying person's thoughts?

Jick was tired after his brutal on-call night, and red wine always had a soporific effect on him when he drank earlier in the day. It was mid-morning. Within a few minutes, he was fast asleep on the couch for a midday nap.

TWENTY-FIVE

Jick awakened at about four-thirty in the afternoon, feeling refreshed. The previous night on call had been a bad one, and not only because of the trauma cases. The mask incident had made it a downright shocking experience. For now, he put it out of his mind and planned to enjoy Walter's retirement party. "Enjoy" to the extent of roasting someone about to retire and knowing he was next. "Tolerate" would be a better word. He did not like departmental parties, anyway. It was a forced camaraderie among people who worked together during the day and other than the job, had little else in common. At least Mireille would be there. The last time they had done something social had been about ten days earlier when they had gone to the rom-com, which Jick did not enjoy. And the evening had ended much the same way as the happy hour at Julio's.

He dressed in a casual pair of slacks, golf shirt, and loafers. Walter's retirement party was in one of the conference rooms at Fox Vale golf club. Fox Vale was one of Dallas' ritzier golf clubs with all the usual amenities, including golf course, swimming pool, and a restaurant with a stellar reputation for its chef. Jick was not a member but had been there on social occasions like his neighborhood association meetings and work-sponsored parties like this one.

He wrapped the railroad pocket watch in a sheet of tissue wrap and put it in a small black gift bag. He had a retirement card, such as it is, and he scribbled a generic message from the department and put it in the bag.

He set off at quarter to six. It was a beautiful Saturday evening, and since he was post-call on Saturday, he was off for the rest of the weekend. As he drove, his thoughts wandered back to the mask.

The more he thought about it, the more it seemed to make sense. This mask replayed the flood of memories as the brain loses power and all the neurons disintegrate. What he could not figure out was its purpose. Why was it made?

His thoughts wandered along philosophical lines about the meaning of life. People are just a collection of memories, held in place by a continuous stream of energy in the form of blood sugar and glycogen. The entire organism, the entire collection of organs, the senses, all locked together in an evolutionary drive to preserve genetic material for the next generation. So the genes may propagate but the memories are fleeting, only held in place by the individual until death. Unlike other animals, humans are unique in the ability to preserve some memories, thoughts, and ideas through the use of language, both verbal and written, after the individual dies so successive generations can build on them. So the species advances. But the individual? Once an individual ceases to exist, that's it. *Done. C'est fini. Exit Stage Left.* He felt the Black Cloud lurking closer at the end of his musings.

He pulled into the golf course driveway and stopped at the valet parking station. A young woman in a starched white blouse and red vest opened his door. He got out with Walter's present, collected his valet ticket, and went inside. There was a sign by the clubhouse entrance pointing to the conference room with "Madison retirement party" stenciled in red. Someone had drawn a skull and crossbones, a grim reaper, and a smiley face underneath. A plastic skeleton with movable joints had been set up, an obvious Halloween prop, pointing in the direction of the party. Jick sighed and walked down the hallway in the sign's direction.

About half-dozen members of the department had already arrived, along with the guest of honor and his wife. Walter Madison and his wife sat at one of the large, circular tables, facing the entrance. A bar had been set up along one wall, and there was even a DJ playing music. It was not exactly raucous music, but at least it was lively. Along the wall opposite from the bar was a buffet table with several empty serving racks. A hostess stood inside the door to the conference room, and she took the bag with Walter's present and placed it in an adjoining room. Jick glanced into the room. An ornate rocking chair made of what looked like black wood lacquer was there with a brass plate affixed to the back.

The inscription on the plate read "To Walter Madison, M.D., in Appreciation for Thirty years of Service. From Your Friends in the Department of Anesthesiology," along with his dates of service.

Jick strolled back to the main conference room and went straight to the bar.

"What are you having?" asked the bartender.

"What red wines are you serving?"

"We have a California cabernet and a zin."

"A glass of cabernet, please."

The bartender poured a glass, and Jick stuffed a dollar bill into the tip jar. He walked over to Walter and his wife and parked himself next to Walter, leaving an empty chair between them.

"Hi, Jick," said his wife. "We haven't seen you in quite a while. How was the cruise? I bet you must have had so much fun."

Jick kept a neutral face.

"Hi, Barbara. It was OK," he said. "I met some interesting people but overall, it didn't bowl me over as much as I thought it would."

"Oh, that's too bad," she said. "Next time you should go with someone. It is so much more fun than going alone."

That was the point, he thought. *To meet someone.*

"You're right," he said. *Next time I'll go with Mireille. Now that would be a romp.*

"Weren't you on call last night?" Walter asked.

"Yes."

"How was it?"

"Brutal. The knife and gun clubs must have had a membership drive. Or it was initiation night for the gangs. One woman arrived in the ER with a gunshot wound through the chest. Got all the major vessels. She was sitting in her car, minding her business, and got shot. Only reason she survived even as long as she did was because it happened down the road from the hospital. Apparently, the car alarm went off and that alerted someone right away."

"Too many guns on the street," Madison said. "I wonder if they caught the person who shot her?"

Jick's thoughts went back to the mask incident in his office, seeing the killer silhouetted in the back seat. He just shrugged in answer and took a large sip of wine. He changed the subject.

"So, old man, what are your plans after retirement?" Barbara spoke.

"Well, we're planning to get an RV and do some traveling around the country. We may even take our passports and make our way into Canada. I've never been to Alaska, and we're thinking of leaving the RV in Seattle and hopping on a cruise to see the glaciers. Or, if we go into Canada, it would be an adventure to drive through western Canada and go into Alaska that way."

"Well, that sounds like fun," he said, taking another sip. Road trips were not really his thing any more than cruises.

"How about you, Jick," said Walter. "What are your plans? You're a year behind me and I am sure you won't work until you're eighty."

"Ouch," Jick said. "Thanks for reminding me. I hoped to remain in a state of denial until the bitter end." The Black Cloud tried to rear its head, so he pushed it back down with another swig of wine.

"I don't have any specific plans," he said. "I can retire next year, but I plan to do some things. Not sure what. I think I'll be more active in cultivating a social life."

Just then, Jick saw Mireille walking in with three of the nurse anesthetists. Jick marked his spot with an unfolded napkin and excused himself. He strolled over to the group.

"Hi, Dr. Arnsson," one of them said.

"Hi, folks," he replied. Mireille looked radiant in her dress. *I should cool it with socializing with her tonight*, he thought, not wanting to start tongues wagging.

He engaged the group in conversation for a few minutes, and it was obvious the four of them had planned to sit together. They excused themselves and headed for the bar. He rejoined Walter and Barbara's table. Three other physicians had joined the table.

"Fantastic day today for the market." It was Bob Foster, who loved reading the Wall Street Journal every morning.

The other physicians did not want to engage Bob in his favorite topic and in a few minutes, the conversation turned to golf.

"So, have you played the course here?" It was Ross Mortimer.

"Oh, yeah, it's great. My best score here was an eighty. That was a few years back, when I was younger," said Bob Foster.

"Oh please," Jick said. "You're still young." He took another sip of wine.

"How about you, Jick?" he said. "How's your golf game?"

"It's OK," he said. "I know how to play but I always like to joke that I shot a sixty-four… on the front nine."

The conversation changed from golf to the younger generation and what their children planned to do in college and employment. Some of his colleagues already had grandchildren.

As they chatted, Jick noticed the hotel staff setting up dinner. Being bored with the conversation and by now nursing his third glass of wine, he sauntered over to the serving line to see what the department had selected for the evening's menu.

The department had sprung for quite a lavish meal. The main courses included slow smoked ribeye for the carnivores, grilled salmon for the pescaterians, and grilled portabella mushroom and spinach pie for the vegetarians. A creamy mushroom compote was an accompaniment for the salmon, although Jick thought it would also go well with the steak. Grilled artichoke hearts done in olive oil and black pepper, along with Texas-sized soft rolls, a rice pilaf, potatoes, and salad rounded out the meal. Next to the serving line was a metal multi-tiered dessert tower with at least ten staggered levels, each inviting guests with an assortment of pies, cakes, and petits fours. All told, an eminently satisfying meal.

The hostess sounded a dinner gong, and they made their way to the various tables after serving themselves. The tables had an even number of seats, so the empty seat next to him was conspicuous. But the wait staff was attentive in keeping glasses filled so both drinks and conversation flowed.

By the end of the evening, one undeniable and somewhat depressing fact struck Jick: He had very little in common with his colleagues. Most of his age contemporaries were married, had grown children, and talked about retirement, golf, stock market, vacations, and how their children did in school. Some of them showed off pictures of their grandchildren. Jick felt like the proverbial "red-headed stepchild" at these gatherings. He was sixty-four, divorced, an aging bachelor who probably drank too much, did not take vacations or like cruises, and wallowed under the Black Cloud.

As he drove home from the party, having had enough wine to be mellow but not enough to get pulled over, he realized one thing: *As soon as I get home, I will have another glass of wine.*

TWENTY-SIX

Four days after Tiffany's death, the medical examiner's office released the body. The case was straightforward, and the only formality was to collect tissue and fluid samples for toxicology. That could take weeks. In the meantime, there was no formal autopsy as the cause of death was obvious.

Jonas received a call from the medical examiner's office.

"Hello," he said.

"Jonas Jensen?"

"Speaking."

"Hi, this is Angie Wilson from the medical examiner's office. Please allow me to offer my condolences for your loss. I'm sure it must be very difficult."

"Thanks," said Jonas. "I've been managing with help from friends and relatives."

"The M.E.'s office has completed their work and will release the body to next of kin. Is there someplace you have already designated to receive the body?"

"Uh, no. I hadn't even thought of what to do next."

"That's OK. We have an arrangement with some funeral homes in the area, so we'll send her body to Morton's Funeral Home." She read off the address and phone number to Jonas.

"You can call them to make funeral arrangements. What are you planning to do for the funeral?"

"We're shipping her back to Utah. Her parents wanted it that way."

"Oh, OK. Morton's can take care of all the arrangements. If there's anything else we can do, please let us know."

"Thanks." He hung up, picked up his wallet and keys, and headed for the door.

He went to Morton's funeral home, parked, and went inside.

"Hi, may I help you?" the receptionist asked.

"My name is Jonas Jensen." He showed her his driver's license. "My wife Tiffany died last Friday. I got a call from the medical examiner's office that they're sending her body here."

"I'm so sorry for your loss," the receptionist said. "Did you have any thoughts on what you would like to do?"

"Yes, we're sending her back to Utah. We are from there and all our folks are there. So we're doing the funeral there."

"I understand." The receptionist looked sympathetic.

"Here's the address for the funeral home in Utah. Her parents wanted her sent there." He handed over a sheet of paper with the contact information for the funeral home in Salt Lake City. Tiffany's father had told Jonas their family had used this funeral home for generations.

"I didn't think I'd be using it for one of my kids," he had said in a heavy voice.

"This is delicate, but do you know if she had any funeral insurance?" the receptionist asked. "I doubt it because most young people don't think about this kind of stuff."

"No, she didn't. Her dad, Ron Peterson, gave me a credit card number to give to you. He will pay the shipping costs."

"We won't be able to accept a third-party credit card without verification. Do you have a phone number for Mr. Peterson so we can verify the billing address?"

"Yes," Jonas gave them Ron's contact information.

The receptionist entered all the information into her computer, printed an agreement for Jonas to sign, and gave him a copy.

"As soon as we confirm billing information, we're ready to go. We'll take care of it from here, Mr. Jensen. We'll make sure she's sent back home with all the proper care and respect."

"Thanks."

He drove back home and sat at his desk. He studied a wall calendar for a few minutes and picked up the phone to call Tiffany's parents.

"Hi, Norma," he said when Tiffany's mother answered.

"Jonas," she replied. "It's good to hear from you. How are you holding up? I still can't believe this is happening."

"I'm hanging in there."

"Poor Tiffany." He heard a sound like a stifled sob. "My baby."

He waited until she had gathered herself and resumed talking.

"When are you coming here?" she asked.

"That's what I called about," he said. "I got back from the funeral home. They will call Ron to verify his billing information and then ship her back straight to the funeral home in Salt Lake. We should set a date for the funeral so I can book my flight. Maybe I should talk to Ron?"

"Oh, yes," Norma sounded glad to pass off the details to Ron. She raised her voice, "Ron. Jonas is on the phone."

Ron came to the phone.

"Jonas, it's good to hear from you."

"Hi, Ron," Jonas said. "It's good to talk to you. I told Norma I had got back from the funeral home here and they are planning to ship Tiffany back home in a few days. I wanted to get my flights booked, so I called to confirm dates."

"I talked to the bishop, Jonas," Ron said. "He said we should have a viewing and funeral on Monday. We will have a short reception afterwards. Still can't believe this is happening."

Perfect, thought Jonas. *That works great.*

"OK. I'll plan to catch a flight on Sunday and stay until Tuesday."

"OK." They exchanged goodbyes and Jonas hung up.

He booked his tickets and after receiving purchase confirmation, leaned back in his chair and closed his eyes. His face was expressionless as he thought through what he was about to do. *Just one more piece of unfinished business*, he thought. The corners of his mouth pulled up into a smile.

*   *   *

"Sorry to drop in unannounced," said Fishburn.

Fishburn and Cook had stopped at Jonas' house without notifying him.

"No problem," said Jonas. He stood at the door, one hand on the door frame and the other holding the knob. "What can I do for you?"

"May we come in? We have some more questions."

"Right now?"

"Yes, right now." Fishburn had a fixed smile on his face. "It won't take long."

Jonas let go of the doorknob and swung the door open. "Come on in."

They sat in the same seats as the first time and Fishburn consulted his tablet.

"It's just you and your wife, right? No pets and no kids?"

"That's right."

"And you're gone for much of the day at work."

"Yes."

"And your wife didn't work outside the house."

"No, she didn't."

"Why didn't she work outside the house?"

Jonas frowned.

"Why is that important? We had our reasons."

"What did she do during the day to keep busy? Did she have any hobbies or any activities?"

"She worked out at the gym. Went shopping, made dinner, the usual things. Where are you going with this?"

"You don't need to sound defensive. We are trying to build a picture of what she did during the day to see if there is any connection with her murder. Could she have met someone who may have wanted to harm her?"

"I wouldn't know."

Fishburn segued to the next topic.

"Do you know anything about her online activities?"

"No."

"She seemed to have an active online presence. And you knew nothing about it?"

"No. What kind of online activities?"

Fishburn glanced at Cook. He shut his tablet cover.

"Mr. Jensen, to give you an update on the investigation," he said, without answering the question. "We have opened several lines in our investigation and may have found a possible suspect or at least, a motive for her death. In other words, this may not have been a random event. For now, we have to leave it at that. We wanted to find out how much you knew about her online activities. But rest assured we are doing everything we can to find your wife's killer."

"Thanks, I appreciate that," Jonas said. "If I come across anything else, I'll let you know for sure."

"You do that," said Cook.

The detectives left. When they were in the car, Cook looked at Fishburn.

"He doesn't want to talk about it, does he?"

"No, he doesn't."

*   *   *

Jonas shut the door and went back to his desk. He sat back in thought for a minute and then picked up his phone.

"The cops were here," he said. "They wanted to know about her online activities."

He listened for a minute.

"Yes, OK, I know. I'll be careful."

He hung up the phone.

Just one more piece of unfinished business, he thought again.

TWENTY-SEVEN

Six days after Tiffany's murder, Harvey Michaels was at home in Houston. His wife Jeanine and two teenage daughters were scurrying to get out the door for a trip to New Orleans to visit her mother. Jeanine had taken two days off work to add to the weekend. The girls' summer break had started, making it a perfect time to visit grandma.

Harvey planned to stay behind. Over time, his relationship with his mother-in-law had deteriorated into an adversarial one. His mother-in-law felt Jeanine could have done better in life than marry a welder and had never been subtle about her assessment of him. She had always found his indolence irritating. Then his welding job had ended some years ago after an on-the-job injury left him on disability. Jeanine ended up working in airline reservations for a major airline while Harvey stayed at home with their daughters. His mother-in-law had not hesitated to voice doubts of the severity of his disability.

During one particularly heated visit, Jeanine's mother had spat out, "Now that the girls are older and don't need as much attention, why can't you get a job? So Jeanine don't got to work so goddamn hard?"

Harvey had told her off and since then had refused to visit. Jeanine and the kids had planned to leave yesterday, but the weather delayed their departure.

Harvey was glad the weather was fine this morning. There would be no further delays. He expected a visitor the next day and another delay would have been problematic. After all the virtual trysts he had had with Madeline online, tomorrow was the real deal. He suppressed his excitement, waiting for Jeanine and the girls to leave so he could get the house ready.

It was ten o'clock.

"Hurry," Jeanine yelled to the daughters upstairs. "We need to leave in thirty minutes. It's a long ass drive."

"OK, mom," came a shout from above.

The doorbell rang, and Jeanine went to answer it. She peeked through the side window first and noted two men in suits standing outside. One was middle-aged, somewhat tall and thin. The other was a younger man, shorter and stouter, with sandy brown hair. She opened the door.

"May I help you?"

"Hello, ma'am," said the older man. He held out his ID. "I'm Detective Ed Fishburn, and this is my partner Detective Sam Cook. We're with the Dallas police department. Are you Mrs. Michaels?"

"Yes."

"Is your husband Harvey at home?" Cook flashed his ID as he glanced over her shoulder.

"Yes, what is this about?"

Harvey strolled to the door.

"Mr. Michaels?"

"Yes."

"May we have a few words with you? We're investigating a case about a woman in Dallas named Tiffany Jensen."

"I don't know any Tiffany Jensen," Harvey said. He felt his jaw tighten.

He turned pale hearing the "in Dallas" part.

"We have reason to believe you do," said Fishburn pleasantly. "May we come in?"

"No," Harvey said.

"Yes," Jeanine said, looking at Harvey with a quizzical expression. "Yes, please come in."

They walked into the living room and sat down. Jeanine looked at Harvey, who looked uncomfortable, and then at the detectives.

"Can I get you something to drink?" she asked.

"No, thanks."

Fishburn and Cook sat on single chairs, and Harvey and Jeanine sat together on a love seat. Fishburn held a tablet and he consulted it.

He cleared his throat and began.

"We're with the Dallas police. Six days ago, a young woman in Dallas, one Tiffany Jensen, was murdered in her car in a neighborhood called Deep Ellum. It's a neighborhood east of Dallas, close to downtown, known for bars, galleries, and its music scene. Ms. Jensen had parked in an unpopulated area of Deep Ellum, on a side street in a parking lot. She had waited, maybe to meet someone, but our analysis of the crime scene and from the phone company records leads us to believe the murderer may have led her there and may have waited in the darkened lot for her to arrive. We believe it's more likely than not she knew the killer."

"I don't know any Tiffany Jensen," Harvey repeated.

"Hang on, sir, let me finish. As part of the investigation, our forensics team also has a cybercrime forensics unit. We always look through computer search histories, social media accounts, any online financial transactions, etc., to find any clue that may give us information and lead us to the perpetrator. It's very difficult nowadays to not leave a digital footprint."

"What's this got to do with me?" Harvey asked. "I already told you, twice now, that I do not know any Tiffany Jensen." He raised his voice at "do not know" to emphasize his point.

"We believe you knew her under the screen name Madeline," said Cook. He waited for the comment to sink in and then continued. "We are going through a list of her social media contacts, and we have reason to believe you're prominent on the list."

At the mention of Madeline, Harvey's eyes widened. A nervous sheen appeared on his forehead as he sank back into the couch cushions. His wife looked at him, her quizzical expression replaced by one of glaring anger as she noted the change in his demeanor.

"What the fuck?" she said. "Harvey, who is this Madeline?"

"I, I don't know," he stammered. "I've never met her. You have to believe me."

Fishburne asked, "Mr. Michaels, I'm sorry about this but we need to know. Where were you last Friday night, on the night of the 14th?"

"Here," he said in a plaintive voice. "I didn't go anywhere. I was here."

"Can you vouch for that?" Fishburn asked Jeanine.

Jeanine crossed her arms. "Yes, he was here. Why are you asking him? Everyone has tons of social media contacts now. What was Harvey doing with this... Madeline? It must have been quite something because y'all came here all the way from Dallas?"

Detective Fishburn glanced at Cook and then at Jeanine, pausing before replying. "You should have that discussion with Harvey after we leave. His involvement with Ms. Jensen was more than as a casual contact. He knew her well enough that if he didn't have an alibi, we could consider him a person of interest."

"Harvey, have you been having online affairs? You piece of shit! I work all day while you sit here on disability having online affairs? My mother was right about you." She burst into tears.

She finished with, "I'm leaving for New Orleans and I may not be back." She almost spat out the last part at him.

Harvey sat quiet and meek, not saying anything.

Fishburn turned to Harvey.

"How long have you known Madeline?"

"Just a few weeks," Harvey mumbled.

"A few weeks?" Jeanine exclaimed. "Damn it, Harvey."

"And during those few weeks, you never met her in person?"

"No."

"Did you plan any meetings for the future?" Cook asked.

A pause.

"No," Harvey lied.

Jeanine opened her mouth to say something but Cook continued.

"Mr. Michaels, we have transcripts of your online chat sessions."

"No," he said again. "I never planned to meet her." His breathing had quickened, and a trickle ran down the side of his face.

Fishburn flashed a glance at Jeanine's fuming countenance and decided not to press the point further.

"That's fine for now. We'll leave it at that," Fishburn said. "All we are doing at this point is trying to establish where any likely persons of interest were at the time of the murder and verify alibis. We will be doing some deeper digging later as well as likely asking for a statement." He smiled at Harvey, who looked anywhere but at the two detectives.

"Now, we need to have a word with anyone else who lives in the house. Y'all have a couple of teenagers living here at home, right?"

Harvey squirmed.

"Do you really need to talk to them? I'm telling you I was home on Friday."

"We'll be sensitive. Please call them and if y'all could step out for a minute, that would be appreciated."

Jeanine yelled for their daughters to come down.

"Molly! Mandy! Come downstairs for a minute."

Two teenage girls thundered down the stairs a minute later.

Mom's got the stronger genes, thought Cook. Both girls looked like miniature versions of Jeanine.

Harvey and Jeanine excused themselves and Fishburn turned to the girls.

"We'll be quick. My partner and I are with the Dallas police. We need you to verify something for us."

A puzzled blank stare from both girls.

"Last Friday, that would be the 14th, do you remember what you did that day?"

The older one, Molly, spoke first.

"I was at home most of the day and then I hung out with some friends. Probably got home around midnight."

"And you?" Fishburn turned to Mandy.

"I was home all day."

"Were your mom and dad home that day too?"

"Mom went to work and got home around six, like she usually does. Dad was home all day."

"He didn't leave the house at all during the day?"

Mandy thought for a minute.

"I was upstairs in my room most of the day. I guess if he went to get groceries or something, I wouldn't know. But I'm pretty sure he was home all day."

From their frank and earnest expressions and their body language, both Fishburn and Cook felt they were telling the truth.

"OK, girls, that's it. We don't have any other questions."

He shut the cover of his tablet with a sigh. Both he and Cook stood to leave. The girls called Harvey and Jeanine to come back into the living room.

Fishburn handed one of his cards to Harvey and one to Jeanine. "We may have more questions. Be available."

Harvey nodded. As the detectives walked to the door, Cook turned to Harvey.

"Is there anything else you want to tell us?" he asked.

"No," said Harvey.

Harvey squirmed under the stare from Cook, but Cook did not say anything else to him about the case. The detectives thanked Harvey and Jeanine for their cooperation and left. The girls had gone back upstairs.

"Jeanine...," Harvey began.

"Fuck off, Harvey," she snapped at him.

"Girls, come on, we're leaving," she shouted up the stairs.

"Just a minute. We're almost ready."

She turned to Harvey, trying not to raise her voice. "What have you been doing online, you piece of shit? What did you do with this Tiffany Jensen? Did you send her dick pics? Did she send you naked pictures?"

Her voice rose.

"Did you plan to sleep with her, like this week when I'm gone with the girls? I know you, Harvey. You planned to meet her, didn't you? I could tell you lied when those detectives asked you."

She did not wait for an answer. As she walked away, a thought crossed her mind. She spun around.

"How the hell did you plan to meet her? I'm taking our car."

She sucked in her breath in a soft gasp of realization.

"Did y'all plan to meet *here*? Were you going to fuck her in our bed? Or did y'all plan to go somewhere together?"

She did not wait for an answer. Her voice rose again. "You know what, Harvey, you are one worthless piece of shit. If this poor girl wasn't dead, I bet she woulda showed up at the house. I bet one Miss Tiffany Jensen woulda come here this week, wouldn't she?"

"Jeanine, no," Harvey said pleadingly. "It's not like that. There's no one that was coming here." He felt a morbid sense of relief that Tiffany was dead.

"That cop asked you if you planned any future meetings and I could tell you lied. He could tell you lied. I bet you had already planned something online, and it was plain bad luck and bad timing that someone killed her before she got here."

Their daughters came downstairs, so Jeanine stopped her tirade. Both girls looked at their parents with puzzled expressions.

"What's up, Mom?" Molly asked. "Why were those cops here? And why did they want to know about Dad?"

"It's not important," Jeanine said. "Don't worry about it. Let's go."

She pierced Harvey with one last glare. He stood meek and silent, a downcast expression on his face. She and the girls loaded their bags into the car and drove off.

Harvey went back into the house. He went straight to the refrigerator and pulled out a beer. He unscrewed the top and slurped the foam that raced to the top.

"Holy shit," he breathed, sinking into a couch. It was exactly like that. That was exactly what he had planned, to meet Tiffany this week when his wife left town. He mentally kicked himself for divulging his address to Tiffany.

He took a swig of his beer and ruminated about Tiffany.

Was I really gonna leave my old lady for Tiffany? Nah, he thought. *She needed to hear that, and I needed to get laid. No harm in that.*

He felt bad for the feeling of relief he experienced knowing she was dead. As he drank his beer, he let his thoughts wander to the video of her sitting on the chair, legs splayed, T-shirt tucked above her exposed breasts, the expression on her face as she climaxed. He put the cold beer down on the bulge in his pants. *Damn, too bad she's gone.*

"I'll never do that again," he swore.

TWENTY-EIGHT

It had been a week since Tiffany's death, eight days counting the night she died since she died before midnight. Jonas had already taken a few days off work. He was calm and expressionless as he went through his morning routine. At eight-thirty, he called Second Chance.

"Hi, Cindy."

"Hi, Jonas," said Cindy, the receptionist. "How are you doing?"

"I had been planning to come in and work for a few hours to distract myself. But I'm still not feeling good today, so I'm not coming in. I need to back up some server data so I'll log in through the VPN and do it from here. I'm going back to bed for now but call if you need anything."

"OK. Take your time, Jonas. Please don't feel you have to come in. It's only been a few days. Poor Tiffany.

"Have the police found out anything yet?"

"No, not yet. They're thinking some random guy took a shot at her from behind the car. They are hoping there's some surveillance video from a building nearby that could help. They're trying to look at video from all the shops and bars nearby. Problem is it was dark so it will be difficult. So far, nothing."

"How are you holding up?"

"I'm doing fine, sort of. It's been rough. Tiffany's folks didn't plan to come as there was nothing they could do. I made arrangements for her to be sent back to Utah. They will do the funeral there so I'm leaving on Sunday and will be back on Tuesday. I'll plan on coming back to work after that. So I'm hanging in there."

"I am so sorry. Take your time and don't rush back. Let me know if there's anything I can do to help. Do you need a ride to the airport on Sunday?"

"No, I'm good. I'll only be there for two days, so I'll leave the car at the airport."

"OK, but like I said, let me know if there's anything I can do to help. I'll tell Mary you're not coming in," she said. Mary was the clinic manager.

"OK, thanks, 'bye." He hung up.

He logged into the clinic's computers through a virtual private network and set an auto backup utility to do its thing on a preset schedule. He logged off and powered his computer down.

He examined the second burner phone. It was set up to spoof Tiffany's number but was also set up to forward calls from his regular phone to it. It was powered off. He put it in his pocket.

He picked up his gun, a Glock 17 chambered in 9 mm rounds, and checked it to make sure he had loaded the magazine. He put it into a small duffel bag along with a change of clothes and an outback hat.

He went to the pantry and grabbed some protein bars and some bottles of water. He stuffed these into the duffel bag.

He left his phone in his office and went out to the garage. He climbed in, backed out of the garage, and rolled out onto the street. He headed out of the neighborhood and navigated the streets of Dallas until he was at the shed where he had done work a month earlier. There was now a truck with a camper top parked outside. He parked his car next to the truck, stepped out with the duffel bag, and locked it. He went into the shed where the truck's keys were hanging on a hook.

He opened a drawer and took out a flat box. He inspected its contents and then satisfied with his inspection, put it in his duffel bag.

He tossed the duffel bag into the truck, locked the shed, and set off. He made his way to I-45 southbound and headed to Houston. He looked at a piece of paper to double check the address. He did not want to use the navigation app in his burner phone, so he had written the instructions on a piece of paper.

He drove non-stop for a little over three hours and arrived in Houston. He stopped at a rest stop north of Houston for a restroom break and to fill his car. He put on the hat and got out of the car. Almost all surveillance cameras were mounted high, so a wide-brimmed outback hat effectively shielded his face.

There was a Burger King attached to the gas station, so he also had lunch there, paying cash. He navigated his way to the address he had written on the piece of paper. It was in a working-class neighborhood; single-story homes with pastel vinyl siding, matchbox-sized lots with waist-high front fences, single-car garages or car ports. He parked a few houses from the target address and surveyed the neighborhood. It was quiet, except for the soft melodic clanking from a wind chime. After watching for a full ten minutes, he felt satisfied that the neighborhood was quiet. It was almost twelve o'clock.

He made his move. He started the truck and nosed it ahead for a few houses until he was outside his target address. He looked around. Still nothing going on. He pulled the gun out of the duffel bag and tucked it into his waistband.

He got out and walked to the house. It was two minutes past twelve. He knocked on the door.

TWENTY-NINE

Harvey awoke the next morning feeling like crap. After the visit by the police and subsequent row with Jeanine, he had lost count after the fifth drink. He had decided he would call her tonight. *But what am I going to say?* he thought. He resolved to begin with a groveling apology and wing it from there.

He started stressing about making the call and decided he would nurse his hangover with "just one drink." Within two hours, the hangover faded, replaced by a buzz after his fourth or fifth drink.

By twelve, Harvey had worked himself into a distressed lather. Jeanine had been royally pissed off, he thought, and he started second-guessing whether he should call her tonight or was it still too soon. He decided he would call her tonight and downed another drink. He staggered to the couch and dropped into it with a heavy sigh and picked up the remote. He turned on the TV and channel surfed over to the sportsman's channel to watch some fishing show.

He heard a knock at the door.

He looked outside and saw a tall, dark-haired man standing outside. As soon as he cracked the door open, the man kicked the door and stormed in. The force of the kick pushed Harvey off balance, and he staggered backwards. With the alcohol coursing through his system, he was unable to regain his balance and he hit the opposite wall, crashing to the ground. As he fell, he caught the edge of an end table; it turned over with a crash, spilling mail and magazines stacked on top. One of the legs hit him in the ribs and forced out a grunt of pain. When he looked up, the man had pulled a gun out of his waistband; it was pointed at him.

"Who are you? What do you want?" Harvey asked, anger and fear trembling his voice.

"Shut up!" the man said. "Do exactly what I say and you won't get hurt. Understand?"

Harvey nodded.

"I don't have any money or drugs."

"I said shut up."

"Are you at home alone?" the man asked.

"Yes," Harvey answered.

"Where's your wife?"

"She's not home."

"Where is she?"

"She's gone out of town."

"Where?"

"To New Orleans. Why the fuck do you want to know?"

"Shut up, I'm asking the questions. Did she go alone?"

Harvey looked puzzled. "No, she went with our daughters. What business is this of yours?"

"I said, I'm asking the questions. Who is she seeing there?"

"Her mother."

"Why didn't you go?"

"I can't stand her."

The man had heard enough to confirm he was at the right house.

"All right, get up, walk to the door, and walk down to the road. No sudden moves."

The man put his hands in his pocket, the gun barrel pushing through the fabric at Harvey. Harvey lurched to his feet, steadied himself against the wall. There was a pickup truck parked by the side of the road. It had a camper top.

"Open the back and climb inside."

"Now wait a minute. Where are we going?"

"You'll know when we get there," the man said.

Harvey opened the back of the truck, lifted the camper flap and sat at the edge of the tailgate, legs dangling over the edge. The man kept his right hand in his pocket.

"Don't move from this spot or I'll shoot you."

"What do you want with me? Who are you?" Harvey asked. The effects of the drinks had been replaced by an adrenaline shot of fear.

The man opened the driver's door and reached for the flat box next to the floorboard. He looked around. High noon, working class Houston neighborhood, nobody around, nobody home. He walked around to where Harvey sat and jabbed him in the thigh with a syringe.

"Ow, what the fuck?" said Harvey, flinching and jumping off the tailgate. The man shoved Harvey hard, and Harvey fell back into the pickup, collapsing on the bed liner. He tried to stand again but could not. He had become weaker, and his legs wobbled. His vision became blurry as the man reached down and lifted his legs, pushing him all the way into the truck. The world around him faded to black.

*   *   *

Jonas injected him with another syringe and closed the tailgate and camper top. He did not want to risk a gunshot that someone could hear or that could go through Harvey and damage the truck. He looked around the neighborhood. No one around.

Jonas had confirmed Simon's identity. Now that Simon was incapacitated in the back of the truck, Jonas started the pickup and drove down the road. He knew that after the most recent hurricane, the area around the Houston known as the Bolivar Peninsula was littered with many destroyed beach houses. Which meant many deserted lanes that led to the water. He also knew that with the people gone, the main inhabitants of the area along the south Texas coastline were the alligators. He drove east along I-10 until he saw the exit to the Bolivar Peninsula. He drove for a few miles until he saw what looked like a dirt road that led in the general direction of the intracoastal waterway. Undisturbed weeds encroached on the tracks, which meant a low likelihood of habitation. He bounced down the lane to the end. He could see the slow-moving water of the intracoastal waterway some ten yards ahead. A dilapidated, concrete boat ramp angled into the water. Weeds crisscrossed the top of the ramp. The track leading up to it had dwindled to parallel wheel ruts.

He turned the truck around and backed it to the edge of the ramp. He got out and walked around to the back of the truck. He took out his gun, opened the back of the camper top, and tailgate, and looked in. Harvey moved around on the floor, still weak and unable to coordinate his limbs.

"Wake up," Jonas said. "We're here."

Harvey had difficulty focusing his eyes and moving his limbs. Jonas waited until Harvey was awake and sufficiently recovered from the injected drugs. Harvey sat up and looked around.

"Where are we? Why did you bring me here?" he asked, angry but with a hint of fear in his voice.

"You'll know. Now get out of the truck."

Harvey got out of the truck with some effort. His strength had almost returned to normal, but he wobbled as he stood, holding the tailgate.

"Now walk over to that boat ramp."

"What the fuck, man?" Harvey said, but he obediently lurched forward a few steps.

"Now turn around."

Harvey turned around. Now he was awake and aware of what was about to happen. He trembled and his expression turned to one of terror.

"Oh, God, man, please. Who the fuck are you? Why are you doing this?"

"Hey, Simon," Jonas said. "I'm Madeline. I told you I was desperate and that I'd be here on the twenty-first."

Harvey's eyes widened in surprise. Jonas aimed the gun at Harvey and fired twice. The first shot hit Harvey on the left side of the throat. A pulsing crimson stream jetted out from the left side of his neck. Jonas had aimed the second shot at Harvey's groin, but it missed slightly to the right, hitting him in his left hip. Harvey's shriek of pain ended in a wet cough and he collapsed to the left, his hip shattered by the second shot, unable to support his weight. Jonas lowered his gun and walked over to Harvey, who lay on the ground looking up at Jonas, helpless, staring, the look of the prey before the kill. Harvey tried to talk but could not. Jonas stood there, expressionless, looking down at Harvey. Harvey rolled around with difficulty, writhing in pain. A third round in the head would have been a *coup de grâce,* but Jonas did not fire a third round. He stood there, motionless, watching, waiting.

Harvey rolled over and as he did, the crimson stream, now weakening, pointed in different directions. Tiny rivulets of crimson flowed down the boat ramp toward the water, picking up particles of dust and fragments of dried leaves. Blood soaked the left side of his waist and hip area. After two minutes, Harvey let out a final wet wheeze and died. Jonas poked at Harvey with his boot. No movement.

Jonas walked back to his truck and took out a knife. He bent over Harvey's motionless figure and ripped open the front of Harvey's shirt. He ripped down the length of each sleeve and took off the shirt in pieces. He ripped open the front of Harvey's pants down the length and took them off. Finally, with a few more strokes of his knife, Harvey's wet underpants slid off. His nude body, glistening from perspiration and blood, lay on the concrete boat ramp, arms and legs askew. Jonas paused for a second. Then, on an impulse, with his lips pulled back in a savage grin, he grabbed Harvey's penis and sliced it off with one quick stroke of his knife. He flung it into the water. Jonas rolled Harvey's body down the incline toward the water and with one last shove with his boot, the body rolled under water. A stream of bubbles rose to the surface.

"Hope there's plenty of gators," Jonas said. Two alligators lay on the opposite bank, motionless, enjoying the sun. When Harvey rolled into the water, one stirred into action. It hoisted itself on its short legs and nosed into the water in the general direction of the body and disappeared. The second alligator followed a few seconds later. Faint, wedge-shaped ripples from the alligators converged in the general direction where Harvey had disappeared.

Jonas collected all the scraps of Harvey's clothing and walked back to the truck. He tossed the clothing scraps into the back and shut the tailgate and camper top. He pulled the change of clothes from the duffel bag, changed, got back into the truck and drove back along the rutted lane. He stopped to fill gas and restock a few protein bars and water bottles. Then he headed back to Dallas. Along the way, he stopped at three rest stops and discarded Harvey's clothes and his own bloodied clothes in different dumpsters.

He had not needed the second burner phone after all. He had brought it, spoofed to Tiffany's number, just in case. He had left his phone at the lab at the University, also just in case.

They won't even begin looking for Simon until his wife's back, Jonas thought, as he drove back home. As soon as he neared home, he discarded the burner phone, still off, into a nearby storm drain.

In two days, he would leave on a brief trip to Salt Lake City to attend Tiffany's funeral.

THIRTY

"What have we got?" It was Ed Fishburn.

He sat at a table at the police station with Detective Cook and two other people in charge of other aspects of the investigation like the cybercrime angle. A third person was one of the field investigators named Joe.

"So, here's what we've been able to put together. Tiffany headed to a rendezvous near Deep Ellum. When she got there, she sat in the car waiting and someone shot her. We never recovered her phone, but luckily for us, her mobile phone provider archives text messages for five days. From the phone company's records, we know someone sent some text messages in the minutes leading up to her being there. The contents of those text messages show she was led to that spot. A couple of hours before those texts, there was a phone call from her husband Jonas to Tiffany. Before the call, there was a brief exchange of texts between them. Nothing incriminating so far.

"Someone also sent two pictures, but we don't have those yet, so we are not sure of their significance. Someone sent those pictures between the text messages, so she had to have seen them. But, by the way she was found, it appears she sat in the car and turned around to look in the back. The trajectory of the bullet was through the back window, then through the front seat, and then into the victim. The perpetrator fired two rounds, one hit her and the other missed completely, hitting the dashboard."

"So, the killer was outside the back of the car?" asked Cook.

"We think so," Joe said. "But we can't be sure."

"We might know more when we see those pictures," said one of the other staffers.

Before Joe could say more, there was a knock at the door and a police station staffer stuck her head in the door.

"This is for you," she said, handing a folder to Detective Fishburn. "We got this a few minutes ago, and we printed it out. They're the pictures from the victim's phone."

The detectives opened the folder to inspect the contents. There were two pictures, each showing a black area, with a neon green and orangish splash of color on the side. One picture was in better focus and a "D" and "E" could be seen.

"Holy shit, that's the Deep Ellum sign," said Detective Cook. "The sign right in front of the car."

"Well, here's the deal as I see it," said Joe. "From how the car was parked, someone could have been standing in the dark, stepped out, taken those pictures, and hidden again. They also could have taken those pictures before she even got there. This is less likely as whoever took the pictures wouldn't have known where she would park. The angle of those pictures looks like someone inside the car or standing outside on the right side."

"Why take those pictures at all?" mused Fishburn.

"To scare the shit out of her," said Cook. "Which makes it more likely he was in the car all the time, hiding in the back."

"We could be wrong because, after scaring the shit out of her, he could have also stepped out from where he hid, gone to the back of the SUV, and fired twice. One round hit her, the other hit the dashboard, and the horn sounded. The guy takes off."

"I see," said Fishburn. "But why even shoot from the back of the car? It's dark, why doesn't he run around to the driver's side and take the cleaner shot at her?

"The other possibility is, he hid in the car all along, took the pictures from the back of the car, scared her like he wanted to, she turned, he shot her, and jumped out and ran to the back and fired another round to make things confusing. That takes some smarts."

Fishburn was leafing through another folder. He turned to one of the other people who sat at the table.

"Anything from the cybercrime angle so far?"

One of the others, a computer guy named Tom, spoke.

"We'll look at the metadata from the pictures now that we have them."

"Metadata?" asked Fishburn.

"Yes, Ed," Tom said with a smile. "Metadata. When you take a picture with a phone camera, it stores all kinds of data, stuff you wouldn't believe. We will know the model of the phone used, the approximate location, etc. But there won't be anything useful as far as where exactly the person took the picture. The date/time stamp will tell us when so we can establish if it was taken when she was already there and parked or taken earlier.

"Also, with image enhancement, we may get something. That picture looks zoomed and grainy. Maybe some surrounding stuff will tell us something, like whether it was taken through a windshield or from the outside. The surrounding stuff will be different if the picture had been taken from inside versus the outside of the car."

"Makes sense," Cook said. "And if it was from inside the car, it has to be the husband."

"What about the phone? The one that sent the pictures?"

"We traced the phone to a shop in the Latino area of Dallas. No one remembers the sale because it's been a few days. The security cameras are also useless because they overwrite data after forty-eight hours."

"What's the story on the husband's alibi?" asked Fishburn.

"We checked the University's security cameras, and he arrived at the lab at about seven o'clock. Footage shows him leaving the next morning, like he said. We checked his cell phone, and it was at the lab all evening. We also talked to the lab personnel, and they can vouch for seeing him there at seven. But they left by seven-thirty, so it does nothing to support his alibi. His client also verifies he was there doing work on the server."

"Hmm," said Fishburn. "If whoever did this hadn't sent those pictures to her phone, we could say this was a random killing. Some unlucky person in the wrong place at the wrong time. But this was premeditated. Someone knew her number and was on purpose trying to get her attention, presumably to turn and face him before he shot her. We are certainly talking the personal motive. And damn it all, it has to be the husband. We talked to this "Simon" guy. He's a loser in Houston who made some dumb choices and got into the wrong situation. He's lucky it ended the way it did for him. If he had done something dumber, like met Tiffany and screwed her, his wife would have killed him. But there is no way he killed Tiffany. His wife says he was home Friday night and besides, he lives in Houston so it would have been too long a round trip to go to Dallas and kill Tiffany without his absence being noticed."

"Did she have any other online contacts?"

"Yes, a few others. But none with the same degree of involvement as this "Simon" guy. Not someone who would be pissed off enough at her to kill her."

"So what's our next step?" asked Cook.

"We keep pushing," Fishburn said. "Try to pierce the husband's alibi. If he's guilty and made even the slightest mistake, we need to find it. Try to find as many surveillance videos as you can from the bars and other shops around there. We could luck out and see something on one of them."

"All right."

"You know, this picture angle has me convinced it has to be the husband. Tiffany was dressed like she was meeting a guy. And Simon had planned to meet her. I bet not that night. I bet the husband found out. Some of the shit she had written to Simon was suggestive. I bet they even went as far as having phone sex and the husband found out. That's the only explanation for all of this. I bet we will find out Jonas planned all of this. Either he was in the back of the car or he steered her to that parking lot, and he waited there to ambush her."

Fishburn had been glancing through pages in a folder when he stopped at one and frowned. He put a finger on the page and his gaze intensified as he traced his finger down the page.

"What's up," said Cook.

"It's the husband," he said.

"Why?"

"Look at this. It's the transcript of the report from EMS. It says when they arrived at the scene, the car alarm was on, and the horn was blaring."

"Yeah?"

"We assumed the horn started sounding when the bullet hit it. That was a mistake. It's unlikely a bullet hitting the horn would cause it to stay on and if it did, it would be a continuous sound. This was the alarm. That means Tiffany probably sat there in a locked car and someone opened the door, *from the inside*, without realizing the alarm was set. And if it was someone inside the car, it was the husband."

Cook leaned back in his chair.

"Could the alarm have gone off when the rear window was shot out?"

"I doubt it. All the doors would still be locked. If he had shot her from behind the car and reached in to unlock the car, then yes, the alarm could have gone off. But the other windows were still closed. Only the rear window was shot out. So he had to have been inside."

"Wow, you're right. And I just thought of something else. When the passersby showed up, they just opened the front door because it was already unlocked."

"Exactly. So, the alarm must have been triggered by someone opening the car door from the inside."

As they concluded the meeting, the door opened and one of the receptionists stuck her head in the door.

"Phone call for either Detective Fishburn or Detective Cook; it's Houston PD."

"We'll take it here," Cook said. "Wonder what they want."

The light on the phone blinked and Cook picked it up. "Cook here."

He listened for a minute with a slight frown on his face.

"Really, when?" he said. Then a pause. "And no one saw anything?" Another pause. "Well, that's interesting." Another pause. "OK, got it. I'll pass it along."

He hung up and turned to the group.

"That was from Houston PD. It was a courtesy call to let us know of a development in the Tiffany Jensen case. Harvey Michaels' wife and daughters stayed longer in New Orleans than they had planned, not surprising given how the trip started, and got back yesterday. It's been eight days.

"Guess what," he continued. "Harvey Michaels is nowhere to be found. His wife filed a missing persons report yesterday."

"So maybe he was involved. And he's fleeing?" said Fishburn.

"I don't think so. They said when his wife got home, she found his wallet, keys, and phone but he was gone. His bed looked like he hadn't slept in it for days. There was an end table near the front door. Someone had knocked it over and the stuff on it was all over the floor."

"What the hell," said Fishburn. "This isn't good. Well, Houston PD will let us know if they find anything. Let's get to work."

The meeting adjourned. The staff left the room, leaving only Cook and Fishburn behind.

"I've got a bad feeling about this," Fishburn said. "Do some more digging into the husband's past. What kind of guy is he? Does he have any priors? Is he the type of guy who, if he found out his wife screwed around or was about to screw around, would go batshit and kill both her and the other guy?"

"I'm worried about this end table being knocked over. Sure indicates a struggle of some sort. Too much of a coincidence that this kind of shit would happen days after we talk to him about a murder."

"We can try to look in the husband's past," Cook said. "It won't be easy. If he had any mental health crap as a minor, those records are sealed. We can find out about priors. Harvey's been gone for a week. There is no way to find out when exactly he disappeared so we can't cross check that with the husband's location at any specific time. Even if he drove to Houston and did something to Harvey, which I think is possible but unlikely, he is smart enough to cover his tracks. Maybe we should have been tailing him."

"I'm not sure that would have helped."

"Well, let's hope Houston PD finds out something."

THIRTY-ONE

A paroxysm of coughing almost awakened Paul Albrecht.
He shifted, uncomfortable, grimacing in his sleep, trying to
rearrange the flattened cardboard boxes that served as his
mattress. He tried to adjust the rolled-up clothing that
doubled as his pillow. It was no use. Another spasm
awakened him, and he sat up, sputtering. It felt like a wet
worm had crawled up his throat and he turned to the
concrete wall behind him and spat it out. He had been trying
to sleep under a freeway overpass. The constant dull roar of
the passing cars punctuated by the cadence of the tires
slapping against a seam in the concrete above him created a
"gray noise" that lulled him to sleep. He knew he was
somewhere under Interstate 30 in Dallas near Deep Ellum.

Paul Albrecht had been a sheet metal worker. After high
school, he had joined the National Guard for four years.
After finishing, he had decided he would become a sheet
metal worker. He got a job at an HVAC company,
fabricating ductwork and within a year, he had married. An
industrial accident soon after his marriage led to the partial
loss of use of his left hand. He embarked on a two-year
journey of trying to get disability, being denied, reapplying,
and finally getting approved. He had received a monthly
payment that was a pittance compared to what he made
while employed. Within a year of his injury, he had turned to
the bottle on a more regular basis and within a year of that,
his wife had left him.

The first ten-year arc of his life as an adult had started
uphill from military service to apprenticeship, to a job, and
marriage. The abrupt downturn started with the injury and
swept him down slope into the 4 D's: disability,
despondency, drink, and finally divorce. He lost his house

and with no other options, had gone to a homeless shelter. Ten years had elapsed since then. On disability and in a homeless shelter, finding work was impossible and after a year, his enthusiasm for work had waned to the point he no longer cared. For the second ten years of adult life, he had been living in and out of shelters. In the summer months, he found it more satisfying to sleep on the streets rather than the crowded confines of the shelter.

He coughed again. This cough had begun with a raw, scratchy sensation in his throat three days earlier. It had progressed until he now produced greenish sputum and felt febrile. His throat felt like someone was parked back there with a piece of sandpaper and scraped a raw patch every time he swallowed.

Crap, he thought as he spat out another mouthful of phlegm. He decided he felt bad enough to go to the nearest free clinic. *What was the name of that place?* he thought. *I think it's Second Chance.*

He stood and stretched, feeling various stiff joints creak and pop. He collected his meager belongings, mostly contained in a backpack and an old, wheeled suitcase, and stretched again. He left the cardboard boxes he had slept on but took the boxes that served as his panhandling signs, "Homeless Vet, Anything Helps, God Bless" and "Visions of a Cheeseburger."

His suitcase had three worn wheels and an exposed metal flange where the fourth wheel had been. He shuffled down the road; the suitcase made a scraping sound every time the corner without the wheel contacted the road. He squinted at the sky; it seemed to be about nine. The road crawled with cars, pausing and contracting at the traffic lights and then stretching out when the light turned green. As he walked down the sidewalk, he sensed the averted gaze of most drivers and a jaundiced glare from a few. He had learned to ignore them.

"Hi Paul," said a voice. He saw Phyllis, another homeless person, sitting on the side of the road.

"Hi Phyllis," he said and coughed again. He spit out another wad of phlegm. "I feel like crap."

"Where you headed?" she asked. Phyllis was older than him, mid-sixties, stringy grey hair, poor dentition, thin, and smelly. Like every homeless person, she had a story that began with varying degrees of fortune, or lack thereof, and ended on a downward spiral that landed on the streets. Phyllis was a long-term inhabitant of the streets and had no family and no resources. *And she's a little nuts*, he thought. Like many homeless people, Phyllis was not entirely "there" between the ears.

"Clinic up the road," Paul said. "Second Chance."

"Oh, OK. Don't let them stick a finger up your ass." She cackled.

He continued to walk up the road. He glanced at the sun. *I shouldn't be this cold*, he thought. He still felt chilled and had occasional shivers. *Probably have a fever*, he thought. He made his way to Second Chance and pushed open the door.

The waiting room had about a dozen seats and only three or four were occupied. He shuffled over to the registration window.

"Can I help you?" asked the receptionist.

"Don't feel good," he said. "Nasty cough, started a few days ago, now getting worse."

She went through the usual routine with registration. He had not been there before, so she gave him a new patient questionnaire on a clipboard and pointed at the waiting room with the back of her pen. She asked him to take a seat and fill out details about his medical history. He filled it out, writing slowly and laboriously with the pen she had provided. He handed it back to her, and she asked him to take a seat again and wait until he heard his name.

After thirty minutes, the people ahead of him had already gone back, and they called him next. The medical assistant ushered him to the back and measured his vital signs. He sat in a small exam room and had another episode of coughing. He reached for a few tissues and spat into them. A few minutes later, the door opened, and a young woman entered the room. She wore a starched white coat with a stethoscope draped around her neck.

"Hi, my name is Meghan Payson," she said. "I'm one of the nurse practitioners who cover this clinic."

"Ain't there a doctor here?" Paul asked.

"We have a supervising physician but for most routine things like coughs and colds, we are capable of treating it."

"Oh, OK," he said.

After the customary questions, she asked him to lift the back of his shirt. He complied, and Ms. Payson plugged a stethoscope in her ears. She asked him to open his mouth and breathe in and out with slow deep breaths while she listened to his lungs. The breathing elicited another round of coughing and he reached for more tissues. She asked him to stick out his tongue for a throat swab. He obliged, gagging as the tongue depressor and a cotton swab pushed against the back of his throat. Afterwards, she left the room, telling him she would be back in a few minutes.

Ten minutes later, she returned.

"Well, your strep test is positive and you're running a fever. Your lungs sound clear, so I don't think it's pneumonia yet," she said.

"What does that mean?" he asked.

"It means you're sick with a bacteria," she said. "It's nothing to worry about. We will give you something here today to start to clear it up."

She tapped a few keys on her tablet.

"We will give you a shot today," she continued, "But since you don't have a place to live and all that, we can't give you a prescription for pills. So, you will need to come back tomorrow and the next day and get a shot each day. Can you remember that and do that?"

"Yeah, sure," he said.

"You should be better by then, but it is important to get all the shots." The clinic realized the futility of passing out prescriptions or even pills to the homeless, given their lack of any support.

As he left the clinic, Meghan Payson finished his chart and signed off. The clerk at the front desk had already entered all his medical history, including his social history and the circumstances that led to him being homeless.

The clinic stored the electronic medical record at a remote location. Second Chance had an IT guy who stopped by three or four times a week to check on things. He happened to be in the office that day. As Paul left the clinic, the IT guy sat at his desk, looking over Paul's medical and social history. His expression changed as he sat there, twirling a keychain on his left index finger.

THIRTY-TWO

Paul Albrecht left the clinic and shuffled back toward his roost. He coughed again and he winced, holding his hand against his chest. He still felt feverish, but the clinic had explained they had given him an extra-strength dose of acetaminophen along with the antibiotic injection so he knew he would feel better soon. The clinic had also given him a blanket. They had a supply of blankets donated by a local charity and passed them out as needed. They also gave him some chewable children's acetaminophen to take with him, anticipating the difficulty the homeless face in getting fresh water to swallow tablets.

Paul walked back to his haunt under I-30, adjusting the angle of the suitcase every time the corner with the missing wheel scraped against the pavement. He reached his spot and settled on the pavement. As he sat, he broke out and felt clammy. He wiped his face on his grimy sleeve. The fever had broken, and he felt a little better. He reached for his bottle of water and took a long drink.

He watched the people walking along the street; their shadows had shrunk to almost nothing. It was almost lunchtime, and he felt hungry. He mulled over holding his "Visions of a cheeseburger" sign but decided he was too tired to move for now.

A familiar figure came up the sidewalk. It was Phyllis. She saw him lying in his usual place and changed directions to head toward him.

"How did it go?"

"Fine," Paul said. "They listened to my lungs, swabbed my throat, gave me a shot, gave me some Tylenol, and told me to go back tomorrow for another shot. I gotta go back every day for the next, I dunno, two or three days and get a shot. They also gave me some chewable tablets I can take every few hours if I feel cold or shivery."

"Did they stick a finger up your ass?" she asked.

"No, Phyllis, they didn't," he said. Then, with his stomach growling in impatience, "You got anything to eat?"

"No, you hungry?"

"Yeah."

"I was going to find something. I'll bring you back something."

"Thanks. I'm gonna take a nap," Paul said.

He rolled over, facing toward the overpass. He ignored his growling stomach and soon fell asleep. He awakened with a start a while later. He squinted at the sun and estimated he had been asleep around four hours. Phyllis had not returned with anything to eat. Or maybe she had, and he'd slept through it. He had another episode of coughing but did not feel feverish anymore. Now he was ravenous.

He sat up, surveyed the street. He felt strong enough to stand, holding his "Visions of a cheeseburger" sign. He rose to his feet, unfolded the piece of cardboard, and shuffled to the road's edge.

In the first few minutes, a few cars stopped, and he gathered a few dollars. After he had enough money for a meal, he decided he would trudge up the road to the burger place to see if he could scrounge some food. He wondered where Phyllis went. *Probably forgot about it as soon as she walked up the road*, he thought. As he was about to fold his sign, a black Toyota Camry slowed to a stop next to him. The passenger side window rolled down, and the driver leaned over.

"Hey there," the man said.

"Hi," said Paul.

"You hungry for a cheeseburger?" the driver asked.

"You bet."

"Why don't you hop in, and I'll take you to get a cheeseburger."

"That's OK. I don't know you. And I got enough money to get me one."

"Your name's Paul, right?"

Paul scowled. "Yeah. How did you know?"

"I work at that clinic you went to earlier. You didn't look too good there this morning. We gave you a blanket and the medicines for your fever. I saw you by the side of the road and wanted to get you a cheeseburger."

"Oh, ok."

Paul climbed into the passenger seat and the car moved off. The driver was friendly and chatted with Paul.

"You know today's July 4th, right?" the driver said.

"No, I didn't. Doesn't make no difference to me. Every day's the same. Just on July 4th, there's more cars, and there's more noise."

"How long have you lived on the streets?"

"Dunno. Ten years, I'm thinking," Paul shrugged.

"Every day's the same," he repeated. "Except when it gets cold all of a sudden. Or gets hot all of a sudden. Or rains all of a sudden."

A block ahead, Paul saw a McDonald's. They drove past the golden arches and Paul looked at the driver, puzzled.

"Ain't we goin' in there?"

"I'm going around the block. There's another place there that has better cheeseburgers."

He made a right turn after the McDonald's into a back alley. There was no entrance to the McDonald's from here, but there was also no traffic. And no witnesses.

"I'll just cut across this alley to the next block. The cheeseburger place is up ahead."

Paul knew this neighborhood, these streets, these alleys. He knew there was no cheeseburger place ahead. He was about to ask the driver where he was going when the driver suddenly lunged toward Paul and jabbed something sharp into his left forearm. As the driver pressed the plunger, Paul jerked back, and the needle furrowed across his arm, leaving a red streak. A red bead bloomed from the puncture site and tracked down the red streak on his arm. The driver slammed the brakes.

"Hey, what the fuck?" Paul yelled.

He tried to reach for the door handle, to open it and roll out. He grasped the door handle and pulled. The handle moved in and out, but the door would not open. After a few frantic pulls on the door handle, Paul's grasp slipped off the handle. As he tried to reach for the handle again, a second jab followed.

"Ow!" he yelled.

He managed to grab the handle and as he did, his hand stopped following commands from his brain. His grip weakened. He tried to pull his left arm away from the assailant, but it moved like it was embedded in quicksand. He slapped at the door handle as his ability to direct his movements weakened. His vision blurred. The driver opened a small plastic bag. Paul felt a wad of cloth pressed against his mouth and nose. A strong, sweet and acrid penetrating chemical odor assailed his nostrils.

He tried to speak but a rasping sound was all he could manage. His attempt to pull the cloth away was weak and clumsy. Now his arm also stopped following commands from his brain. The last thing he remembered was another sharp jab in his arm. He blacked out and his head lolled to one side.

*   *   *

Jonas leaned back, panting from the exertion. He leaned over Paul and pushed the seat recline button until it whirred almost flat, and Paul was no longer visible from the outside. In the broad daylight, anyone stopping next to the car would have seen Paul. He reached behind the front seat and pulled out a blanket. He covered Paul's face and body, making sure no part of Paul was exposed. He positioned a loose fold of blanket over Paul's left arm with another syringe handy, just in case, nearby.

He pulled out his phone and tapped out a text message: "Good to go."

He put the car in drive and eased away from the curb. He drove the few miles through the streets of Dallas until he came to the industrial area with warehouses and sparse traffic. He drove a few more blocks, and the road became narrower and rutted. He made his way to the lot with the shed in which he had set up equipment two months earlier.

As he drove around to the back of the shed, a man came out the door. He had already unlocked the shed door and had slid it open. Jonas drove his car into the shed and parked. The sound of the generator intruded in the background.

Paul's left arm moved, and Jonas jabbed him with the syringe. Paul stopped moving.

He got out of the car and the other man came over. Without a word, the two of them pulled Paul out of the car. He was heavy and being unconscious, seemed heavier. Together they heaved Paul onto the aluminum table. They both paused, panting with exertion.

The other man turned to a metal cabinet with drawers. He slid open the top drawer and extracted a shiny object, a scalpel handle. From another drawer, he took out a blade and with a small hemostat, slid the blade onto the handle where it clicked into place. He turned to Paul's still figure. Jonas had pulled Paul's shirt up and bunched it under his armpit, exposing his flank.

"Let's get to work."

Fifteen minutes later, Paul's inert figure lay on the bed of the pickup truck. A pool of blood had begun to gather around him. Jonas climbed into the cab and started the engine. He drove off the lot and turned right, heading deeper into the greenbelt surrounding the river. About a half-mile away, he stopped by a bush and looked around. It was quiet.

He opened the back of the truck and noted with alarm that Paul was moving weakly.

What the fuck! he thought. The other man had injected Paul in the heart with a drug that was meant to stop the heart immediately. But either it had not worked, or his accomplice had done it wrong.

He held Paul's arms and dragged him out of the back of the truck. Paul landed on the ground with a soft thud, next to a bush, sprawled in an awkward pose. Jonas pulled out his gun, held it against Paul's chest at point-blank range, and fired a single shot. He climbed back into the truck and sped off.

THIRTY-THREE

Jick had planned to call Vic a few days ago to see if he could tag along on one of his calls. Then things got busy at work, and he had not followed through. He planned to keep the mask a secret, until he figured out more about it. He hoped since Vic was a beat reporter who covered crime for Dallas' biggest newspaper; maybe he could get to crime scenes early enough and get close enough to see what this mask could do. He was excited at the prospect.

As Jick got home, his phone rang.

"Hi, old man." It was Vic. "You doing anything for the 4th? Any plans with la belle femme?"

"No, nothing planned," Jick said.

"Wanna come over for dinner? Sam and I are staying at home to watch the July 4th fireworks on TV."

"All right, that sounds good. I'll just freshen up and head over."

He put the mask in a backpack, slung it over his shoulder, and headed out in a few minutes.

This would be good. Jick looked forward to one of Sam's foodie experiments. She usually succeeded when she tried out various cuisines. Being married to Vic, she had also mastered many Indian dishes. A mouth-watering aroma wafted into his nostrils as Vic greeted him at the door.

They went into the kitchen and Vic poured Jick a drink. Both Vic and Sam wore aprons and Vic had been chopping vegetables.

"Hi, Jick," Sam said. "Glad you could make it."

"Thanks for having me over. I wasn't doing anything anyway. La belle femme, as Vic put it, had other plans.

"So, Vic," Jick said, "anything going on work-wise? Any hot crime leads?"

"Nothing so far," he replied. "It's been kind of slow. Surprising, given how warm the summer has been. Tempers seem to flare more in hot weather, and we get more knife and gun club events."

Jick added, "Say, Vic, when you go out to these crime scenes, are you allowed to take someone along?"

Vic looked at Jick. "Generally, no. Why? Do you know someone who is interested in this stuff?"

"Yes, me."

"Why?" Vic asked, surprised.

"No particular reason. I usually see more trauma than I care to. But when they come to the operating room, they are already sedated. And obviously if they are already pronounced, they go straight to the morgue. I am interested in what happens at the exact moment of death. The ER would also be a good place to observe this, but I wanted to see what happens out in the field. I've always been curious about what happens at that moment of death, at the point between being alive and aware, to being dead."

"I didn't know this moment of death stuff interested you so much."

"Well, maybe it has to do with my getting old and not coping with it very well." Jick reached for the wine and took a sip.

"You're wondering what will happen to you at your moment of death? Wow, Jick, you are getting old.

"OK. If I get a hot tip on a crime and the victims are lying there bleeding and about to die, and my contact in Dallas PD calls me, and you're available, you are welcome to tag along. However, there may be times when a cop at the scene is a hard ass and does not want any unauthorized people around, but if it's someone I know, it should not be a problem."

"OK, perfect," Jick said. "Send me a text whenever you get a tip and if I can make it, I'll race over and meet you there."

Jick lifted the lid on one of the dishes. Sam had made a creamy chicken tandoori, first marinated and flame-grilled and then deboned and stirred into a creamy sauce. For a side dish, she had made a vegetable medley in coconut gravy. A chopped cold salad of cucumbers, tomatoes, cilantro, lime juice, and green chillies rounded out the meal. Deep fried *papadums* filled a breadbasket.

"Wow, Sam, this looks fantastic."

After dinner, they enjoyed a *digestif* of Rémy Martin XO and watched fireworks coverage on one of the local channels. To Jick, fireworks seemed to be a waste of time, not to mention money, because it was the same celebration every year. One more checkmark of cynicism on his chart of getting older. Any birthday, even one celebrating the birth of the country, seemed unwelcome. He took another generous sip of the magnificent cognac and thought, *No Black Cloud tonight.*

Just then, Vic's phone rang. He answered and his expression changed. After a few "yesses," "uh-huhs," and a "where", he hung up and said, "Your wish may come true, old man. We have a crime scene."

Given Vic's longstanding connections with the Dallas police, one of his contacts called him when a report came in about an unusual crime. Because of this, he had a knack of "scooping" other reporters. The relationship was mutually beneficial as he was respectful to the police and his florid prose was especially complimentary to law enforcement.

"What is it?" Jick asked.

"A murder," Vic replied. "Kind of unusual. A jogger found a body and thought it was a sleeping homeless guy by his clothing. But he was sprawled out in an awkward pose, not moving. So she went up to him. She almost lost her dinner at what she saw. She called the police, and that's all I've got."

"What did she see?" Jick asked.

"Don't know yet. Fazio told me to get there ASAP. Do you want to go along?"

Fazio was one of Vic's contacts in the police department.

"Let me get my backpack," Jick said. He felt a little thrill at being able to go along on one of Vic's calls. "Let's hurry."

They made their way around downtown Dallas and to the nearest parking spot to access the Trail. As they approached the site, they noted several police officers, two women in full body covering garb, and police tape. Vic was the only media presence so far. A few curious joggers had stopped to look but stayed at a safe distance behind the tape. In the background, scattered fireworks had begun for the July 4th festivities.

"Vic Arnsson," Vic said. And "Hi Jerry" to the officer standing by the police tape.

"Oh, hi Vic," the officer said. "They're almost done and about to bag the body," he added, pointing over his shoulder with his thumb.

"You can go look," he said, while looking at Jick. "Who's he?"

"My brother, Dr. Jick Arnsson," Vic said. "Is it OK if he goes in also?"

"Hmm, department policy is no bystanders but since it's you, and he is a doctor," he looked at Jick, "what kind of doctor are you?"

"An anesthesiologist."

"Is that a regular MD?"

"Yes."

It was not the first time Jick had heard that question.

Jerry hesitated, "OK this time."

They walked to where the body lay. It was a man, Jick guessed forty-something, lying on his left side, facing away. His shirt was slashed from the button and had gathered in a loose bunch around his shoulders. He still had his pants on, so his abdomen and chest were uncovered. From any reasonable distance, he looked like he might be asleep. But he wasn't. Standing next to the body and looking down revealed a large incision on his right flank. His right kidney was missing. A trail of dried blood from the incision snaked over his belly and joined a dark wet patch on the ground. A small hole was visible on the left side of his chest. It was surrounded by dark powder burns indicating the point-blank distance of the fired shot. A larger hole bloomed on the other side of his chest from the exit wound. A large puddle of blood had spread down across his left chest wall and onto the ground. A second puddle of blood oozed from his mid-abdomen, also spilling across his body and onto the ground. One of the women in full body covering garb rolled him over on his back. A second incision was visible on his left flank. It was difficult to see this incision, but judging from its position, Jick surmised his left kidney was also missing. He leaned over the body and was greeted by a metallic stench.

As a physician, Jick had seen it all, especially during his gruesome experiences in the Trauma room. Even by those standards, what had been done to this man was horrific. Yet Jick found the dead man's expression oddly counterintuitive; it was peaceful. In many murders, the victims know what is about to happen and their last expression reflects either surprise or fear. Not so in this case. The victim's expression was peaceful, almost like he had been asleep when this happened. Asleep, but alive. Jick felt a shiver. Organs were routinely donated by the dying for organ banks, but the process needed to be done immediately upon expiration of the donor to keep the organs viable. It seemed clear to him this was organ harvesting at its worst.

His peaceful expression aroused Jick's professional curiosity. To be deeply asleep, deep enough to not awaken as your kidneys are being removed, would require a general anesthetic. Had someone anesthetized him before taking out the organs? And would an anesthesiologist be complicit in this type of organ harvesting?

He sauntered around to a nearby bush and stepped behind it. One of the police officers glanced at him and looked away. *Probably thinks I'm about to either puke or take a piss*, Jick thought. He took out the mask and put it on. Nothing. No feeling of dizziness or disorientation, no visualization of this man's last moments. There was nothing. He could see through the eyeholes of the mask at the crime scene from behind the bush. He took off the mask and put it back in his backpack.

He walked back to the group. He caught the end of their conversation. They speculated about this murder and how long he had lain there. Based on a preliminary survey of his body, the assumption was that he had been there for at least an hour, if not longer.

Jick was not surprised he saw nothing with the mask—the poor guy had been dead too long.

They headed back to Vic's place.

"We should help Sam clean up," Jick said.

As they left, he heard the staccato of fireworks and in the distance, giant expanding multicolored mushrooms of light lit up the night sky as July 4th celebrations kicked off. The mushrooms faded into tinsel that drifted to the ground. But Jick knew that one less person would witness it this night.

THIRTY-FOUR

A few days after the eventful July 4th evening, Vic had called to let Jick know he had a bit of information on the crime scene. He had also mentioned that Sam had called him to say she would be late and would grab dinner on the way home for herself. So Jick offered to take over some dinner to Vic's. He stopped at the Burger Barn, known for its juicy gourmet burgers and to-die-for onion rings. He picked up two large cheeseburgers with mushrooms and jalapeños, two large orders of onion rings and for good measure, and to assuage any guilt about his unhealthy food choices, two side salads with vinaigrette dressing.

Vic sat at his desk looking at his computer.

"Here's dinner," Jick announced. "Burger Barn with onion rings and a side salad."

"Oh, that sounds good. Just what the doctor ordered. Put it in the warming drawer for now. Oh, help yourself to some wine. I already have some."

Jick poured a glass of zinfandel and joined Vic in the study.

"His name was Paul Albrecht," said Vic. "He was a homeless guy living in the streets near Deep Ellum. Nothing unusual. Unlike many homeless people who have mental problems and can't get proper care, Paul Albrecht did not have any mental issues that we know of. He was a down on his luck sheet metal worker. After a year or two of living in the street, a certain inertia sets in and you're in a rut. By this time, it is more difficult to extricate yourself and get back to a reasonable and productive life.

"The police have a tough time keeping track of the homeless. If they are seen in either the healthcare system or criminal justice system, there is some record. Many of them wander around, foraging around population centers, stopping at soup kitchens, etc., until something goes wrong. Sometimes one of them, especially the mental cases, will go bonkers and if there is an assault, or something worse, the criminal justice system will have a record.

"For Paul Albrecht, there was nothing. He kept a low profile and wandered around. The only reason they identified him was because the police ran a picture of him in the paper without divulging details about how he was found. It was one of those 'Do You Recognize This Missing Person' pictures, like the kind you see on milk cartons for missing kids, and someone called the tip line and identified him."

"Any idea who called?" Jick asked.

"No idea," Vic said. "There is an ex-wife somewhere. Maybe her. But that's all I got."

As he talked, Vic went through his emails. One of them was from his police contact. He clicked on it and noted he had sent four attached pictures along with a brief note. He clicked on each one, downloading it to his desktop.

"I can use these pictures in my reporting," he said. "The police are stumped. Someone drugged him and took him to a location where they took out kidneys. His autopsy showed needle puncture marks and bruises on his left forearm. They transported him in a vehicle, based on drag marks and tire tracks, and dumped him off by the Trinity, rolling him out of the vehicle, which explains his position. My guess is that it was the back of a covered pickup truck since it would have been easy enough to hose out the back of a truck and that would be that.

"That email was from Fazio. I can't get any pictures of the crime scene, but he sent some pictures of the area around Deep Ellum where Paul lived."

He opened the pictures on his desktop. They looked like pictures of a squatter camp under a freeway. It could have been anywhere in the U.S. as no localizing landmarks could be seen in the pictures. One picture was a close-up of the dead man's face, eyes closed, peaceful, like he was asleep. There was a picture of a roller suitcase and what looked like a backpack. Two cardboard signs leaned against a concrete pillar in another picture.

"I'm sure the police will keep investigating but this isn't exactly a high-profile victim," Vic continued. "Not only that, but there's also very little to go on. The homeless crowd does not particularly like the police, so they are not going to go out of their way to volunteer information."

Jick walked around to stand behind Vic.

"These are pictures of where Paul lived?" Jick asked. "And that's his stuff?"

"Yes."

He glanced at the pictures; one of them looked familiar, and he drew in a sharp breath.

"That picture looks familiar."

"Which one?"

"That picture of his belongings. That piece of cardboard next to that bag says 'Visions of a Cheeseburger.'"

"What about it?"

"I'm pretty sure I've seen this guy. It was a few weeks ago. When I had gone shopping for Walter's present, I drove around Deep Ellum and there was a homeless guy holding that sign. It was dinnertime, so I bought him a cheeseburger combo meal. I remembered the sign because I found it amusing.

Jick's trivia-aware nerdiness asserted itself.

"That Venus flytrap and 'Feed Me Now' was unforgettable. Did you ever see the original 'Little Shop of Horrors'? Jack Nicholson was in it as the masochist. There's a flesh-eating plant in it that bellows 'Feed Me Now!'. This guy was holding that sign. He had been dancing on a street corner waving that sign and doing pirouettes to attract attention."

"Poor guy," Vic said.

Jick felt a deep sense of poignancy looking at that picture of the cardboard sign. Here was a man minding his own business, eking out a living on the road, with nothing to his name. Someone had targeted him and murdered him. They had erased him. Forever. For his organs. No one would even remember him or miss him. He had ceased to exist. Jick shivered as a goose walked over his grave.

"There's something that doesn't quite add up. He was a normal-sized guy. There is no way anyone could have done what they did to him unless he was under anesthesia or already dead. If the goal here was to harvest organs, he would need to be alive. Organs do not last long when someone is dead. And if we assume there was organ harvesting going on, they would need some infrastructure. Drugs to knock him out, machines to keep him asleep, surgical tools to remove the organs, some professional know-how, and equipment to keep the organs viable."

"Out of curiosity, how would you knock someone out and keep them alive?" Vic asked.

"Good question," Jick said. "There are several drugs that could do it. Intramuscularly injected succinylcholine would paralyze someone, but it could take two to three minutes for full effect. During that time, your muscles would weaken, and your vision would become blurry. However, during those two or three minutes, the victim would still have some ability to fight back. Maybe someone used a higher-than-normal dose.

"Injected ketamine, at much higher-than-normal doses, would create a dissociative anesthetic state in which it blocks the sensation of pain. It would probably be the ideal drug to knock him out, along with succinylcholine, and then harvest his organs."

"But with both drugs, they could still fight back for a while, right?" Vic said.

"Yes, they could. But if the killer also used a wad of gauze soaked in ether or chloroform to their face, with that combination, sleep could be almost instantaneous. It would still take some effort on the part of the killer to hold them down for a few seconds."

"Where would someone get all this stuff from?" Vic asked.

"That," Jick paused, "is an excellent question. If I had to speculate, the killer, or someone he knows, has medical knowledge or is in the medical field, and has access to drugs.

"This could also be the start of a wacko serial killer who just wants the organs, and, in that case, he would not need to be alive."

"Oh, he was alive, all right," Vic said. "The preliminary autopsy results showed that."

"The autopsy was already done?" Jick asked, surprised. Autopsies often take weeks to months to complete.

"Just the preliminary," Vic said. "All the lab and toxicology stuff will take longer. Maybe then we will find out what drugs, if any, they gave him."

"There's a good chance the toxicology results won't be helpful. I believe succinylcholine breaks down in a matter of minutes and ether vaporizes almost in an instant. Maybe ketamine has some metabolites that will show up on the toxicology tests. I'm not sure it makes a difference, anyway. We know someone drugged him before they gutted him.

"What happens to him now?" Jick asked.

"What do you mean?"

"I mean, what kind of funeral does he get? And who pays for it?"

"Oh, that. Usually, the police try to contact some next of kin. Most homeless people have some next of kin who, if they can afford it, claim the body. Many times, there is no one to claim the body, and the city pays a fee to the funeral home. There is a list of funeral homes that are on a rotating 'call' list. They call whoever is on deck. Sometimes they hold a memorial service at the gravesite, and it would surprise you how many homeless people show up. Often, this is the only family these people have and after years together, they are closer than their biological family."

"That is sad. And to think I bought this guy a meal a few days ago."

"Yeah, I know. The police need to catch the guy who did this."

"For sure."

"Let's eat," Vic said. They got the burgers and onion rings from the warming drawer, the salads from the fridge, and another round of wine. The crunchy, beer-battered rings were, for sure, to-die-for. The burger was great as well, but

Jick had trouble finishing it with images of the cardboard sign fixed to his brain.

Later Jick headed home deep in thought about this murder. He got home at ten, had his daily nightcap, this time a South African port, and went to bed.

THIRTY-FIVE

Taylor Potts sat by the side of the road and behind and above him, could hear the constant roar of the cars on the freeway. He also heard the occasional voice and without bothering to look for the source, replied. There was no one around him. Passersby would stare at him for a second and look away. He knew he should have been on some medications.

When he needed to eat, he would hold his piece of cardboard out to traffic. A few coins and fewer one-dollar bills would appear. He would shuffle off to the alleys and nearby restaurants, sometimes getting handouts, sometimes rummaging in dumpsters, and sometimes exchanging the dollar bills and coins for food.

But today he had a splitting headache and did not want to bother with the cardboard sign. He had found some cans of food that had pull tops in a nearby dumpster and settled for them for a meal. He squinted through his headache and tried to work one open.

As the top of one of the cans snapped off, he felt a sudden sharp pain in his left thumb and thought, *Ah, shit*. A small ribbon of crimson appeared on the pad of his thumb where he sliced it open on the sharp edge of the open can. The crimson ribbon elongated and drops of blood ran down to the base of his thumb and fell on the ground when he shook his hand. He stuck his thumb in his mouth, sucked at the wound but stopped after the volume of blood was copious. He pulled his thumb out and spat a wad of crimson. He held pressure for a few minutes, but the bleeding continued.

Shit, he thought again.

He held pressure again and stared around, undecided. Another round of bleeding started as soon as he released pressure. Holding his thumb against his index finger, he shuffled down the road.

"Hi, Taylor," said a voice. It was Phyllis.

"Hi, Phyllis," he said.

"Where you headed?" she asked. He told her what had happened. He told her he was headed to the free clinic a block away, Second Chance.

"Don't let them stick a finger up your ass!" she admonished, cackling.

"I won't," Taylor promised.

He made his way to Second Chance and went in.

"Can I help you?" the receptionist asked.

"I cut my thumb."

He held out his hand and showed her the dried blood. As soon as he lifted his index finger, the ribbon reappeared. The receptionist gave him a wad of gauze to hold pressure on his thumb and gave him some paperwork to fill out.

"Won't be long," she said. "It's not too crowded today."

Taylor stared at the paperwork, helpless, and then back at the receptionist. She helped him fill it out. They called his name soon afterwards and the medical assistant took him back. He stopped at a vitals station where the medical assistant measured his vital signs, recorded them in Taylor's chart, and took him back to an exam room. A few minutes later, a man in a white coat entered the room. He was young, African-American, and with a perpetual smile on his face.

"Hi, I'm Dr. Williams," he said. "They say you cut your finger. Let's see what we have here. May I take a look?"

Taylor extended the thumb, holding the gauze pressed against it. Dr. Williams lifted a corner of the gauze and a tiny spurt of blood arced over his thumb and landed on the floor. Dr. Williams pressed the gauze back on the cut.

"Looks like you sliced open a small arteriole," he said. "Quite the bleeder. But not to worry. We'll numb it and throw a little suture or two and you'll be OK. Come back in a week and we'll take out that suture."

"OK, OK, OK," he said, first to the doctor and the second and third time, to whoever resided in his head.

Dr. Williams was back in a few minutes. Taylor sat in a chair and extended his hand. Dr. Williams lifted the gauze and swabbed the area with an alcohol wipe, holding pressure on the cut. When he released pressure, the bleeding started again.

"I'm going to inject some numbing medicine," Dr. Williams said. "It has something in it that should also slow the bleeding a little."

He took a small syringe with a tiny needle and injected a little local anesthetic on both sides of the cut. Taylor winced a little but did not move. After two minutes of holding pressure, Dr. Williams took out a suture mounted on a small, curved needle. With a small tool that looked like a needle-nose pliers, he guided the needle through the edges of the cut with the hemostat and tied off the suture. Most of the bleeding stopped almost immediately. He placed a second suture next to the first and as soon as he tied it off, the bleeding stopped. He smeared some antiseptic ointment on the cut, covered it with clean gauze, and placed a sterile wrap around the thumb.

"There, good as new," he said. "Don't forget. Come back next week, OK?"

"OK, OK, OK," Taylor said, holding his left thumb out.

Taylor smiled as he left the clinic, holding his thumb out like he was trying to hitch a ride. Dr. Williams finished the brief note about the encounter. There was not much to write because except for his head and his left thumb, there was nothing wrong with the twenty-eight-year-old Taylor Potts.

*   *   *

As Taylor shuffled out of the clinic and made his way back to his spot on the side of the road, searching for his uneaten can of food, the IT guy at Second Chance watched him from a back window. He looked over the electronic medical record for a few minutes. He picked up the phone and pressed a few buttons.

He listened to the other end and then said, "Yes, I'm sure."

He spoke again for a few seconds and then hung up. He opened a drawer in his desk, took out a small box, put it into the pocket of his blazer, and walked out of the clinic.

*   *   *

Later that evening, Taylor sat at his usual haunt, under the Interstate 30 overpass, engaged in a voluble discussion with the imaginary inhabitants in his head. He had missed his usual foraging at the restaurant dumpsters since he was at the clinic. He was hungry and decided to head to one of the soup kitchens.

As he was about to shuffle off, a black car pulled up alongside the curb. A window rolled down, and the driver leaned out.

"Hey, Taylor?" the man said.

"Yeh, that's me," Taylor replied.

"You hungry?"

"Yeh."

"Why don't you hop in? I'll get you something to eat."

"Who are you?" Taylor asked.

"I work at the Second Chance clinic. You went there earlier today," the man replied. "I felt bad you waited there for so long and wondered if you missed a meal."

Taylor did not remember that he had been there that long, but he was hungry. He got into the car. The man shifted the car into drive, and they pulled out. As they drove down the road, the driver chatted amiably, asking Taylor what he liked to do and what he liked to eat. They arrived at an intersection as it turned red. The shadows had lengthened, and some streetlights flickered to life.

The man reached into his pocket and took out a keychain. He started to twirl it. There was something fluffy attached to the end. Taylor stared at it in fascination, almost hypnotized by its metronomic quality. The man noticed

Taylor's fascination and kept up the twirling. The light turned green, and the car moved on. A few blocks later, they had driven out of the populated areas near downtown Dallas and the traffic on the road became sparse. They headed toward the Trinity River. At the next stoplight, there was a sudden movement as the driver lunged toward Taylor with his right arm. Taylor felt a sharp sensation in his left forearm. Within a few seconds, his vision became blurry. Between the driver's seat and door, the man grabbed another syringe and jabbed it at Taylor's left forearm. Taylor felt the sharp needle, but he had difficulty jerking his arm away. He slumped against the passenger door. The man took out a wad of cloth and held it against Taylor's face. Taylor blacked out.

*   *   *

The light turned green, and Jonas drove the rest of the short distance, past several warehouses, to a lot. He turned right and drove straight to what looked like an abandoned shed. Taylor stirred, and Jonas jabbed him again with the two syringes. As he pulled up to the shed, there was a sound of a motor. It was a generator, and it was on. He drove around to the back and into the shed. Two large industrial floor lights had been set up on pedestal stands. Inside the shed was a pickup truck with a camper top and next to the pickup was a table with a smooth metal top, some metal boxes that now made a bubbling sound, and various surgical tools hung on the wall. A man stood next to the table. Jonas motioned him to come over.

The second man opened the passenger door of the car and the two men struggled to get Taylor out. Taylor was a deadweight. With difficulty, the two of them positioned Taylor on the table. Jonas jabbed Taylor again with both syringes. Taylor did not move. The two men rolled Taylor on his right side and pulled his legs up so he would maintain the position without assistance.

"Let's get to work," the second man said.

He reached up to a shelf and took down a case. He opened it to reveal several surgical scalpel handles gleaming in the light. He donned a pair of surgical gloves. He opened a smaller box inside the case and with a pair of forceps, took out a surgical blade and attached it to one of the handles. The first man pulled up Taylor's shirt to reveal his left flank. The second man placed the scalpel along the left side of Taylor's stomach and traced a line from front to back. In the scalpel blade's wake, the skin parted to reveal deeper tissue that immediately turned red from the laceration of many deeper small blood vessels. The second man continued to work without talking. In a scant two minutes, the left kidney lay exposed. He clamped the vessels in two places and transected them between the clamps. The kidney slipped out with ease. Jonas opened the lid of one tank in which a liquid bubbled. The second man placed the kidney in the tank and shut the lid. They rolled Taylor over and the second man performed the same procedure on the right side. After the right kidney was also out and placed in its tank, they rolled Taylor on his back. They thought Taylor may have winced, and the second man motioned to Jonas to jab him again.

All this had taken place without a word being spoken. Now the second man spoke.

"Let's load him in the truck. Hurry up. I need these by tomorrow morning for the next phase."

Jonas loaded the metal boxes into his car. There was a small oxygen tank attached to the boxes. Each box was plugged into a small power pack that was also loaded into the car.

"Good," the second man said. "I have thirty minutes of power for the oxygenator."

"I can manage here," Jonas said.

"OK, but remember," the second man said. "Not like the last time. Don't go to the edge of the river and fire your gun like a dumb ass."

"Hey, it was you that didn't inject him properly," Jonas protested.

"Fine, but go someplace more private, not out in the open next to a jogging trail."

The second man pulled out another syringe and placed the long needle on the left side of Taylor's chest. He pushed it through the ribs directly over the heart. When he was at the right depth, he drew back on the plunger. Dark blood swirled as it mixed with the clear liquid in the syringe. He injected the contents of the syringe directly into the heart and pulled out the syringe.

He climbed into the black car and left with the organs. Jonas dragged Taylor's bleeding corpse into the back of the covered truck and shut the tailgate. Blood had smeared the back of the truck, so he sprayed the back of the truck with a garden hose. He drove out. The black car had turned left to head toward town.

Jonas drove for a mile and arrived at a row of industrial warehouses. He turned between two buildings and cruised around to the back until he saw a dumpster.

Sunday evening, no one around, thought Jonas.

He pulled up next to the dumpster, checked in all directions to make sure no one was around, and clanged open the dumpster lid. He backed the truck until its tailgate was lined up with the edge of the dumpster. He dragged Taylor to the edge of the tailgate and hefted him over and into the dumpster. He pulled the lid shut and drove off.

*   *   *

The clang permeated old Jeremiah Jackson's dreams and he awakened with a start. The early evening sun had disappeared behind the warehouses.

He rolled to the side on his bad hip and staggered to his feet, favoring his bad knee. He limped to the edge of the warehouse and looked around the side.

Some forty yards away, a pickup truck with a camper top, its tailgate open, backed up slowly until it lined up with the edge of a dumpster. A man got out and walked to the back of the truck, facing away from old Jeremiah. He leaned into the truck and started pulling at something. He struggled to drag it to the edge of the dumpster and Jeremiah's eyes widened as he realized it was a body. Sensing he may be in danger if spotted, Jeremiah slunk back behind the warehouse. He dropped to the ground and with a sense of morbid curiosity, peeked around the edge of the building. The man had pulled the dumpster lid shut.

A minute later, the engine started, and the truck drove away.

Jeremiah staggered to his feet and walked over to the dumpster. He lifted the lid and peered in. It was a body. He looked at it for a moment and thought the person was still breathing. He noticed a leg move slightly.

Jeremiah let go of the lid and it clanged shut. He sprinted as fast as his bad hip and bad knee would allow him. He waved frantically as soon as he reached the main road. A police car, parked under a nearby tree, sprang to life and its light bar started flashing. The occupant nosed the vehicle across the road, and it stopped next to Jeremiah.

The window rolled down.

A police officer stuck his head out of the window.

"Anything I can help you with?"

THIRTY-SIX

"Another one, hurry up!" Jick answered his phone, and before he could say hello, Vic was telling him to hurry.

"Another one what?"

"Another murder like the last one."

"What?" Jick cried.

"This one's more recent. Fazio said a homeless guy saw a body being dumped into a dumpster in south Dallas. I'm heading there right now. I'll text you the directions and GPS coordinates if you want to come check it out."

Jick had spent his Sunday doing odd jobs around the house and had already begun the day with a couple of drinks at lunch. For the rest of the afternoon, he had nursed a few more. He shook off the effects, grabbed the backpack with the mask, and raced out to his car, phone clamped to his ear.

Vic filled Jick in on the few details he had as Jick drove to the site. He knew he needed to get there as soon as possible to have any chance of testing if the mask could repeat what it had done with Tiffany Jensen's murder.

He raced as fast as he could. This time, the location was much closer. In an industrial section of Dallas, a homeless guy had witnessed a body being unloaded into a dumpster off the back of a truck. It was Sunday evening and traffic was light. At some sparsely populated intersections, he glanced in both directions and drove through, ignoring the stop signs. At one intersection with a traffic light, he arrived as it turned red. There was no cross-traffic, so he looked in all four directions and ran the red. *No cops, no stops*, he thought.

He made his way to where Vic had told him to go and noticed Vic's car was already there. Vic had just gotten out of his car and jogged over to where a small group had assembled. The usual professionals had arrived to process the crime scene. An officer strung yellow tape around the scene.

Jick noticed Vic introducing himself to the police officers present. He lifted the yellow tape and ducked underneath. Jick parked next to his brother's car. They had already set up a field light next to a dumpster. He was only fifteen feet away from the body. No one paid attention to him, and he reached back and grabbed the backpack. He took out the mask. It appeared to be more alive now. It did not glow as such, but just seemed more "alive", like there was a life force within it. Jick stared at it, stunned, anticipatory excitement mounting over what he might see. He put the mask on.

The same feeling of dizziness and disorientation washes over me. Everything around me is shrouded in gray clouds. Fuzzy gray shadows move in a procession. A few fuzzy human shapes walk by. My head swivels one way and then the other, as if I am in a conversation, but I see no one. One of the fuzzy gray shadows detaches from the procession and pulls up beside me. As I walk by, its shadowy outline coalesces and becomes sharper: a car with its window being rolled down. I detour toward it in response to a summons from the driver and open the passenger door. As I get in, the images sharpen further. Finally, the images sharpen enough to see the driver in silhouette. Now and then, the driver turns to me and says something.

Finally, the car slows, stops. A red glow bathes the dashboard from outside. I see the driver fish something out of his pocket, a key ring with something that looks like a tassel attached to the ring. He idly begins twirling it in his left hand. I stare at it, unable to take my eyes off the object.

The glow from outside turns green and the car moves on. At the next intersection, with a sudden move, the driver lunges at me. He has put away the keychain and has taken something out from the left side of the driver's seat. I look down at my left arm, below my elbow, where a needle has jabbed me. I look at the driver and within a few seconds, my vision blurs. The driver does something with his left hand. He lunges at me and holds a cloth to my face, obscuring my vision. I try to lift my arms to push the cloth away but cannot.

It is blurry and getting blurrier by the second. Another jab at my arm and everything in the car turns darker and darker until it fades to black...

Jick pulled off the mask, drenched in sweat, fighting a wave of nausea. He looked at the mask. It was no longer "alive."

What he had seen in the mask had shocked him to his core. The mannerism he had seen was so familiar and so unexpected he could not believe what he had seen.

Tiffany Jensen's murderer!

It was impossible and made no sense but Tiffany Jensen's murderer and the man who had murdered this vagrant were the same person.

He put the mask back in the backpack. He grabbed a towel out of his backpack, wiped his face, and got out of the car. He tried to go over to where Vic stood with the forensics guys. One of the police officers blocked his access.

"Sorry, sir, no bystanders allowed," he said.

"It's OK, Carl," Vic called out. "This is my brother. He's a physician. He's been helping me with some of my story writing, to get the medical stuff straight."

"Oh, OK." Carl waved Jick through.

"Did you run all the way here?" Vic asked, glancing at his brother's face.

"Feels like it," Jick said, without elaborating.

The body lay in a twisted heap on the ground. Two technicians had managed to pull it out of the dumpster.

"A homeless guy was having a nap around the side of the building," Vic said, indicating Jeremiah, who was standing by engaged in an animated discussion with one of the detectives.

"He spotted someone trying to get rid of the body," said one of the detectives. "He swears he saw the guy breathe and move a leg but by the time we got here, he had expired."

The detectives rolled the body to a supine position. Jick knelt by the body, his right knee protesting. It was still warm. A cursory glance at the body revealed a similar scene as the Paul Albrecht murder. The peaceful expression, the lateral incisions over the kidneys, it was all there. This time, there was no bullet wound on the chest. Jick squinted in the light and noticed a puncture wound on the chest. Jick's knees creaked and popped as he stood.

He knew from what he had seen in the mask that the murderer injected something into his victims to knock them out first and then murdered them. *At least they didn't feel pain*, he thought grimly. It appeared this victim had died more recently, and he had gotten to the scene sooner, so he had been able to see more in the mask.

After they completed the work of crime scene processing, two forensics technicians loaded the body into a body bag and carried it to one of the waiting vans. There was nothing else to see at the crime scene, so they left.

After Jick got into his car, he glanced at the mask. It was again drab, lifeless.

As he drove home, his mind reeled from what he had seen while wearing the mask. The mysterious person who had shot Tiffany Jensen from the back seat of her car had the same mannerism as the person who had been in the car driving this latest victim around, most likely to his death. It was also likely this same person had murdered Paul Albrecht. Jick could not put any of this together. No one else knew of this connection between two unrelated murders. Nor could he tell anyone without sounding like a kook. He needed to figure this out. Before more victims faced a gruesome death.

On his way home, on an impulse, he decided to go to a movie. He wanted a complete distraction from the recent events so he could gain a new perspective. He picked a random matinee thriller and tried to focus on the plot of the movie. It was a partial success, as the day's events kept intruding on the plot. The plot was enthralling enough that by the end of the movie, he had forgotten about the case. But as soon as he got into his car, the mental image of the murderer twirling the object in his left hand crashed into his thoughts again.

THIRTY-SEVEN

The twin cones of light from Jick's headlights swept over his garden as he turned into his driveway. He pulled into the garage and turned off the engine. The chorus of chirping crickets mingled with the ticking sound of the engine as he exited his car. The sound of the garage door clattering shut drowned out the sounds as he went into the house. Jick did not think he could sleep; he felt too wound up from the excitement of the evening. The distraction of the movie had not helped much. His head still reeled from what he had seen replayed in the mask.

He surveyed the contents of the freezer and took out a TV dinner. It was too late to order anything, and he was too tired to do anything more than heat something in the microwave. He stared at the hypnagogic effect of the turntable until the microwave dinged. *Not quite Sam's cooking,* he thought as the aroma of the TV dinners permeated the kitchen.

He poured a glass of wine and tried to think this through. Two murders, one a crime of passion, a gunshot to the chest, and the other, a methodical drugging, killing and gutting with removal of organs. What was the connection? Given the *modus operandi*, there was no doubt the earlier murder of Paul Albrecht was also by the same person. It was unlikely the police had made the connection between the killings. His vision becoming blurry while watching through the mask seemed to confirm his educated guess that a combination of injectable and inhaled drugs knocked out the victims. The most likely combination was ketamine, succinylcholine, and ether or chloroform.

He thought about telling the police about this but realized it was not possible at present. There was no plausible way he could know the same man murdered Tiffany Jensen as well as one, and most likely two, homeless men. And no plausible way that he could tell anyone that he donned an ancient mask and saw the final moments of someone's life. If he had been told that a few weeks ago, he would have had the person committed himself! And if an anesthesiologist said that? People would think he had been sniffing some of his chemicals.

Perhaps an anonymous tip? The movie's protagonist had planted ideas about maintaining anonymity online. But to whom would he send an anonymous and untraceable email? He decided the most logical recipient should be Vic. He was sure Vic would notify his buddy Fazio on the police force and it would get things moving.

He spent the next fifteen minutes creating a new e-mail account using fictitious names. He sent a cryptic three-liner to his brother.

Tell the police to check if the Tiffany Jensen murder from a few weeks ago has any connection to the murders of those two homeless guys. You will not regret it. They were done by the same guy.

There. That should get his brother's investigative mind racing.

Jick was not sure how far the police had gotten in their investigation of the Tiffany Jensen murder. Certainly, by now they would have checked out her immediate family, friends, and coworkers. Since he had heard nothing on the news about a suspect being held for that crime, likely everyone had an alibi. So there had to be someone else in her wider circle of friends, acquaintances, colleagues, or relatives who had enough of an axe to grind with her they would want to murder her. How would that person have any remote connection to two murders of homeless men, especially in the horrific manner in which they had died? It made little sense. *At least I'm doing what I can to help the police,* he thought with some satisfaction.

THIRTY-EIGHT

The setting sun illuminated the Dallas skyline in a radiant orange-pink as Jick headed home on Friday evening. He had a long and exhausting day and he looked forward to his first glass of wine. Mireille had taken the day off as she had some relatives from Canada visiting, so Jick could not ask if she wanted to go out on a Friday night. And, he was not sure he wanted to anyway as it had been an interminable day; he had covered the pediatric ENT room again. Working in that room was the short straw and every time he covered it, he came home exhausted. He felt they should have a department policy that the older anesthesiologists with the most seniority should be exempt from covering pediatric ENT. He resolved to mention it at the next staff meeting.

The murder of the second man had been five days ago, and he had been so busy at work he had little time to think about it.

He pulled into his garage and got out. He went into the house and sat at the edge of his bed with a sigh. Shoes and socks came off, and he lofted the socks in a high arc into the laundry hamper. Work clothes came off and followed suit. He washed his hands, splashed water on his face, and headed to the wine fridge for a bottle. He started mulling over his dinner options.

He switched the television on and noted that it was almost six-thirty. Jeopardy time. He thought back to Vic's comment about being a nerd. He was right. He was an aging nerd. He was not ashamed of it. He enjoyed learning things for the sake of learning them. Having a deep well of general knowledge at his disposal had been helpful and had made him a well-rounded person. Not that it had paid off, he sadly reflected. No big winnings on Jeopardy and no one in his life to sit and watch the program with him either.

He shook off his gloomy introspection and opened a bottle of wine. He poured a glass and sank into the couch. Jeopardy had begun. The first category was "State Capitals" and Alex Trebek read out the first clue.

"This is the only state capital with three words in its name."

Jick said, "Salt Lake City."

One contestant buzzed in successfully while one of the others clicked his button in a rapid-fire pattern in desperation.

"Salt Lake City," she said.

Before they revealed the next clue, his stomach growled, reminding him it was time to eat. He pulled himself out of the couch, right knee protesting, and walked to the kitchen drawer where he kept a stack of menus. As he started leafing through the stack, his phone rang. It was Vic.

"Hey, old man, what's up?" Vic asked.

"Nothing. I got home, poured a glass of wine, and I'm chilling on the couch watching Jeopardy."

"Figures you would watch Jeopardy."

"Are you doing anything?" Jick said.

"No. Sam's gone out with one of her friends. Betty. You don't know her. Sam has been more stressed and anxious about the baby thing. And Betty is having problems with her husband and wanted to hang out with Sam to talk about life and the universe over drinks. They are at a downtown bar somewhere."

"Want to come over?" Jick asked.

"Sure. That's why I called."

"Want to bring dinner?" Jick asked.

"Hmm, can't pass up that deal. Sure. What do you feel like?"

"I haven't had good Indian food in a while; I just have TV dinner stuff. How about Royal Curry House since it's by your house?"

"OK," Vic said. "I'll get some stuff and head over."

Jick went back to watching Jeopardy. Alex Trebek chatted with the contestants after the first commercial break. Vic arrived twenty minutes later. He walked in the door carrying a large brown paper sack. The aroma from the sack was noticeable in an instant. Jick's mouth watered, and his stomach growled with insistence. Vic glanced at the TV as he walked into the kitchen.

"Nerd alert," he said, putting the bag down on the kitchen counter.

"Pour yourself a glass," Jick said, ignoring the gibe. Vic poured himself a glass and came into the living room.

"If you don't mind, I will go ahead and start eating," Jick said. "I'm famished."

"Go ahead. I'll join you as soon as I finish this first glass of wine." He plopped down on a couch.

Jick examined what Vic had brought. There was chicken tikka masala, shrimp vindaloo, cucumber raita, spinach paneer, and samosas. Naan and basmati rice rounded out the meal.

"Man, this looks good," he said.

He served himself and sat down. He savored the first bite and waved a thumbs-up at Vic.

Vic took a sip of his wine. For the next few minutes, they watched Jeopardy. Jick's fund of knowledge was far better than Vic's.

There was a question about the number of states that border Canada.

"Twelve," said Vic, staring at an imaginary map in the air.

"Thirteen," Jick said. "You probably forgot Alaska."

"Damn." It was thirteen.

Finally, after Alex Trebek had asked the last Jeopardy question and the closing credits rolled, Jick asked his brother a question.

"Anything new with this latest murder investigation?"

"Very little," Vic said. "They don't even know his name. Of course, it's only been five days since they found him. They did one of those 'Have You Seen This Missing Person' things in the local newspaper yesterday and today, but so far, no luck. From what little I got from Fazio, his fingerprints did not show up in the database either, so he is not a habitual criminal. Most likely he was a mental case and lived on the streets.

"As I'm sure you know, mental illness is difficult to treat, and we have limited resources. I have written a couple articles on the subject, and it is a real social issue. Many hospitals, lacking access to psychiatric beds, turn patients out as soon as they are physically able to be discharged. Families don't want mentally people at home and the bar to push them out of the house and fend for themselves is low. Many of them become chronically homeless. If you look at aggregated data from multiple studies, it's safe to assume that about a third of homeless people are mentally ill. That is much, much higher than the general population."

As Vic talked, Jick ate a few more bites of the delicious repast.

Vic continued. "They found one clue, however. His left thumb was sutured from a recent injury. There was clean dressing over it. So that means he had to have sought treatment somewhere. But it could be in any of several urgent cares and emergency rooms, so digging around will take some time. I'm sure they will ask nearby hospitals and urgent cares to run a database search of their records for the billing code for sewing a laceration in the past few days. Or he may not have gone to an urgent care or ER at all. He could have gone to a regular doctor's office, so that makes the haystack that much bigger."

"There is some organizing behind this," Jick said. "There has to be. These are normal-sized guys and yet someone knocked them out and took out their organs with surgical skill. That cannot happen just anywhere.

"What I don't get is the 'why' part of this. I don't get the impression this is a serial killer. It's someone, or more than one person, harvesting organs. But for what? They cannot use them for transplantation through any licensed facility as UNOS does not accept any old organ. It would be exceedingly difficult to ship them out of the country, although I suppose they could do it in a clandestine fashion.

But if organ harvesting was the goal, why not go to some Third World country where it is easier to cover up this sort of thing? So, what does this person or persons want with these organs?"

"What's UNOS?" Vic asked.

"United Network for Organ Sharing," Jick explained. "A quasi-government organization that organizes and maintains the organ transplantation database."

"Well," Vic said. "They found one on the Trinity Skyline Trail and the other in a dumpster in an industrial area. But that doesn't mean they died nearby. And even if the murders did take place nearby, it is a sizeable area to search. I didn't get any pictures or anything else about this murder. Since they don't know who he is or where he lives, they have essentially no place to start."

Jick refilled their wine glasses.

"I'm getting some dinner," Vic said. "That delicious smell is overpowering me."

He went into the kitchen to serve himself. He returned and sat back on the couch.

"You know, Jick," Vic said, "I think I will start doing some investigating on my own."

"How so?"

"I don't know. Snoop around. I think I'll start near where they found the bodies and work outward, visiting areas where the homeless hang out and asking questions, showing pictures of them, talking to people, etc. Someone must have known this guy. I'll try to look like one of them."

"It is an extensive area," Jick said. "The bodies were found some miles apart."

"I know. But I have to start somewhere. Hope I find something before there's a third murder."

Jick had not thought of that.

Vic knew Jick was exhausted after his strenuous day at work. By ten o'clock, they wrapped up their evening. Vic offered to leave all the leftovers.

"I'm married to a marvelous cook," he said with a smile, "so you can have the leftovers. It was wonderful stuff."

"Thanks for the dinner," Jick said. "Do I owe you?"

"No, of course not," Vic said. "Well, I'm heading out."

"Sounds good. I'll pick up the tab next time."

Jick put the leftovers away. *It'll taste great tomorrow,* he thought. Indian curries taste great for a few days as most of them are slow cooked for the rich flavor. Chinese food, much of which is stir-fried, tastes best on the day they make it when the vegetables are crispy and tender. By day two, the vegetables are mushy, and the flavor is not as good. Except hot and sour soup. That tastes great on day two or three.

Shortly after Vic left, Jick turned in for the night. As he lay in bed, he realized he had forgotten to steer the conversation with Vic to ask him about any earlier murders that had taken place in the city. If Vic had seen the email Jick had sent him about the connection with Tiffany Jensen's murder and taken it seriously, he would have mentioned it. He decided he may have to resend it the next day.

He fell asleep with a satisfied sigh after the scrumptious meal they had had.

THIRTY-NINE

Vic sat at the kitchen counter, stirring his coffee. Sam had gone to work earlier than usual. The microwave dinged as Vic's croissant sandwich of eggs, sausage and cheese was ready. He stared into space as he munched his way through the sandwich, thinking about the murders.

Two men murdered, both homeless. The media had not yet latched onto these stories as much more than a footnote. The police's official statement was, in each case, simply that a homeless man was found dead. Vic had been asked to not reveal more circumstances at this point, and he had honored that to retain his strong connections with the force. If this was the start of a serial killer, it would be all the more reason to get on top of things as soon as possible. But it would be difficult. Homeless men leave very little of a trail on the grid. With their nomadic lifestyle and no permanent address, tracking their movements and whom they interacted with would be challenging. And homeless people are not eager to talk to police officers. It would be difficult.

Vic decided to do some investigating on his own. He bought a giant wall map of Dallas County and pinned it to the wall in his office. He looked at the area around downtown. The Trinity Skyline Trail was where they found the first body and the second body was in the dumpster.

"They found them here," he said, marking a small black "X" near where the perpetrator dumped the two victims' bodies. He consulted his notes and looked back at the map.

He marked the map with a different colored X to identify areas where the homeless congregated. He planned to drive around, making an arbitrary decision to start with the area closest to the Trinity River and moving outward. Dallas had many bridges and overpasses that served as a natural habitat for the homeless. He identified five likely targets to focus his search.

Later that night he told Sam his plans. He decided he would not shave for a few days, not shower, and not use deodorant either.

"You'll sleep in the guest room," Sam teased.

For the next three days, he did not shower, shave, or use deodorant. It bothered his sense of hygiene not to shower daily. He also slept in the guest room as it seemed to be the courteous thing to do. On the third day, he dressed in shabby clothes and made his way to the first area he had chosen from his map. He parked a few blocks away and began walking down the road. Soon, he approached the first likely place. Several homeless people milled about.

Vic walked up to an older man and sat down on a grassy embankment. The man turned to look at him. He had scraggly gray hair and one eye was glassy and unfocused. He tracked Vic with his good eye.

"Hi," Vic said.

"So?" the man replied.

"How ya doing?" Vic asked.

The man scowled and turned away.

Vic sighed and got to his feet. He shuffled over to another group. They seemed receptive to his opening questions. After a few minutes of idle chitchat, he asked them if they knew Paul. Most homeless were on a first name basis unless there was more than one person with the same name. This group did not have a "Paul" in their circle. He produced the pictures.

"Are you a cop?" one of them asked with suspicion.

"No. I'm trying to find out what happened to Paul and this other guy."

"What happened to them?" asked one of the other men.

"I don't know," Vic said. "Someone killed them, and we need to find out what happened and who did it."

"They was killed? Think someone's going after us 'cause we on the streets?"

"I don't think so. I'm a reporter, by the way. I would much appreciate any help. Look at these pictures and see if you recognize any of them."

He passed the pictures around, but no one recognized Paul Albrecht or the other man.

"Hey, so you're a reporter, right?" one man asked Vic. "Since you're a reporter, can you do something about us?"

"What do you mean?"

"Can you let folks know there's a lot of homeless and if y'all could get a place for us to stay and get a meal, it would be great."

"Well, I'll see what I can do," Vic said. He was not getting anywhere fast. No one knew Paul or the other guy. After a few fruitless hours of walking around, he tabled the effort for the day.

The next day, he parked in a different neighborhood. With his shabby clothes and lack of deodorant along with facial stubble, he looked more and more like one of them. As he emerged from his car, the contrast between his air-conditioned car and the weather outside was stark. As soon as he stepped out of his car, the heavy air settled around him like a warm blanket. He could feel sweat trying to push through his pores.

He had the same fruitless experience as his first day. He had made a mental note to not divulge his occupation. Once again, no one seemed to know Paul Albrecht or the other man. By the end of the day, his dogs barked something fierce. He climbed into his car and took off his shoes. Trying to ignore the overpowering smell, he massaged his feet to relieve the aching.

The next morning, he awakened in the guest room as he had done for the past few days. *I can even smell myself*, he thought distastefully. He grabbed his wallet and keys and headed out. He did not even want to go into the kitchen and make coffee. He made a mental note that he would have a shower soon but would hold off shaving until he gave up this quest for information. He stopped at a drive-through for a large coffee and a breakfast sandwich.

On the fourth day of the mind-numbing task of driving around, parking, wandering, querying, moving on, and becoming frustrated, he was in Deep Ellum. He parked on a side street and got out. On each day, he had dressed in the same shabby jeans and rumpled shirt, not shaving, and not using deodorant. He wandered around with the two pictures in his hip pocket, asking random people if they had heard of the recent murders and if they recognized any of the men. He mentioned Paul's name and asked if they hung around the area. He was met with the same suspicion, denials, blank stares, and outright hostility from a few.

He began to think he was on a wild goose chase. Or the haystack was larger than he had anticipated. It was possible these murders took place far away from here and whoever did it drove the bodies to the Trinity Skyline Trail and the dumpster just to throw off the scent.

At lunchtime on the fourth day, he saw an older woman with a rusted shopping cart sitting on the edge of the sidewalk where a patch of grass met the concrete sidewalk.

"Hi," he said. "I'm Vic."

The old lady fixed her rheumy eyes at Vic for a long time, longer than a normal quick appraisal.

"So what?" she said. "I'm Phyllis."

He asked a few random questions and then brought up the subject of Paul Albrecht and the second victim. He took the pictures out of his pocket.

"Yeah, I know them," she said. "Don't need to see no pictures."

He had expected another denial and for a moment, was unsure if he had heard what he thought she said.

"What? Are you sure?"

He put the pictures back in his pocket and sat down next to her. His feet ached from walking around all day, and he relished the brief respite. He feet signaled their appreciation as he curled and uncurled his toes in his shoes.

"They from around here," she continued, pointing to the Interstate 30 underpass next to Deep Ellum.

"I warned them."

"Warned them? About what?"

"Warned them not to go to that place. Told them if they went there, they should be careful not to get a finger stuck up their ass," she cackled.

"Oh," he said, a little deflated. *Her elevator does not make it to the top floor,* he thought. *Another dead end.* He hoped she had something a little more concrete. He was about to stand but his feet signaled otherwise. *Maybe a few more minutes.* He continued the conversation.

"Where did they go?"

"To that clinic, Second Chance."

"Second Chance?"

"Yeh, both of them went to Second Chance."

"When did they go missing?"

"I don't know, maybe the same day, maybe one, maybe two days after they was at the clinic."

"Did they go on the same day?" He wanted to take off his shoes and massage his feet. He continued curling and uncurling his toes.

She thought for a minute, her eyes drifting up as if counting the days on an imaginary calendar in the sky. "No. They went about a week apart."

"And then what?"

"And then nothing. They just disappeared. Maybe they moved someplace, but I don't think so."

"Why not?"

"Because they from around here," she said matter-of-factly. "They got no place else to go."

"Do you know why they went there?"

"Paul felt like crap with a fever and Taylor cut his finger," Phyllis said. "Paul had been feeling bad and then he started coughing. Coughing, coughing, coughing. Decided he had enough. Taylor cut open his finger, and it was bleeding, bleeding, bleeding. Wouldn't stop."

"The second guy's name was Taylor?" he asked. *Maybe this is not a dead end after all.*

The police had not identified him yet, so knowing his first name, if this batty woman was right, was a huge break. The ache in his feet receded as his attention focused on the conversation.

"Taylor, yes, yes. Don't know his last name."

Vic wanted to confirm that crazy Phyllis was talking about the two victims. He took the pictures out of his pocket again. He held them out to her.

"This them?" he asked.

Phyllis looked at the pictures.

"Told you I don't need to see no pictures. But yep, that's them. Paul and Taylor."

"So they both went to Second Chance, about a week apart, and after they went there, they disappeared? On the same day or a day or two later."

"Yep. Do you know what happened to them?"

"Were they friends of yours?"

"We's all friends and family here. Unless you take something that ain't yours. Then we ain't friends."

"Phyllis, I'm sorry to tell you they're both dead."

"Dead?" Phyllis looked shocked.

"They were killed. I'm trying to find out who did it and why."

"What happened?"

Vic did not want to divulge too many details.

"I can't go into that. But they were killed, and we need to find out who did it."

Phyllis leaned back on the grass.

"Poor guys. I did warn them to be careful or they'd get a finger stuck up their ass." She cackled again but Vic could see her eyes glistened. She dragged a grimy sleeve across her face and sniffled. He got to his feet.

This was a definite, solid lead. Both Paul and Taylor had gone to Second Chance, and both died soon afterwards. Vic also remembered the important clue from the second victim: the sutured cut on his finger. It made sense he had it treated at Second Chance. He felt a slight throb of excitement at this development. He made a mental note to stop by the clinic for a visit as soon as possible.

"Thanks for your help. I'll be heading over there to check it out. Where is it?"

She pointed north.

"That way, maybe two, maybe three blocks, on the left."

"Thanks." He was about to leave when she stopped him.

"Got anything to eat?" she asked. "Or money?" She hoped for a reward for her information. After their conversation, she already knew he was not one of them, despite his appearance.

"Hang on a second," he said. "Wait here and I'll be back."

He walked up the block until he saw a fast-food restaurant. He did not want to go in because of his unkempt appearance and the odor that trailed in his wake. He approached the drive-through window. There was a sign stating there would be no service for walk-ups. He knocked on the window. A young man in a dark blue uniform and a paper hat waved him away. He pointed at the sign.

Vic flashed some money. He also showed the man his driver's license through the window.

"Hey, I'm a reporter. I'm dressed like this to get some information from some homeless people around here," he said. "I didn't want to come in like this because I smell pretty bad. Haven't showered in a few days. Let me have one of your burger combos right quick. I'm using it to get some info from a woman over there, a block away."

The fast-food worker looked at him with suspicion but relented after seeing the driver's license and the money. He slid the window open, and the aroma of French fries rolled out of the window and over Vic like a warm olfactory embrace. He ordered an extra burger and fries for his drive home.

Vic paid for the meal with a twenty and accepted the meal and the change through the drive-through window. Vic paused and looked through the window at the milkshake machine.

"Give me one of your chocolate shakes too, please." He paused. "And make it a large."

He paid for the shake and stuffed the rest of the change into his pocket.

"Thanks."

He went back to Phyllis and handed her the meal. He also gave her the change from the twenty.

"Here you go."

"Thanks." She stuffed the money out of sight, casting a furtive glance one way and then another.

"Folks steal stuff when you're sleeping. If they know you have stuff. Like money," she explained. "Then we ain't friends."

He handed her the chocolate shake, and her eyes widened.

"You're OK," she said. "So who are you?"

"Just a guy doing some investigating. I'm trying to find out what happened to Paul and Taylor. I'm going to Second Chance to get more information. Thanks for the tip."

Phyllis looked alarmed. "Don't let them stick a finger up your ass," she warned as she took the burger out of the bag. She peeled the paper wrapper off the straw and let go of the wrapper. It fluttered away and swirled into a corner with other debris. She pushed the straw through the top of the milkshake and took a deep draw on the chocolate shake. She sighed in satisfaction.

He went back to his car parked a few blocks away and got in. He started the car and turned on the air conditioner.

"I'm an idiot," he said out loud. He had already known after the Albrecht murder that Paul Albrecht's usual haunt was in Deep Ellum. And Jick had told him he had bought him a cheeseburger there once. Vic realized he should have begun his search here rather than near where they found the bodies.

I could have saved myself days of smelling bad, he thought. He ate his burger and fries, savoring the meal and the cool air. He threw the debris from his meal into a nearby trash can. He slowed as he drove past Second Chance but decided he would come back for a visit after a shower. He might get more information if he looked more presentable rather than as a homeless bum. He headed home.

FORTY

Vic noticed Sam's car was home when he arrived. He went in through the back door, yelled "I'm home" and ran upstairs. He undressed and jumped into the shower. He had a long and luxuriating hot shower, allowing the water to bounce off him, making sure every nook and cranny of his body felt the warm water. He felt the accumulated grime of six days of investigative work wash away.

This feels so damn good, he thought.

While in the shower, he ruminated about these murders. Both men had gone to Second Chance for minor problems and within a day, someone killed both men. This was a solid lead and not a lead the police could discover easily. He had been lucky in stumbling across Phyllis. He was rather proud of his investigative work. He decided not to put off visiting Second Chance and planned to go back as soon as he finished his shower. He debated notifying Fazio but decided to visit the clinic first.

He turned off the water and stepped out. Clouds of vapor hung in the air and covered the mirror after his long shower. He turned on the exhaust fan and opened the door. He wiped off a part of the mirror with his towel and followed his shower with a shave. He splashed aftershave on his face, savoring its bracing citrus-flavored smell. He applied deodorant and stepped out of the bathroom, feeling fresh. He stepped on the carpet in his bedroom and curled and uncurled his toes, enjoying how it felt after several days of walking around several neighborhoods in uncomfortable shoes. It was three o'clock in the afternoon.

He had a towel wrapped around his waist and with a start realized Sam had entered without a sound and stood in the room looking at him. She walked over and sat at the edge of the bed, looking coquettishly at him. She pointed at him, palm up, her right index finger outstretched and pointing at him. She curled her index finger slowly, back and forth, motioning him over to her.

"Come here, stinky boy," she said. "You've had six days to investigate this case. Now investigate this."

He walked over to her obediently. She reached up and pulled off his towel. He stood there naked. Beads of water still glistened on his shoulders and his hair was still spiky and wet. She reached up and fondled him, holding his now erect penis, and pulling him closer. He had been so immersed in this investigation he had not realized it had been six days without making love. He allowed her to pull him closer and pretended to trip, falling next to her, pulling her to the bed. She was still clothed.

"OK," she said. "Get to work. Start investigating."

He took his time investigating, unbuttoning this and unzipping that, feeling this and breathing in that. Finally, after immersing all five of his senses in her, he came up for air, "This investigation is almost complete. I have almost found what I'm looking for."

She smiled and bit her lower lip as he rolled over on his back and pulled her on top of him. She pinned his arms to the bed as she smothered him. After six days, it was intense and explosive.

"I felt my eardrums bulge," he said, as he pulled her down for a kiss.

"Mine too," she said, nuzzling against him. "The French call it *la petite mort* for a reason."

After they finished and got dressed, Vic said he planned to go to Second Chance and ask some questions.

"Don't be too late. Dinner will be ready by six."

"But you've already had dessert so dinner may be an anticlimax, so to speak," she smiled and winked at him.

Vic drove to Second Chance, his thoughts once again occupied by the murders. He mulled over some ideas about how to approach the staff with his questions and decided on the direct approach. He parked a block away and walked to the clinic. He pushed open the door and stepped into the waiting room. It was not crowded. A faint body odor greeted his nostrils, now hypersensitive after days spent wandering around with the homeless. The smell emanated from the patient sitting near the door. The receptionist at the check-in counter looked up at him.

"Can I help you?" she asked.

"Maybe," he said. He flashed a smile. "I need some information and hoped you could help me."

"Who are you?" she asked. "And what kind of information do you need?"

"I'm a beat reporter investigating a recent crime." He reached into his pocket.

"Do you recognize these men?" he asked, showing her the two pictures of Paul Albrecht and Taylor Potts.

"Can't say," she said.

"Did they come in here in the past few weeks?"

"We get a lot of patients. I told you I can't say. I can't answer questions about patients."

"This guy, Paul Albrecht, had a cough," he said, pointing to Paul in the picture, "and this other guy, Taylor something, had a cut finger," Vic persisted, now pointing at Taylor.

"I'm sorry, I can't answer any questions."

She continued. "You aren't with the police, right? Do you have a warrant? Do you have a release of information from the patient or, if they're not available, a power of attorney? If the answer to all three questions is no, I can't answer any questions."

"Is there anyone else here I could talk to? Is there a clinic supervisor?" Vic kept up with the questioning, hoping for a break.

"These guys are both dead," he continued. "These are the guys who were in the news, the guys who were found on the Trinity Skyline Trail and in the dumpster with their kidneys cut out. I believe they were both seen here before they died."

He tried a persuasive approach. "Did you know you can reveal anything you want to about them to me since they are both dead?"

Her expression changed to one of irritation. She picked up the phone and murmured a few words to someone. In a few moments, the door opened, and a man came in, twirling a keychain in his left hand. Vic looked at him. Tall, about six-two, medium-tan complexion. The man parked himself behind the receptionist and stood there, twirling the keychain. Some patients in the waiting room had glanced at the mild commotion at the check-in desk.

"Thanks, Jonas," she said. Then, turning to Vic, said, "You must leave now. I can't answer questions about any patients. Period. End of discussion."

"What if this guy kills again?" he said. "Don't you want to prevent another death? Any information you tell me could save a life."

"Leave right now or I'm calling the cops," she said.

"OK, OK," Vic said. "I'm gone. Here's one of my cards. Please call me if there's anything you can think of or if you're allowed to say."

With that, Vic turned, opened the door, and left. Once outside, he smacked his right fist into his open left palm. That was frustrating, he thought. He could tell from the receptionist's body language that she knew the two men. Since he had gotten nowhere, he decided he would mention it to Fazio. It might help the police in their investigation.

*   *   *

"What was all that about?" asked Jonas.

"It was some guy who seemed to think those two homeless guys found murdered on the Trinity Skyline Trail and found in that dumpster were our patients. You know, those guys who had their kidneys taken out."

"He did? Wonder why he thought that?"

"He didn't say, and I didn't ask him."

"Was he a cop?"

"He said he was a reporter, but you never know."

Jonas looked at Vic through the window as he walked away. *How the fuck did this guy connect them to Second Chance so quickly?* The two guys had no family, no friends, nothing. No one knew who they were or where they went. He was determined to find out.

"Well, I'm going back to my cubicle," he said. "If he comes back again, let me know. Oh, and let me have his card."

Jonas took the card and sauntered back to his office. He tossed the card on the desk and then loped down the back hallway, letting himself out the back door. He ran around the corner and saw Vic a block ahead. He quickened his pace and caught up to him.

"Hi there," he called out.

Vic turned around.

"Yes?"

"I overheard the last part of what you and Cindy talked about and asked her after you left."

"And?" Vic asked.

"I want to help. I'm the IT guy at the clinic. I know about patient confidentiality and all that, but these guys are dead, and they were a couple of homeless men, nobody looking out for them, if you know what I mean. If there's anything I can do to stop this guy, it would make me feel better. Say, are you a cop?"

"No, I'm not a cop. I'm a beat reporter. So, those guys were patients at the clinic?"

"Yes," Jonas said. *Good, he's not a cop.*

"One of them came in with a cough and fever and the other guy cut his finger open. Think he needed a few stitches, and he was OK."

"The first guy's last name was Albrecht," said Vic. "Off the top of your head, you wouldn't happen to know the second guy's last name, would you?"

"Potts, I think."

"Potts. Thanks for the info."

"No problem, you're welcome," Jonas said. "Say, how did you know they were patients at our clinic?"

"I got a lucky break," Vic said. "I drove around town where the homeless hang out, asking questions, getting replies that cops can't, and I ran into a crazy woman earlier today who talked to both of them on the morning they came here before someone got to them."

"I see," Jonas said. *So the cops had not made this connection yet.*

He wondered if he should ask Vic if he knew the name of the crazy woman. She was also a loose end. He decided against it as the chances of her being questioned again were slim to none. And he did not want to raise Vic's suspicions.

"Why do you think she was crazy?"

"Oh, you should have seen her and heard her talk. I didn't think she knew Paul and Taylor until I showed her their pictures. Then I realized even though she was nuts, she was right about them coming here."

Jonas shrugged. "Oh, OK. I don't have any more information about these guys. But if I find out anything else, I'll let you know."

"OK, no worries," said Vic. "Thanks for your help." They shook hands and parted.

He headed to his car. Jonas watched Vic until he got into his car. Then Jonas walked back to the clinic. *Shouldn't have done those guys so soon after they were here*, he thought. *The cops can't know there's anything in common with those guys. Or I'm fucked.*

FORTY-ONE

Vic had planned to drive home when Sam called.

"Hi, honey," Sam said. "I'm going to leave a bit later and hang out with Betty again. She called. She is still stressed about life. I'll leave your dinner in the warming drawer."

"Oh, ok, that's fine," Vic said. "In that case, I'll stop by the office to review my case files. I might email Fazio about going to Second Chance."

Now Vic sat at his desk and stared at the computer screen. He opened his email program and quickly scanned his Junk Mail folder to sort through any important mail that may contain. He had received an anonymous e-mail asking him to investigate a connection between the murders of two homeless men and a seemingly unrelated random killing of a woman in her SUV. The email was in his Junk Mail folder and Vic had not seen it for a few days. And then he had spotted the subject line: "Important! Connection Between the Murders You're Investigating." Its contents surprised him. *The same person?* He knew that both homeless men lived in the Deep Ellum area and Tiffany Jensen's murder also took place in Deep Ellum. Coincidence? Or something more. He wondered who could have sent it to him.

He decided he would look into the archives of the Tiffany Jensen murder. Her murder had been about a month ago. She was a young homemaker who lived with her husband, Jonas Jensen, in Dallas. They had no kids and no pets.

He decided he would share this development with Sam to see if she had any insight. He also wanted to confirm whether her outing with Betty tonight was really about Betty. Or something else. He picked up the phone and called his house. Sam was still home.

"Hi, honey," he said.

"Hi, Vic," Sam said. "What's up?"

"Wanna hear something weird? You know I've been looking into those murders of the two homeless guys. I was scanning through my Junk folder and there was an email telling me the same guy did the Tiffany Jensen murder. You remember that one? The Deep Ellum murder a few weeks back. That woman who sat in her car and someone shot her?"

"Sort of," Sam said. "It was in the news for a couple of days and then faded out of the news cycle. From what I remember, the police suspected the husband, but nothing came of it. It is still an active investigation. Why would you get an email now to look into it?"

"This email says they are related. Says the same person did all the murders."

"Really? The murder of those homeless guys and the murder of that woman? How are they related?"

"That's what I am hoping to find out. This email may be a hoax but there is no reason for that and why would someone email me rather than the police? So I thought I'd call you to see if you might think of something. I can't see how they're connected."

"That is weird. I can't think of anything helpful. Oh well, I'm heading out in a few minutes."

"So, this thing with Betty tonight. Is it just about Betty or...?" He left it hanging.

A pause.

"I'm fine."

"Sam, there are many options so let's meet with a fertility specialist and see what we can do. Nowadays women are having babies into their fifties."

"I know, I know. We have been trying for so long. And fertility treatments are awfully expensive."

"We'll manage. At least let's meet with a specialist and see what options there are."

"OK, I have to go now."

"All right, I'll see you when you get back. Say hi to Betty from me. Love you."

"Love you too." Sam hung up.

With the number of murders in the United States, the only reason Tiffany Jensen's murder was even newsworthy was because it was a young white woman, murdered in her car while going out for a night on the town. It had faded from the news cycle after a few days. He logged in to his newspaper's archives section and started looking through some articles. He retrieved some articles from other news outlets that had also covered the story and read through them. The police still considered it an unsolved killing.

Tiffany Jensen had gotten dressed in a manner suggesting she had planned to meet someone. Initially, the police did not know why she had not gone to a bar or public meeting place but had pulled into a parking lot in a somewhat unpopulated area of Deep Ellum. As she waited there, ostensibly to meet this mystery person, someone had shot the unfortunate woman while she sat in her car.

Vic kept reading.

After reviewing Tiffany's phone, investigators suspected whoever had murdered Tiffany had most likely been texting her from the back of the car. Her phone's message thread contained two pictures, each of the Deep Ellum sign, visible through her front windshield. The first picture was taken through a piece of fuzzy cloth to make it less obvious that it was the Deep Ellum sign. The second picture was clearer and was also sent from the burner phone. Whoever had murdered Tiffany had wanted to build up a gradual sense of terror. That suggested a crime of passion.

Vic kept reading.

Although the ballistics analysis was inconclusive because the back window was also shattered, indicating someone could have stood outside the SUV and fired the shot from behind it, based on an analysis of pictures sent to Tiffany's phone, the police had concluded the perpetrator probably fired the bullet from inside the car.

That meant someone she knew.

That meant someone who hid in the car when she left her house, lying in the back of the car.

That meant most likely her husband.

Occam's Razor.

Vic kept reading.

Tiffany had been having an affair with someone online, but it was a long-distance affair with suggestive texts and progressively revealing pictures. Several texts on Tiffany's phone gave her directions to the parking lot in Deep Ellum. The police traced the number to a burner phone, but the perpetrator had already deactivated it. The shop where the murderer had bought the phone was identified, but the person who had bought the phone and its minutes had used cash. The store where the phone was purchased had a security camera system. But it was the type that overwrote data every forty-eight hours in a continuous loop. It was useful to identify perpetrators who might rob the store. It was not useful in identifying who had made purchases days later. The articles never identified if investigators had determined who the online paramour was. Certainly, an affair indicated passions and a crime could evolve from it. But he was sure the cops would have already gone that route.

Her husband, Jonas, had an airtight alibi. He worked as a consultant IT specialist for a company that covered several clients, including some clinics around town and the University. His specialty was database and server maintenance and management. On the night of Tiffany's murder, one of his clients at the University had a server crash, and he had been at the site until midnight with the client rebuilding files, a slow and painstaking task. He had been too tired to drive home and had slept on a couch in the lab until the next morning. Surveillance cameras proved those facts. Tiffany was murdered around ten o'clock. The police questioned him, but he denied any knowledge of the murder. He also denied knowing anything about any of her online relationships, if she had any.

The texts on Tiffany's phone had a phone number from the Houston area, presumably the person she had an affair with. That person, with whom she had an online affair, was positively identified by investigators who traced his location and pinpointed it to the Houston area. His phone number was still active, but there was no way he could have committed the murder. He was at home with his wife and children.

No doubt revealing his role in this murder was not good for his marriage, Vic thought.

The police concluded the murderer set the burner phone to spoof Simon's phone so Tiffany would think Simon had texted her to meet in the parking lot. That again focused suspicion on the husband as he was an IT guy and would have the expertise to plan something like this. But, with his alibi, he couldn't have murdered her either. So, for now, Tiffany Jensen's murder was still an unsolved killing. The police had very little else to go on.

His chair creaked as he leaned back. He still did not see how this murder had anything to do with the murders of the two homeless guys.

Vic resumed reading.

Without having much to go on, Vic dug into the Houston angle. He searched for any information about this "Simon" character.

After Tiffany's murder, the police had shown up at Simon's house in Houston one morning after discovering he was the "Simon" with whom she had been sexting. This revelation had led to a row between him and his wife. She had planned to go to New Orleans to visit her mother and the four-day trip turned into a weeklong trip. When she had finally returned a week later, Simon was nowhere to be found. She found his wallet, phone, and keys but he had disappeared. None of the neighbors had seen or heard anything. It was still an open missing persons case.

"Hmph," Vic said out loud. "That's weird. So the most likely suspect in Tiffany's death is her husband. The guy she has been having phone sex with goes missing a few days later. But the husband has an airtight alibi based on the testimony of his client who says they rebuilt a crashed server. The police will investigate if this alibi is as airtight as it seems. To me, the most likely explanation is that beloved hubby discovered his wife catted around. Or planned to. He probably went berserk and murdered the wife and I guess he could have also murdered Simon. I'm sure the police have all this figured out and they are watching the guy. But how does this connect to the murder of two homeless men? I do not see a connection here at all.

"Besides, even if it was the husband, there is no way the husband, an IT guy, would have the know-how to carve open bodies and take out their kidneys. I don't think there's any connection here."

He decided he would email Fazio about the link between the homeless guys and Second Chance.

As he was about to wrap up reading about Tiffany Jensen murder, he noticed that one of the archived articles had a thumbnail link to pictures that had been in the original article about Tiffany Jensen. Vic clicked it, mostly out of curiosity to see what Tiffany had looked like. The picture showed a smiling young couple, probably taken during some formal event, as Tiffany was dressed to the hilt and her husband wore a nice, tailored dark blue suit.

Vic stared at the picture in shock. The smiling face of the husband looked very familiar. In fact, Vic had seen him earlier. *The husband was the IT guy at Second Chance, where both Paul Albrecht and Taylor Potts had gone a few days before their death.*

"Oh, Jesus," thought Vic. He chair creaked as he stared at the picture. He picked up his phone and dialed a number.

FORTY-TWO

Jick had invited Mireille over for dinner and she had accepted, which surprised Jick. Even though their relationship had been plodding along in fits and starts, the overall picture, depressing to Jick, was that she viewed this as more of a platonic friendship rather than as a "friend with benefits," in today's vernacular. In his mind, the age difference was the most likely reason, a significant impediment, the deal breaker. He had already decided that no matter what happened in their relationship, it would not affect them at work. He had realized the age difference probably meant she saw him more as a father figure than romantic interest. *But if that's the case, why did she accept a dinner invite? Oh well, I'll play along and not overthink it.*

For dinner, he had ordered out and had stopped on the way home to pick up the order. Knowing Mireille's fondness for spicy food, he ordered that delicious Chinese food and included an order of kung pao chicken with lots of red boys, and hot and sour soup, and a few other dishes.

She'll eat this spicy food and get all sweaty again, he thought, thinking back to their first lunch together at work. He put that thought out of his mind. *I had better stock up on some beers. Goes better with spicy food.*

Jick stopped at the grocery store and bought two six-packs of microbrew beers that, according to the shelf tags at the store, sported a four- or five-star rating. He surveyed the labels. Both contained higher alcohol at about eight percent. One was a dark beer, and the other an ale. As soon as he got home, he filled a chest with an ice and water slurry and dunked all twelve bottles.

Mireille arrived at about six. She had finished working out and had changed into her usual after work shorts and T-shirt. Jick popped the top off two bottles of beer and handed her one. They clinked the bottles together.

"Here's to more dinners together," he said, keeping it to the point.

The television set was on, broadcasting the evening news. He had put the Chinese food in the warming drawer and the aroma wafted from the kitchen.

"That smells divine," said Mireille. "You didn't make anything, did you?"

"I was up early in the morning and slaved in the kitchen getting it all ready before going to work," he joked. "Actually, no, it's takeaway from my favorite Chinese restaurant in this area. We can eat anytime you want."

"In a little while," she said. "I'm hungry but I want to relax and enjoy a beer or two. By the way, this beer is fantastic." She studied the label on the bottle and made a mental note for future reference.

"I'm glad you like it," Jick said.

They were on their third beer on an empty stomach when Mireille made an unexpected comment.

"One of the reasons I left Canada was a broken relationship."

Jick took a swig of his beer.

"Oh? What happened?"

"It just didn't work out. He was much older than me. But that's not the reason the relationship fizzled."

"How much older?" Jick tried to sound nonchalant.

"He was in his sixties. I'm forty-five."

"Forty-five?" Jick sounded incredulous. "Mireille, you look great for forty-five. I thought you weren't a day over *thirty*-five."

"You're sweet," she said. She leaned over and pecked his cheek. The cloud reappeared under Jick's feet, and he felt like he had levitated.

Jick pulled down another swig of his beer. Things between Mireille and him had taken a sudden turn for the better.

His brain churned as he thought about what to say or do next. As he mulled his options, the phone rang. Vic's name and work phone number flashed on the television screen. Jick excused himself and went to his office to answer the call.

"Hi, Vic."

"Got a minute?"

"Sure. What's up? Oh, but before you start, Mireille's here and we were about to have a drink and then dinner. So yes, you're interrupting."

"Oh," Vic said. "Good for you, old man. I won't be long. I need to tell you something real quick."

Vic told him about the investigative work he had been doing for the past several days and mentioned a happenstance meeting with an old homeless woman named Phyllis. She had told Vic that both Paul Albrecht and the second man, whose first name was Taylor, had gone to the Second Chance clinic for treatment shortly before their murders.

"That's a good lead," Jick said. "Have you told the police yet?"

"No, not yet," Vic said. "I was about to. But I did go to Second Chance to ask some questions. They were tight-lipped because of patient confidentiality. They would not even confirm or deny that Paul and Taylor were patients there.

"Anyway, the major reason I called was because of something else weird, could be an odd coincidence.

"A few days ago, I got an anonymous email from someone," he said. "The sender asked me to investigate a connection between the Tiffany Jensen murder and the murders of those homeless guys. It was in my Junk folder, so I didn't see it for a few days. Anyway, I went through all the archives of articles about the Tiffany Jensen murder, and I think I found something.

"I stumbled across a picture of Tiffany Jensen with her husband. You're not going to believe this. *Her husband is the IT guy at Second Chance.*"

"What?" Jick said. Jick knew the same person had murdered Tiffany Jensen and the two homeless men. Vic had discovered that both homeless men had gone to Second

Chance for treatment and Tiffany Jensen's husband worked there.

Jick had a sudden, terrifying thought as the final piece clicked into place.

"Vic, I want you to think of something. This is important. You met the husband?"

"Yes."

"What was he doing?"

"Nothing," Vic said. "I guess he was in his office and came out when the receptionist called him. He stood there, providing a physical presence as support for her because I was being a nuisance with endless questions. She was almost ready to call the cops. She ordered me out of the clinic, but he ran up to me about a block away and said he wanted to help."

Jick frowned. "He came out of the clinic and caught up with you a block away? What did he want?"

"Nothing much. He said he wanted to help. First, he asked me if I was a cop. I told him I was a reporter. Then he told me why Paul Albrecht and Taylor Potts visited the clinic. He told me Taylor's last name, by the way. He asked me how I figured out they were patients at Second Chance, and I told him I had met that woman, Phyllis."

"Did he have an odd mannerism when he stood there in the clinic? Did he twirl something in his left hand? Think, Vic," Jick said.

Vic paused. "Actually, yes, he had a keychain or something and he took it out of his pocket and started twirling it around in his left hand when he stood behind the receptionist. How do you know about that?"

A sudden cold pang of fear settled in Jick's stomach like a brick. He felt the skin on the back of his neck crawl, accompanied by an involuntary shudder.

"Any chance he knows where you work?"

"He might. I left one of my cards with the receptionist."

"Oh my God. Vic, you need to get out of there right away."

Jick raised his voice.

"Get out of there! Stay on the phone with me, go home, get Sam, and go to a hotel right now. Call the police as you're driving home, don't wait, and tell them you know the IT guy at Second Chance is the also the murderer of those two homeless men who had their kidneys removed. Tell them it's Jonas Jensen, Tiffany Jensen's husband. Go, now!"

*   *   *

Questions cascaded through Vic's mind, but he listened to Jick's advice. He shut his computer, grabbed his bag, and left the office, thundering down the stairs two at a time down to the parking garage, his phone still clutched in his hand. From Jick's reaction, Vic realized he had inadvertently stuck his hand into the hornet's nest by going to Second Chance. Jonas had come out after him to see how much he knew and whether the police had made the connection yet. Vic had revealed that he was a man who knew too much, a loose thread.

His phone was still on, connected to Jick. He stopped talking as the sound of his footsteps echoed on the metal stairs.

"How do you know this about him?" Vic said when he reached the bottom. "I know it's an odd coincidence that Tiffany Jensen's husband works at Second Chance, but how can you be so sure Jonas is the murderer?"

As Vic talked, he arrived at the door to the parking garage. It was the standard metal fire door with an aluminum crash bar. There was a red and white sign affixed to the inside: "Fire Door, Keep Closed." The hinge spring had malfunctioned, and the door had not shut all the way. Since he held his bag in one hand and phone in the other, he spun around and backed into the crash bar, pushing it with his butt, to open it all the way. He spun around again, only to see Jonas Jensen standing there, five feet away, at point blank range, pointing a gun at him. Jonas had to have heard the last thing Vic said into the phone as he backed into the door.

"Oh God, please don't," were Vic's last words.

"What?" came from his phone's speaker. "Vic, what's going on?"

The explosion from the gun reverberated on the walls of the parking garage and echoed back and forth. The back of Vic's head exploded in a cloud of red that splattered the red and white "Fire Door, Keep Closed" sign. He crumpled to the ground.

                *   *   *

"Vic, no!" Jick screamed into the phone. Mireille walked into his office, curious about the commotion.

"Vic, Vic!"

No answer. But the call was still connected.

                *   *   *

Jonas picked up the phone. He heard the metallic voice through the phone's tiny speaker. The screen showed the call connected to "Jick Arnsson."

"Vic, talk to me," Jonas heard the phone's speaker, the voice distorted from the shouting at the other end. "Are you OK?"

Jonas disconnected the call. He pocketed the phone, looked around on the ground. The spent casing from the shot lay next to the parking garage wall. He picked it up, still warm, stuffed it into a pocket, and raced to the nearest stairwell. His shoes clattered down the single flight of stairs to the ground level and he exited the parking garage. By now, two minutes had elapsed. He opened the texting app and sent a text to Jick.

"Some guy took a shot at me from outside the parking garage. He was behind the wall. He missed. I'm OK. He ran. I'm heading home. I'll call when I get there."

He thumbed through Vic's contact list until he found what he looked for. As he walked away from the parking garage, he noticed the storm drain between the edge of the sidewalk and the parking garage. He paused for a second, powered off Vic's phone and dropped it into the drain. He ran to his car, got in, and sped away.

FORTY-THREE

Mireille had heard everything that had transpired.

"It had to have been Jonas," Jick said, frantic with worry.

"Who is Jonas?"

Jick did not answer but hung up the phone and quickly dialed 9-1-1.

"9-1-1 operator, can you please hold?" the voice said.

"No, I fucking cannot hold," Jick screamed. But it was too late. He was on hold for a minute, although it seemed much longer, after which an operator came on the phone.

He told her someone had shot his brother in the parking garage of the Dallas Times newspaper. "You need to get someone over there right away," he almost shouted.

Jick's phone dinged as he was on the phone with the 9-1-1 operator. It was a message: "Some guy took a shot at me from outside the parking garage. He was behind the wall. He missed. I'm OK. He ran. I'm heading home. I'll call when I get there."

"OK, we'll send someone over right away," the operator said.

Jick read the message again then said, "He just sent me a text saying he's OK. But ... please send someone over to the garage. Someone just shot at my brother." Jick hung up.

"Why didn't he just call me?" He looked at Mireille.

Jick called Vic's number, and it went straight to voicemail. He left a quick message and hung up. He sent a text, telling Vic to be careful because Jonas was dangerous. There was no reply. *Probably still driving*, he thought.

Frantic with worry and not knowing what else to do, Jick called Sam.

She answered on the third ring.

"Jick, what's up?"

"Are you home?"

"No, Betty and I are at a bar downtown, just hanging out, talking. Why, what's going on?"

"Don't go home. I already told Vic the same thing. Go to a hotel or go home with Betty. But don't go home."

"Why not?"

"Vic's investigation has uncovered something dangerous. I'll tell you more tomorrow."

"OK." She sounded hesitant.

Jick hung up and called Vic again. It went straight to voicemail. He sent a text to Vic and waited. He put the phone down and paced in his living room.

"Something must be wrong. He's not answering."

Even though as an anesthesiologist Jick was taught to foresee the unexpected and he had always believed in the mantra that *"anticipation is the key to survival"*, the events of the past few minutes were so far from normal and so devastating, he could not have foreseen what was about to happen, that Jonas might murder Vic and then head straight over to his house to tie up a last loose end.

As he paced in his living room, the doorbell rang. Caught unawares, Jick opened the door. As soon as the door cracked open, the front door slammed open, the force knocking him back. Before he could assimilate what had happened, a man walked in. He held a gun and pointed it at them.

"Well, well," he said. "You must be Dr. Jick Arnsson. How are we doing today?"

Jick and Mireille stood where they were, too stunned to register or accept this development.

"Who are you?" Jick stammered. "Get the fuck out of my house!"

"Now, now, doctor, just sit there and be quiet. We are expecting another guest in a few minutes. Soon, everything will be answered to your satisfaction."

The assailant walked around the room in a semicircle with the gun trained at them. Mireille had not said a word, but a sheen of fear-induced perspiration covered her face.

Jick felt a trickle under his arms as his guts felt like someone had twisted them from the bottom up.

For a few minutes, no one said anything. The man walked over to Jick.

"Put your arms behind your back and turn around," he said.

Jick did as he was told. The man put down his gun for a moment, watching him for any sudden moves, and pulled a wrist tie out of his pocket. Jick clasped his hands together and clenched his muscles, channeling his dad's teachings, trying to keep his wrists apart as the man quickly tied his wrists together.

The man motioned Mireille to do the same. After securing her wrists, he sat in a chair, pointing his gun at them. A small keychain with a tuft of something furry appeared in his left hand and he started twirling it. Jick stared at the mannerism with shock and recognition.

"Jonas Jensen," Jick said. "It was you. You killed Tiffany and those two homeless men. You were in the back of her car. You're her husband."

"Guilty," Jonas said. "Oh, and that nosy reporter. I also killed him. Blew his fucking brains out."

Jick stared at him, the color draining from his face. He tried to say something, but his throat felt constricted, and he could only stare at Jonas. He felt a sudden helpless rage wash over him. There was nothing he could do.

The sound of the front door opening interrupted them; Professor Art Marlow walked in. Jick's jaw dropped open. He felt his masseters slacken and his mandible drooped.

"Hello, Jick," Marlow said, smiling. "You can close your mouth."

Jick had difficulty swallowing. "What...," he got out, "...are you doing here?"

Marlow did not immediately answer. He stared at Jick and Mireille and sat down.

"Jick," he began, "I wish it didn't have to end like this. But even though I don't owe you an explanation, I'll answer your question."

"You're planning to kill us," Jick stated, "aren't you?"

Mireille's expression of fear gave way to sobs.

Marlow ignored the question.

"Jick, as you know, I have been doing research on genetic transmutation. My model was to take a sample of DNA and grow organs compatible with the source. Think about this. This was to be the actual holy grail, the holiest grail if you will, of organ transplantation. Using pluripotent stem cells, my model was designed to allow cellular differentiation while controlling the local host environment. We could grow specific organs. That's right, made-to-order organs, all from one stem cell. The office of translational research had already lined up angel investors and other venture capital funding. They even created CellGenEX, LLC. Even though the university owned the intellectual property, as a founding member of the limited-liability corporation, I would have been rich and famous. My name would have been mentioned in the same breath as other cellular biology greats and a Nobel prize would have been guaranteed."

"So what happened?" Jick asked. He clenched and relaxed his wrists as Marlow talked, hoping his wrist ties would loosen.

"It failed. We could not get the cell lines to differentiate as we had hoped. We did not have a working prototype. We tried six times over several years and each time, the result was less than optimal. The investors would pull the funding in a year, and I needed to continue my research.

"I'm sure you've heard of Peter Northrup, that rich piece of shit whose wife left him over that escort business. He was one of our main funding sources. When my research ran into problems, I tried to convince him to give me another million and he said no. I offered him a majority interest in CellGenEX and he still said no. I'm glad that stupid shit is dead. Imagine if he had continued funding me and I had succeeded not only with the kidney but also the heart. Maybe I could have saved him."

Jick did not say anything. He had not known that Marlow and Peter Northrup were acquainted. Marlow continued.

"Anyway, I took a leap of faith. I took an existing organ and tried to transmute its DNA based on the source. Not quite the Holy Grail, but at least it would have led to genetically compatible organs and would have obviated the need for immunosuppressant drugs. And finally, I would have had samples of histologically compatible organs to show to the investors. And it would have worked."

Jick tried to wrap his mind around what Marlow had said. "What do you mean by 'existing organ?'"

"What I said, Jick, 'existing organ.' I procured existing organs and tried to transmute the DNA to make genetically compatible organs."

"Holy shit," Jick breathed as realization dawned. "You and Jonas are killing these homeless men to steal their organs. During your Grand Rounds, you described having a kidney model. Now it makes sense."

"Jick, I hope you realize it's for the greater good. I did not want to do it this way, but I had no choice. I was in a tough spot. The investors had pulled all the venture capital. I only had a few months of funds remaining and I had to move quickly to get some meaningful results. I could not wait for donated organs, and I was in a severe time crunch. I had to get existing organs and at least show the viability of my work. As soon as I could show the viability of my work, there would have been no further need for organs. No one would miss a few homeless men. I must admit at one point, I had a revenge fantasy about taking Peter Northrup's kidneys. It would have been karma for denying me. But it would have drawn too much attention."

Jick shook his head. "But you *killed* two people to get their organs, Art. You're a doctor. You cannot justify it for the 'greater good.' That's what doctors did in Nazi Germany."

"Jick, Jick," Marlow said. "No need to be melodramatic. The sacrifice of these two men will result in thousands of lives being saved. From the standpoint of collateral damage, it was minimal."

"They did not get to make that choice. They did not deserve to have their lives taken from them. And what about Vic? Was he also collateral damage?"

"I'm sorry about Vic. I didn't realize he was your brother. Jonas told me a reporter had stumbled across the connection between the two men. It was unfortunate for him. I wanted two random choices, but Jonas made a poor decision.

"Jick, you don't understand. My model is close to success. Soon, I'll have the genetic transmute model working for existing organs and that alone will secure enough funding to move back to the *de novo* model. Like I said, once I get the funding secured, I won't need existing organs anymore. I'm sorry you stumbled across what was going on, but it truly is for the greater good."

"What's your involvement?" Jick asked Jonas. "Why are you helping Art?"

"Money," Marlow answered for him. "Lots of it. I've always known Jonas had a mean streak, a sociopathic tendency if you will, and the lure of money was easy bait."

"What do you mean 'always known'? How long have you known Jonas?"

"All his life," Marlow said. "He's my brother."

"What?" Jick exclaimed.

"Actually half-brother. My parents divorced years ago, and my father moved back to Utah. The divorce was not pleasant in the beginning and afterwards, my mother remarried. She had my surname legally changed from Jensen to Marlow. My father married a younger Brazilian woman and Jonas was born in Utah. There was a little tension between my mother and his second wife, but it smoothed out over time. I went to Jonas' wedding. I knew him on and off for much of his life. He had problems in school. We are alike in some ways, probably too much like our dad. I was able to work through my issues and become productive. Jonas was also productive but had more difficulty with self-control. I'll leave it at that.

"Now, since I have answered your questions, I'm sorry to do this. OK, Jonas," Marlow said, glancing at Jonas and motioning toward Jick and Mireille with a nod.

"Wait," Jick said, frantic. The wrist ties had not yielded as much as he had hoped.

Then, turning to Jonas, hoping to buy time, he said, "Why Tiffany?"

Jonas stood in the corner, near Jick's desk and display shelf. He had put away his furry keychain thing and had picked up the mask, examining it on both sides.

He looked up at Jick, surprised. "How the hell do you know about Tiffany?" he asked.

"He probably didn't tell you," Jick said to Marlow. "He ambushed his wife from the back seat of their car and shot her. Cold-blooded murder."

"Oh, that," Marlow said, as if Tiffany's murder was inconsequential. "I already knew about that. Tiffany had an ongoing sexting relationship with some guy. She planned to leave Jonas and when he discovered it, he went berserk. He came to me the day he had discovered it and he lost it. He told me he would kill her. He spoofed Tiffany into thinking this guy wanted to meet in person. I did not want him to do it and draw attention to himself. But he was berserk, and I couldn't reason with him. I still needed him for my work and could not let him get arrested. He was the obvious suspect. So, I made sure he had an airtight alibi rebuilding a crashed server the night he killed her. He also left his cell phone with me so when the police investigated phone records, it would show his presence in my lab that night. He arrived at the lab before midnight right after the murder and crashed on the couch. That server was in one of my labs and I was the client who provided the alibi.

"He also drove to Houston and killed the guy she was leaving him for. Again, I did not want him to do it, but I could not convince him otherwise."

"Yeah," Jonas grinned. "It was great. Tried to shoot the stupid fuck in the balls and missed. But I watched him die. Then I cut off his dick and fed it to the gators."

Mireille's face somehow conveyed both terror and revulsion at Jonas.

"But how do *you* know about Tiffany?" Jonas asked Jick.

"Figure it out," Jick replied.

Jick felt a surge of fear as he stared at Jonas. This man had killed for profit, passion, and pleasure. He felt a sudden desperation as the wrist ties did not loosen much. He detected some slack in the ties but not enough for him to get one of his hands out. He struggled, pushing his wrists together, desperate, hoping he could work one of the ties off.

I'm about to die, he thought, in a sudden panic, his breath quickening.

Jonas held the mask in his left hand and the gun in his right. The mask seemed to have the same pull as it did on Jick the day he bought it. He held it up to the light to study it.

As he watched Jonas examine the mask, Jick had a sudden flash of blinding clarity and drew in his breath, eyes widening in realization.

He understood the reason for the mask.

He understood why it replayed memories of a dying person. He understood why it was made and what purpose it had served in the past. The knowledge of its unique abilities, and the reasons for its existence, had faded over time. It had lain dormant in boxes and on dusty shelves until it was bought by a person whose proximity to dying people revealed its abilities, but he had not been able to figure out its purpose. Until now.

It had to be. There was no other reason for anyone to make a mask that replayed the entire life of a dying person.

A crazy idea formed in Jick's mind.

"Put that down, please," he said, hoping Jonas wouldn't.

Jonas didn't. Instead, he put it on and looked at Jick through the eyeholes. Jick could see only the black eyes staring at him, not Jonas' eyes.

"Jonas, stop fooling around and let's get done and get out of here," Marlow said.

The mask was on Jonas. *He does not know what it can do. But I do. Hope I can figure out how.*

Jonas swung the gun toward Jick with his right hand as he lifted his left hand to his face to lift the mask off his head.

Do or die. Now or never.

He leaped off the couch and charged at Jonas, his right knee protesting at the sudden stress. Jick positioned his chest as close to dead center to Jonas' line of fire, thrusting his chest out with his hands tied behind his back. Jonas must have thought Jick was about to jump on him.

He fired, while still wearing the mask.

Jick felt the bullet hit. It felt more like a firm shove in the chest. Before the pain registered, a glow emanated from the mask, and he was now co-conscious with Jonas, with his life being replayed in the mask.

In the altered reality of looking through the mask, Jonas did not know what had happened. At the precise moment of shooting Jick, the first few seconds would have been a sudden and unexpected barrage of sights from Jick's earlier years. Both Jick and Jonas inhabited the mask, but only Jick knew what it could do. Jick felt himself inside Jonas. He did not know how the mask did what he felt sure it could do. He felt a surge of control that he could not explain and at that moment, wrenched the mask off.

He swayed, dizzy and nauseated. *But it had worked.*

Jick looked down at his body. There was a look of uncomprehending horror on his face. Jonas looked around from inside the body and tried to talk. He could not. Blood bubbled out of his mouth, and he coughed. He rolled on the floor, hands still tied behind him. The legs moved a little, another cough, another feeble attempt at a roll and speech, and he was still. From shot to the end, it took less than a minute.

Jick stood, holding the gun in his right hand and the mask in his left. It still glowed but dimmed as Jonas faded into oblivion.

"Stupid fool," Marlow said with some impatience. "Instead of a clean head shot, he made it worse for himself.

Come on, enough fooling around, make it quick with her and let's go."

Mireille shook and sobbed in fear. She looked at Jick with an expression of wild-eyed terror. "Please, please, no," she rasped through a parched mouth. Jick steadied himself and gripped the gun. It felt unnatural. His arms felt younger, stronger, more in control. He put the mask down.

"OK," Jick said in a stranger's voice. "Art, look at me."

Art Marlow faced Mireille. He turned his head toward Jick.

Jick looked at him, eye to eye. His right index finger was already on the trigger, squeezing. He cupped his left hand under the gun's grip.

"This is for Vic."

Jick raised the gun, pointed it at Marlow, and fired twice, a double tap. The two rounds hit Art Marlow on the left side of his chest and exited straight through, leaving a fatal trail across his left lung, ascending aorta, mediastinum, right lung, and out. Marlow let out a grunt and an expression of astonishment and pain crossed his face. He toppled to the right, a crimson pool spreading out from the exit wounds. His face made several wordless changes of expression. He tried speaking, but nothing came out. In a few seconds, he was still.

On the table, the mask started glowing again. Jick stared at it. Art Marlow's memories, everything he had been, played back in the mask. But there was nowhere for the essence of Art to go. After a while, the glow dimmed and faded. Art was gone.

Jick tucked the gun in his waistband. Before Mireille had time to process what had happened, Jick strode to the desk drawer, walking like Gumby. He took out his pocketknife, walked over to her, stumbling at the strangeness of his legs, and cut her wrist ties apart.

"If you promise you won't tell anyone I was here, I won't hurt you," Jick said. "Make up something. Tell them Dr. Marlow broke in here, there was a scuffle, Dr. Arnsson got shot, and you grabbed the gun and shot Dr. Marlow. Do not tell them about me. If you promise that, I'll let you live."

She nodded, mute, staring at him, face transfixed in terror. Jick's brain was already thinking a few steps ahead. He realized he needed to get away from there. He was also aware he needed some time to plan his getaway. He needed Mireille to not say anything right away. He regretted scaring her into silence but at that moment, had no choice.

He wiped off any surface he thought Jonas may have contacted. He walked over to his desk and picked up his wallet. He would need access to some money. He walked over to where his body lay. A strange feeling came over him, looking down at it. He had learned in medical school, in one of his psychiatry lectures, that loss of a body part after an amputation causes a grief reaction like losing a loved one. He had not had time to assimilate that he had lost his entire body. Nothing would be the same anymore. He picked up his phone.

But he was alive.

Or am I?

Jick leaned over his still body and cut the wrist ties apart. He needed to support the narrative of the scuffle so it would not do to have his body with hands tied. The hands fell apart and the left hand fell on his outstretched hand holding the knife. He drew in a sharp breath and jerked his hand back, staring at the still warm, familiar lifeless hand. He pulled the gun out of his waistband and Mireille jerked back against the couch. He wiped it off as well as he could and walked over to Mireille.

She had not moved, staring at Jick in fear, not believing he was not going to harm her. Jick grabbed Mireille's hand and she reacted like she had been stuck with a cattle prod. She flinched and tried to pull away. He forced her hand around the gun and squeezed her hand to imprint her fingerprints on the handle. He wanted to place the gun on the ground between Art's body and her. But, since she had seen Jonas kill Jick, the thought crossed his mind that she could lunge for the gun on the floor and shoot him. He placed the gun on the desk, safely out of reach but easy for her to get after he left.

He turned away, picked up the mask and knife, and went out the door, wiping it as he left. He paused to look back at Mireille, who had a beautiful glowing expression of relief, astonishment, and befuddlement. He took one last regretful look at Mireille.

"Remember, I wasn't here." He made a slashing gesture toward his throat with the knife and shut the door.

FORTY-FOUR

Jick wiped off the doorknob. He went over in his mind all the surfaces Jonas had touched inside and hoped he had remembered everything. He had Jonas' wallet, his phone, the mask, the pocketknife, and whatever was in Jonas' pockets. He folded the knife and stuffed it into one of the pockets.

He ran to the end of his driveway and looked up and down the street. He felt in his pockets and pulled out a set of keys. He pressed the unlock button on the key fob. Nothing happened. He tried to imagine what Jonas would have done. Jonas would have parked down the road a few houses away to the south if he came from downtown, near where Vic worked. His car should be in that direction.

He turned right and jogged down the road for a few houses, pausing every fifty yards and clicking the unlock button. Nothing. He came to a church parking lot. When he pressed the unlock button, a nondescript black sedan, a Toyota Camry, on the edge of the parking lot chirped and its lights flashed once. He ran to it, opened the door and tossed the mask onto the passenger seat. He got in and, noting that the seat and mirror adjustments fit perfectly. He took a deep breath, held it in, and exhaled. He looked at his phone and put it in airplane mode and turned off location services. Hesitating for a moment, he powered it off. He pulled out of the parking lot, turned in a direction away from his house, and drove off.

As he headed down the road and after he had made a few turns, he pulled into the parking lot of a busy shopping center. He took out Jonas' wallet and looked at the license. The address was a few miles away. He took Jonas' phone from his pocket. It was locked. He held his thumb over the fingerprint sensor, and it unlocked. He gave it directions to Jonas' house, and it started navigating him there.

Son of a bitch, he thought. *It recognizes my thumbprint and voice.*

As he drove, the thought crossed his mind that the passenger seat was where both Paul Albrecht and Taylor Potts had met their end.

Jonas' place was a small one-story house in Oak Cliff, one of Dallas' more modest suburbs, close to downtown. Jick knew from Vic telling him about his investigative work that it was just Tiffany and Jonas. No pets, no kids. The thought of Vic and their last phone call clutched at his throat. He forced himself to not think of that now—he had too much to do if he had any chance of survival now. He pulled into the carport and shut the engine.

The house was dark. He looked at the bunch of keys and put what looked like the right one into the lock. On his third attempt, the back door opened. He hoped there was no alarm system. He stepped in and turned on the light. With Tiffany gone, the house appeared to be reverting into a bachelor pad. Dirty dishes filled the sink. He looked in the refrigerator. Not much in there.

He walked around the house, looking for personal effects so he could learn the part. He knew he was now a man on the run. He created a mental checklist of things he would need to do as soon as possible. He would need to look through Jonas' personal effects like photo albums, files, tax records, etc. to find out everything about him, including knowing about members of his family who might identify him. He would need to go to Second Chance tomorrow and quit. He would need to get all the money out of Jonas' accounts and close the accounts. He would need to sell the car and get another one, requesting only a temporary title, using his address and not Jonas', and dropping off the grid as thoroughly as possible.

He had considerable assets that, on his death, transferred to Vic. Now that Vic was dead, it would pass to Sam. *Poor Sam*, he thought.

He undressed and in a pocket of his pants was the keychain with a furry tassel. He stared at it. This was what had allowed him to connect Jonas to all the murders. He tossed it into a drawer. The only clothes available were Jonas'. He had to wrap his mind around putting on his underclothes. A part of him found the experience revolting. Another part of him rationalized those same underclothes belonged on this body.

He slept the first night in Jonas' house. It was difficult. He tossed and turned and kept waking up, feeling strange and very out of sorts in this body.

At six the next morning, he jolted awake. He lay in bed, not moving. For a moment, he experienced a feeling of disorientation as his limbs behaved in a way he was not used to. He was also in a strange bed. He swung his legs off the bed and stood. The bathroom door was ajar, and he walked toward it, a little stiff-legged. It was still dark, although dawn had broken, and a colorless gray tinge suffused the room. As he walked to the bathroom, he could see the outline of his form in the mirror through the open bathroom door, increasing in size as he stepped toward the bathroom. He groped around the inside of the door frame for a light switch, felt one, and flicked it on. He started at his reflection and jumped back. *Jonas' evil face looked back at him.* It was the first time he had seen his reflection and the full reality of what he had done hit him.

Jick thudded back against the wall and slid to the floor. He buried his face in his hands. *What have I done?* Now that the initial shock and excitement of what transpired yesterday had passed, a feeling of horror engulfed him.

Several thoughts went through his mind, starting with the reality of realizing that from now on and for the rest of his life, every time he looked in the mirror, Jonas' face would look back at him. This face was already associated with memories of Jonas pointing his gun at him in his house. This face was the last person Vic saw before he was killed and the memory of Vic's last words over the phone, *Oh, God, please don't,* were going to haunt him forever. This face had also owned these hands, the hands that had brutalized Paul Albrecht's and Taylor Potts' bodies. Jonas was dead, but this face would always be a daily reminder...

His bladder and bowel signaled a need for relief. The sensation was odd and familiar. He stood and walked to the commode, studiously avoiding looking at the mirror. He pulled down his pants and sat down. He looked at his penis, his legs, his feet. All alien, all normal. Relieving himself and having a bowel movement felt familiar and unnerving. *What the fuck have you done, Jick?* he thought. *Is this really happening?*

After attending to his personal hygiene, all the while avoiding looking in the mirror, he walked back into the bedroom. He took a careful inventory of his body parts, noting that Jonas was essentially a normally developed male human. To the extent possible, he did a cursory physical exam on himself, checking his pulse, feeling all appendages, trying out various movements, testing muscle strength. Everything seemed fine. This body was also a hell of a lot younger than his previous one. It would take a lot of time to assimilate all this and get used to it. But his knee did not bark at him daily.

Later that morning, he went to work at Second Chance and told them he had to quit. He told them the anguish of dealing with Tiffany's death was too much to bear and he needed to take some time off and refocus on what he needed to do. He thought of Vic and this helped him force out a few tears. The clinic staff was supportive and kind. The clinic manager wished him well and told him he was welcome to come back whenever he wanted.

He went to the bank and closed the accounts belonging to one Jonas and Tiffany Jensen. The bank verified his photo ID and fingerprints. There was about three thousand in total and he extracted it in cash. He went to a different bank and rented a safe deposit box big enough for the mask. He prepaid the rent for five years and left the mask there. He took one last look at it. It stared back at him through its black eyes, drab and colorless as usual.

"Let's leave you here for a bit," Jick said to the mask. "You have caused enough trouble."

He closed the safe deposit box, pocketed the key, and walked out of the bank vault.

He returned to Jonas and Tiffany's house at about noon. There was nothing to eat in the house. Even though he was hungry, the stress of what had happened in the last twenty-four hours still weighed on him and his appetite was shot. He rummaged through the pantry and found a box of protein bars. He sat at the kitchen table to munch a protein bar and think. After finishing the protein bar and a glass of water, he had to go to the bathroom again. He opened the door and went in, keeping his gaze averted from the mirror so he would not have to look at himself. Afterwards, he was back at the kitchen table.

What was his next step going to be? *I have no clue what to do next, none at all,* he thought. Even now Mireille could be talking to the police. Even now the police could have discovered that it was Jonas Jensen who had committed these crimes.

I need help, he thought. *I need an anchor to keep me sane in these uncharted waters. But who?*

FORTY-FIVE

Jick spent the next day in a daze. He did not remember what he did, but it vacillated between paranoia that the police would arrive at any minute to arrest Jonas for murder, to elation that he was now much younger, to fear that he was in limbo, trapped with no way out.

He needed an anchor. Someone he could trust with the details of what had transpired. Someone level-headed and rational. Only one person came to mind and that was Sam. He would have to tell her. It would be the most outlandish narrative she would hear in her life. But there was no way he could wander around the country, indefinitely untethered from the grid. Even if he decided to live like a hermit in the wilds somewhere, at some point he would need access to at least some trappings of civilization. At times he wished he had not done what he did, and he also wondered if it would have been better if he had ended it all. As an anesthesiologist, he could have concocted any number of ways to a painless end.

But looking in the mirror every day would be damn near impossible to get used to. *I guess I have a strong survival instinct and will to live*, he thought.

He also realized if he had not succeeded, Jonas would have murdered not only him but also Mireille. At this very moment, both Art and he would have been pushing ahead with their horrific plans. Maybe even harvesting more organs. So, from that standpoint, he was glad he had thwarted their plans.

But he was in a new phase of his life and floating in uncharted waters. So Jick would need an anchor. And that would have to be Sam. So he called her.

Jick picked up the phone in Jonas' kitchen. After listening for the dial tone, he pressed the keys to block caller ID and dialed Sam's house. She answered on the second ring.

"Hello."

"Hello, Samantha Arnsson please," he said.

"Speaking."

"Hi, Ms. Arnsson," Jick said, before taking in a deep breath and then getting straight to the point. "You don't know me, but I have some information about your husband's death. I wanted to meet with you in person, to tell you all that I know." He waited for it to sink in.

"Who is this?" she asked.

"I know this is difficult but for now, I would prefer not to say," he continued. "We have to meet in person. For your peace of mind, would you be willing to meet in a public place like at a restaurant? I plan to tell you everything, but for reasons that will become clear later, it has to be in person."

"No, that's not going to happen," she said. "If you have information about Vic's death, you can tell me now or I'll call the police."

"Calling the police won't help. I'll hang up and you won't get the information I have about your husband's death. Like I said, let's meet in a public place and I'll tell you everything I know."

"I don't know about this," she said, hesitating, but also drawn to finding out more about Vic's death. So far, the police had identified no persons of interest.

"Do you have a gun, Ms. Arnsson?" Jick asked, knowing she did. Sam had a concealed carry permit and sometimes carried a Beretta Nano 9 mm for personal protection.

"Yes."

"If it would make you feel better, bring it with you. I will be unarmed."

"Well," she hesitated, and then deciding, "OK."

Jick breathed a sigh of relief. Convincing Sam to meet with a stranger could have been difficult. Given the unusual nature of the request, she could very well have said no. But his reassurances that he would be unarmed, and she could bring a gun may have helped. This was the first hurdle. Now on to the second.

"I have one request. Please don't call the police. I know I have to trust you on this, but this is important and after I have told you everything, I'm sure you will understand."

"OK."

And the third and final hurdle.

"Would you like to choose the place to meet?" Jick asked.

"How about Julio's?" she suggested. "It's a Mexican restaurant near Highland Park with an outdoor seating area."

The one place Jick did not want to go to was Julio's. He had serious misgivings about going to a place close to where he had lived and worked. The chief reason was Mireille. She knew what Jonas looked like and had seen him shoot Jick and Art. What if she was there? But he had no choice. He could not tell Sam he did not want to go to Julio's. If he suggested an alternate location, she may think she was being steered into a trap. Being a weekday evening, Jick hoped Mireille would not be there. It was only a few days after his "death".

What kind of funeral did I have? flashed through his mind.

"I know the place," Jick said. "A nice busy street, and the restaurant has an outdoor patio. That sounds great. Do you want to pick the time?"

"Let's meet at five. About an hour from now."

"OK. I'll be wearing shorts and a T-shirt. No place to carry a weapon," he added, "so you'll know I'm unarmed.

"I'm about six-two, about two hundred, dark hair, olive complexion."

Describing himself was difficult. Jick walked over to Jonas' closet with his left shoulder scrunched, phone pressed against his ear. He looked through Jonas' clothes. "I'll be wearing brown shorts and a blue and white T-shirt with the Dallas Cowboys logo on it. Oh, and a baseball cap with the Texas Rangers T logo." He hoped with a baseball cap and sunglasses, even if by some chance Mireille was there, he would not be recognizable.

She acknowledged what Jick said and hung up. He placed the phone down and took in a deep breath and exhaled. *I hope she doesn't change her mind about the cops,* he thought.

He glanced at the clock. Almost four. A half-hour to kill before needing to head to Julio's. It was a restive time. He went over in his mind how he would begin the conversation. There was no way to plan or rehearse for it. He would have to wing it. He debated having a drink to calm his nerves but decided against it. So he turned the television on and watched something, although none of what he watched registered in his mind. He thumbed through a magazine, but nothing he read registered either.

At four-thirty, he set off for Julio's in Jonas' car. At four-fifty, he pulled on to the street and Julio's was ahead on the right. There was curbside parking and a parking lot in the back. He spotted Sam's car in one of the curbside spots. He knew Sam well enough to know she would have arrived early, conducted a brief survey of the area, and sat with the exits already mapped out in her mind and her back to a wall. She was in the patio outside, her back to one of the trees on the patio, sunglasses still on. She had her purse in her lap, no doubt for easy access to her gun. A member of the wait staff had placed a glass of water in front of her and stood by the table, presumably asking her if she was ready to order a drink. As he watched, he saw Sam shake her head and say something to the waitress who nodded and left. He could almost hear her say, "not yet, I'm waiting for someone."

Jick scanned the street. There was no obvious police presence. He parked in the back and walked around to the side of the restaurant. The main entrance was along the side street. He pointed toward the patio and told the hostess he had plans to meet someone who was already there. The hostess waved him through.

He pushed open the patio door and walked over to Sam, approaching in her line of sight so she could see he was unarmed. He pretended to scan the patio as if he did not know her. There was no one else on the patio he recognized. He was thankful Mireille was not there. Sam noticed his brown shorts, Cowboys T-shirt, and baseball cap and waved to him. He walked over.

"Ms. Arnsson?" he queried.

"Yes."

He sat across from her and placed his hands on the table. A smooth, non-threatening gesture. He took off his sunglasses so she could see his face. He sat with his back to the rest of the dining area and would thus be unrecognizable even if Mireille happened to arrive.

"Thank you very much for agreeing to this meeting," Jick said.

"So how did you know my phone number?" she asked.

"I'll get to that," he replied. "When I'm done with my narrative, you will know everything."

She got straight to the point. "You said you had information about my husband's death."

"Yes," he said. *Where do I begin?*

He decided to start at the very beginning.

Jick told her about his work at the hospital and what he did for a living.

"You're an anesthesiologist? My...," she paused, "late brother-in-law was also an anesthesiologist."

"I know," he said. "I knew him."

"What is your name? I'm sure Jick would have mentioned you, maybe in passing."

"I'll get to that in a little," he said. *So far, so good.*

The waitress stopped at the table. She placed a glass of water in front of Jick. Jick ordered a Corona with a slice of lime and for the table, some Julio's *nachos especial* from the appetizer menu. Sam declined an alcoholic beverage.

"By the way," Jick grinned at Sam. "I don't have any money. No, I am not a broke doctor. There is a back story I'm going to get to so I hope you can cover this."

Sam looked startled and displeased.

"Yes, I am an actual doctor," he guessed what she thought, "so here goes my story."

Jick began his narrative about needing to buy a gift for a retiring colleague and stopping off at the antique shop in Deep Ellum. He mentioned finding a nondescript mask that looked like it had been lying there for many years. He told Sam he had bought it because it was called the Healer of Life. Since he was also a healer, it seemed appropriate, and he thought it would look good in his office. He filled in the details about taking it home, then taking it to his office, and hanging it on his office bookshelf. His narrative continued with a description of the gunshot trauma victim who had died on the table. He told Sam he had gone to his office to decompress for a few minutes after the victim had died and about the presence he had felt in his office. Later in the day, when he had gone back to his office, the feeling had disappeared.

"What does any of this have to do with my husband's death?" she asked, sounding impatient.

"I'm getting there," he said. "Please bear with me."

He told Sam about Peter Northrup and how he had died in the operating room after a catheterization related complication. When he had gone back to his office a few minutes later, he had again felt a presence. When he put on the mask, for a fleeting moment, he had seen what looked like apparitions bending over him before they disappeared, leaving behind just a view of the office through the mask.

Sam looked at Jick with an inscrutable expression. Jick knew her well enough to know her irritation level had risen. He paused for a sip of water and plunged ahead.

He continued with a narrative about Tiffany Jensen's death and the otherworldly experience he had had in his office when he put on the mask. He told Sam he had seen a vague outline of a man committing Tiffany's murder and had surmised the mask must have had a way of replaying brain activity when a person is about to die and the energy from the dying brain ebbs. He described the murderer's keychain-twirling mannerism.

Sam looked skeptical.

"This is fascinating," she said. "Vic mentioned this woman's murder to me the day he was killed, something about there being a connection between her murder and some other murders he had looked into. You're telling me this mask somehow replayed the last moments of this woman's life and you had some intuition or sixth sense about knowing who killed her? Again, what does any of this have to do with my husband's death?"

Jick pressed on. He told Sam he had assumed the sooner after a person's death the mask was donned, and possibly in closer proximity, the better the imagery would be as more of their life was replayed and therefore, more of their life would be visible. To test this theory, he needed to get in touch with someone who had a more "on the spot" type of job in responding to violent crimes. The only person he could think of was Vic, a beat reporter with direct access to crime scenes.

"Vic knew you?" Sam asked. "I still don't know your name and he has never mentioned knowing any anesthesiologists at the hospital other than his brother."

Jick paused before delivering the bombshell.

"Yes, he knew me. To get closer to crime scenes, I called him and then stopped by your house one night. It was the night of the Albrecht murder, the first homeless victim, on July 4th. I was a little nervous about the mask as I had slowly realized its abilities and I wanted to get closer to crime scenes and as soon as possible after the crime was committed. I had the mask in my car and by coincidence, Vic got the call about the Albrecht murder that evening. You are an exceptional foodie, Sam, and that evening we had marinated chicken tandoori in a creamy sauce, a vegetable medley in coconut sauce, a cold salad of chopped cucumbers, tomatoes, cilantro in lime juice, and fried *papadums* on the side. And the *digestif* afterwards, the Rémy Martin XO, was sublime."

FORTY-SIX

Sam's face blanched. As tough as she was, this narrative was beyond belief. Her right hand rested against her purse, and she pushed her hand deeper, almost by reflex, reaching for her gun. She stopped. With her left hand, she had gripped the table edge and she let it go.

The arrival of the waitress with their food interrupted Jick's narrative. She held a large serving tray with Jick's beer and the nachos, served with chips and guacamole. She transferred everything to their table along with two thick-walled earthenware bowls of Julio's special salsas, a green and a red. Sam said nothing but just looked at Jick. In the background on this warm Texas evening, the Spanish music from the bar and the sound of silverware clinking from nearby tables provided an acoustic backdrop, punctuated by the sound of an occasional passing car or motorcycle.

"Can I get y'all anything else?" she inquired.

Jick shook his head. "No, we're good for now. Thanks."

Once the waitress had left, Sam's expression changed to one of anger.

"Who the hell are you? And how do you know about my house and what we ate that night?"

"I'm sorry, Sam," Jick said, now calling her by her preferred nickname rather than "Samantha" or "Ms. Arnsson."

"You'll have to assimilate this and wait a few more minutes. There is more to this story and by the time I get to the end, I will have answered all your questions, including questions about Vic's death."

He pressed on, now far beyond the point of no return.

"When Vic called me about Taylor Potts' murder, he was the second homeless victim, its discovery was sooner after they killed him than the Albrecht murder. I put on the mask close to Taylor's body and watched his interaction with the murderer before he died. I had an experience similar to what I saw with Tiffany Jensen's murder. The murderer had a mannerism, twirling something in his left hand; it was the same mannerism that Tiffany Jensen's murderer had. I was flabbergasted at this.

"Tiffany's murderer and the person who murdered the homeless men were the same guy! I emailed Vic to investigate any connection between Tiffany Jensen's murder and the murders of the homeless men."

Sam interrupted.

"Vic mentioned he had received an anonymous email informing him of this. So, it was you."

"Yes, it was I who emailed Vic. Vic, in the meantime, had been investigating the murders of the two homeless men. He had stumbled across the fact that both men sought treatment at a free clinic near downtown called Second Chance. When he went to the clinic and later looked into Tiffany Jensen's murder, he discovered the IT guy at Second Chance was Tiffany Jensen's husband. He also noticed the twirling keychain mannerism but did not know its significance.

"This IT guy, Jonas Jensen, must have wondered how a reporter was already asking questions about the two murdered guys and their connection to Second Chance. He went out to Vic and talked to him. When he realized Vic had discovered this earlier in the day and had not told anyone yet, he decided to tie off a loose end and kill Vic as soon as possible, before he had a chance to inform the police. He knew where Vic worked because Vic had given the receptionist at Second Chance his business card."

"What?" said Samantha, almost rising to her feet. "You know this IT guy at Second Chance killed my husband? Let's go tell the police right now."

"We cannot," Jick said. "There's more to the story."

Sam sank back into her seat.

He continued. "I doubt the police will believe a story of visions from a mask as evidence to pursue Jonas, anyway. But there is still more.

"I was on the phone with Vic when Jonas shot him. I heard Vic's last words and heard the gunshot."

This was difficult. Jick paused and swallowed.

Sam looked distressed at the mention of Vic's last words. She gathered herself, cleared her throat, and interrupted.

"You still haven't told me how you know what we had for dinner. You're telling me what we had for dinner like you were there. And you were not. Now you're telling me Vic was on the phone with you when he was killed. Jick called me the day Vic was killed to warn me not to go home.

"I don't even know you. This had better not be some elaborate hoax. Did Jick tell you about dinner at our place that night and you're using it to propagate some bullshit? What's your angle? Money for information?"

"Please, Sam," he implored. "We're almost there."

Jick continued. "After Vic was killed, since the phone was still on, Jonas must have seen my name on the call screen. He sent me a text from Vic's phone saying he was OK and then headed straight to my house to tie up another loose end."

He paused for a moment. "He came to my house. I was there with Mireille Lavoisseur, one of our nurse anesthetists. He was armed and made us sit still until his partner in crime arrived. It was Art Marlow, an assistant professor at the university.

"Jonas had tied our hands behind our backs. Marlow told us everything about his research, that his models for controlling the environment for growing genetically compatible organs had failed and as a result, he had to get existing organs to carry out his research. So, he enlisted the help of his half-brother, Jonas, to murder homeless men to get their kidneys. After explaining everything to us, he ordered Jonas to kill us."

Sam stared at Jick. It was possible a glimmer of what he was about to say had already registered, but there was no way her rational brain could wrap around it. She said nothing and waited for him to go on.

"While Art Marlow explained everything, Jonas wandered around the room. He picked up the mask, studied it for a while, and put it on. My efforts at working the wrist ties loose were unsuccessful."

Jick took a deep breath, paused, took a swig of beer, swallowed it, and exhaled.

"OK, here goes," he said.

He delivered the second bombshell.

"It was at that moment, Sam, that I knew why the mask was created. It was meant to be worn by someone at the same time someone else was killed nearby. Since it began replaying the dying person's life immediately, if it was worn by someone else, the dying person would have the ability to transfer their consciousness into the person wearing the mask, *if they knew about its abilities beforehand.*

"I had a crazy idea, Sam. I was about to die. I was caught between Scylla and Charybdis. I had no choice. I was near the mask. Jonas had put on the mask. There was a chance, an infinitesimal chance, with the immediacy of my death and the mask already being on someone, that it would preserve me. There was no other reason why someone would create something like this mask. So, the fact that he already had it on would mean all of me would be replayed in his body. I did not, could not, wait to think this through, but I was already a dead man anyway. They were about to kill us. In that moment of mortal danger, I jumped in front of Jonas. A leap of faith, with my hands still tied. The gun went off, and the bullet hit me in the chest. I was in the mask with him in an instant. He did not know about the mask. We were co-conscious for a second and then I felt something I can't describe and felt myself reaching up to take off the mask. I stood there for a second, not able to believe what had happened. Art then ordered Jonas to kill Mireille. I asked Art to turn and look at me. When he did, I said 'This is for Vic' and shot and killed him as revenge for Vic."

Sam had just gone pale from the earlier revelation about knowing what they had for dinner that night. But this revelation about the mask and what he had done was, in a literal sense, beyond the pale. It was almost too much. For the first time since Jick had known her, the tough exterior faded and for a few seconds, he thought she would faint. She realized the person she sat with was her husband's killer. She steadied herself and reached deeper into her purse.

"You bastard," she said. "You killed Vic and somehow found out that other stuff about Jick."

"Sam, please," Jick implored. "I am Jick."

He felt tears well up but kept his composure. "I know this is difficult to believe. If I wasn't living it, I would not believe it either. Every morning I have to look at the face of the man who killed Vic, killed me, killed his wife, her online lover, and two innocent homeless men."

He held up his hands. "These are the hands that perpetrated those crimes, Sam. There has been blood on them. Literally. And Jonas is dead. He died a dog's death on the floor of my living room with his hands tied behind his back. Whatever he was has ceased to exist. And the mastermind of the operation, Art Marlow, is also dead."

Sam regained her composure. Sensing the sincerity in what Jick said may have convinced her that he was not Jonas perpetrating some fraud. If what this man had told her was true, this Jonas person had been a violent man, not the type of person to orchestrate an elaborate fraud. If he had thought Sam was a loose end, for whatever reason, he would have killed her without compunction, like he had killed Vic. She pulled her hand out of her purse.

"There is another problem," Jick said. "Jonas is dead but there is no way to prove it. So I am, and now you are, in the somewhat surreal position of having to cover up for him. Vic's murder will have to remain unsolved."

Sam's eyes widened. She had not thought of that. She had come to the rendezvous hoping for information about her husband's death. She now knew who had killed him, but if she believed this man, Vic's murderer was dead, and Vic's murder would have to remain unsolved.

She took a long sip of water. Neither one said anything for a full two minutes. One of the high school students working at the restaurant came to the table, did a side pour out of her pitcher into Sam's water glass to dump some ice cubes, and topped up her glass. During that time, Sam looked at Jick, then at the nachos, then at the sky, then at the chips and salsas, and finally back to Jick. Finally, she spoke.

"Jick, I am glad you're alive."

Jick felt a wave of relief wash over him. He wiped his eyes and took a large swig of beer. He burped from the beer bubbles, making his eyes tear up more. He wiped his eyes again.

"Thanks, Sam," he said. "I don't know what the hell I did but I am here, alive, at least I think I'm alive. This could be quite the philosophical mind-fuck about what being alive is. *Cogito ergo sum*? Is that all it is to be alive? I died on the floor of my living room from a gunshot wound to the chest. Mireille probably thinks Jonas and Art had a falling out, so Jonas killed Art. She saw Jonas shoot me."

"Sam, I told you because I needed an anchor, someone grounded in the real world I could turn to. Somehow, I need to cover up traces of Jonas' existence, try to cover up his involvement in Vic's or my murder or, for that matter, the murder of Paul Albrecht and Taylor Potts, and somehow make sure the police are not after Jonas for murder.

"I don't know what to do. Wander around keeping a low profile, I guess. Try not to get into trouble. As much as I loathe this body and looking at it every day, this body is also only about thirty-five years old. Mine was sixty-four, healthy, but still sixty-four. In some ways, I feel like I have a new lease on life."

"Let's go back home," she said. "We have a lot to talk about."

"And now you know why I don't have any money. I can't use any of Jonas' credit cards and he didn't have too much cash. There was some cash that I took out of his bank account, but I left it in an envelope at his house. I have his ATM card, but I don't know his PIN."

"Actually, Jick," Sam said, now smiling at him. "I shall inherit your estate as Vic was your beneficiary and officially, both of you are gone. So don't worry about it. The beer and nachos are on me."

"True," he said. "Sam, you can have all of my estate. I'll call you if I need an allowance."

The banter continued until they parted ways in the parking lot. Jick got into Jonas' Toyota, started the engine, and paused for a moment, hands on the steering wheel. He took in a deep breath and exhaled a shuddering sigh of relief. He made his way out of the parking lot and toward Sam's house.

FORTY-SEVEN

"Oh God, please don't."

I startle awake and jerk to an upright position. My breathing comes in short gasps, like a bellows. I am in Sam's guest room. The nightmare fades and I cannot recall details. Did I hear it through my phone? Or did I hear it in person, standing in the parking garage, hear it from Vic's mouth, at his moment of death?

I am both exhilarated and terrified about what I have done. How can I ever be sure Jonas is gone? I took a leap of faith and landed in a living netherworld.

I lie back in bed and shut my eyes, try to focus on nothing except my breathing, try to go back to sleep.

*   *   *

The day after their rendezvous at the restaurant, Sam and Jick sat on the patio, an oscillating fan between them, sipping a lemonade. Sam had recovered from her initial shock but still managed to flash incredulous glances at Jick.

"I don't think I'll ever get used to seeing you like this," Sam said.

"Me too. At least I only have to look at myself by choice, like when I shave. You have to see me like this all the time."

"It will take some getting used to."

They sipped their lemonade. Jick swirled his drink and stared into his glass.

"I had never shot anyone," he said. "Until Art."

"How did it feel?"

"I felt a sense of savage satisfaction at the time. Afterwards, when I had time to reflect, it felt surreal. Art deserved it but I dispensed vigilante justice."

"I'm glad you feel that way. If you had enjoyed it and had no regrets, I might worry about it."

"Me too," Jick agreed. "I think I'm all here and it is all me, but I'll never know if all of Jonas' memories disappeared.

"I had a nightmare last night. I heard Vic's last words. But so did Jonas. So, the nightmare didn't help."

"So where is this mask?"

"I put it in a safe deposit box."

He sipped his lemonade and leaned back, ruminating about the mask.

"Imagine what life must have been like when this mask was used regularly," Jick wondered. "In essence, if you use it, you're stealing someone else's body."

"I imagine they would have made it into some type of ritual," Sam said. "So the person being sacrificed would be a willing participant."

"Would you use it, say, if you were terminally ill? You could ask some unsuspecting person to put it on and then kill yourself. You would be committing the perfect murder."

"But it wouldn't be the perfect life afterwards, would it?"

"That's for damn sure." Jick nodded. "I'm stuck in a living netherworld, unable to do what I was trained to do, unable to travel freely, depending on someone else for money. I may not even be able to find a job if I wanted one. And I could get arrested any moment for murder." A hint of desperation crept into his voice.

"But I am thirty-five years old now. How many of us, when asked if we could go back to being young again, have said 'I would love to go back, but with the maturity I have now'? I know I have, and in this surreal manner, my wish came true. I died, and I am alive now.

"By the way, how was my funeral?"

"It was awful, at least for me. I was in a state of shock. On Monday, we had had Vic's funeral. His was a closed casket funeral," her voice broke, "and there was an odd finality about seeing a closed coffin and realizing he's gone forever."

She pulled a tissue from a box and dabbed her eyes.

"We scheduled yours for Tuesday evening. There was a large turnout and I think pretty much everyone in your department who was not at work was there. Even a few members of the media showed up because of the sensational nature of the deaths.

"Since there was no next of kin, as such, the funeral home asked me, and I did not want one of those morbid open casket affairs. I was not in a proper frame of mind to make such decisions, anyway. So, it was a closed casket affair with members of your department making brief eulogies. Several other people, probably various staff from the hospital, also attended. Then the next day, you called, saying you had information about Vic's murder. Could not have imagined anything like this. I still feel like I have been dropped into an episode of the Twilight Zone."

The discussion then turned to arranging Jick's disappearance. The police were undoubtedly continuing to investigate Tiffany Jensen's murder and must have been wondering why her husband had disappeared.

"I don't know what I am going to do," Jick said.

"Let me think about it for a while.

"There's no point in learning anything about Jonas. You're not him and you won't be able to fake it. And, as a suspect in a murder investigation, it's only a matter of time before he's caught."

Sam organized a list of things Jick needed to do. She realized that for Jick to evade capture by the police, they must think he was already dead. She came up with a plan in which Jick would write a suicide note and then disappear. Her organizational skills were on full display; on how he should write a note; how he should crumple and smooth it to show sad, tragic desperation; how he should never go back to Jonas' house; and how to arrange a disappearance in which no body was found.

They arranged a scheme in which Jonas' burned-out car would be found near an alligator-filled waterway in South Texas, somewhere near Houston. Copious amounts of Jonas' DNA would be left in the form of drops of blood, along with spent casings and a gun. Perhaps authorities would assume he had tumbled into the water and the body was consumed by alligators. Whether it worked or not, Jick knew he would always have to be vigilant in the future.

Two days later, they were back in Dallas. They had carried out Sam's scheme as best as they could. Both were exhausted and the stress of the long drive had left Sam feeling under the weather. She complained about feeling nauseated and decided to retire to bed without dinner.

The next day, they were on the patio, talking about Jick's future. He talked about wanting to leave and do some traveling around the country by bus.

"Keeping my fingers crossed our mock suicide scheme works."

He leaned back and laced his fingers behind his head.

"You know, I think this is the end of the line for the Arnssons," he said.

"How so?" Sam asked.

"Well, Vic is gone, and all of my body is gone too. No more Arnsson DNA to propagate the gene pool."

"That may not be true." She smiled at him.

"What do you mean?" He looked at her, puzzled.

"I'm pregnant." She tossed out the bombshell with nonchalance.

Jick stared at her, unable to speak for a moment.

"What?" he said, astonished. "You're pregnant?"

"It's Vic's. After he did all that investigating for days without showering, we were intimate the day he had his shower.

"After the shower, of course," she smiled.

"We had some pregnancy tests lying around as we had been trying. Looks like it happened. I did not feel great last night. I first thought I had eaten something bad during the drive to Houston and, on an impulse, decided to check. It was faint but positive."

Jick stared at her, dumbfounded.

"That's fantastic," he exclaimed. "It's the best news I've heard in a long time."

His thoughts drifted to Vic, and he felt a slight tightness in his throat.

"Poor Vic," he said. "This will not be easy for you, Sam. You know, I never asked Vic your age. I assumed there was about a ten-year age gap so you would be about forty-four?"

"I'm thirty-nine, almost forty."

"Really?" he said and then added with some haste. "Not that you look older, Sam. You look great. It's that in speaking with Vic, I assumed there was an approximate ten-year age gap between you guys. I guess it was more like fifteen years."

"Nice recovery," she smiled. "Yes, I'm thirty-nine."

"That son of a gun, the age gap between Mireille and me was nineteen years. For all the crap Vic gave me about chasing a younger woman…"

He let the sentence trail off.

"Well, that's good that you're only thirty-nine, but it still places you in the high-risk pregnancy category."

"I'll make sure I set up an appointment with an obstetrician as soon as possible."

"Do you want me to stick around?"

"No, you don't need to. I have my sister and parents around and they will be more than willing to help."

"All right. But I'll still plan to be back around the time of the delivery. I won't be able to place your epidural, though," he quipped.

The next morning, bright and early, Sam dropped Jick off at a bus station. He had altered his appearance as much as possible, by trimming his hair short and not shaving. He also wore the Rangers baseball cap and dark glasses.

He leaned over and gave Sam a goodbye hug.

"Be careful," she said.

"I will."

"Goodbye, Jick."

"Goodbye, Sam. I'll call you every now and then, see how you're doing."

He walked into the building. He got in line at the ticket counter and when it was his turn, the agent asked, "Destination?"

Jick scanned the board.

"One please," he said. "Let's try Albuquerque."

GLOSSARY

Several medical terms and other phrases appear in this story. Some of them may not be familiar to the layperson. With apologies for assuming the reader may not be familiar with these terms, the following list is provided:

Cholecystectomy: surgery to remove the gallbladder.

Clubbing: enlargement of the fingertips with downward sloping of the nails. Typically caused by chronically low levels of oxygen in the blood.

End-tidal CO_2 monitor: If the breathing tube is in the right place, i.e., in the trachea, and the patient's heart is putting out blood, carbon dioxide is produced and is exhaled through the lungs. An end-tidal CO_2 monitor monitors the presence of CO_2 in exhaled gases. Even if the breathing tube is in the right place, if the heart is not pumping properly, no carbon dioxide is produced.

Endotracheal tube: a breathing tube designed to be inserted into the windpipe or trachea.

Fetal decels: when monitoring fetuses in the uterus, the fetus' heart rate is the most sensitive indicator of fetal distress. A slowing heart is called fetal deceleration, abbreviated 'fetal decels'.

Grand multip: a multiparous woman has delivered more than one baby. A grand multiparous woman has delivered more than five babies who have lived beyond a certain age, usually 24 weeks.

GSW: abbreviation for gunshot wound.

Idli: steamed rice and lentil cake from South India, served with sambar and chutney.

Intubated / extubated: process of placing a breathing tube in or removing a breathing tube from the trachea.

Masala dosa: a thin crepe-like pancake from India, usually savory, served with sambar and chutney.

<u>Midazolam</u>: also known by its brand name Versed, a mild
   sedative and anxiety-reducing drug.

<u>Milligram epi</u>: administer 1 milligram of epinephrine.
   Epinephrine, also known as adrenaline, is a hormone
   that causes the heart to race, opens airways that are
   closed due to asthma or anaphylactic attacks, and raises
   blood pressure.

<u>Perfed</u>: medical jargon for perforated.

<u>Pressor agent</u>: drugs administered to maintain the blood
   pressure.

<u>Sambar</u>: a lentil-based soup from South India, usually
   cooked with vegetables, tamarind, and spices. Served
   with cooked rice, dosas, or idlis.

<u>Stat sections</u>: urgent cesarean sections.

<u>Sternotomy</u>: an incision done with a scalpel and a bone saw
   down the middle of the sternum or breastbone.

<u>Thrill</u>: In medicine, a thrill is a vibratory movement or
   resonance heard through a stethoscope.

<u>V.fib</u>: short for ventricular fibrillation, basically a flat line
   EKG. Not compatible with life.

END

Made in the USA
Las Vegas, NV
18 March 2022